S0-AGQ-158

Love Rejected

"Brett," she whispered, holding his gaze with hers. "Do you love me? If you do, I'll wait forever for you."

Brett stared back at her, his whole soul pained. He'd known she would feel this way, she could never understand the utter, final ruthlessness of the aristocracy. If he ever admitted his love, he doomed her to an endless, futile lifetime of hoping. He swallowed hard, clenching his jaw with the effort of returning her pleading gaze. "No," he finally murmured, almost choking on the lie that dimmed the beautiful light in her eyes, "I don't love you."

Cerissa

Jessica St. Claire

Book Margins, Inc.

A BMI Edition

Published by special arrangement with Dorchester
Publishing Co., Inc.

If you purchased this book without a cover you should be aware
that this book is stolen property. It was reported as "unsold and
destroyed" to the publisher and neither the author nor the publisher
has received any payment for this "stripped book."

Copyright © MCMLXXIX by Jessica St. Claire

All rights reserved. No part of this book may be reproduced or
transmitted in any form or by any electronic or mechanical means,
including photocopying, recording or by any information storage
and retrieval system, without the written permission of the Publisher,
except where permitted by law.

Printed in the United States of America.

Chapter One

The tiny village of Bainwater was blooming with the tender greens and pale yellow pastels of an English spring. The winter of 1682 had been cold and hard, and every one of the town's three hundred and twenty-two inhabitants were already busy in the just warming fields, trying to rush the crops that would ease hunger pangs left by cold weather. Cerissa Hammond brushed a wisp of her heavy chestnut hair out of her blue eyes without pausing in her work, her hands reaching deep into her apron pockets to grab another handful of seed peas, her feet kicking at the muddy furrow to open it farther as she walked its length. This particular spring meant more to her than to most—who thought only of a more bountiful table. This spring she would be sixteen, traditionally the age to marry. In a few days less than a full month, her Aunt Mary and Uncle Wat would decide for her which one of her several suitors to accept. The betrothal would commence immediately, the wedding would follow in June.

With an unconscious, restless sigh, the girl moved to begin another row of seeding. Ye Gods! What a choice! John, just eighteen, son of a farmer whose lands adjoined her Uncle Wat's; or Matthew Spire, whose father was the village blacksmith; or Garlen Rickey who would inherit his father's prosperous dairy one day. Of the three, John was the handsomest, but Garlen the best catch. His family was the nearest thing to wealthy that Bainwater possessed. If only he weren't so ugly, so gangly and awkward, his teeth protruding over his bottom lip like a mouse's.

"Lordy, Cerissa, hurry up. I've got my rows all done already." The high pitched, faintly whining voice of her Aunt Mary's fourteen-year-old daughter interrupted her thoughts, and Cerissa straightened her back, stretching wearily.

"Annie, you're not supposed to do it so fast. Did you get the seeds down far enough in the dirt this time?"

"Oh, Cerissa, don't be such a . . ."

Both girls broke off their bickering long enough to whirl around and stare at the road that wound by the field, the faint sounds of a party of horsemen galloping there erasing all thought of the planting. Visitors, even by the weekly coach, were infrequent in Bainwater, and such a large troop of individual riders might be the fabled nobility. Cerissa had often heard stories of them but had never seen them. Bainwater was hardly a fashionable spot.

"Lordy, do you think they be quality?" Annie's voice was soft and muted in awe.

Cerissa shrugged, trying to conceal her own rising sense of excitement. Oh! Just once to see a real lord or a gorgeously gowned lady! Just one memory to glow in her dreams to make bearable the dull years stretching ahead as a farmer's wife in Bainwater. Unconsciously, she smoothed her tangled hair back from her forehead with muddy hands, smearing her forehead with black dirt as she stared at the troop drawing ever nearer.

"Excuse me, ladies, is this the town of Bainwater?"

Muffled laughter followed from the other men as the two girls stood stricken dumb in awe and fright—squinting stupidly into the setting sun to try to better see the rich velvets and bright-hued satins of their clothing. "Try again, Ardsley," a deep voice called laughingly to the first speaker, "I do believe the sight of your face has turned the girls to stone."

As if in a dream, Cerissa shifted her gaze from the first man's face to find the second's. As her blue eyes fixed on his green ones, her heart stopped still for a long moment, then galloped on again at twice its normal rate. Her every thought of handsome sat embodied in the lord. Thick wavy dark hair—black, or was it deepest brown?—eyes clear and emerald green, straight nose, strong jaw and a mouth, curled now in a teasing smile, that drew her like a magnet.

Suddenly aware of the girl's intense gaze, the lord swept his plumed hat gallantly from his head, his eyes sparkling in amusement as he made a mock bow to her from his saddle. "Have you a blacksmith here in Bainwater? We had heard so, but..."

"Aye, my lord, a fine one. Master Spire be his name and ye'll find him at the crossroads ahead—look for the smoke of his bellows." Annie's childish voice broke the spell and Cerissa started guiltily, turning her face away from the dark haired lord, blushing with shame at her terrible manners. Unlike Annie, whom she lived with, Cerissa had been carefully instructed by her Aunt Mary in "quality" manners and proper speech. The why of that instruction had remained a mystery, though she'd often pleaded for an explanation. "Some day perhaps ye shall know," her Aunt had replied always with a smile at once searching and sorrowful, "Some day."

Forcing a deep breath into her lungs, Cerissa made a deep curtsey, hauling hard on her cousin's hand to make her follow suit. "Please forgive my poor manners, gentlemen. I am Cerissa Hammond and this is my cousin, Annie Miller. Can we be of some service to you?" Even to Cerissa's untrained ear, her speech sounded stilted and oddly formal after Annie's. Her eyes lowered shyly to the ground, she missed the quick glances of surprise and amusement which the mounted men exchanged.

"Would she consider warming my bed tonight an allowable service, do you think?" One man asked another in a voice far too soft for the girl to hear, provoking even greater amusement among the party.

The lord named Ardsley chuckled to his dark haired friend and then addressed the girls patiently. "One of our servant's horses has thrown a shoe. We need a smith to hammer a new one—and an inn to have some ale in while we must wait."

The girl hesitated a minute in indecision, staring at the muddy ground, not daring to lift her eyes again lest they find the dark haired lord's green ones and start her brain whirling helplessly again. The blacksmith in town was probably competent to shoe a horse, but there was certainly no inn in Bainwater worthy of the name. Honesty urged her to admit that fact and direct the men on to the "Boar and Bull," some twelve miles down the road in Bywater,

7

but her whole soul rebelled at the idea of having these gorgeously dressed lords—especially the black haired, green eyed one—ride out of her existence so abruptly. Never before had she felt so keenly the eerie call of fate. It was as if something deep within her claimed her whole being for an instant, refusing to allow her to release this strange moment, this impossible meeting. If this was all she would ever see of the world beyond Bainwater, she must hold it a little longer.

"Mrs. Tyler is a widow. She lives in town proper, and sometimes lets rooms overnight. She has ale, I think . . . and she bakes the best tarts in the whole county." Startled by her own words, Cerissa quickly dropped her head, scolding herself for sounding so much a country child. Tarts! Why would these noblemen care about a stupid tart? They had custard trifles and cream pastries every day by the hundred if they wished. And besides, when they saw what she'd recommended as an inn . . .

"Which house is hers?" the dark lord questioned softly, sending waves of giddy ecstasy through the girl.

Without thinking, she flashed him a grateful smile, her deep blue eyes catching in the magic snare of his green ones. "The big one," she murmured weakly at last, managing to pull free of the spell, "across from the small weaver's shop. You can see it from the crossroads—there's a sign out in front and a stone gate."

"You're not actually considering stopping there." Ardsley stared at his dark haired companion incredulously. "Why the food'll be awful and the beds likely full of bugs. Besides, Bywater . . ."

"I'd rather stay here," the dark lord shrugged almost apologetically. "Damn if I know why . . . Maybe I have a yen for a strawberry tart."

"Strawberry tart, my ass," the blond grunted, his grin good natured though his eyes were puzzled. "You have a taste for an innocent country wench more likely, Lindsey."

The man named Lindsey chuckled and shrugged again. Maybe Ardsley was right, maybe it was the girl who attracted him so. To the two girls, who still stood frowning up into the sun, ankle deep in field mud, their faces bright with rapt wonder, he merely nodded his head and smiled. "Thank you for your recommendation, ladies. Perhaps you might be so kind as to take us to this Mrs. Tyler's yourselves—if you have a minute to spare, of course."

Cerissa glanced longingly down the road but shook her head in answer. "Forgive us, my lord, but we really mustn't. My Uncle Wat would take a strap to us if we didn't get these peas all planted and it's

8

growing dark already." Helplessly, feeling oddly as though she'd just done something terribly wrong, terribly final, she kicked at a furrow in aching resentment. Her one chance to be with quality and these lousy seed peas of Uncle Wat stood in her way. "Perhaps this evening though, after supper . . ."

The frown cleared from the lord's face, replaced by a quick smile, showing teeth white and even in his deeply tanned face. "Come to the inn whenever you can get away. If we aren't there, tell the woman you're waiting for us—Lord Ardsley," he gestured toward the good looking, ruddy blond who rode beside him, "Or myself, Lord Lindsey. Have a few of those tarts you spoke so highly of if you'd like, and put it on our bill."

Cerissa curtseyed quickly again, her heart pounding in renewed excitement, not untouched by fear and wonder at her own unusual boldness. When she finally managed to pull her gaze away from the retreating figures of the lords, she found Annie staring at her, eyes huge in speechless horror.

"Lord almighty, Cerissa! What'd you go and say that for? You know we won't be allowed to go anywhere tonight—we never are. And to meet strangers—lords!—at a rooming house . . . You know how my Dad thinks of them quality folk. He'll give us both a whipping for even talking to them!"

"Oh, hush Annie, please. I don't know why I did it, and you don't have to go if you don't want, but I . . . I'm going to be married in June. I'm not a child any longer. What harm can it do just to talk to a handsome lord once in your life? Pretty soon I'll be an old married drudge, making porridge and bearing children. I'm going to ask Aunt Mary to let me go, just this once. She may let me."

"Well, I'm not going, Cissy, and that's a fact! Why it scared me half to death even looking at 'em—so grand and so bold . . . I'm a farmer's daughter and I'll be a farmer's wife no doubt and that suits me fine." Trembling and still pale, the younger girl suddenly turned and sped away for the security of the cottage, leaving Cerissa to finish the last row of planting alone.

Though her body made the necessary motions, Cerissa's mind was miles away from the muddy field. Her bravado in front of Annie deserted her quickly as she trudged the muddy furrows alone, remembering her unbelievable and inexcusable boldness with a kind of numb amazement. Even now, half of her urged caution, the other recklessness. A hundred times she asked herself why, and each time, in silent answer, the dark Lord Lindsey appeared in her mind, water-green eyes smiling down at her like some handsome, ancient pagan god, miraculously reappeared on the earth for her to adore. This helpless giddy confusion, this half-fright, half-eagerness awakened her woman's soul as nothing else in her life had done. Something she had never felt with John, or Matthew, and certainly not with the buck toothed Garlen. And perhaps, this was what some instinctive sense buried deep within her had longed for, craved for, knew intuitively that she was missing. She'd hardly noticed the other men once she'd seen Lord Lindsey. There had been four or five amongst them dressed like quality, yet she remembered only his face clearly. Over and over she repeated his name softly in spellbound wonder, savoring the sounds like sweet music.

With a start, Cerissa realized that she was almost to the door of the cottage and she hesitated uncertainly, her day dreams evaporating slowly as morning mist, her doubts returning. What could she, Cerissa Hammond, a country wench, offer a fine lord like him? All she knew was farm life and village news. It had seemed enough until now, yet he would never be interested in such nonsense. And, as handsome as he was, he could have his pick of all the fine Court ladies, gorgeously gowned, their hair piled high and glittering with jewels, eyes painted to enhance their color. Lord Lindsey fall in love with a country wench? Never. Why, for all she knew, he could be married already.

Cerissa's shoulders slumped in sudden anguish. Feeling foolish, and suddenly bewildered, the girl opened the cottage door slowly to see Aunt Mary's solid frame waiting just within, silhouetted by the uneven light of the rushes.

"Come in child," the woman murmured kindly, "I want to talk to you."

Cerissa's breath caught in her throat, more from excitement than from exertion, as she arrived at Mrs. Tyler's gate. Never in a million lifetimes would she have guessed that Aunt Mary would allow—no, actually encourage—her to do such a daring thing. And why she had was a mystery, but Cerissa had wasted no time on the wondering, just kissed the cheek of the kindly, round woman who had been as a mother to her. Then, before her aunt could change her mind, Cerissa had fled for town. Now, pink cheeked from her long run in the crisp March evening air, Cerissa paused to fluff her freshly washed, waist length chestnut hair over her shoulders before stepping into the hearth room. Aunt Mary had given her a gingerbread loaf to bring to the widow, providing some excuse for

Cerissa's visit. The lords would leave in the morning, and Cerissa would have to live the rest of her life among these simple people—and simple people had simple morals. An unmarried girl did not go out at night to meet a man, not any man, not even the king himself. So Cerissa had not come to see the charming Lord Lindsey again. She had merely brought a sweet loaf to the widow.

"Hello, child," Mrs. Tyler's weathered face softened in a maternal smile. Cerissa Hammond was a favorite of hers. Not only was she such a pretty little thing, but more importantly, she was kind and sweet tempered with it. "How nice of Mary to think of me," she smiled, "I have special guests in the house tonight and I am beside myself what to offer them."

"Special guests?" Cerissa echoed in pretended ignorance. "Who?"

The white haired widow lowered her voice conspiratorially to answer, telling the girl nothing she didn't already know well. "Imagine me entertaining royalty!" she finished at last, shaking her head.

"Oh, Mrs. Tyler!" Cerissa exclaimed, feeling a quick flash of guilt for her deceitfulness. "How I'd love to see them!"

The widow glanced quickly at the girl's eager face. She certainly could use the girl's help this evening, but Cerissa was a mite too pretty to be let loose amongst the gentlemen—they'd snap her up like honey cakes in January. That tall, dark haired one especially...how could an innocent like Cerissa resist his attentions? Why, she herself would be near fifty next birthday, and even she had blushed like a school girl. But, she hesitated a moment, considering, if she recollected rightly, he was already off to his rooms upstairs. And the other gentlemen seemed mighty engrossed in their card game.

Waiting for an answer, Cerissa felt as though eons had passed, her heart plummetting in quick despair. The whole plan was for naught—Mrs. Tyler would say no. Just then, the widow nodded, smiling at the girl as she remembered her own youth. How important such a thing could seem at sixteen. Besides, the men were all under her roof. She would keep an eye on them.

Her heart soaring with excitement, Cerissa followed the widow into the small parlor, serving as a private dining room tonight. She scanned the room eagerly for sight of Lord Lindsey's dark hair and broad shouldered frame. By the third silent search, her heart plummetted again. He was not there.

"Excuse me, my lords," Mrs. Tyler's interruption of the card game was hesitant. "Cerissa here has offered to help me serve your desserts and spirits. Please tell her your pleasure." She turned and walked to the doorway, still uneasy about leaving the girl alone. Suddenly, she stopped in the doorway, the knob already turned in her hand, whirling around to face the men. "T'is only fair to warn you that she's a sweet, innocent child, and dear as my own flesh to me. If one of ye lays a hand on her, I'll boot you out in the mud—lords or no!"

Ardsley was the first to recover from the shock of the widow's forth right declaration, and his handsome face broke into a disbelieving but amused smile. "I'll be damned," he swore softly to his companions, his eyes dancing to betray the limit of his mirth. "I shall watch out for her myself, Mrs. Tyler, I swear. Don't worry."

Apparently satisfied, though she glared silent warning at each man once more, the widow nodded and left.

"Hello, darlin'," the blond lord grinned to the nervous girl, beckoning her over to stand by his chair. "I'd given up on your coming."

Cerissa shrugged, trying to force a smile, not sure now whether Lord Lindsey's absence disappointed or relieved her. Now that she was actually here, she was trembling in terror, almost wishing she were safe at home in the bed she and Annie shared.

"How about fetching us some of those tarts you recommended so highly, sweetheart," Ardsley continued, his eyes gleaming in merriment to see her terror. "And several more bottles of chilled ale as well."

Thankful for a job to do to keep her mind from whirling into a hopeless spin, Cerissa mumbled an answer and fled for the door to the kitchen, stumbling clumsily on the edge of the frayed rug as she went.

Behind her, Ardsley and the others laughed softly and winked at one another. "Well, damn, but that's another wager I lost to Lindsey today," one said in mock disgust. "Who would have believed the devil's charm would even work out here in God's country!"

"Don't give him your guineas yet, Harry," Ardsley grinned. "She may be here, but she's far from sharing a bed with him. I promised to keep an eye out for her, mind, and I think she'd run like a frightened deer if he even touched her."

"Do you?" the first speaker, Lord Martin, chuckled unpleasantly. "Like to make a bet on that?"

"Hell, yes, I'll bet you ten pounds," the blond retorted, his eyes no longer amused. "But there's no use making a wager on that.

Brett's taken his leave and gone to bed already. He won't be back down."

"Tired out from last night's tumbling, no doubt. Well, no difference. We'll simply send the wench up."

Ardsley frowned. Sometimes, as now, he sensed something unpleasant in Harry's nature begin to surface. "And how in hell do you plan to get the girl to do that? She won't go willingly, I'll be bound."

"I think she will. Give her a few minutes to lose her flightiness and we'll ask her to take a note to Brett for us. I didn't believe she'd have the boldness to even come tonight, but since she did . . ."

Ardsley frowned again, studying the amber colored liquid in his glass. "I'm not sure about this, Harry," he murmured finally. "I really think the girl is an innocent—barely more than a child. I did say I'd look after her, and I don't want to be responsible for . . ."

"Hell, Ardsley, you're getting virtuous as an old Roundhead anymore. Brett Lindsey is not the man to rape the girl, is he? You're always prattling on about him as though he can do no wrong. Are you saying now that you don't trust him to be decent to the chit?"

Ardsley shrugged and forced a grin, feeling vaguely out-manuvered. Harry was right. Brett wouldn't harm the wench. No man who attracted women like that bastard did would need to! "Ten pounds!" he agreed at last with false heartiness. "Go write your note."

By the time Cerissa returned to the room with the sweetcakes and four more bottles of chilled ale, she had regained some of her composure. And when Lord Ardsley, with a beguiling grin, invited her to share his seat at the card table, she smiled and nodded eagerly, enjoying the men's conversation as much as the game. The stakes of the game had astounded her at first, for to her, a pound was a significant sum of money. Why a single pound would pay for a new dress for herself and Annie too. But these lords bet a pound and more just on a single hand. And evidently such stakes were not unduly high as these games went, for when she had finally dared to whisper her incredulity to Lord Ardsley, he had responded with an indulgent laugh that many more-serious games at Court anteed with twenty or thirty pounds.

Gradually, the girl settled into a sort of fairy tale contentment, feeling protected and secure under the blond lord's kind attentions to her. Her heart had nearly calmed to its normal rhythm when one of the lords suddenly swore and slapped his cards face down on the table, startling everyone.

"Oh, damn, Harry," Lord Martin, swore again, glancing

13

covertly at the blond lord who had the girl balanced precariously on his knee, "I forgot to tell Brett Lindsey something important."

Ardsley frowned faintly, refusing to help Harry. He had almost forgotten their earlier agreement in the pleasure of the evening. Cerissa was not only a stunning natural beauty, she was a sweet child, truly an innocent and a refreshing change from the jaded, over-painted, over-experienced Court women. He had no taste now for the game he and Harry had thought to play with her.

Lord Martin frowned impatiently, kicking Ardsley beneath the table in annoyance. The blond lord responded only by a curt shake of his head.

"Leave it go, Harry," he muttered, tightening his arm protectively around the girl. Bewildered, sensing that the interchange between the two men somehow concerned her, Cerissa's face pouted in a pretty frown, her blue eyes troubled.

Shrugging in ill-concealed irritation, Lord Martin ignored his companion's disapproval and spoke directly to Cerissa. "Hey, pretty little country girl, I'll give you five pounds to deliver a note to Lord Lindsey for me. All right?"

Astounded by the mention of such a huge sum for such a petty errand, and startled at the sound of that magic name, Cerissa gaped at the man, thinking to see a teasing glint in his eye. But there was none. "Five whole pounds for just that?"

"Five whole pounds for just that," Lord Martin echoed with a faint jeer.

Cerissa studied the man's face in momentary consideration. She saw a too-sharp chin, and small ferret eyes, adding up to a faintly unpleasant expression. Surprised, she realized that she didn't like Lord Martin, noble or not. He looked like a weasel, in fact, with an unpleasant glint in his tiny, dark eyes. But five whole pounds.... Why Aunt Mary could buy so much they needed with that sort of money. It would repay her aunt's trust, too, in letting her come tonight. And yet, she hesitated, feeling Lord Ardsley's disapproval. Was there a real reason for the blond lord's reaction? Or was he merely a bit hurt to think she would leave his company so easily? Too, she thought, her heart jumping at the idea, it would be a chance to see the handsome Lord Lindsey just one more time.

Cerissa turned to search Ardsley's face, asking mutely for his help. He returned the gaze for a long moment, seeking signs of her own feelings perhaps before responding. Finally, noticing the blush occasioned by the mere mention of Lindsey's name, he nodded his head. "Go ahead if you want, sweetheart. Brett won't hurt you."

Cerissa smiled, reassured, and secretly thrilled to have such a chance when she had long since resigned herself to not seeing the green eyed lord. Impulsively, she leaned forward to kiss the blond lord's ruddy cheek, thanking him for his kindness. Five whole pounds, she thought again in amazement, for something she really wanted to do anyway. "I'll be right back," she promised eagerly, never doubting that she spoke the truth.

"Of course, sweetheart," Lord Ardsley smiled back, patting his knee with the flat of his hand. "I'll save your seat."

Cerissa grabbed the note in one hand and her long skirts with the other, turning only once at the foot of the stairs to see the blond lord still staring at her, a strange expression on his face. But as she hesitated, he smiled and waved her on. Heart thudding in wild excitement, she turned to run up the winding stairs.

"You sent her to Mrs. Tyler's with a gingerbread, Mary?" Wat Miller's voice was frankly irritated as he stared helplessly out the cottage's single window toward the dark, distant village. "Didn't you know there was quality staying there tonight?"

"Yes, Wat, I knew that. The girls told me they'd seen them on the road," Mary answered calmly though her heart thudded loudly in her ears. If her husband ever guessed the true reason for the girl's eagerness to go ... "I thought it would be a good chance for Cerissa to see such folk first hand. And besides," she added hastily, noting Wat's quick anger, "Mrs. Tyler is like to need some help with a full house."

"I've told you before to let it go, Mary, but you refuse to heed me. That girl may have been born quality—if the ramblings of a fever crazed old nurse are to be believed—but she's got no family but ours. From what I remember of the old crone's mumblings, both sides of the girl's families disowned the parents for marrying against their wishes. So it be pretty doubtful they'll welcome the offspring of such a match. Besides, Garlen Rickey's father has offered a share in his dairy for the girl's hand. T'will do no good for the girl to be fretting about her life as a simple man's wife here in Bainwater."

"And I've told you before, Wat Miller, that you're wrong to think as you do about that. Whether there be a place for her or not, the girl's got a right to know the facts of her own ancestry. You agreed years ago that we'd tell her on her sixteenth birthday, and leave the choice in the girl's own hands. Now you got your eye on a piece of that dairy and you be wishing to change your mind. But I think you are being unfair to the girl. She ought to see those fancy lords down at Mrs. Tyler's tonight, give her a chance to see what she'd be choosing between. Besides, you were at Bridger's when the question come up, so I couldn't ask your yea or nay. She knows to be home by midnight, Wat, and Cerissa's a good girl. She'll be no problem. In a few hours, she'll be sleeping in there with Annie just the same as ever."

"A couple of hours with the likes of those quality folk are plenty of time for trouble to happen," the man grunted. "You may be regretting your foolishness by then."

Aunt Mary kept her head down deliberately, staring at her darning, hoping desperately that her husband was wrong about her decision to send Cerissa into the village. What other real choice had she had? Given the child's background—all a secret to her so far—surely the girl at sixteen should have a chance to try to find a place amongst her own kind. At least this night might give Cerissa a reason for choosing. It might open her eyes to the realities of her alternatives. A simple life with Garlen Rickey might not seem so bad to the girl if the quality men grew coarse or over-familiar with her. Troubled, she glanced quickly at her husband's scowling face. Oh Lordy! she realized suddenly. That girl best be home safe and innocent by midnight or she'd have the devil's own to pay with Wat for ever letting her go.

Cerissa knocked softly on the door, trembling in a mixture of terror and excitement. She had no business being up here, all alone at this time of night, rapping at a strange man's bedroom door. Five pounds or not, she had been crazy to have agreed to this errand. In sudden fright, she whirled away from the door, starting back to the stairs.

"Come in," a deep male voice called from within, "the door's open."

As though frozen, her feet dragged reluctantly to a halt, the sound of his voice playing havoc upon every fiber of her being, her heart racing in renewed terror while the blood roared in her ears. Could she ever forgive herself for lacking the courage to see Lord Lindsey one more time? After all her effort to get to Mrs. Tyler's tonight . . . Helplessly, feeling as drawn to doom as a moth seeing firelight, and every bit as helpless to resist, she watched her hand reach out slowly to turn the latch of the door, pushing it open. Almost hypnotized, she forced her feet forward into the room, stopping in sudden shock at what she saw.

16

Lord Lindsey stood half-naked, only his velvet, fawn colored breeches on, shaving with a silver straight edge razor by the dubious light of a flickering candelabra. Horrified, her embarrassment mingled with the strange and unsettling sensation of unfamiliar stirrings in her belly, Cerissa gasped and dropped her gaze immediately to the floor, half-turning her back to the man, unable to say a single word.

"Well." The dark haired lord drawled the word slowly, staring at the girl in obvious surprise, a smile spreading to make white creases in his sun-browned face. "Cerissa Hammond. I thought you wouldn't be coming."

Cerissa stood trembling, longing to flee from the room yet totally unable to do so. She kept her eyes on the floor, afraid to see the man's broad, muscled shoulders and chest, the lean taut belly. Whatever that stirring sensation in her loins had been, she was afraid to reawaken it. "I had to wait until my Uncle Wat left to help a neighbor birth a mare after supper," she explained in a barely audible voice.

Brett waited patiently, expecting her to continue her conversation, intent upon his own lathered reflection in the copper mirror. When the silence persisted, he threw a quick glance at the girl. The scarlet blush on her cheeks, her averted eyes and trembling hands surprised him. Damn if she didn't look as though she'd just caught him stark naked in bed with someone else's whore! With a sudden grin, he shook his head in rueful comprehension. He was so used to the sophisticates of Court he'd forgotten that, to such innocence as this, his bare chest was probably every bit as startling. In London, there might be the wild living of the Restoration Court, but here in the country, old Oliver Cromwell and his puritannical morals still held much sway. "I'll be done in a minute, Cerissa. Please sit down," he explained solemnly though his green eyes danced with private amusement.

The girl obeyed wordlessly, sitting down on the very edge of the chair, every muscle in her body poised for instant flight, Lord Martin's note totally forgotten.

"Does your Uncle Wat do the local animal doctoring?"

Cerissa shook her heavy chestnut hair in mute denial, struggling to find her voice. "No . . . ," she managed to stammer at last. Forcing more strength into her tone, she continued to explain. "No, the Bridger's own a farm near us and they're distant kin. He just went to help Mr. Bridger."

"I see." Brett nodded, cautiously because of the sharp razor in his hand. "I have a mare due to foal this month myself. Do you like horses?"

Cerissa coughed quietly, trying to force some moisture into her dry mouth. "Yes," she replied haltingly, "but we don't have any ourselves. My uncle says they're too dear to keep when he and the boys can do the planting without them." Numbly, she realized how dull and stupid her conversation was. Lord Lindsey was more likely to fall asleep than fall in love with her if she didn't gather her wits soon. Desperately, she searched her mind for a witty comment, even a piece of village gossip to break the silence. Unconsciously, her hands clenched in concentration, and she felt the sharp edges of the paper crumple in her fist. Remembering her errand, she smoothed the paper out and held it up toward him. "Lord Martin asked me to give this to you."

Brett set the razor down, wiping the rest of the lather from his face with a small towel. "Harry did?" he questioned in some surprise, a faint frown of puzzlement drawing his brows together over the finely bridged nose. Now what the devil?

Cerissa backed away as the dark haired lord approached her, feeling strangely like a cornered animal. She had not realized how tall he was on horseback. Now, his solid six feet looked like ten as he drew closer, following her retreat.

"Hold still girl," he laughed at last, "I'm not going to bite you. I just want the note."

Mortified, Cerissa dropped her head and handed him the paper, agonized to see that her hand trembled as her fingers brushed his.

Lord Lindsey opened the folded paper quickly, scanning the brief scrawl. "Ardsley has laid ten pounds against your success with the girl. H." Quickly, he glanced at the girl to see if she had guessed the game being played. Somehow, he thought not. As skittish as she was, the wench would never have come up so boldly for that. Even though her every move bespoke an intense attraction to him, she was obviously terrified to even be in the same room with him. Well, he had coaxed recalcitrant women before, he would coax this one.

"You are afraid of me," he scolded Cerissa gently, his voice soft and husky, his eyes searching the girl's face. Lord! What a beauty she was with her hair clean and free-flowing over her shoulders, her big, cornflower blue eyes lowered modestly, her breasts heaving in her agitation. As he expected, his words produced a hasty, though obviously untrue denial. "Yes, you are, Cerissa," he laughed softly. "Though I don't know why. Do you truly think I mean to harm you? Or are you so shy with all men?"

"Oh, no," Cerissa shook her head hastily, fearing to hurt the lord's feelings by admitting her terror. "I'm just . . . I've got to be home by midnight and it's likely growing late."

Lord Lindsey's eyebrows arched in silent surprise. He couldn't remember the last time he had been with a woman who had a curfew—except for a few with possessive husbands, of course, who might wonder at an all night absence. The girl was beginning to intrigue him for herself rather than for Ardsley and Martin's game. It was oddly comforting to see such innocence still alive in the world, oddly arousing to smell the strong clean country soap smell of her thick chestnut hair, oddly intriguing to look into a face whose beauty did not depend on paint. He wasn't going to rush the girl. He would talk to her, soothe her as he would a flighty filly. If midnight came before she had come willingly into his arms, then so be it.

"Come sit by the fire with me, Cerissa. I'll pour us some wine while we talk," he suggested gently, nodding his night dark head toward the small, two-cushioned sofa by the hearth. He noticed her hesitation, the quick lowering of her eyes, and he reached out to take one of her hands and pull it toward him. "Please, Cerissa, just for a few moments. I swear I won't hurt you. I'll have you home by midnight if need be. All right? Please?"

Cerissa smiled in spite of her fear, the warmth and gentleness in his eyes destroying her last attempts to resist his charm and the powerful pull he, seemingly without knowledge and without effort, exerted on her very soul. Shyly, she nodded.

Brett seated himself on the sofa, the girl beside him, exerting himself fully and enjoying the effort. The challenge of the situation lent its novelty, he decided, smiling slightly at his own intensity. Usually women courted him rather than vice versa. Ardsley's good natured envy of his conquests had long been a standing joke between the two men, so he did not resent his friend's wager against him. Besides, from what the girl said, he gathered that the blond lord had been rather taken with the wench himself, for it was very unlikely for the man to be so protective.

Cerissa perched on the sofa, ready for instant flight if the dark haired lord made a move toward her. But gradually, under the influence of the warm fire flames nearby, and Lord Lindsey's careful attention, she began to relax, the full bodied wine sending a tingle throughout her body, her head feeling pleasantly dizzy. All the wine she had ever consumed up to now had been heavily watered, and the strong burgundy was having an effect on her. She began to giggle at the lord's stories of Court life, and finally grew bold enough to tell a few of her own, feeling immensely clever and successful as he chuckled in appreciation. Soon, in response to his urging, she found herself agreeing to call the dark haired lord by his first name, Brett, which he explained was shortened from Bretegane.

"Brettegdene?" she giggled helplessly, finding the name absurdly impossible to pronounce.

"Bretegane," he repeated slowly with a grin, his green eyes dancing with amusement at her growing inebriation. "My mother was Scottish. Bretegane was the name of her ancestral home there. A wild, rocky place, she often said, but beautiful."

"You're beautiful too," she smiled, flushing scarlet as she realized what she'd said. "Oh, forgive me, please," she stammered, aghast at her runaway tongue, and terribly conscious of the burning blush which flushed her face. "I'm afraid I've had too much wine." To her horror, she began to hiccup, the fire suddenly feeling uncomfortably warm.

Brett's grin broadened as he watched her embarrassment. "Here, sweetheart, take a few sips of water and swallow slowly," he advised, putting one arm around her shoulders as he lifted the glass to her lips. "You don't feel sick do you?"

Cerissa could only shake her head in denial, her mouth full of water. The warm weight of his arm seemed to set her body on fire, yet the burning was the most exciting, pleasurable sensation she had ever felt. The wine making her reckless, she leaned into his shoulder, aware that her heart was racing and her breath growing ragged. The dark haired lord's eyes darkened with a strange emotion as they met hers, sensing her beginning surrender.

When he spoke again, his voice was lower, soft and strangely husky. "You're a beautiful girl, Cerissa. Have you ever been kissed?"

"No," she answered breathlessly, her eyes staring up into his emerald green ones in a kind of hypnotized trance, her lips parting unconsciously, begging for his touch. Vaguely, she realized that her whole body had begun to tremble.

"Would you like to be?" he asked gently, beginning to bend his dark head down to hers.

"Yes, I think so," she answered in a whisper, too relaxed to heed the warning that a distant part of her brain was insisting she heed.

Brett's head dropped slowly, to meet hers, his lips warm and dry and tasting sweetly of wine as he covered her mouth with his own. Cerissa's eyes closed instinctively, her body melting against his, molding itself closer and closer. The single kiss seemed to last for timeless eternity to the trembling girl, all her senses vividly acute and all concentrated on the incredible ecstasy of his touch.

At last he raised his head, his green eyes dark as lake water in his growing desire. The expression on the girl's face answered his unspoken question. Her eyes still closed, her mouth parted in welcome, her body warm and yielding in his arms. With a faint smile, he bent his head again, pressing gently against her to force her back on the cushions as his hands sought the laces of her bodice.

Cerissa started in surprise and fear as she felt his hands on her breasts, caressing the soft flesh and taut nipples with skillful fingers, gentle and patient. The last fleeting vestige of self-control forced a cry of anxious protest. "Please please, I can't . . ."

"Hush, sweetheart, I won't hurt you, I swear," Brett murmured huskily against her ear, never pausing in his love-making, his lips touching her throat and neck even as he spoke.

"But I mustn't . . ." she murmured helplessly, far too enraptured to make a move to escape him, her body tingling and demanding in a way she'd never known before. "I have to be back by midnight."

"I'll have you back by midnight, Cerissa, I promise," Brett whispered patiently, his voice low and comforting, his body beginning to tremble in response to the girl's.

Helplessly, Cerissa moaned, closing her eyes again and locking her arms around the dark haired lord's neck to draw him closer again. She knew she shouldn't be doing this, she knew she would regret it in a few moments, but she couldn't resist to save her very soul.

At last, his breathing heavy and his manhood hard and demanding relief, Brett moved from the sofa and bent to pick the girl up in his arms, carrying her to the bed. She surrendered her youthful innocence to his bold embraces, her thick chestnut hair falling in heavy waves across his shoulder and down his arm.

He laid her gently on the bed lowering himself carefully down upon her, his hands moving quickly to free them of their clothing. At last, the girl lay completely revealed to his gaze, the soft firelight casting a golden glow of warm light and dark shadow over her perfect young body. With a soft oath of pleased surprise, he paused a moment to enjoy her beauty, his eyes lingering on her perfect fine features, her high, firm, full young breasts, her slim hips and long legs. If she were bred from the stocky country folk, he'd be a ladies handmaiden.

Cerissa stirred, wondering at his hesitation, opening her

21

smouldering blue eyes wide and reaching her arms up to him in welcome. With a faint smile, he lay down against her, drawing her eagerly to him, his hands moving to caress her velvet soft skin, his lips covering hers, his tongue seeking the sweetness of her mouth as the girl sighed and pressed hungrily against him. In a moment, he slid one hand down from her breast, over her flat belly and down between her thighs, his fingers searching for her warmth. Cerissa flinched instinctively under his unexpected touch, her body beginning to draw away from his. Quickly, he moved his hand away, sliding it back up to caress her breasts, and back to stroke her thighs and buttocks, letting his fingers touch her in their passing but never dwell until at last she relaxed again against him, her body pressing back against his touch, welcoming him and trusting him.

Brett shifted his weight onto his elbows, moving his hips over to lay between the girl's legs, his dark head bending down to caress her nipples with his tongue, then lifting it to find her mouth again, nipping gently at her soft lips until they parted hungrily and licked at his.

Gently, with deliberate care, he slid down resting just barely within her body, his hips rocking slightly against hers. Cerissa was not the first virgin he had taken, and he knew that any impatience or roughness on his part would surely ruin it for her. And so he forced himself to agonizing slowness. His jaw clenched white with the effort to control his own demanding passion, he moved gently within her until her moans grew louder, more urgent, her face flushed and her body writhing beneath him in the height of her need. At last, he abandoned his caution and plunged fully within her, the patience he had forced on his body rewarded by the joyous and eager welcome she gave.

Cerissa's blue eyes were wide in astonishment as waves of incredible pleasure rocked her whole body. The tearing pain did not diminish the ecstasy at all. In wonder, as it finally passed, she stared down at Brett's dark head, buried against her shoulder as he moved violently within her, his own passion nearing fulfillment. Grateful for the incredible delight he had given her, wishing to return it to him, she covered his black hair with kisses, tightening her arms around his neck, drawing her knees up instinctively to allow him deeper within her. In the space of a heartbeat, she felt him shudder in her arms, a soft groan escaping from his lips before he lay still and spent, heavy upon her. Tenderly she stroked the thick black hair back from his damp forehead and laid a soft kiss there, wanting to thank him but unsure of the words.

At last, Brett raised his head, a lazy smile on his face as he kissed her lips once again, very gently. "Thank you, Cerissa," he murmured. With another kiss he rolled away from her reaching one arm out to draw the girl's head against his shoulder.

"That was..." Cerissa whispered, still overwhelmed by the splendor of the experience, unable to think of a sufficiently expressive word.

Brett grinned in reply, his eyes bemused. Was there anything in the world as marvelous as a newly awakened woman? He glanced down at Cerissa's face where it nestled contentedly against his shoulder, and kissed her love-tangled thick chestnut waves, tightening his grip around her. The girl sighed and snuggled closer, her eyes closing reluctantly as the wine and the lovemaking combined to make her terribly sleepy and overwhelmingly content.

"Don't you have to be home soon?" the dark haired lord prodded reluctantly. He had enjoyed her immensely, but he didn't want any irate kin storming into his bedroom with pistols.

"Yes," she nodded drowsily, never opening her eyes, "but I just have to rest a minute."

Brett smiled indulgently, feeling warm and generous in the afterglow of his pleasure. "Go ahead and sleep then, sweetheart, I'll take this watch," he offered.

"Don't let me be late," she murmured almost inaudibly.

"I won't."

Still smiling, Cerissa fell asleep almost immediately, secure and content in her lover's embrace. Lord Lindsey reached cautiously across her to extinguish the candle burning by the side of the bed, then leaned back, stretching luxuriously, enjoying the touch of the girl against him, the country scent of her hair, and the changing shadows cast by the bright, almost full moon outside. Thoroughly satisfied with himself and the whole evening, Brett laid his dark head back upon the pillow, smiling into the darkness. If there were time, he'd enjoy taking the girl a second time. There wouldn't be as great a need for care this time—he could show her the joys of a more reckless type of lovemaking. With a soft sigh, he glanced through the half-shuttered window at the still rising moon. Not enough time left before midnight. He might as well just rest for the few minutes that were left.

Chapter Two

Cerissa bolted upright in the bed, her blue eyes wide with surprise. That couldn't be sunlight coming through the window! With a quick cry, she leapt from the bed and ran to the narrow glass pane, staring in stricken disbelief at the first light of dawn, the sky streaked mauve and yellow along the horizon, the burning gold of the newborn sun a hazy semicircle above the greening meadows.

Behind her, Lord Lindsey struggled to raise himself on one elbow, his eyes still clouded by sleep. He frowned at the girl in drowsy irritation. "For God's sake, wench, what's the matter?"

Cerissa whirled around, dismay on her face, "Oh Brett, it's morning! It's morning already!"

The dark haired lord stared at the girl in confusion, shaking his head at last to try to force his brain to function. Obviously the girl was terribly distraught about the fact.

"So what?" he shrugged, raising one hand to shield his eyes against the increasing brightness. "Why shouldn't it be morning? That's a normal enough occurrence following nightime."

"But I had to be home by midnight—don't you remember? You promised to keep watch . . ." her words trailed off as she buried her face in her hands. "Oh Lordy! Uncle Wat'll be like to have my head for this."

At last, Brett began to remember. Wincing in quick realization of his guilt, he swung his long legs off the bed, walking swiftly toward the softly sobbing young girl. He couldn't believe it was the disaster Cerissa seemed to think it, but he owed her enough to be kind to her.

"Hush princess, I'm sorry I must have fallen asleep myself," he said, dropping a consoling arm around her hunched shoulders. "Get your clothes on and give me a minute to wash my mouth out. I'll take you home."

"You don't know my uncle, he'll . . ."

"Just get your clothes on," he snapped impatiently, immediately regretful as he saw the girl's eyes blink in hurt surprise, fresh tears sparkling on her long black lashes. "Oh hell, I'm sorry, Cerissa, I'm not at my best in the morning—especially this early. Don't worry about your family. I'll think of something to tell them."

The dark haired lord turned away, reaching for his breeches and a clean linen shirt, trying to appear as good natured as he could about the whole thing. But he wasn't used to having to escort women home from his bed at dawn, especially when an irate family probably waited for him. "Damn!" he swore silently. "These innocent country wenches had some drawbacks to them."

Cerissa was dressed and waiting at the door—astonished to see Lord Lindsey pause to gulp a swallow of last nights Burgundy wine. She averted her eyes, suddenly aware of a pounding in her head and the uneasiness of her stomach. The next time she drank any wine, she would be sure to water it herself. How could she have done what she'd done last night? Let herself be used for one evening like the commonest whore. Worst of all, she could not even deny how pleasurable it had been.

"All right sweetheart, let's go."

Without further speech, the pair walked out into the dark hallway of the large house, Brett pausing a moment outside the door to get his bearings. "I have to tell Ardsley I'm going. You wait here," he cautioned as he stepped into the room just down the hallway. Without protest, feeling more than half dead anyway from humiliation and dread of Uncle Wat's sure rage, Cerissa nodded.

"Ardsley, wake up," Lord Lindsey ordered sharply, allowing a

25

frown to draw his black brows together now that the girl was out of sight. "I've got to go somewhere."

The blond man scowled back, his eyes sleepy and thoroughly annoyed.

"What the hell? What time is it anyway?"

"Too damn early," Lindsey muttered disgustedly, "and also too late."

"What?"

"Never mind. I won't be long. Don't leave without me."

"All right, just go away," Ardsley growled, shoving his head back under a plump pillow. "Jesus Christ, what a time for going visiting."

Brett walked back into the hallway, trying to force a smile of reassurance for the girl, but it just wouldn't come. Shrugging, he moved off down the hallway, beckoning Cerissa to follow him.

"Oh Brett, no. I can't go that way. Mrs. Tyler will see me and know I've been here all night!"

Frustrated and impatient, he nodded his understanding and reversed his steps anxious to get finished with this nonsense and get back to bed.

"Is there a back stairs in here?" he questioned abruptly.

Helplessly Cerissa replied that she didn't know. She had never been upstairs here before. The impatient anger in the lord's green eyes struck the last lingering bits of joy from the girl's heart. Wiping the tears away with the back of one hand, she followed him dejectedly, wishing with all her whole heart and soul that she were dead. The wine and her own wishful thinking had so bedazzled her last night that she had honestly believed the lord cared for her—as something more than a one-night wench. His scarcely concealed impatience and frustration with her this morning had dispelled that romantic notion. How she would ever face anyone in the village again . . . how she would ever be able to meet Aunt Mary's accusing eyes . . . or to live with herself for that matter, remembering her shame . . . especially when she had only herself to blame.

"Here, Cerissa, be careful on these stairs." Lord Lindsey warned, taking her arm to steady her as they descended.

They stepped out together into the now light stable area, Brett tossing a small gold coin to the stable boy to have him bring the horse quickly. As they stood silent in the cool air, he glanced down at the girl's face—surprised to see streaks of tears glistening on her downcast face. Immediately he damned himself for a selfish bastard and struggled to act a little kinder. But the girl didn't respond in the slightest and he finally abandoned his efforts. Swinging her easily into the saddle before mounting himself, they rode in silence down the deserted street, the warmth of the horse's breath making small clouds of mist in the cool March morning air.

Suddenly Cerissa stiffened, her mouth opening in horror. There was her uncle walking swiftly toward them, the whipping cane in his left hand.

"Brett," she whispered, her throat instantly parched with fear. "That's Uncle Wat."

The dark haired lord reined the horse in, dropping easily to the ground and reaching up to grasp Cerissa around the waist to swing her lightly to the ground. Cerissa caught her breath as his hands brushed her breast, astonished that, even in the midst of her terror, his mere touch could recall such memories that wild, giddy excitement flooded her soul. Startled, she gasped and swiftly drew farther away.

Wat Miller stalked stiffly toward the girl, ignoring the green-eyed lord who stood near her. His square jawed face contorted in rage, he drew one powerful arm back and struck her hard across the face, knocking her into the dirt. "You filthy slut! We've taken you into our house, shared our food with you, treated you like kin and this is how you repay our charity? By whoring with a devil-spawned Royalist the first chance you get!" Enraged he brought the whipping stick down across her shoulders and her buttocks with all his strength, swearing viciously, completely forgetting the man who stood nearby until a strong hand reached out to grasp his wrist, wrestling the cane away to hurl it away down the road. The stocky farmer looked around in surprise to find a pair of glittering green eyes darkened with anger staring down at him, their expression dangerous.

"Stay out of this—this be a family matter. You've no cause to interfere," Miller snarled, snatching his wrist away, turning back to the cowering girl.

"I disagree," Lord Lindsey's quiet drawl held an unmistakable warning, and despite his hatred for the lord—for all nobility—Cerissa's uncle hesitated.

"You're being unnecessarily harsh on the girl. I'm to blame for her lateness," Brett spoke quietly, struggling to keep his own temper in check. He had been stunned with surprise to see the man go after the girl so brutally, and his instinctive reaction was to kill the brutal farmer outright. But the girl had to live on in this village—killing her uncle would surely not help. Her only chance was to have him

27

smoothe the situation over diplomatically. He had a responsibility to the wench to keep his iron fury in check until he accomplished that.

"I don't doubt for a moment that you were responsible for her lateness." Miller sneered, his face lurid in rage. "And now that you've taken your pleasure, you're bringing the trash home to dump back in our lap."

"That isn't so," Brett denied his green eyes flashing. "I was tired last evening and retired early. Cerissa was kind enough to bring up a note from my companions, and I asked her, as a favor, to stay and keep company with me for a while. We drank some wine and . . ." he shrugged, hating to degrade himself by this cowardly deceit, but understanding too well Cerissa's precarious position in the tiny village, "when we awoke, it was dawn."

Wat Miller stared back into the young lord's face, his hands clenching almost spastically in fury. He longed to throw himself at the arrogant bastard to let his hands go around his throat, but something in the man's green eyes stopped him. He had the feeling that any attack he made directly on this tall stranger would make him a dead man. He knew the man was lying . . . lying at least by omitting an important fact. He had been enraged this morning to realize Cerissa was still at Mrs. Tyler's yet he had clung to foolish hope—thinking she might have been staying there at the widow's behest. Even when he'd seen the pair of them riding toward him, the girl nestled close against the man's chest—he'd hoped it was only the cold air which drove her to it. But when he'd seen the man reach up to swing her from the horse . . . seen the easy familiarity he'd handled her with . . . then, as a man, he had known.

"So the evening be spent all in innocence, eh?" he spat, knowing it for a lie.

Brett merely stared back at him, neither agreeing nor denying the statement, his stance apparently careless though his right hand rested lightly on the hilt of his sword.

"Then you won't mind me calling the midwife in to examine the slut?"

On the ground where she lay, Cerissa had listened to the exchange with growing surprise, amazed that the dark haired lord should take it upon himself to try to pacify her uncle, deeply grateful that he had. But the last question rang in her brain like a knell of doom, dashing her faint hopes. A midwife could see at once that she was no longer a virgin. Dear God! What would her uncle do with her then? Hopelessly, she sobbed anew, burying her head in her arms.

A few feet away from her, the two men still stood staring at each other. But in contrast to Cerissa's reaction, Brett had only smiled faintly at the farmer's last threat, shrugging his broad shoulders in careless concern. A midwife could tell that Cerissa was no virgin any longer, but she couldn't tell how, or when, or by whom she had been deflowered. He knew that. And more importantly, he knew that Cerissa's uncle did too. But whether that might help the girl's plight or simply worsen it...

In helpless fury, Wat Miller turned away from the dark haired lord, unable to hide the hatred in his eyes any longer.

"Get out of my town," he muttered, his voice thick with a desperate, barely restrained killing urge. "You and the rest of your ilk."

Lord Lindsey stood motionless a moment, struggling to unclench his hand from his sword hilt before he shrugged and turned to grab the reins of his horse. He had done what he could for the girl. The whole thing was obviously hopeless and going from bad to worse. His prolonged presence would only infuriate the obstinate farmer further. His face grim, and his strong jaw hard, Brett swung himself up on the black horse, hauling hard on the reins to whirl the animal around, kicking the stallion into a swift canter back toward the village crossroads.

Cerissa lay still, knowing her punishment was far from over, her knees drawn up against her belly in pathetic self defense as she cowered and whimpered in terror, waiting for the blows to start again—the worst pain of all hearing the rapid echo of hoof beats that meant Lord Lindsey had ridden out of her life forever. That alone would have been punishment enough without her uncle's savagery.

Wat Miller stared a moment at the black horse and his rider, his envy and his hatred welling up inside him like a bitter poison boil. The trembling figure of the girl caught his eye again and he turned back toward her, the force of his hatred bursting free to focus on her and all her noble birth represented. He might not be able to punish the arrogant lord as he wished to, but the girl...the girl he had sheltered and who had betrayed him to the class he hated so deeply, she was within his reach. In unreasoning fury, he bent and seized the stout cane again, raining blows and curses and kicks upon the helpless girl, seeing Lord Lindsey lying there instead of her, wanting him dead and bloody and filthy in the road.

Cerissa could only cringe in abject terror, helpless to defend herself against the man's brutal strength, unaware of how her whimpering and moans of agony goaded the man into further viciousness. With a sort of dazed bewilderment, she began to realize that her uncle wouldn't stop now until she were dead. In numb agony she only prayed for her life to end quickly, for the pain and the shame and the horror to be over.

Intent on his victim, Wat Miller didn't hear the sound of approaching hoof beats—the gratification of the girl's terror filling his whole soul. Without warning, he felt himself being hurled backwards, his body landing heavily in the dirt. Astonished, he looked up to see the dark haired lord standing over him—jaw clenched in fury, green eyes dark with danger. The farmer lay motionless, not even daring to breathe, every instinct in his soul warning him that any movement or any speech might mean his end.

"You bloody son of a bitch," Lord Lindsey grated, his voice hoarse with rage and contempt. "I ought to take your head for this. Get up you motherless whoreson and try taking your cane to me. Or does your courage desert you when there isn't a helpless girl under your stick?"

Wat Miller didn't move, didn't even dare to blink, his breath almost bursting in his lungs, his heart pounding in sick fear as he stared up into Lindsey's burning eyes.

At last, with a vicious oath, his handsome face ugly with disgust, Brett turned his back on the motionless farmer and walked quickly toward the girl who still lay whimpering in the road. He knelt beside her on one knee, drawing a deep breath to try to banish his own murderous fury. "Hush, sweetheart, it's all right now. He won't hurt you any more."

Cerissa lifted her chestnut head slowly, not believing she actually heard his voice. For a long moment, her wide, tear-filled eyes stared incredulously at lord's face. Then with a huge wracking sob, she flung herself against his chest, unable to speak, clinging to him with desperate hands.

Brett let her cry against his shoulder for only a moment, saying nothing but placing a gentle kiss on the top of her head as he held her. Then he stood, pulling her up with him.

"I think you'd better come with me, Cerissa," he murmured wearily, glancing over his shoulder cautiously to see what the girl's uncle was doing. The farmer was several yards away already, crawling backwards with great caution, his fearful eyes still pinned to the lord's sword hand.

"You mean leave Bainwater? And Aunt Mary and Annie?" Cerissa's eyes grew wide in immediate distress, fresh tears gathering in their blue depths.

"You really have no choice," Brett sighed. Unfortunately, neither did he, he thought grimly. If he left the girl here, he had no doubt that her uncle would actually beat her to death for her indiscretion. Surely she realized that too.

Cerissa's head dropped forlornly, understanding the impact of his words slowly. "Lord Lindsey, I'm so sorry . . . I've been nothing but trouble to you . . . Why didn't you just let my uncle finish his task?" She whispered miserably, unable to meet his gaze. "It's what I deserved."

A faint half-smile, a shade ironic, touched the man's lips. In a way, perhaps the girl was right. He had certainly gotten more than he'd anticipated this time. Instead of a pleasant bout of loving, and a sweet goodbye kiss at the finish, he was saddled with the wench at least until they reached London and he could find a decent place for her somewhere. He made a mental note to leave country wenches well alone after this encounter. They were much more troublesome than the pleasure was worth. Still, it really had been his fault that the girl was in this wretched situation. He could hardly have ridden away and left her to a brutal death, much as he might have wished to.

With a heavy sigh, he wiped the tears from the girl's face as best he could, and set her on the horse. Ardsley and Martin would laugh themselves sick when they saw what he'd gotten himself in for.

Chapter Three

It was twenty-three miles to Bywater, the next stop, and the day grew cloudy, damp and chill. With Cerissa perched precariously on the horse's withers, in front of the leather saddle, only Brett's one arm around her waist to balance her, their travel was far slower than usual. Much of the time passed with the men talking of things completely beyond Cerissa's limited knowledge, and she contented herself with simply listening, grateful to the blond Lord Ardsley for occasionally directing a little of the conversation her way. He had not—by so much as a raised brow or quirked lip—expressed the slightest regret or annoyance that she had come along, and Cerissa smiled at the man in deep gratitude. Lord Lindsey continued to be kind to her, though in a sort of vague preoccupied way. He said or did little to acknowledge her presence other than to offer her a cloak when he noticed her shivering in the sharp wind.

After a lunch outside, of cheese and brown bread and sweet dried apples, conversation had lagged until Lord Martin urged his horse up closer to the others, a faintly malicious expression narrowing his already narrow eyes further.

"Lord Lindsey! I guess your charm has deserted you at last," he snickered. "I'd have never guessed you'd be reduced to dragging a sixteen-year-old country wench along to keep your bed warm at night!"

Cerissa, her face flaming, stared intently at the coarse black hair of the stallion's mane while Brett simply pretended not to have heard.

Ignoring a warning glance from Ardsley, Lord Martin plunged recklessly ahead. "I hope you're planning to be generous with your new whore, Lindsey, I'd like to find out first hand what magic the girl has."

Ardsley suddenly spurred his bay gelding hard on one side, sending him jumping sideways into Harry's horse, knocking the lord nearly off. By the time Martin had regained control of his mount, he had apparently forgotten the trend of the conversation he had been pursuing and they rode again in silence.

But Cerissa had not forgotten. The word whore echoed in her horrified mind, blotting out every sight and sound of the English countryside. A whore, she thought, her soul suddenly sick with humiliation, so that's what they consider me now. No, she realized with even greater bitterness, that's actually what I am now . . . what I've become. In the space of only a single, foolish day.

She felt Lord Lindsey's arm tighten around her waist slightly, and looked up in surprise to see him smiling faintly at her, his eyes kind with reassurance. Gratefully, she smiled back tremulously and lifted her chin. So long as he did not join in the man's condemnation of her, she didn't care what the rest of the world thought . . . or what that nasty Lord Martin said. She was Cerissa Hammond, and she'd done what she'd done because she loved the man who rode behind her, and yes, damn, she would do it all again. Shyly, she turned her head and reached up to kiss Brett's cheek. He grinned down at her, surprised, but seeming pleased with her gesture, and Cerissa dared lean closer against him as they headed into Bywater.

It was already dusk by the time they reached the "Boar & Bull"—a good sized inn, with loud voices and firelight and the smell of rich, spicey stews promising a warm welcome to the small party. One of the servants went in to secure three rooms, and baths, and to reserve a private dining room for the three lords and Cerissa to eat supper in. The two squires, part of the original group, had ridden west this morning and the servants, of course, would sleep in the commons room. Cerissa was amazed to realize how quickly she had accepted the distinction between the classes. Though the three manservants had ridden the whole long journey with them, at a discreet distance behind, of course, she had not even thought to ask their names. Now, with a swift pang of guilt, she hastened to question Brett and said goodnight to each one of the men by name.

The inn's rooms were clean and nicely furnished, much larger than the ones in Mrs. Tyler's house, and Cerissa murmured her delight, not seeing the lord's indulgent smile at her delight as he turned to close the door behind them. She tucked her chin down to her chest, peering at the unfamiliar wrong-sided clasp on the cloak Brett had lent her, fumbling ineptly at the closure for several minutes before it sprung free. As she shrugged the heavy wool from her shoulders, she felt Brett's hands on them, turning her gently around to face him, his dark head bending down to cover her mouth with his own, his tongue parting her trembling lips and thrusting deep within. Cerissa was breathless by the time he finally raised his head.

"I've been wanting to do that all day," he smiled.

Cerissa smiled back at him, beginning to understand the strange, dark expression in his glittering green eyes, and welcoming it. She slid her arms over his broad shoulders, looping them loosely around his neck. At least, in this one situation his coolness melted and she could pretend he was as glad of her company as she was of his. "Before dinner?"

Brett nodded slowly. "They'll understand if we're a little late," he murmured, bending his head down to her face, his hands reaching behind the girl to cup her buttocks, pulling her hips forward against his.

Involuntarily, Cerissa flinched and gave a soft cry of pain.

"What is it? What's the matter?" Brett questioned sharply, frowning in confusion.

Quick tears burned in the girl's blue eyes at the obvious frustration showing on the lord's dark face. "Nothing," she lied, closing her eyelids and raising her lips up for another kiss, pressing her body closer to his. "I'm sorry."

Lord Lindsey stood, staring down at her, still frowning. In a moment he had whirled her around, his fingers working at the buttons of her long, homespun wool skirt, leaving it drop to the floor around her ankles, then starting on her petticoat snaps.

Cerissa remained motionless, not daring to utter a protest

though her heart hammered in disappointment and something near to fear. Was he going to take her just like this? Without even another kiss or a single caress?

"Jesus God!" the dark lord muttered softly, staring in sick surprise at the girl's buttocks and thighs. Both were covered with long red and purple welts, raised and swollen and angry looking. "My God, girl, why didn't you say something about these? Riding all day...you never complained..." he shook his dark head in impotent rage wishing the girl's uncle were under his sword hand now. He'd had no idea the man had beaten her this long before he had glanced back and seen them. "I'll send one of the servants for some salve. You'd best take it easy tonight. I'll have your dinner sent up."

Cerissa stood in helpless silence, seeing only the black temper on his hard face, not understanding that it was directed at her uncle and not at her. Her heart hammering in sudden, sick fear she forced a trembling smile, trying to press coquettishly against the angry lord. He was disgusted with her infirmity—she could read that plainly, flickering in his water dark eyes. He might leave her here. Not take her with him.

"Don't worry about these, my lord," she murmured desperately, catching at his arm in a pathetic effort to dispel the anger. "They hardly hurt me any more. I can still do whatever you desire."

Lord Lindsey scowled at her, his mouth hard. "For God's sake, girl, what kind of low-life do you think I am? I don't ride a lame horse, and I'm not going to..." Suddenly he stopped, drawing a deep breath, realizing belatedly that the girl had only been trying to please him. "Oh hell, forgive me Cerissa. I'm only so damn mad at your uncle. I should have killed him when I had the chance." Disgustedly he shook his dark head, turning away. At the doorway, he paused again, turning back to face the girl, his smile warm if a touch strained. "Don't you worry, sweetheart, I'm not angry with you. Just get a good bath and put some balm on your hurts. Don't wait up—I may be late playing cards downstairs."

Cerissa nodded, grateful for his change of temper, her smile radiant now that she understood his rage. "Win a...a hundred pounds," she wished him sincerely, naming the hugest sum she could think of.

Brett's smile deepened at the wide-eyed wonder on the girl's face as she mentioned the amount. "If I do, I'll give half of it to you," he promised. "Now do as I told you and I'll see you for breakfast." He acknowledged the kiss Cerissa blew him with a salute and stepped into the hallway, closing the door. Immediately, his face transformed into hard, angry lines revisualizing the ugly weals left by the uncle's stout whipping cane, his eyes growing dark and glittering with menace. If I ever see that son of a bitch again, he's a dead man, he promised himself. Only a little comforted, he strode off down the hall to join Ardsley and Martin below.

It was late morning, and her stomach was growling with hunger before Lord Lindsey reappeared at last. Cerissa jumped up happily to greet him, her smile radiant with relief, for she had begun to believe he had ridden off and left her.

"Well, princess, you're up early," Brett smiled easily, his eyes light and calm, reflecting renewed good nature. "Hungry, I hope."

"Famished!" Cerissa agreed quickly, delighted at his much improved mood. "But why do you call this early? Lordy, but the sun's been up for hours . . . you're not just now getting to bed?" she asked in astonishment, her blue eyes wide.

He chuckled as he drew on fresh clothing, glancing over his shoulder to reply. "Maybe you farm wenches get up at dawn—but we don't. Not unless we have to. And it isn't too unusual for us to go to bed about this time—except out at sea. Then I follow an earlier schedule."

"At sea?" Cerissa echoed in surprise. "You have a boat?"

"A ship," he corrected smiling still. "Actually several of them. I get tired of Court life pretty quickly so . . . I go privateering."

Cerissa's brows pulled together in quick disapproval, "You mean you're a pirate?"

Brett looked at the girl sideways, his eyes dancing with amused surprise. "I'm not a pirate, I'm a privateer. Cerissa. There's a difference."

"Uncle Wat said they were one and the same thing," she argued. "Only one was legally wicked and the other wasn't. I forget now which was which."

Brett grinned, shaking his head patiently, "You don't like pirates?" he teased, lacing his shirt.

Cerissa stared at him a moment in confusion. How could she say no when he was evidently one of them? "Well . . ." she answered slowly, "I never met one before, that's all."

The lord chuckled as he bent to pull his boots on. "A very diplomatic reply," he conceded, his face revealing his mirth.

Cerissa fell silent, vaguely uneasy. He seemed to be laughing at her, but she wasn't sure. Perhaps she'd be best to drop the subject for now. "Where did you sleep then since you didn't come back here?" she asked.

Brett frowned at her, not entirely pleased with the question. It was one thing to bring her along—entirely another for her to start nagging him like a jealous wife. But, seeing the artlessness in her eyes, he merely shurgged, deciding she probably didn't realize that she shouldn't ask. "In another room," he answered shortly, omitting any reference to the inn's barmaid who had shared it with him. No sense causing a useless quarrel.

Cerissa pouted, confused and puzzled. She opened her mouth to pursue the topic further but was interrupted by the arrival of their breakfast. She jumped to her feet staring at the trays of food in astonished delight. "Oh Brett, look here!" she cried excitedly running to the small table. "There's eggs, and fried ham, and cheese and fruit and sweet cakes and jam, and . . . what's this?" she asked, peering at a thin inky liquid distastefully.

"That's called coffee, sweetheart," he smiled. "Don't you like it?"

"I don't know," she replied slowly, dipping a finger in it to taste the dark brew. "Ugh, no." she decided, making a face. "It's bitter."

"Tea then for the lady," Brett smiled to the servant, tossing him a silver coin.

Cerissa sat at the table, still studying the various dishes in a kind of reverent awe. Two days before she had eaten a half-bowl of porridge for her breakfast and thought herself fortunate. Brett must have ordered this feast especially for her. Eyes shining, she turned to thank him, all thoughts of his nightlong absence fled.

"Well, you're welcome of course, sweetheart. But why all the fuss? We eat like this every morning."

Cerissa gazed at the food, feeling like a terrible fool. Of course a lord wouldn't eat porridge in the morning. She would learn not to jump to conclusions.

"And why does that fact steal the smile from your face, Cerissa?" Brett questioned gently, studying her downcast face shrewdly. He sensed that he had taken much of her delight in the meal away, but why?

"No reason," she replied quickly, forcing a faint smile back on her face. "I was just thinking of my life in Bainwater."

Brett continued to look at her a moment longer, sensing there was another deeper reason, but not knowing what. Finally he shrugged, forgetting about it. "Here then . . . try some of these shirred eggs, sweetheart, and pass the coffee over to this side. The boy will bring your tea up shortly."

Cerissa and Lord Lindsey had been waiting downstairs for Lord Ardsley for several minutes before he arrived. But as soon as the blond lord caught sight of the girl, he turned with an oath and started back up the stairs. Cerissa glanced quizzically up at Brett's dark face, but he only shrugged his ignorance and watched the stairs. At last, Lord Ardsley reappeared, a feather pillow tucked under one arm.

"How much?" he asked the inn-keeper, holding the pillow high in the air with one hand.

The man quickly said, "One pound." He could buy four good pillows for that much, and he knew these eccentric lords would pay the inflated price.

"Here then," the blond lord grinned, giving the pillow a sharp toss in his friend's direction as he turned to pay the innkeeper.

Brett managed to grab the thing with one hand before it hit him, and he glanced impatiently at Ardsley. "What the hell is this for?"

The blond lord arched his brows in seeming surprise. "Don't you think your lady friend's nether regions deserve some special consideration for awhile. Your stallion's withers are hardly a comfortable saddle on the best of days."

Brett nodded quickly, understanding at last, and a bit chagrinned that he hadn't remembered about the girl's hurts himself. "Thanks," he muttered quickly. "Let me pay you back."

Ardsley just chuckled, dismissing his friend's offer with a wave. "Don't bother, Brett. You lost enough to me last night at cards. I can afford to be generous."

Cerissa accepted the pillow Brett handed her with mumbled thanks, her face burning in embarrassment. Her "nether regions" as Lord Ardsley had called them, were a very private matter to her. She was horrified to think Brett had been discussing the condition of them with everyone in the inn. And what did the blond lord mean about winning so much money? How much had Brett lost? She wondered about that silently all the way out to the stableyard, wanting to know but afraid to ask. She didn't want Brett to think she was prying.

But finally, the worry made her ask him, her voice soft and tentative.

To her relief, Lord Lindsey only chuckled, no sign of displeasure darkening his emerald eyes. "You don't really want to know, princess. You'd think it a horrendous amount and worry all day."

"That much?" Cerissa gasped, her eyes wide in dismay. He must have lost ten, even twenty pounds, to talk like that.

Ardsley and Brett exchanged quick, amused glances, the dark haired lord shaking his head in mirth.

"Don't be over-concerned, sweet," Lord Ardsley grinned teasingly at her. "He's not a total pauper yet. And you know what they say—Lucky in love, unlucky at cards."

Cerissa smiled back at the blond man, liking him greatly and terribly pleased that he thought Brett lucky to have her love. "I'd like to learn how to play that card game myself, Lord Ardsley," she announced, her eyes sparkling at the idea of being so wicked, for gambling was a vice, she had been taught so from birth. "Maybe I'll win some money back from you!"

Ardsley and Brett exchanged swift surprised glances before bursting into loud laughter. This was the first time the girl had shown the courage to break free of her narrow, country up-bringing and the two men approved the change whole-heartedly. "Mind he doesn't try to cheat you," Brett chuckled as he swung into the saddle behind her.

"He wouldn't dare," Cerissa assured him with great confidence. "I've got a pretty sharp eye."

She was puzzled by Brett's laughter for she could think of nothing funny in what she had said. But when he bent his head to kiss her hair lightly, she forgot all about it in the pleasure of his caress. In great contentment, despite her aching buttocks, she leaned happily against him, lost in her daydreams.

Chapter Four

Lord Martin and his manservant met the rest of the party at a crossroad late that afternoon, and Cerissa tried to conceal her displeasure at his reappearance. She had assumed that he, like the squires, had turned aside to pursue a different route, but evidently he had only made a small detour and now intended to accompany them to London.

Cerissa heartily disliked the man, almost feared him, though she tried to ignore those feelings. She certainly had no real reason for her attitude, except for a few minor comments he had made that had embarrassed her, and she could hardly protest his presence to Brett on the strength of those. And yet, try as she might she couldn't forget him. And every time she happened to glance around unexpectedly, she found him staring at her with a very, unpleasant expression in his pale, narrow eyes.

It was the third night out of Bainwater, the second they had camped out under the tall, royal oaks along the main road. The men preferred the mild discomforts of the outdoors to the dubious quality and cleanliness of the inns on this stretch of the journey. Tomorrow, Brett had commented—noticing the trouble she had had the night before in finding a comfortable position for her sore back, rump and thighs on the hard ground—they would reach Oxford. And from there on into the city of London there were plenty of good inns—well kept and frequented by a higher class of travelers.

Now, with supper over, the three lords and Cerissa sat on blankets inside the large tent, a lantern lighting the small space as the inevitable card game began again. Cerissa watched in contented silence, curled up like a small kitten at Lord Lindsey's side, smiling and laughing with them at their varying fortunes and misfortunes as they played.

Suddenly, Ardsley grinned at the girl, beckoning her to sit forward into the circle. "Didn't you say something about wanting to learn to play this, sweetheart?"

Cerissa nodded, but spread her hands apart in denial. "I don't have any money," she demurred, not really too disappointed to simply sit and watch.

"Oh that's no problem. Brett here can stake you," Ardsley chuckled, enjoying his friend's surprise.

"I will not," Lord Lindsey denied quickly, though he grinned at the blond lord good naturedly. "I lose enough money to you just paying my own debts."

"Oh, go on," Ardsley urged, laughing and giving Brett's leg a quick jab. "Don't be such a miser with the wench."

"Leave Lindsey keep his money," Lord Martin interrupted smoothly, his light-blue eyes glittering with a disturbing expression as he gazed at Cerissa. "Let her play like the ladies do at Madame Ribot's. Let her use herself as her stake."

Both Ardsley and Brett frowned at the man's suggestion, all humor vanishing from their faces. Cerissa squirmed uncomfortably. She had never heard of Madame Ribot's and didn't understand what the man meant by using herself as her stake, but she distrusted and disliked him and guessed he meant no good.

And the two men, who were familiar with the notorious gambling house and brothel located just off fashionable St. James Park, liked Lord Martin's idea no better. It was custom there for ladies of the Court to arrive incognito, a mask concealing their faces, and play cards or dice in an unusual way. They would take a seat at a table and proceed to gamble the night away. Each time they lost a hand or a throw of the dice, the winner would choose one item of their clothing to remove. The man who won the last piece claimed the woman's body as well, at least until dawn.

"Back off, Martin," Brett warned softly, his green eyes glittering, his mouth hard.

His mouth sullen and stubborn, Lord Martin took another swig of brandy, apparently unperturbed at the dark haired man's anger. "My Lord, Lindsey!" he complained heatedly. "You're the stingiest man with his whore that I ever saw. It's fine for you, of course, you've had company in your bed every night of the journey, but for the rest of us..." Without warning, he lunged forward, his hand cupped, reaching to grab Cerissa's breast.

Instinctively, the girl twisted and leaned back behind Lord Lindsey's shoulder, wordlessly, seeking his protection. She heard Ardsley swear in anger, and sensed rather than saw Brett's hand go for the dagger in his belt. She grabbed for his arm desperately, crying a warning to the blond haired lord.

Ardsley jumped between the two men quickly, hauling Lord Martin backwards out of the tent into the cool night air, swearing viciously at him as he moved.

Cerissa let go of Brett's arm, pale with fear at how he might react to her interference. Surprisingly, he said nothing, his face reflecting total concentration in controlling his black temper. At last, he sighed and gave the girl an absent-minded pat. "If he weren't Ardsley's cousin, I'd enjoy slitting that son of a bitch's throat. He's one of the most unpleasant..."

Cerissa drew a deep breath, relieved that he wasn't angry with her, and astonished that the detestable Lord Martin could be kin to Lord Ardsley whom she liked so well. At least that explained a few things, she mused silently, for she had noticed Brett and Ardsley exchange irritated glances at the man's behavior several times along the way, and she had wondered why they tolerated his continued presence. But of course, since he was family...

"I'm sorry, Brett," Ardsley had reappeared into the tent, his normally ruddy complexion nearly maroon in anger and exertion. "He must have had too much brandy."

"Better caution him to drink less in the future, then, James. I'll kill him next time."

Lord Ardsley nodded agreement, a little surprised that Brett's quick temper hadn't murdered the dumb bastard already. Not that he'd mourn his cousin overmuch anyway. "Well, I don't feel like playing anymore. Shall we just turn in?"

Brett nodded, turning around to spread the blankets out smooth. Cerissa hesitated a moment, knowing she couldn't go to sleep yet, but embarrassed to say anything. Finally, red-faced she murmured something to the men and went outside searching the darkness for a relatively private place to relieve herself.

On her way back in, she felt a man's arm slip around her waist, and she turned to face him, sure it was Brett, welcoming his attention. The sight of Lord Martin's face pressed close to hers so startled her that she froze for a moment. Then belatedly tried to jump away, terrified to feel his arms lock around her, pulling against him. Instinctively, she opened her mouth to scream for Lord Lindsey, but Martin clamped his hand across it before she could make a sound. Cerissa writhed and kicked at his legs, desperate to escape. At last, she managed to get her mouth partly free of his smothering grip, and she screamed again and again in mounting hysteria.

Ardsley bolted through the tent flap first, Lord Lindsey on his heels, running hard toward the screaming girl, Lord Martin released the girl and stepped backwards, scowling in anger and fear.

Ardsley stopped between his cousin and the trembling girl, wordless in his rage.

Brett stopped to throw an arm around Cerissa's shoulders, his face, pale in the faint light, drawn with anger. "Cerissa, are you all right?" he questioned brusquely, staring at the girl's frightened face. She started to nod, then her eye catching a movement behind him, gasped and cried a hasty warning.

"Look out, Brett, he's got a sword!"

Lord Lindsey whirled to face the smaller man, jumping backwards quickly to avoid a slashing thrust of Lord Martin's sword. In an instant, he had drawn his own in reply, shoving Cerissa toward the protection of Lord Ardsley.

"Harry, you damn fool, put your sword up!" The blond lord ordered, his voice hoarse with rage.

"And let him slit my throat, James? No thank you." Lord Martin hissed back, his gaze never wavering from the tip of Lord Lindsey's sword, gleaming dully in the fitful moonlight of the cloudy night.

"For God's sake, man, don't be a total idiot," Ardsley snapped in reply. "Do you think for one minute that your waving that thing around is going to deter a swordsman of Brett's caliber from killing you if he decides to? Now put the damn thing away."

For a long moment, no one moved. Then, reluctantly, Lord Martin lowered his sword, licking his lips fearfully as he stared at

43

Lord Lindsey's furious green eyes. "Don't let him kill me, James," he whined piteously, starting to back away. "You promised."

Ardsley glanced quickly at his friend, his eyes anxious. "Please, Brett, for my sake. God knows he's given you reason enough, but leave it go. I'll send him packing tonight. I've had a bellyfull of his company myself."

Brett shrugged reluctantly and sheathed his sword with deliberate slowness, pausing to stare for a long moment at the cowering Harry, his eyes pitiless and unforgiving, glittering dangerously in the soft light. Then he turned on his heel and strode swiftly toward the tent.

Ardsley caught at Cerissa's arm as she turned to follow Lord Lindsey, his kind eyes troubled as he searched the girl's pale face intently. "I'm sorry sweetheart. He . . . he didn't hurt you?"

Cerissa shook her head quickly and pulled away, anxious to be away from Lord Martin and safe inside the tent with Brett. By the time she reached the flap and stepped inside, Lord Lindsey was already stretched out under the blankets, laying on his stomach, his head resting on his folded arms. Cerissa noticed his boots and his jacket lying neatly near the small table, but the swordbelt which usually lay with them was missing. She turned to look for it and saw it lying on top of the blankets, at Brett's side. Cerissa shivered at the implied menace, but said nothing. Quickly she kicked off her tiny shoes and reached to extinguish the lantern, kneeling at Lord Lindsey's side to reach down and rub the tight muscles of his neck and shoulders. At last, she felt them relax and soften under her touch. After a time his light, even breathing told her that he slept, and gratefully, she lifted an edge of the blanket, careful not to disturb him, and crawled blissfully against him. She was momentarily amazed at the tremendous warmth he always seemed to radiate, even sleeping, and then, in another moment, she nestled her head closer to the strength and protection of his shoulder. There, she listened for what seemed like hours to the sounds of Lord Martin's hurried departure, hearing Ardsley's soft curses and exhortations to haste, and finally the rapid rhythm of hoofbeats galloping away. And only then did she sleep.

Cerissa awoke at the first light finding her long years in the country routine hard to break. As usual, both men were still sleeping soundly. She paused to raise the blankets higher over Brett's shoulders, then tiptoed carefully out into the cool, late March morning, waving a hello to the two manservants who were gathering wood to boil water for coffee. Both lords were adamant about starting the day with several mugs of the black, bitter brew.

Ardsley even refused to put his boots on without its fortification. Cerissa still preferred the milder taste of tea, and that was enough of a luxury for a country wench used to spring water.

Breakfast done, the small group mounted up, Cerissa still balancing gingerly on the feather pillow, but enough accustomed now to her perch to allow the men to canter and even gallop the horses at times. The initial strangeness between the two men, caused she guessed, by the confrontation last night, evaporated quickly in the sunshine of the fine spring day. Ardsley chatted amiably, amusing the girl with wild tales of Court life, describing the sights she would see in London City.

Cerissa listened intently, terribly aware of how important this casual information might be to her future. Despite all her efforts, she had never managed to get the taciturn Lord Lindsey to confide anything of his background, his thoughts, or his feelings. Actually, of late, she had found herself wondering whether he even had any—feelings, that is. His attitude toward her had been unfailingly kind, unfailingly considerate—and unfailingly distant. At first she had assumed his manner was due to some lingering resentment at having to bring her along in the first place, yet he never admitted to that, no matter how much she questioned him. She had finally been forced to admit to herself that she sensed no anger toward her on the lord's part; only a faintly cool, faintly vague indifference she increasingly found more frightening than anger. It was as if Brett hardly recognized her presence except when some need of her's impinged on his consciousness. As if he felt only the distant kindness he might show to any living creature dependent on him. In contrast, her adoration of the dark haired lord had grown to awesome proportions. And unless she could somehow manage to strike a spark, to breach the wall of that indifference.

"Cerissa, aren't you listening to me?" Lord Ardsley's complaint was delivered with a grin, and the girl smiled ruefully in return, shaking her head.

"I thought perhaps you weren't, sweetheart," Ardsley laughed, "So let me repeat myself. You really ought to reconsider, and turn your affections from Brett to me. After all, he may be titled already, but he's only a baronet, and I'll be an earl when my father dies. Besides, I'm a much nicer fellow overall than this black haired devil you ride with. He'll take off for the high seas anytime again like the pirate he is and leave you waving a tearful farewell from the docks. Now I—I'm far more stable than he is and far more considerate. I stay put in England. And I..."

"You amuse yourself with dice and cards, and Court whores,

and entirely too much brandy," Brett laughed. "Which is far less conducive to longevity than piracy."

"And I'm almost as rich as he is," Ardsley continued to tease, pretending not to hear his friend's retort.

Cerissa smiled at the blond lord, aware that his teasing was mostly just that, even though much of what he said in jest was really true. Why hadn't she fallen in love with the blond lord instead? Why this enigmatic, moody man who remained a stranger despite her efforts to touch his heart? Suppose she accepted Lord Ardsley's offer? Would Brett even protest? She thought not. Yet her love belonged to him regardless. Fool that she undoubtedly was.

Gradually, the men's talk drifted to other things and Cerissa tried to force the apprehension Ardsley's words had caused from her heart. She could not help herself, she admitted ruefully at last. She loved where she loved, though there was precious little reason for it to lie there. And whether Brett remained a mystery, or if he indeed left her on a dock as Ardsley said he well might, she could not change the course of that love. And though she realized the bleakness of her future, the hopelessness of her affection, she continued to smile radiantly whenever Lord Lindsey spoke or glanced at her, feeling as though God had given her the whole, beautiful world in the person of this tall, black haired stranger with gleaming green eyes.

They made their way slowly toward London, detouring once for several days to visit a noted resort, famous for its healthful waters. Ardsley, of course had been the one to suggest the stop, pointing out that one of the party had some unmentionable hurts which might be eased by a good soaking. Brett had agreed though with little enthusiasm, that strange darkening expression playing on his face as he smiled at the embarrassed girl.

And on their next stop, Lord Lindsey had marched the bewildered Cerissa into the local dressmaker's, ordering two new outfits for the astonished girl. In Bainwater, these clothes would last for a whole year, maybe more!

"I don't need any more." Cerissa protested softly, a look of wonder on her face at the countless bolts of brightly colored fabric. Tentatively she touched Brett's hand feeling hope stir in her heart. Was this unbelievable generosity sign that the lord's coolness was finally beginning to change? With London only days away...

Lord Lindsey merely arched his eyebrows in disagreement, a half smile curving his lips at her reluctance to spend any of his

46

money. Most women were quite the opposite. Normally, he found Cerissa's attitude charming but just now ... she'd had those same clothes on for the entire week he'd known her and they were getting a bit stale. "Two." he repeated firmly to the waiting seamstress.

"What style?" the woman asked the bewildered girl.

Cerissa shrugged helpessly. She'd never in her life seen any fashion other than what the country women wore in Bainwater.

"Like these, I suppose," she answered at last. "I'm used to these."

The dressmaker looked toward the tall lord, obviously expecting him to disapprove. But Brett shrugged his shoulders in acceptance and turned away, a faint smile still lingering on his lips as he walked toward several bolts of brightly dyed calico cotton.

"And a day gown out of this," he said, holding up a corner of sky-blue material, printed all over with tiny bunches of long stemmed white daisies. "Something fairly modest but not too childish."

Cerissa looked at the material in awed delight, thinking it the most beautiful thing she had ever seen. She gazed at Brett with adoration in her blue eyes, wishing she could jump to her feet and throw her arms around his neck in thanks.

The dark haired lord smiled back at Cerissa as he turned to the door, a little embarrassed himself by the radiance of the girl's pretty face. "You get fitted here, sweetheart, then go back to the inn. Ardsley and I will be out hunting all day, but I'll meet you for dinner." He started out the door, turning suddenly as he snapped his fingers in belated rememberance. "And a dressing gown too," he called over his shoulder to the amused seamstress. "By tonight."

Cerissa blushed hotly as the shop women exchanged laughing glances, but she soon forgot her uneasiness in the exciting bustle of the clothes-making. The shop's owner, an older woman with a kindly eye, soon realized that the girl was totally ignorant of high fashion and she scolded herself silently for pushing the child into making such a poor choice on her outfits. There was no help for it now. The linen shirts were already cut, the wool skirts nearly so. At least she could guide the girl about the laced bodices she would wear over the shirts.

"Becky!" she called, a warning glint in her old eyes. "We seem to be out of the brown wool for bodices. Make one of the emerald green velvet, and the other of that new rose pink. Lord Lindsey won't mind the change."

In pretended innocence, she spent the day chatting gaily to the sweet young country girl with the pretty name. Cerissa, she mused, no farmer's wife thought that one up. And the girl had a certain fineness, as well, a certain air of quality. Realizing she would never know, the woman shrugged her curiosity aside, concentrating on teaching the ABC's of current style, doing it in such a way that the child never guessed she was being taught.

Finally, all was settled except for the dressing robe, and here the woman hesitated for a long minute, wondering whether modesty or seduction should be her goal. At length, her memory of the dark, good looks of the girl's young lord decided her. He was one gorgeous hunk of man and he deserved something extra special.

Smiling secretly, her eyes gleaming, the older woman described the cut of the gown to the apprentice who would make it. "And the bodice, very high," she mused aloud. "The neckline low ... very revealing, but sew in a generous ruffle of the same material. That way, it closes up for modesty, opens for ..." She laughed aloud as she made a suggestive gesture, delighted with her own cleverness. Now, what should the fabric be? Silk would be cooler, and oh, so very clinging and seductive ... But silk was also very expensive. Perhaps Lord Lindsey would be angered at the cost. Brocade too stiff for the design, and velvet too ... Oh! But that new bolt of lightweight robin's egg blue—yes! That would be perfection. Hadn't the lord himself selected a blue calico to match the girl's lovely, large blue eyes? And with the girl's rich, dark brown hair, touched with the auburn glints ... yes, perfect. Intrigued with the whole prospect, anxious to have the gown done by evening, the woman clapped her hands imperiously, hurrying the apprentices, pulling the confused Cerissa toward the private, curtained fitting room in the shop's rear. Oh! What she would give to see Lord Lindsey's face when he saw the girl tonight ...

Cerissa was bathing when her dressing gown finally arrived. The shopkeeper started to bring another of the everyday outfits along as it was finished but she had decided against it at the last moment, turning back around to return it to the shop for the night. The girl might just be innocent enough—or ignorant enough—to dress herself in that instead of the blue robe. Helpfully, she assisted the girl into the gown, demonstrating the clever way the neckline could change shape. At the embarrassed blush that reddened the girl's face when she turned the ruffle down, the woman sighed and shrugged helplessly. Well, she had done what she could for the child anyway. If the girl chose to hide her beauty behind the fabric so be it.

As the door closed after the shop woman, Cerissa stared

wonderingly at her reflection in Brett's small traveling mirror, amazed and rather delighted with the apparently sophisticated young woman who stared back at her. Daringly, holding her breath and feeling horribly wicked, she turned the velvet ruffle down, revealing the shadowed creamy softness of her high, full breasts.

At the sound of the door opening, she turned in surprise, forgetting to pull the blue velvet back up. Brett stood motionless in the doorway, his eyes wide with amazement as they dropped slowly down to the gown's hem and then returned to her face, a slow smile of approval spreading over his handsome face. "Holy Jesus!" he breathed at last, forgetting that he was cold and wet from being caught in the rain as they hunted, "How beautiful!"

Cerissa stood hesitantly, a shy smile on her face at his obvious delight. But then, as his gaze swung back to her bosom, she remembered her near nakedness in horror and reached quickly to pull the velvet back together.

"No!" Brett commanded swiftly, coming out of his near-trance at last to move quickly toward her, catching at her small, fine boned hands to draw the blue velvet away again. "Leave it like that."

Cerissa blushed guiltily and dropped her hands, her head whirling dizzily from the hot expression gleaming in his dark green eyes. Shyly, she reached her hands up around his neck, her soft blue eyes locked with his, her own breath coming in shallow, rapid gasps as she felt him press against her, feeling the trembling beginning in his body. Brett dropped his head, crushing her lips under his, his tongue thrusting deeply within her mouth, urging, seeking, wondering. Cerissa returned his kisses with a fierce longing of her own. Being so close to him all these days without being able to taste the delights of his loving again . . .

At last, Brett raised his dark head, eyes emerald in passion as he asked huskily, "Is it all right yet, sweetheart? Your back . . ."

Cerissa smiled her answer, not caring if it left her in sobbing agony, then pouted and cried softly aloud in disappointment. "The bed isn't made up yet! The servants said they would do it while we ate dinner . . ."

Brett only smiled, searching the room for an alternative. There by the fire lay a deep, oval sheepskin—soft and fluffy and terribly inviting just now. "Who needs a bed?" he questioned, his voice soft and almost hoarse in his eagerness.

Without waiting for her answer, he bent and carried her over to the rug, pausing only to throw a couple more logs on the small fire. Cerissa had never gotten accustomed to the luxury of burning wood—the poorer country folk used peat instead—and she always kept a fire on the edge of extinction. Shrugging off his wet cloak and tossing it impatiently near the hearth, he turned back to the girl, dropping quickly beside her on the soft fleece, covering her mouth possessively, one hand reaching down to cup her soft breast.

Cerissa gasped with the violence of the hot, giddy flashes that stabbed her loins, writhing urgently against Brett's body in desire. In a moment, he started to fumble at the closings of her gown, his fingers strangely clumsy in his haste. Cerissa dropped her hand down to caress the length of his taut, trembling body, her fingers finding the front of his still wet breeches, gasping in redoubled passion to feel his manhood swollen and hard under her touch. With a muffled groan, Brett pulled the edges of the velvet apart, exposing her whole body to his caresses. Quickly he slipped the buttons of his breeches open, groaning again to feel the warm touch of her flesh against him, and he bent his dark head to bury his face in the sweet darkness of her breasts, his mouth covering her nipple as he touched her with his tongue.

Cerissa sighed in ecstasy as she felt him enter her, thrusting deep within her in mounting violence. The world whirled and stars burst in her brain as she clutched his hips greedily against hers. In a moment, she felt Brett convulse and cry aloud—an instant later she followed him. And it seemed like days later when she reopened her eyes and drifted back into the lazy contentment of the moment.

Brett's head lay heavy and damply warm on her breast, his face flushed, his breath still ragged. At last he raised it slowly, smiling ruefully as he met her gaze. "I'm sorry, sweetheart, I was too quick for you this time." He sighed heavily and rolled to lay beside her, still fighting for breath, marvelling at the intensity of his own desire for the girl. "Jesus, I think the last time I made love with my breeches on, I was fifteen..."

Cerissa smiled, feeling immensely successful though she didn't quite know at what, snuggling contentedly against the wet linen of his shirt. "What did you mean, too quick?"

Brett threw her a swift startled glance. "Well, I meant... Was the loving fulfilling this time? I figured that I didn't..."

Cerissa smiled a cat's smile of secret satisfaction, pleased to see his expression change in answering knowledge, though she was still puzzled over his words.

"Well, one of these times, maybe you'll know what I meant about 'too quick,'" Brett smiled teasingly, "And then again maybe not."

Cerissa reached out to caress his face, combing her fingers

through his thick dark hair. She started to ask him when dinner would be, then stopped hastily, realizing he had fallen sound asleep. Quietly, she reached for the edges of her gown, drawing them back together, unready to move yet herself.

A soft knock at the door startled her and she jumped to her feet, snapping her robe front together, flipping the ruffle closed as she ran to the door. "Who is it?" she called softly.

"Me—Ardsley," a deep voice answered. "May I come in?"

"Oh . . ." Cerissa paused a moment, smoothing her hair back and straightening her gown self consciously. She knew that Ardsley understood the relationship she had with Brett, and yet it continued to embarrass her—especially for him to walk in now, when he would surely know what they'd just been doing . . . Hurriedly, she glanced around the room, searching for any tell tale signs of their loving—horrified to realized that Brett's breeches were still unbuttoned. "Just a minute, Lord Ardsley," she called hastily, running back to Brett to keel beside him, her fingers pulling gently on the front of his still damp pants as she tried to slide the buttons through without waking him. Suddenly, she raised her head, feeling his gaze upon her.

"After me again already, wench?" Lord Lindsey smiled lazily, looking not unpleased with the idea.

Cerissa smiled back at him, the affection in his green eyes giving her the courage to reply saucily as she withdrew her hands. "Hardly so, you conceited thing! Your friend, Lord Ardsley, is knocking at our door, and I was only trying to make you decent before I let him in."

Brett grinned, enjoying her pertness, his hands reaching out to grasp her wrists as he pulled her down against him, covering her mouth possessively for a long kiss. At last, reluctantly, Cerissa raised her head, tracing the outline of his lips wistfully with one gentle fingertip, and gestured toward the door.

"Go away, Ardsley," Brett called lazily, never moving from where he lay stretched out full length on the warm rug, "We're busy."

"The hell I will go away," the voice behind the door responded. "You've time enough for that after dinner."

Lord Lindsey grinned and sat up, buttoning his breeches before he stood. Then, as the turned to the door, he noticed the girl's downcast face, and hastily knelt beside her, his eyes soft with concern. "What is it, sweetheart? What's the matter? Is it your back?"

Cerissa shook her head, trying to smile but her lips were

51

quivering "I'm sorry, Brett. I'm just being silly."

A fleeting smile flashed across the dark lord's face before he responded. Most of the time, the things that women chose to cry or sulk about he did find silly. As long as he hadn't hurt her...

"It's only that..." Cerissa murmured softly, her tear filled eyes intent on the floor "Well, I hate the way that people look at me sometimes... like they're laughing at me because they know that I... you know, with you."

Brett studied the girl's face for a long moment, wondering what he could say to her. It was true what she said, the girl was right. Of course people looked at a man's whore that way. What did she expect? "Ardsley doesn't think the less of you for sleeping with me, sweetheart. He only likes to tease you."

"Oh, I know, Brett, and I like Lord Ardsley an awful lot... but it still embarrasses me to have him know. I'm sorry, I know its silly."

Lord Lindsey was silent, his eyes troubled. Of course he should have realized—the girl was too naive to know what to expect in this new type of life she'd been plunged into. But if Ardsley's affectionate teasing bothered her, how in the world would she ever face the more hostile opinions? The open lechery in a man's eyes or the cruel, appraising mockery of a woman's? "Listen, sweetheart, I think we should have a longer talk about this. I want to explain a few things to you—prepare you for what you're liable to meet with when we get to London—but for now... we'd better let Ardsley in before he breaks the door down. OK?"

Cerissa nodded, grateful and a little surprised at the lord's patience with her. Brett got halfway to the door and started to chuckle, realizing that in his previous haste to get Cerissa in his arms, he had neglected to bolt the door. "Come on in Ardsley—the door's open."

The blond lord came in quickly, shaking his head in exaggerated frustration, "Jesus, Lindsey! I'd stood out there in the hall so long it was starting to feel like home! Not much question about what you two were doing in here while I..." He caught the warning shake of Brett's head, his glance toward the girl, and he stopped uncertainly, wondering what was wrong.

"I was only napping." Lord Lindsey's voice was solemn, though his green eyes danced with amusement.

The blond lord noticed his mirth and relaxed again. "Napping, my ass," he chucked, "You were..."

Brett shook his head again, harder this time, a slight frown forming. "Only sleeping."

Ardsley fell silent, staring at his friend in confusion. At last, noticing the embarrassment on the girl's face, he began to understand, and nodded slightly toward Brett. "So, he spends a whole day away from you, out hunting, and the best he can manage when he finally gets home is to fall asleep? With such a lovely creature as you to welcome him?" Ardsley walked over to drop a teasing arm around the girl's shoulders, "I have half a mind to steal you away from him and show you how a pretty girl ought to be treated! I wouldn't neglect you like that, believe me."

Cerissa smiled shyly, blushing a little bit in confusion. Lord Ardsley made it sound as though Brett had failed somehow in his responsibility to her. She hated to hear him criticized—especially when she knew it wasn't true. Uneasily, she glanced sideways, up through her full lashes at Ardsley's good natured face, totally unaware of how seductive her look was. "He doesn't neglect me," she murmured defensively "Why you should see all the clothes he bought for me today."

The blond lord arched his eyebrows, looking sufficiently impressed even though, of course, Brett had told him about it earlier while they were hunting. He listened attentively, nodding slowly. "And a gown too? Out of the most beautiful cloth in the world?" he echoed teasingly "Well, that kind of event should be marked by a celebration, don't you think, Brett?" He looked at his friend inquiringly, his blue eyes shinging with mirth.

Lord Lindsey grinned and nodded in response "Definitely. Though the gown won't be done until tomorrow."

"Tomorrow night, then. We'll all go to dinner at the "Cock & Quail," he said, referring to a noted tavern in town recommended for its good food and ale, and frequented by whatever members of the nobility found themselves staying here in Lichester.

Cerissa nodded ecstatically, her eyes shining with eager anticipation and pride. The rest of the evening passed without strain. Brett ordered their meal up to the room, refusing to allow her to change her new velvet robe for the grimy, travel worn old clothes. And when Ardsley bid them goodnight, laughing that he assumed—since Lord Lindsey was so over fond of napping that he would doubtless want to turn in promptly—the warm exuberance of the evening prodded Cerissa to reply teasingly as well. "I have other plans for Lord Lindsey tonight," she had smiled, winking mischievously at the blond haired lord.

Both men had exchanged pleased, surprised glances, and Lord Ardsley had gazed seriously down at the girl's flushed face, his eyes kind and fond "You grow up a little more every day sweetheart," he had smiled as he left, feeling just a tiny bit envious of his friend for possessing such a treasure. "Whatever you do, enjoy!"

Cerissa was almost breathless in excitement as the three of them sat down at a fireside table at the "Cock & Quail," Brett on her right and Ardsley seated across from them. The tavern was crowded with richly, and gaily dressed people. The tables were heavy oak, polished and gold, with a narrow strip of linen placed down the center, a vase of yellow spring jonquils in the center. This was the first time she'd seen Brett and Ardsley wearing formal clothing— their knee length, lace-cuffed jackets fitted snuggly, the shoulders wide, waist narrow. The breeches matched the fabric and the color of the brocade coats—Brett's emerald, Ardsley's burgundy. Instead of the high riding boots, they had on white silk hose, gartered below the knee with wide satin, and black tie shoes.

Ardsley had a pen wig on beneath his large brimmed hat, but Brett preferred the coolness and the comfort of going without that.

"What do you want to eat?" Lord Lindsey smiled at the girl's obvious awe, wondering whether her blue eyes mightn't just pop all the way out of her face when she saw the real splendor and magnificence of the London restaurants. The gilt chandeliers at the "Four Ponies" or the sparkling fountains of "Le Trianon."

Cerissa turned to him quickly, unsure of what exotic dishes she might find in such a glorious place. "Oh," she replied cautiously, "whatever you're having."

Brett smiled, recognizing her common ploy when confronted by her unsophistication. "I'm having venison chops if they've got any—stuffed hen quail if they don't."

Cerissa considered that a moment, then decided quickly. She had tried venison one night at an inn and found it a shade too gamey for her taste. "I'll have the quail."

Brett nodded, satisfied with her choice. He had thought she might enjoy the small game bird. Ardsley poured wine into the tall crystal goblets, amused at the interplay between the two.

The dinner was ordered and arrived in good time, and the evening quickly grew gay as the wine bottles emptied. Cerissa giggled and glowed under the men's flattery and attention, believing she really did, as they insisted, look every inch a queen in her new gown.

"Lord Lindsey, Lord Ardsley," a strange man, well dressed and obviously known to the two seated, stopped at their table, sweeping his hat off and bowing slightly. "My God, Lindsey, where'd you find such a pretty wench?" he grinned admiringly at the delighted girl. "You always did have a reputation for keeping the best looking whores!"

Cerissa's face flamed and she dropped her eyes hastily, barely hearing the rest of their conversation. At last he left and Lord Lindsey turned to the girl, giving her hand a reassuring squeeze, well aware of the reason for her embarrassment. "Don't let that spoil your evening, sweetheart. People don't mean anything by that word—at least people in our circle don't. "'Whore' with us just means...means the same thing as girlfriend."

Ardsley glanced at his friend sharply, surprised to see Brett making such an effort to spare the girl's feelings for he wasn't usually one to bother with that sort of thing. Not that he was deliberately unkind to his women, only that he didn't believe in pulling any punches. Brett was one to explain very clearly to a woman the relationship he expected, then, when the situation became tiresome, or too serious or the woman opportuning, he simply walked out.

Cerissa nodded her dark reddish head, apparently accepting Brett's explanation and the evening grew gay again. Now though, Ardsley found himself studying his dark haired friend's face, noting the strange expression that played in the green eyes sometimes when he looked at the girl, and the gentleness of his fingertips when they played with the shining mass of her hair.

At last, the meal was over and they drained the last wine out of their gobblets, preparing to leave. Brett had turned to slip a cloak over Cerissa's shoulders when a party of a half dozen, obviously well-born diners, stopped at the table. Ardsley frowned as he recognized one of the women in the group. Barbara was an old amour of his—of Brett's too for that matter—and he knew her for a bitch.

Lord Lindsey introduced Cerissa, a faint smile on his face at the awe on hers. She was staring almost rudely at the people, gaping at the magnificent, low-cut, satins and brocades of the women's gowns, the brilliance of their jewelry, the high, elaborate piling and curling of their hair. Suddenly, the girl felt dowdy and plain.

"What was your name again child?" Barbara purred smoothly, running her eyes up and down the girl's modest cotton gown with ill-concealed amusement.

"Cerissa", the girl answered softly, flushing under the woman's scrutiny.

"Cerissa?" Barbara echoed, raising her eyebrows in exaggerated surprise "My, what an unusual name. So quaint, so country-ish," she smirked. Turning to the rest of her group, she said in a loud whisper "Does anyone else catch the smell of cows?" Her friends tittered behind their fans, exchanging quick glances.

Brett studied the woman, a faint smile on his face though his green eyes glittered. "I think that's enough, Barbara."

The woman merely shrugged, ignoring his warning, apparently unperturbed to incur his displeasure. "And since when have you become such a gallant, Brett Lindsey? And when did your tastes start to run to innocence? Although," she murmured, aside to her party, "in this case, he seems to have confused innocence with ignorance."

Lord Lindsey turned his back, taking Cerissa's arm to guide her out of the tavern. "Step aside, Barbara. We were just leaving."

The woman didn't move, staring challengingly back into the man's green eyes. Brett reached one hand out and slowly shoved her away. She gasped and stared at him in furious humiliation, finally whirling around to hiss at her equally embarrassed escort. "Don't just stand there, you ill begotten lout. Don't let him shove me around like that."

Uneasily the man stepped forward, half drawing his sword from its jeweled sheath. "The lady requires an apology, sir," he stated in a nervous voice. He was no stranger to weapons, he, like all lord's sons, had practiced fencing from an early age. But dwelling in the classroom of a teacher was far different than using that skill, refining it, and making it deadly on the deck of a fighting ship as Lord Lindsey had done.

Brett raised his eyebrows, faintly smiling. "I didn't know she was a lady, sir."

Ardsley stepped forward quickly, anxious to avoid bloodshed. "My God, gentlemen, let's not lose our tempers over such an insignificant trifle. Barbara, you know damn well you asked for what you got, and you know Brett well enough to have avoided this whole scene, had you wished to. So, let's part friends. All right?"

The woman's escort nodded, relieved to have found an honorable escape from drawing sword against the dark haired lord. "He's right, Barbara. No use spilling any blood over this."

The magnificently gowned redhead threw the man a contemptuous glance, but turned away with a cool farewell to Lindsey and Ardsley. She glared a moment more at the bewildered Cerissa, then stalked away.

Cerissa held Brett's offered arm tightly as they threaded their way back through the crowded tavern and out into the street for the short walk back to their rooms at the Linchester Arms Inn. Brett seemed already to have forgotten the unpleasant incident at the restaurant, and he talked and laughed carelessly with the girl until she did too. At Cerissa's side, Ardsley was unusually quiet, considering his friend's astonishingly protective behavior with a sense of incredulity. My God, he thought silently, glancing curiously at Brett's dark face in the dimness, for a man who's whored with half of England's ladies, he acts like a green boy with this country wench. If he doesn't watch himself a bit closer, there will be blood spilt over the girl and not in the too distant future. I'm not going to interfere another time. If he's crazy enough to draw sword for his whore, so be it.

Chapter Five

The late afternoon forest was sun dappled and peaceful. Lord Lindsey had promised to hunt fresh pheasant for their meal tonight, and Lord Ardsley and Cerissa sat tossing pebbles into a sweet water stream that bubbled by their feet.

"I wish this were a wishing pool," she murmured wistfully, plopping a smooth white stone into the center of the water.

Ardsley smiled at her, his blue eyes teasing. "And what would you wish for if it were, sweetheart?"

Cerissa closed her eyes dreamily, putting her face up to the warmth of the mid-April sun. "I'd wish for Lord Lindsey to marry me."

Ardsley's eyes opened wide in astonishment as he stared at the girl for a long moment, then threw his golden head back and roared with laughter, wiping tears from his eyes with the back of one hand. Cerissa's eyes flew open, gazing at his mirth with horrified humiliation. After a single frozen heartbeat, she leapt to her feet and bolted away into the forest, blinded by burning tears, running recklessly until her foot caught on a fallen tree limb and sent her sprawling. Too wretched to move, there she lay on the damp, leaf covered forest floor, sobbing wildly.

Ardsley had plunged after her, lost her for a moment in the pathless forest, and now he stood and stared down at her, his face flushed and guilty as he knelt beside her, touching her shoulder apologetically. "Jesus Christ, sweetheart, I'm sorry. I shouldn't have laughed... but I never thought you were serious, sweetheart, please don't cry."

Cerissa could only lay there, crying as if her heart would break. Ardsley stroked her long silky hair awkwardly, struggling to know what to say. At last, the girl sat up, sniffling, her face smeared with dirt from the wood's floor. "Why shouldn't I be serious?" she murmured accusingly, her breath coming in silent hiccups from her tears, her chest heaving.

Ardsley frowned, pitying the girl's innocence, reluctant to hurt her further, "Well, Jesus, Cerissa, you know Brett can't marry you."

Cerissa stared at him, feeling cold dread fill the pit of her stomach. "He's already married?"

The blond lord shook his head, not noticing the relief that filled her blue eyes. "No, not that, princess, but... Hell, child, he's Lord Lindsey... a Baron, with a seat in Parliament, and a family centuries old... he can't go marrying some farm wench whether he would or no. When he finally does marry, it will be to a girl of the same background as his, with family and money and a title, and... He hasn't been promising to marry you has he?" Sudden anger gleamed in the blond lord's eyes and Cerissa hastily shook her head, staring dejectedly at her hands, her eyes filling quickly with fresh tears. She'd been a fool to even let herself think about such nonsense, of course Lord Ardsley was right. How could a lord fall in love with her? Much less marry her! Suddenly, humiliation and hopelessness crushed her, and she flung herself against Ardsley's chest, sobbing again. "Oh, but I love him so much! I thought, if only I could make him love me a little bit too..."

The blond lord held the girl helplessly. Suddenly, for the first time in his life, he was bitterly jealous of his friend Brett Lindsey. Love was an oft-used word in Court circles, but almost never was the true feeling behind it. That precious selfless, deep devotion of one soul for another's... Ardsley felt suddenly weary and old and terribly stupid. He had seen that radiance on the girl's face whenever she looked at Lindsey, how could he have been so blind not to recognize it for love? Just because he'd never seen it before . . . Jesus Christ, did Brett guess the depth of her feelings? Or was he, like Ardsley, too jaded, too cynical to sense genuine emotion . . . "Don't cry, sweetheart. If it's any consolation, I think Brett does love you a little bit." Ardsley had meant the words only for kindness sake, trying desperately to calm the girl's tears, yet he suddenly frowned at the possibility of their truth. It would explain a lot of Brett's reactions concerning the wench . . . his unusual patience, his possessiveness, the quick anger at seeing her hurt . . . Oh, Christ! he groaned inwardly, instantly despising himself for his earlier envy of the man. What a cruel twisted, trick for Fate to play. Offer love on one hand and deny the possibility of its fulfillment on the other. Was Lindsey himself aware of his own growing attachment to the wench, or did he . . .? "Listen, sweetheart, I want to explain something terribly important to you. Marriage and love among the nobility are not related, do you understand? Brett could love you more than life itself and he still wouldn't be able to offer you marriage. If you love him enough to stay with him in spite of that . . . well then, go ahead but don't let false hopes disappoint you along the way."

Cerissa nodded, confused and faintly frightened by the sorrow showing in Lord Ardsley's eyes. Why should he look as though something dreadful had just happened? Wasn't love always perfect and beautiful regardless?

"And another thing, sweet," the blond lord continued seriously, a rueful half-smile tugging at his mouth, "we lords live in a very different world than the one you grew up in. It's jealous, and bitter, and often vindictive. We learn to ignore our emotions or they would destroy us. Politics and power don't set well with the softer side of feelings. So, if Brett does begin to love you, princess, you'll have to be very patient with him. It won't be easy for him to learn to love after a lifetime of deliberately forgetting."

Cerissa forced a tremulous smile, giving Lord Ardsley a grateful hug, though her blue eyes were uncertain and a little puzzled by what he had said. The man acted as though love was more pain than pleasure, and an awesome responsibility to boot! Still, she whispered silently to herself, she wouldn't let him scare her. She loved Brett enough to make anything worthwhile . . . and she'd wait for years if she had to for Brett to return her love. And yes, by God! Someday he'd marry her too, in spite of what Ardsley believed.

"Well, you two," Lord Lindsey's lazy drawl startled both of

them as he leaned against a tree, grinning at the guilt that flashed on both of their faces "If I were a jealous man, I'd wonder what you two had been up to in here. You look like children caught raiding the sweet counter at the Exchange."

Ardsley forced a grin and shrugged, muttering something about Cerissa's tripping and hurting her ankle to explain her tears and his wet shirt. But he couldn't meet his friend's gaze just now. His new knowledge, and his pity for them both, would show too plainly.

Cerissa gazed at Brett's darkly handsome face in open adoration, warmed by the recollection of Ardsley's belief that Brett loved her a little bit too. In a moment, Lord Lindsey's green eyes darkened with that peculiar, exotic expression and she felt herself growing light-headed and short of breath in familiar response.

Lord Ardsley noticed the unspoken exchange that passed between the two and forced another smile as he shrugged and sauntered back to the horses, glad that his friend's attention was too centered just now on the girl to have noted how strained his apparent high spirits had been. "If you two aren't done in a half hour, I'm leaving without you," he called back over his shoulder, trying to feign his usual teasing impatience. Dear God! he thought silently, I wish I could give you years together.

The summers in London were hot, and, especially this August, smotheringly humid and close. The spacious third story rooms of the apartment she and Brett occupied felt airless through Cerissa had left both of the wide bay windows open. Listlessly, she opened her book, a new play by Dryden, which Ardsley had lent her, and began to read, only half interested in the story. Brett was out, as he had been most days since their arrival in early May, pursuing business affairs at Whitehall, petitions in Parliament, checking on the building of a new ship at Braydon-on-Thames, or overseeing the arrival or reloading of the cargo on others, as they sailed into the dockyards by the Bridge. Occasionally he spent a day hunting with Ardsley, or escorting Cerissa to a play or to the Exchange, or took her riding in the shadowed, oak lined paths of St. James Park.

Cerissa missed him during the day but she never complained about his absence, understanding the reasons for it. She never complained about his night life either. Early in the summer she had made that mistake, feeling so secure in her place in his life that she had finally dared to demand Brett cease his coming and going at unpredictable hours. His response had been unequivocal. After a bitter quarrel, she had burst into tears and fled to the bedroom, locking the door against him. She had heard a crash as a chair had been angrily overturned, then the door had slammed behind him. Brett had been gone three full days after that quarrel, and when he finally reappeared early in the morning of the fourth day, she had welcomed him back thankfully, in the joy of seeing him home again forgetting that she had decided to be cold an unforgiving when he returned. He had breakfasted with her, coolly distant, and unmistakable challenge in his green eyes. Some instinctive sense in her woman's soul warned Cerissa that to quarrel again would be the end, so she had said nothing, about the incident ever again. Now, when he was planning to be out all night, he usually sent a note home to her, telling her not to wait up. Often the following morning he would stay later in the apartment, sharing breakfast before leaving her again.

Brett had rented the floor below them for the modest staff of servants—a cook, a groom for the carriage horses, one maid servant to help Cerissa with the apartment and her own, now more sophisticated, toilette, and two burly manservants. If the loneliness of the day bothered her, she often called down for Lina to go out with her, to the dressmakers or the Exchange, but normally she stayed in—always fearing to miss Lord Lindsey if he dropped in unexpectedly. She blamed the monotony of her days for her recently unsettled temper. Compounded, she decided, by the terrible heat and the lateness of her period as well. For London, though unquestionably magnificent, and frantic, and bursting with activity, had somehow disappointed Cerissa and she found herself thinking wistfully of the simple, more real existence of country life. The city reminded her too much of a gilded whore—too much glitter and too much paint and not enough soul.

She blamed the surperficiality of town living too, for Lord Lindsey's apparently unchanging attitude toward her. All these months, she had clung to Ardsley's belief in Brett's affection for her, remembering his warning for patience, but September was coming soon and he still had never once said he loved her, nor offered any commitment for a future together. And, though she forced herself to ignore the feeling, she was becoming increasingly uncertain whether he would ever do so. The strain of living only day to day was growing unbearable to her now. Soon, quarrel or no, she was going to have to force the issue.

The sound of Lord Lindsey's heavy step on the landing drew her instantly from her chair as she hurried to the door, surprising him with kisses, hardly noticing the faint scowl he wore on his face. He kicked his shoes off wearily and crossed to the window, dropping heavily into a chair and stretching his long legs out to rest on the sill. "Jesus, God and Mary, but it's too damn hot!" he muttered sourly, rubbing his face with one hand. He had a wicked headache, and his muscles ached, and his clothes clung damply to his body from sweat.

"I'll ask Lina to bring up some cool tea," Cerissa promised quickly, moving to the stairs. In a moment she brought two tall glasses over to the window seat, handing Brett the one with a sprig of mint. She preferred the sweeter taste of an orange slice in hers.

"I don't remember it being so hot in Bainwater," she murmured, fanning herself futilely with Ardsley's play.

Lord Lindsey smiled faintly and studied the girl's flushed face. "Ever wish you hadn't left there, sweetheart?"

Cerissa shook her head quickly, flashing him a sweet smile in answer. He cocked his head, sipping the tea slowly. "Why not, Cerissa? Why trade the cool country air for this damn roasting oven?"

The girl said nothing, only gazing down into her glass, her mouth curved in a gentle, secret smile. Brett stared at her, his curiosity piqued by her silence. "Because you would have missed seeing London? Because of the plays, or the gowns, or the dinners out? What?"

Cerissa took a deep breath, her head whirling in trepidation. So many times she had thought the words in silence, never daring to give them speech. "Because I love you," she answered softly at last, too shy to look at his dark face as she spoke.

Lord Lindsey frowned at her, his mouth slightly contemptuous as he looked away. Damn if the wench wasn't learning too well the artificialities of London and the life here. The thing he had always treasured most about Cerissa was her honesty, the depth of her emotions, the genuineness of her reactions. "You fit right in here anymore, Cerissa. You ought to do well for yourself here in London after I've gone."

Cerissa felt her world begin to spin, her heart nearly bursting as though someone had seized it within her breast and was squeezing it in an iron fist. It couldn't be mockery she was hearing in Lord Lindsey's voice! "I . . . I don't think I'll stay in London when you've left," she whispered, still stunned by the finality of the rejection.

"No?" he drawled lazily. "Where will you go then? Paris perhaps? Or Venice?" Venetian whores were internationally famous for their beauty—and their artificiality.

Cerissa felt tears fill her eyes, but still she sat in the chair knowing her knees would never hold her if she stood. "I'd go back to the country."

"The country? You're not liable to find another rich lord to keep you in the style to which you've become accustomed," he replied arching his black brows in mocking surprise.

Suddenly, Cerissa's head snapped up, her eyes meeting Brett's cool stare, "Maybe I don't want another rich lord! Maybe I've had a bellyfull of rich lords!" She leapt to her feet, her fists clenched, her eyes wild with hurt.

Brett scowled at her, his headache pounding worse than ever, his face flushed now with anger as well as heat. "I don't like to be criticized by my whores! If you can't hold your damn tongue, there's the door!" he snapped.

The girl stared at the dark lord for a long minute in incredulous horror, her face slowly draining of all color, the blood pounding in her ears. "I hate you, sometimes," she whispered slowly, her voice vibrant with emotion, "Oh God, how I hate you sometimes." She turned quietly, surprisingly calm, her instinctive dignity keeping her back straight and her chin up as she walked toward the wardrobe to pack her things. Brett frowned at her; puzzled and surprised by the violence of the hatred, obviously real, that had showed in her eyes.

"Oh, hell, Cerissa, don't play martyr. Come on, I'll buy you . . ."

"Buy me what?" she spat, turning on her heel in renewed fury "That's all you ever had to give isn't it? Money, dresses, jewelry . . . Well, you never could understand it, but you never bought me, Brett. I was never for sale. I left Bainwater with you because I loved you. And I stayed with you here in London because I loved you. I was never your whore, Brett Lindsey, and I never intend to be. So go find yourself a new wench to keep your bed warm. I'm through with it." Cerissa turned back to her clothes, pulling the simpler cotton dresses out to fold into a canvas travelling bag, her movements deliberate and unhurried.

Lord Lindsey stared at the girl in stunned surprise, the realization of what he'd done, what he'd said, breaking only slowly upon him, making him swallow hard against the sudden nausea that rose in his throat. Dear God! The girl had been altogether serious when she'd said she loved him—it had not been the superficial flattery he'd assumed it to be. She'd made an honest offer of an emotion he had never been privileged to know, and, not recognizing it, too damn cynical to even believe it existed, he had mocked her offer, trampled on the girl's freely given soul, sneered at her...

"Oh Jesus..." he groaned. Gritting his teeth against the sick throbbing every movement caused in his head, he forced himself to his feet, starting toward her. "Please, sweetheart... If I'd had any idea you were serious..."

Cerissa stood absolutely motionless, her eyes filling with tears, longing to turn and run to Brett's arms in forgiveness. But what good could that do her? He was only saying whatever he thought would pacify her... Yet unwilling memories of that long ago summer afternoon in the woods by Lichester with Lord Ardsley stole into her mind. Oh, how Ardsley had laughed... And then he had warned her... "How can you people be so blind?" she murmured softly, after a long silence, turning to face Brett. "Do you live in such artificial circles that nothing genuine ever touches you?"

Brett only stared at her, helpless in such an alien situation. Finally, he shrugged, trying unsuccessfully to force a smile. "God, Cerissa, if you knew how sorry..." he answered, his voice strained and strangely quiet. "Please forgive me, sweetheart. I never meant to hurt you. I'm just so damn tired... and my head hurts like a son of a bitch, and I..." He held his arms out to the girl in a wordless plea, his green eyes searching hers for understanding.

Cerissa could resist him only a moment. Then she ran to him, flinging her arms around his body as she began to sob. "Damn you," she finally sniffled, drying her wet face against the lace front of Brett's shirt.

Lord Lindsey smiled faintly, sighing in deep contentment, bending his dark head down to nuzzle her with soft kisses, his arms tightening around her quivering body. How could he have been so incredibly stupid? he asked himself angrily. Jesus... how close he had come to driving her away...

Cerissa frowned suddenly and took a half step away, remembering his earlier words. "What did you mean about leaving, Brett? Are you leaving London?"

Lord Lindsey only shook his head slightly, a faint smile curving his lips, his eyes soft and a little sad as he gazed at her. Cerissa felt her heart slowly turning to stone in slow, sure dread. "You're leaving England... in one of those ships again..." Even as she spoke, she knew, that often talked about, vague, sometime when Brett would leave to go privateering again. She had lived with it so long that the spectre of his going had become unreal... so far into the hazy future that she believed it would never come. And now it had. "When?" she asked dully.

"Two weeks," he answered, his green eyes gentle and apologetic. "I was trying to think of a way to tell you for these last few days..."

"Oh, Brett, please let me come with you," she begged, her blue eyes bright in sudden hope "I wouldn't be any trouble to..."

"No, sweetheart," he replied firmly, shaking his dark head in warning "Privateering is demanding, and dangerous—and often foul. It's no life for a woman."

Cerissa began to cry softly in hopeless despair, unable to bear the idea of losing Brett for months...maybe for years. "But how long will you be away?"

Lord Lindsey frowned, wondering at the girl's question, finally smiling faintly and shaking his head in comprehension. "I'm sorry, princess. I'll be gone years if I come back at all. No, I've put a thousand pounds for you with Isaac Benjamin, the goldsmith. With your 1,000 pounds and your pretty blue eyes, hell, you'll be quite a catch. You'll be able to marry well, Cerissa..."

"I don't want to marry well!" she flared, quickly angry again at his lack of understanding, "Don't you even listen to me? I love you! I want to be with you!"

"Yes, I know, sweetheart," Brett murmured, his finger touching the pout on her lips gently, "But you'll feel differently when I've been gone a few weeks, maybe. Anyway, you'll have the option." Suddenly, unable to hide his weariness any longer, he sighed, and half-stumbled against the girl, his face drawn in exhaustion. Cerissa tightened her grip around his chest, her eyes dark with concern.

"Brett what is it? Are you ill?"

"No...no, sweet, just awfully tired."

"Here, love, you'd better lie down, then," she frowned, urging him toward the bed. "How in the world did you get so exhausted? What were you doing..."

"Hush, wench. It's all innocence," he sighed, leaning wearily back into the soft pillows. "I've been up for two nights and more. After you went to sleep, I left again...There was so much to do, princess, and I didn't want to upset you yet, so..." he shrugged ruefully, looking oddly little-boyish.

Cerissa frowned at him, again, a little angry at his deceit, a little embarrassed to have been so easy to fool, and more than a little concerned at the risks he had taken with his health. London summers were notorious for fevers and disease. Scarcely more than ten years before, the city had been nearly emptied by a terrible outbreak of plague.

Lord Lindsey noticed her expression and smiled, reaching out to take her hand and pull her toward him. "I'm too big for you to paddle my bottom, so stop looking so grim. Besides, I intend to apologize in style..."

Very gently, he reached up and drew her chestnut head down to his, his lips touching her face, her eyes, her nose, her mouth with exquisite tenderness, his green eyes dark and sweet. Slowly, he reached one sun tanned hand up to loosen the ribbons of her hair, setting it free to tumble its way down onto his shoulders and into his face, smoothing it back again before he reached to unfasten the snaps and buttons of her violet day gown. Cerissa barely breathed, revelling in his unhurried loving, only moving her head a bit to drop a soft kiss on his fingers as they worked. At last, the gown was open, and she waited as he moved the capped sleeves off her shoulders, pulling the dress free to reveal her firm, white breasts, bending forward to kiss her nipples and rest his forehead against their cool velvety smoothness.

At last, her own heart beating faster, Cerissa reached forward to untie Brett's lace ascot, then unlaced the shirt front below it. As slowly as if in a dream, Cerissa watched the dark haired lord slip the linen shirt up and off over his head, his browned arms and torso startlingly dark against the crisp white of the bed sheets. Once again, she caught her breath in admiration at the breadth of his shoulders, the strength rippling in his muscled arms, the glossy raven hair of his chest and the lean, hard flatness of his belly. She raised her eyes adoringly, studying the familiar, strong lines of his face, etching it lovingly into her memory. How perfect the straightness of his nose, his high cheek bones, the square, often stubborn set of his jaw. His lips so changeable—grim, and thin, and hard in temper, now soft and richly formed, a faint smile curving them slightly upwards. And his eyes...those beloved, water-green eyes...depthless and clear as crystal, reflecting his every mood, framed in such long, thick ebony lashes that they looked almost angelically beautiful. Now, the green was changing, shifting, turning to emerald as his body reacted to the touch of her warm, bare skin against his. Slowly, she smiled into those eyes, reaffirming the boundless, eternal love she felt for this restless, dark haired lord, accepting the heartbreak that might lie ahead in gratitude for the beauty of this moment. Cerissa leaned forward, pressing her lips to his, welcoming the quick penetration of his tongue, her head whirling in familiar passion as she breathed the familiar male smell of him, the leather and the lime cologne, mixing with the sweet muskiness of his sweat. She molded her body to his, her leg moving between his, her belly filling with hot eagerness to feel him swell and thrust against her. Suddenly, Brett's arms tightened around her as he moaned with urgency, rolling the two over as one, his body covering hers heavily. Then he was thrusting slowly deep within her, moving gently and carefully as if savoring every sensation of her answering passion, his lips kissing her mouth, and her throat; his hands cupping the fullness of her breasts, his legs spread wide upon the bed, forcing her thighs far apart, her body lying open to receive him. Again and again he thrust deep within her, in measured speed, without violence but more overwhelmingly, masculinely masterful than anything Cerissa had ever known of him. Helpless to move beneath him, unwilling to do so anyway, she moaned her pleasure, her hands running over the trembling, cordlike muscles of his shoulders and back, her head moving restlessly upon the pillow under his searching lips. Imprisoned beneath the weight of his hips, her loins ached with demanding desire, craving more of him, faster, and more again, until she writhed beneath him, nearly mindless, aware only of her need for him, and the slow, deep thrusts of his body as he responded to that need, now growing more rapid at last, growing in violence, filling her hungry body with throbbing warmth. She clutched his hips greedily, drawing him ever deeper, then crying aloud, nearly sobbing in ecstatic fulfillment of her passion, slowly drifting lazily back into the world to find Brett still within her, his body seeking hers, his hips rocking violently against hers, penetrating her again and again moaning in anticipation of her own release. Incredulously, Cerissa felt her body respond to his passion again, her belly stabbed by lightning flashes of greedy need, every fiber of her being vividly acute, extraordinarily sensitive still from her first explosion. Almost frightened by the intensity of her body's reaction, yet mindlessly demanding fulfillment from this uncontrollable new arousal, Cerissa lay helpless beneath Brett's arching hips, moaning and twisting as it came again, exploding deep within her with an eerie completion she had never reached before. And at last, he lay still upon her, withdrawing his body gently from hers to collapse beside her.

It was several minutes before Cerissa could speak, before her lips moved at her command again. She turned her head to return Brett's kiss, finding the movement difficult, her head strangely heavy. "I love you." she murmured at last, gazing deeply into his green eyes, not caring any longer whether he repeated her words or not. This lovemaking had been so different from all the others, without the haste, without the violent urgency on his part, without the dominatingly selfish pursuit of his own gratification. Not that Brett was ever an inconsiderate lover, but his masculine pride accounted for much of that. No, Cerissa decided silently in awed surprise as she caressed his handsome face tenderly, watching for him to sleep. This loving had been a gift from him to her . . . and not a gift of his money, or attention, but a gift of his soul, his very being. Whether Brett Lindsey knew it or not, he was finally beginning to fall in love with her. Silent tears, half joy, half bittersweet sorrow, coursed down Cerissa's cheeks as she gazed at him, lost in the precious gladness of her discovery. One thing was certain now, she decided at last, just before curling against him to sleep, when Lord Lindsey's new frigate sailed, somehow, by hook or by crook, she was going to be aboard it. She refused to let him be gone from her now just when he was starting to learn to love her. And rant as he may, or rage as he surely would, he'd soon get used to having her tagging along, as he had leaving Bainwater. Perhaps in time, he'd even be glad of it.

Chapter Six

Cerissa huddled in the bottom of the large crate, terrified that the sailors would somehow drop her into the water and drown her. For even if she could use her small dagger in time to cut the heavy rope bindings around the box, she had never swum a stroke. And though she could hear Lord Lindsey's deep voice calling orders from the deck of his new frigate, she doubted seriously whether he would jump into the chilly, filthy dock water—especially if he recognized her.

She had decided on this plan weeks ago, and with characteristic tenacity, she had pursued it carefully, listening intently to Brett's stories of life at sea; what to eat, what to wear, how long the trip took, the various compartments of a ship and what went where within them. And she had overheard him urging Ardsley to ship some cargo to Jamaica—there to be sold at the usual huge profit to the isolated colonists. And when the blond lord had agreed, this plan had taken form. She had guessed correctly that Lord Lindsey wouldn't question the last-minute arrival of another crate from his friend. In case he had, Cerissa had carefully placed several bolts of wool cloth from the London Exchange on the false top above her head, still leaving plenty of room for her to curl up beneath, with her water jugs, her loaf of bread, some hardtack, dried beef and salted pork in a small keg, apples to prevent the dreaded scurvy, and, of course, a change of clothes. Her supplies would never last the month or so the sailing to the Caribbean would take—but they didn't need to. Once they were too far away from England for Brett to turn around and return her easily, she would reveal herself...and hope he wasn't so furious that he dumped her overboard, in mid-ocean.

But twelve full days had passed and still Cerissa cowered in the dark hold of the ship, fearing Lord Lindsey's sure anger. Each day she had grown more timid rather than less, remembering the uncompromising firmness of his insistence that she remain in England, remembering the perilous glitter of his green eyes in temper, wondering why in the world she had dared to so defy him. Surely this would ruin instead of aid the small seeds of love that had begun to grow. She should have stayed put, as he'd ordered her, used the thousand pounds—a small fortune really!—while she waited for his return, and Lord! what if she were pregnant besides. She was over a month late now for her period...

Cautiously, she raised the lid of the crate and crept out, listening for sounds of sailors outside the hatchway. Her stores of food had lasted all right because she'd nearly starved herself to conserve them, but her fresh water had run out days ago, forcing her to steal up from the lightless, rat-infested hold where the cargo lay to the next level to fill her water jugs again. The last time she had missed her footing on the dark stairs and had dropped the earthenware vessel with a loud crash, sending her heart into her mouth, sure she would be discovered. With unbelievable good luck, no one had found her then. But this time, if she made the slightest sound...

Cautiously, she pushed the hatchway up, peering anxiously into the crack of light, then hoisted herself up into the galley to secure the water. Suddenly, she was surrounded by shouting sailors, their fierce, be-whiskered faces thrust up close against hers as they grabbed at her, swearing loudly in their surprise and obscene delight. Helplessly, the girl screamed and struggled to fight free of their grasping paws, succeeding onto in aiding their efforts to rip

71

the cotton gown from her body. One warty, black-bearded man seized her long hair, pulling her head back to cover her mouth with his, his hands pawing eagerly at her nearly exposed breasts. Then, with a curse, his fellows dragged him away and another even more foul, red-headed sailor was upon her, bending her slender body backwards under his, his hands hauling her skirts up, ripping her petticoats free.

Suddenly, two new voices joined the clamor, screaming oaths and promising terrible punishment for any man who disobeyed them. With a reluctant growl, the red-haired man let her go, and the others backed away slowly. Cerissa sobbed helplessly, only now aware that, in her terror, she had been crying. She sank weakly onto the deck, too overwrought to even try to cover her breasts, totally numb with shock.

"Jesus Christ." The one man, evidently an officer of the ship from the way the others had obeyed his orders, simply stared at her, not understanding how a wench had managed to suddenly materialize out of thin air.

The other reacted more quickly, moving to grab the terrified girl and pull her away from the muttering, encircling crewmen. "Holy Mother of God, wench, where in the world did..."

"What the hell is going on in here?"

Cerissa's head turned at the sound of that familiar, deep voice and she met a pair of scowling green eyes with her pleading blue ones.

"I don't know, Captain, Wilson and I just got in here ourselves and..."

"Cerissa," Brett breathed slowly, his eyes still wide from shock and stunned incredulity as he returned her gaze. Gradually, in the sudden uneasy silence of the gun deck, his handsome face turned darkly menacing. "By God, wench, you'll regret..."

"Brett please, oh please don't be angry with me," Cerissa pleaded, at the very limit of her endurance, "I couldn't bear to..." Her voice trailed off as she shivered at the unmistakable, unwavering rage in his eyes. Helplessly, she lowered her face into her hands in wracking sobs, feeling even more miserable than she had under Uncle Wat's murderous fury. What if Brett turned his back on her? Left her to the mercy of these leering sailors? Oh God, why hadn't she stayed in England.

With a start, Lord Lindsey collected himself, realizing that the other men were staring at the near naked girl in frank desire, some already licking their lips or fingering themselves in anticipation.

72

He'd better do something fast before the men grew totally out of control. Hastily, he pulled the cold, rain soaked cloak from his shoulders, heaving it angrily at the shivering girl. "Put that around you," he muttered, his anger urging him to smack her, strike her, do something to...

"Shall I take the wench up to your cabin, Captain?" The first mate had noticed the obvious familiarity between the two. He didn't care what the Captain wanted done with the girl eventually, but they'd better get her out of general crew quarters before...

"Yes, Jake, maybe you'd better," the dark haired lord nodded slowly, his green eyes liquid fire as he stared at Cerissa "And lock her in."

"Aye, Captain." Not unkindly, the grayhaired, grizzled old mate took the girl's arm, guiding her up the stairs, across a short expanse of the open, upper deck, and back down another hatchway into the officer's quarters. Cerissa followed meek and silent, shivering from Lord Lindsey's wet, heavy cloak, getting thoroughly drenched and chilled above deck in the cold rain that frequently accompanied the trade winds.

"In here miss," the mate, Jake Oates, opened the door of the stern cabin and ushered the girl inside. "You're to wait here. I'll lock the door on my way back."

"Thank you," Cerissa murmured absently, struggling to hold back her tears. The mate nodded and left. Once alone, she sank into a leather backed chair and let her chestnut head fall heavily onto her folded arms, letting her bitter, frightened tears fall as they willed.

Below, Lord Lindsey shrugged as he spoke to the muttering, dangerous crew. "The girl belongs to me," he repeated firmly, his green eyes glittering as he stared warningly into the dozens of eyes that stared sullenly back, "She belonged to me in London, she belongs to me now. I didn't know she was on the ship, but since she is..." Brett gritted his teeth and shrugged again, damning the wench for her overbold disobedience. "She is my responsibility and my personal property. Any man who lays a hand on her gets 20 lashes for the first offense." Suddenly, he allowed his face to soften a bit, sensing that the crew acknowledged his right to the woman. "And if you manage to behave yourselves for the next couple of weeks before landfall, I'll buy each of you a pint of rum and a night at the best brothel in Port Royal. Agreed?"

Like a tropical storm clearing, the atmosphere suddenly changed. Several men chuckled and others grinned and poked a companion lecherously. The Captain had offered a favorite reward—and a handsome one, too. Port Royal's prices were higher than London's. The tension dissipated gradually, and the men turned away. Lord Lindsey smiled slightly, relieved to have ameliorated such a potentially explosive situation so easily. Then his face hardened again, his jaw line clenched tight and white, his hands clenching unconsciously into fists as he started for his cabin. By God the wench would regret this little bit of devilment . . .

Lord Lindsey had listened to the girl's hesitant explanation in growing rage and disbelief, his long legs trembling as he paced the small cabin, his wet boots oozing water on the polished floor, leaving small puddles as he walked.

"And after all I tried to do for you, you dared to steal passage on my ship?"

Cerissa hung her head, so wretched that she was almost beyond feeling anymore. "I'll pay you if you want," she whispered quietly, staring numbly at the wet floor.

"With what?" Lord Lindsey snapped. "With the money I gave you? You have the audacity to offer me payment with my own money?"

Cerissa said nothing, her head drooping a bit lower, her shivering growing more violent.

"And you took advantage of Lord Ardsley too, using his name," Brett swore and kicked furiously at the table leg, marring the new finish which made him even angrier. "He wasn't in league with you, was he?" he questioned in sudden suspicion. Damn but the blond lord seemed overfond of the wench, unable to resist any . . .

"No, he knew nothing about it," she answered softly, feeling even more guilty. She had never meant to drag the kind Lord Ardsley into this, he had been so good to her . . .

Brett stopped pacing and stared at the girl, unable to totally comprehend the enormity of her daring. Unwillingly, he admitted a perverse sense of admiration for the girl. Damn but she had been clever . . . and even courageous . . . to face the blackness of the hold, the bitter cold, the filth and the countless, fearless, hungry rats . . . "What are you shivering for?"

Guiltily, Cerissa started, trying to suppress her quivering. "I'm sorry," she apologized softly.

"The cloak . . . and the rain upstairs . . ."

"Above deck," he corrected automatically, frowning. 'Well, for God sake then, why don't you change your clothing?"

Cerissa swallowed hard, licking the salt of tears off her lips as she spoke. "It was so cold in there—where the crate was. I put on both pairs of my clothes." Never had Lord Lindsey seemed so cold, so distant. Even his anger was now oddly without warmth.

Brett frowned at her, his black brows drawn together over puzzled eyes. Finally, he realized what the girl meant. "You mean you only brought two pairs of clothing? What did you think to wear in Jamaica? Or were you expecting me to provide another wardrobe?"

Cerissa stared at him a moment, her blue eyes astonished. Was payment of her passage and the idea of buying her a few more dresses so overwhelming? Why had she bothered to go though what she had for this man? Handsome as Lord Lindsey was, tall, broad shouldered, with the strength and grace of a well-muscled panther still . . . she had only been fooling herself, his soul, his love, wasn't sleeping, it was dead. He cared more for his purse than he did for her. Finally she shrugged, looking away. "I only had room for one extra set of clothing. My crate was hardly luxurious. I set more store by having food to eat."

The dark haired lord scowled, a little surprised at the unexpected shift of Cerissa's mood, sensing that the girl was now somehow criticizing him. "You're a troublesome baggage, wench. I ought to throw you to the sharks."

Cerissa merely half-smiled, feeling already mostly dead inside anyway. The sharks didn't bother her. She couldn't swim long enough to live for that horror. If Lord Lindsey wanted to throw her overboard, then so be it. She was powerless to prevent whatever revenge he decided upon.

Brett stared at her, puzzled by her lack of reaction. Surely the girl ought to respond to such a gruesome suggestion. "You know the customary fate of a stowaway is to be sold into slavery in Jamaica. Perhaps that would be more to your liking. At least it would reimburse me for your passage."

Calmly Cerissa met his angry green eyes, her pretty face growing cold and set as she returned his unyielding stare.

"Go to hell," she answered finally, enjoying the surprise on the dark haired lord's face.

Lord Lindsey stared at the girl in momentary shock, then involuntarily, he smiled, turning away to hide his face. Damn but the girl had spirit . . . if he pushed her far enough to forget her country meekness. "Well, you can't sit there shivering, whatever I decide to do with you. If you have no clothes of your own, you'll have to make do with mine. We've a shortage of dressmaker's here in the Atlantic." Silently he stalked to the sea chest, pulling out a pair of woolen breeches and a linen shirt, tossing them carelessly on the bunk.

In equal silence, Cerissa pulled the tattered remnants of her gowns off and dressed awkwardly in the man's clothing, pretending not to notice that Lord Lindsey sat near her, watching her coolly, his green eyes appraising. Unwillingly, she felt her face flush scarlet in angry indignity, and she turned her back on him to finish.

"Have you eaten anything substantial?" Brett queried at last, his eyes going over her thin frame in open disapproval. The girl looked ludicrous—yet faintly, undeniably charming in the male clothing, which, being miles too big for her, gave the impression of a small child playing dress-up.

"No," she responded quietly. She longed to beg for a hot meal, to fill her growling stomach and stop her shivering, but she refused to give him the opportunity to deny it.

"I'll order you something then," he shrugged. "But don't make a pig of yourself or you'll only vomit it all back up."

Cerissa sat down in another chair, her blue eyes fixed defiantly out the porthole in the stern, neither replying nor even acknowledging his offer—and the accompanying jibe.

"For God's sake stop your damn quivering!" Lord Lindsey snapped in sudden hot rage, furious at the girl's wretched condition, and doubly furious to find himself concerned about it. In spite of his anger at her stowing away on the ship, in spite of her reckless defiance now, he had to acknowledge that he was more content with her presence than he had been in the nearly two weeks since he had left her behind, supposedly, in London. Was it only the flattery of being so steadfastly adored that the wench would risk anything to be with him? Or, was it possible—as Ardsley had warned on the eve of his sailing when he had asked his friend to watch out for Cerissa's welfare—that he himself was falling in love with the girl? Damn! What the hell was the matter with him anymore? He was 28 years old, and a man of incredible experience . . . he wouldn't fall in love with a sweet little country whore like some green farmer boy! Ardsley was crazy. His reaction was purely selfish.

Feeling a little easier, Brett stood and began to gather his log book papers to take them above when he took the helm for the next watch. "Cerissa, you're shivering still, now stop it. I won't throw you overboard—much as you deserve it. And I won't sell you as a slave, either."

At last, she raised her cool blue eyes to meet his, surprised to see the anger in them almost gone, replaced by an odd sort of puzzled thoughtfulness. She bit her lip against the tears that threatened to flow again, her emotions reawaking in a painful explosion in response to Brett's gentler temper. Oh why couldn't she ever stay mad at the man? Why did she always melt helplessly whenever that strange confusion clouded his clear green eyes? "I'm not afraid, Brett," she answered forcing her voice to remain cold as she averted her gaze hastily lest he sense her capitulation. "I'm only chilled." Her eyes staring at the porthole again, she missed the quick frown of concern that creased his sun tanned face.

"Well, get into my bunk then, wench, under the blankets. I have to take watch next, but you'll be warmer there anyway."

Wordlessly Cerissa complied, surprised to see the lord stop and pull forth two extra blankets from the huge chest, settling them over her before he left, his long black cape swirling angrily as he stalked out into the gangway.

At last, the mate that had led her up from the crew's quarters came through the door, a tray of hot, steaming stew, crusty bread, butter, cheese and tea in his brawny, tatooed arms. "Hello, missy," he called cheerfully, setting the food on the table "Captain ordered grub for you, so here t'is."

Cerissa clambered hastily from the bunk, her mouth watering at the thick, brown broth of the wine-flavored stew. "Thank you, Mister...?"

"No, mister, miss," the seaman chuckled "Just mate. Jake Oates here, first mate aboard 'The Falcon' and proud of it." With a quick nod at the girl's clothing, he grinned and murmured his approval. "The Captain's got a good idea there. The sight of a woman's skirts at sea... well, that's the surest road to mutiny there is."

Cerissa gaped at him, mystified. She had heard of mutinies, and she knew the dangers involved, but why... "Why would a woman's skirts cause such trouble?" she asked, her blue eyes wide with surprise. Was that why Brett had been so angry with her? Threatening to throw her overboard?

The old sailor shrugged, a bit embarrassed. "Well, miss... It isn't so much the skirts as what lies under 'em. On a trip like this, maybe four, maybe six weeks out at sea... well, men got certain needs, missy, and they get to aching bad from 'em. Understand? But you shouldn't worry. The Captain claimed you personal, and he's a man to hold his own. The crew knows that, and they respect the Captain's sword pretty good—they ought to leave you alone, ok now. 'Cept I wouldn't take no more strolls into their quarters, missy. You're tempting the Devil at that."

Cerissa studied the man, a faint frown on her face, her brows drawn together in a near solid bar. "Do all men have these...ah, needs?" she questioned intently, "Even Lord Lindsey?"

The grizzled mate shrugged, plainly embarrassed by such talk. "Of course, he's got 'em missy. Everybody has...exceptin' them what are buggers...them what likes boys," he explained, shifting his weight from foot to foot, avoiding her gaze.

"Why do you call Lord Lindsey Captain?" she inquired hastily, "And...and he's not a...a bugger is he?"

"Lord, missy, you shouldn't be using such language," Oates frowned, "Of course he ain't no bugger. Why he's one of the gamest men I ever went awhoring with, and..." the mate stopped, his face flaming. That was enough of such talk he decided grimly. T'wasn't fitting to be talking to the Captain's whore this way. Abruptly, he changed the subject. "I call the Captain "Captain' cause that's what he be. He may be a lord on land in England, but out to sea, missy, then he's a Captain. And a damn fine one I may add. I served under him for three years—since he first arrived in Port Royal, looking for crew. And he took plenty of prizes, with plenty of good booty, and he ne'er was one to torture innocents unnecessarily. He stuck close to the laws in the letter of marque he'd got, and he weren't no pirate or scalawag. I be nearly a rich man now, because of him, but I wouldn't let the Captain go sailing without me, no sir. I'd follow him to Hell and back if he ordered."

Cerissa's astonished eyes followed the grey-headed mate as he turned to leave the cabin. The description he gave of Lord Lindsey, the obvious devotion he showed...the man she had known in London, the selfish, cynical, cold-blooded, superficial, bewigged and beribboned grand lord she had lived with in England...he could not command a fighting ship so easily. Nor would he have aroused such deep attachment. Was Brett so different here at sea? And if so, which was the real man? The jaded, artificial, over-sophisticated Court gentleman, making witty ripostes, dealing in intrigue and vicious gossip, intent only on pleasure and self-gratification...or the adventurous, reckless, obviously respected master of a fighting ship? Admired and feared by his own seamen, notoriously the most critical judges in the world?

And which one did Cerissa hope to be the real Bretegane Lindsey? She had fallen in love with the elegant lord...or had she? Had she actually sensed the presence of a more real character

78

beneath the gilded veneer of the Court; and responded to it? Was that the real source of her growing dissatisfaction with Brett while in London? That the very environment had strengthened the artificial aspects of his personality, and dampened the more genuine ones? And here at sea . . . where he was more the man and less the lord . . . how would he react to her? Might she take advantage of the 'needs' Mate Oates had so carefully referred to, and use the honest influence of the sea to bind Brett closer to her?

Cerissa's heart leapt in sudden hope as she finished her meal and crept wearily back into Brett's narrow bunk. Here in the middle of the ocean, she was Lord Lindsey's—no, she amended quickly, Captain Lindsey's only choice if he wanted a woman. Not like in London where every woman of the Court and every apple-cheeked serving girl had invited the handsome lord to her bed. She remembered the one time she had, inadvertently, seen one occasion of Brett's infidelity, when he was leaving a tavern, his arm draped around a beautiful, blond-haired lady whose gown of satin and necklace of diamonds had glittered in the sunshine. Remembered the cold sick feeling in the pit of her stomach to see him stop to kiss her, before Cerissa had hurried the coach driver on, unwilling to see more. Not that he had ever flaunted his infidelities to her . . . Brett was rarely cruel. Yet, they existed, and both understood they would continue . . .

But here on the open sea, Brett could only be with her, at least for the three or four weeks left until they reached Port Royal in Jamaica. She would not have to compete for his attention; she could make him court her for a change. With delicious daydreams of how he would seek her, and how she would surrender at last to his attentions, Cerissa fell sound asleep; the first truly deep slumber since she had left London nearly two weeks before. Her morbid fear of the rats, and the endless, ever-present cold of the ship's hold had interrupted her nights before. Now, like the dead, she slept, dreamless and still, not waking when Brett came in hours later to change his wet clothes, shoving her over against the wall as he climbed in beside her—not waking when the dawn came and he climbed out again, dressing to go above.

When the noon watch sounded and the wench was still asleep, Captain Lindsey began to worry, feeling his anger at the girl return as he blamed her for his concern. Quietly, he had instructed his first mate, Jake, to go below and check the girl every hour, waiting for her sleep to end. At last, with a vicious curse, he handed the levers of the helm over to Oates and left the quarterdeck, dropping easily down the hatchway with the grace of long familiarity, his hands barely needing the stout rope bannister for balance.

In the cabin, he bent over the bunk, one hand reaching out gently to touch the girl's forehead, fearing to find fever beneath his fingertips. But Cerissa was cool, and stirred restlessly at his touch, her blue eyes half-opening, filled as always, with a radiant depth of adoration as she gazed at him before her eyes closed again in sleep.

Startled, and feeling a shade regretful of his earlier anger, Brett withdrew his hand and moved quietly out of the cabin, his suntanned face serious, his green eyes dark with thought as he reassumed control of the ship's course. Damn but there was something about that girl . . . the way that she loved him no matter what he said or did to her. This love made him uneasy, unsettled his thoughts, yet he enjoyed her devotion too . . . had almost grown to need it during these past months. There was no use pretending he was unhappy with her presence, he wasn't. He was delighted. He had missed her while at sea—surprised to find himself picturing her ready, innocent smile, or the way she cocked her chestnut head when puzzled. And yet being loved was a problem, too. It restricted his tempers, fearing to wound her too deeply by a careless word. Sending her notice of his whereabouts when he was planning to be out for the night . . . often enough in another woman's bed. Thinking of her preferences when selecting a play, or choosing a restaurant. Considering her pleasure in bed, as well as his own. And yet, he wouldn't want to give her love up, inconvenience or not. It was incredibly flattering, deeply reassuring that the girl found him worth loving. That he could drop his guard with her, admit to a headache or being tired, not be forced to pretend limitless gaiety, endless wit, exaggerated gallantry . . . Jesus Christ! She had loved him enough to stow away in the cargo hold, knowing how furious he would be, gave up her country and risked her very life. Hell, he couldn't even pretend to be indifferent to the wench. Not that he was ready to admit it to Cerissa, but he was glad she had come along. For one thing, he liked himself better when he was with her, thinking of someone besides himself. Damn if Ardsley hadn't been right on the mark. He was falling in love with the wench—not that he could ever tell Cerissa so. It would be crueler than anything conceivable to do so. He could never marry the girl, and she would never understand why not. But he could keep her as his mistress, treasure her for her unfailing love, even have children with her if Cerissa had the courage to bear them illegitimate. Yet, she had disobeyed his direct orders in coming along, and risked herself terribly... if Oates hadn't heard the crew shouting when they'd discovered her... Yes, he'd better feign anger for a few more days to teach her a lesson.

The bells sounded the evening watch at last, and Brett descended to hatchway wearily, glad to be out of the damp and cold of the upper deck, anxious to see if Cerissa was awake yet.

"Hello, Captain," Jake Oates' leathery face creased in a grin as Brett walked in, shedding his cold cloak gratefully. There were no open fires of course aboard ship—except one for cooking in the galley—but just being out of the chill winds...

Cerissa turned cautiously, her blue eyes searching his tanned face hopefully, eager to find forgiveness. When he answered her with a quick scowl, her face fell. The mate protested swiftly, unafraid of the Captain's wrath.

"Come now, Captain, and give the miss a smile. Ye look fiercer than the squall gathering on the starboard quarter."

Brett frowned hastily at the weathered old seaman. "You seem very fond of the wench, Jake. Maybe I should give her over to you. And may she be the plague to you she's been to me."

Oates grinned, shaking his head reluctantly at the offer. The wench was lovely, and they had been two weeks at sea, but he hadn't gotten to be mate by having rock between his ears. The Captain had looked like thunder all day, but all the while was checking the girl each hour. Aye, he cared for this little wench in spite of his bluffing. Besides, Jake had a sharp eye for wenches, and this girl had a certain glow in her eyes... the slightest roundness to her belly. Mighn't she be carrying the Captain's child even now? Chuckling aloud, Oates shrugged and winked at the dejected girl, turning to leave. "I'll bring in a nice intimate supper for two, Captain Lindsey. And I'll knock first."

Brett sat hastily at the table, stretching his long booted legs out gratefully under the table, hiding the secret smile Oates' comment had evoked. He heard Cerissa come softly up behind him, her arms dropping over his shoulders to pull his head back against the pillow of her breasts, her small hands rubbing his neck and forehead. Brett relaxed thankfully, sighing his contentment, then snapped his dark head suddenly forward away from her touch.

"You're still angry with me?" Cerissa questioned softly, a half-smile curving her lips. She was content to let his anger run it's course. They had weeks before landfall.

"It's not a question of still," he snapped. "The reasons I forbid

81

your coming haven't evaporated, Cerissa, they still exist. A sea voyage like this..."

A knock on the door sounded, and a worried-looking Oates poked his grey head in. "'Scuse me, Captain, but that's one nasty looking squall coming from starboard. The seas are getting higher already."

"Did you order the top-sails furled?"

"Aye, sir, and the mizzen's drawn as well."

"All we can do for now. I'll eat and come back up for the helm." Brett sighed and reached for a bowl of pork and potato stew, breaking off a drumstick from the roasted capon. October and November were always the rainy months in the Indies, but he had hoped to be beyond most of the fiercer storms by leaving later this year. Yet the tradewinds were always unpredictable. Luckily, 'The Falcon' was a brand new ship and stoutly built of seasoned oak. She should be able to weather anything but the direct force of a devil hurricane.

"You'd better find a good book and stay in here, Cerissa," he advised, reclasping a dry cloak around his wide shoulders. "If the seas get too rough, put out the lantern and get into the bunk. The furniture is mostly nailed down, but some of the smaller pieces may move around a bit."

Cerissa nodded obediently, settling herself into a chair, a selection of Dryden's poetry in her hands. In passing, she blessed her Aunt Mary again for struggling to teach her to read and write, wondering for the hundredth time why she had bothered. Had the woman somehow sensed that her life would take this course? In general, only the quality had the leisure time, or the money, to enjoy a library.

Soon, the ship was pitching violently, the timbers creaking and groaning in the force of the squall, the wind howling wild above her head. By straining her ears, she could barely make out Brett's voice on the deck above, shouting orders over the wailing gusts. Determined to be unafraid, she took a deeper seat in the leather chair, and drew the yellow light of the lantern closer to her, unsure of whether the increasing darkness was due to the evening or the storm.

Suddenly, she heard a resounding snap above her, followed by a ringing thud, and she jumped to her feet. She blew out the lamp and grabbed Brett's extra cloak from where it hung drying on the post, pushing open the cabin door, astonished to see water running into the gangway through the open hatch. Above her head, the curses and screams of the crew were muffled by the raging, slashing bitter winds. She hauled herself up the narrow stairs, clinging to the swaying rope guide, pulling her hood up before she raised her head to peer out onto the main deck. At once she noticed the queer tangle of canvas and rope at the front of the ship, the bow itself obscured by a tall, fallen spar which listed at a crazy angle to the deck. Men were swarming over the mess like flies, pulling at companions trapped beneath it, heaving the useless rigging away. Everything seemed to lie behind a misty grey curtain as the driving rain continued to beat down on the pitching ship.

Behind her lay the quarterdeck, roofed and partially enclosed to afford the helmsman some protection from the weather, and she turned towards it, only to feel a strong hand grasp at her ankle, hauling her down into the small gangway again.

"Best get back in your cabin, missy," Oates frowned warningly at her. "The Captain's got his hands full enough without picking you up out of the sea just now."

"Oh, Jake are we sinking?" Cerissa cried, clinging to the mate with fearful hands. "I heard something and . . ."

The sailor grinned, his blue grey eyes twinkling merrily as he shook his head, "Hardly sinking, lass. The Falcon's a good ship, she'd weather worse than this before floundering. No, it's just a little squall coming up from the islands to greet us. But get back in the cabin before the Captain sees you running about or you'll rouse his temper again."

"He's mad at me already," the girl shrugged, unwilling to be sent to her room like a chastised child.

"Oh aye, of course he is," Oates laughed, grabbing the rope line to begin heaving himself up. "Though he checked you every hour all day. Don't you worry about his temper missy, this storm'll take care of that." With a salute he disappeared, closing the hatch after him.

Cerissa stared after him, surprise changing to a secret, delighted smile as his words crystallized in her mind. So Brett wasn't really as furious as he pretended to be, he was only unwilling to admit he had forgiven her so easily . . . She laughed as she walked back to the cabin, blowing a kiss to where she guessed Brett would stand on the deck above her. Oh yes! She had made the right decision in London almost a month ago. And somehow she would get Brett to admit it too.

The storm lasted all that night and through the early morning. Finally, Lord Lindsey appeared, shortly before lunch time, his whole body sagging with weariness, his eyes shadowed as he dropped his cloak carelessly onto the floor and walked straight to the bunk, bending to pull his wet boots off before laying back on the bed, moaning his satisfaction.

Cerissa shrugged off his lack of greeting, secure in her secret knowledge of his concern and carved a slice of cold chicken, dishing out a half bowl of steaming soup to carry it over to him, offering it wordlessly.

"Thanks, sweetheart, but I ate breakfast above deck earlier. All I want to do now is sleep."

The girl nodded, reaching down to unlace his linen shirt, unbuttoning the snug cuffs of the full, gathered sleeves to draw it off, then pulling at the broad leather belt to release the catch.

"Cerissa, I'm not even interested in that just now. Please just leave me alone."

The girl's face flamed and she drew back angrily. "I wasn't interested in that either, Brett Lindsey. I was only trying to help! I don't have to throw myself at you. If you want me, you'll have to ask for me, and then maybe..."

"I don't have to ask for anything from you," the dark haired lord snapped back, "And I'll be damned if I'll grovel for your favors wench. You enjoy me as much as I you, you'll be seeking me..."

"Never!" Cerissa vowed, turning her back on the man haughtily. This was one time she had the upper hand. Brett had no other choice but her out here. She wouldn't taunt him with his words or his pride would refuse to allow him to seek her, but nevertheless, she was going to wait him out. Make him come to her this time...

Brett frowned at the girl, but rolled over into the bunk in a moment. He was too tired to argue the point right now with the wench. Fighting that squall had taken all his strength, all his emotion. Let her think whatever she liked, time would prove who was right. At least his ship was safe now, the broken spar being repaired, the seas calm and the horizon fair. He could sleep a while...

Cerissa laid her book aside, and was stretching the cramps out of her legs when she heard the mate knock softly on the door, bringing their supper. Quietly, she moved to take the trays from the sailor, nodding her head toward Brett's sleeping form in the bunk.

"It's all right, missy. The Captain asked to be wakened for supper," Oates smiled, making a deliberate clatter with the platters, grinning as the dark haired lord cursed viciously and sat upright, staring accusingly at the mate. "Suppertime, Captain. And the boys have finished the spar. Will you wish to inspect the rigging tonight?"

"No, not tonight, Jake," Brett mumbled, looking hungrily at the steaming pewter dishes "But I'll take first watch again in the morning. Bring coffee for me."

The seaman saluted jauntily and disappeared leaving Cerissa and the Captain alone, both feeling a little strained in the silence that hung in the small room. Finally, Brett cleared his throat motioning to the table. "Ladies sit first," he shrugged, smiling a bit self-consciously. He wasn't used to remembering etiquette at sea.

Cerissa smiled, pleased to see that his face had regained its healthy, wind-colored appearance. She could sense that he was in a better humor now, and she could also sense that he was a little uneasy, probably wondering whether she was planning to continue the quarrel they'd begun in the afternoon. "Let's not pretend we're at Court, Brett," she teased, dropping into a nearby chair. "I'm hardly dressed in the height of style."

Lord Lindsey grinned, visibly relieved. "I confess I like you in those clothes," he nodded. "I'm not accustomed to seeing petticoats at sea, anyway. We really live very differently out here away from England, you know. I'd be hard pressed to even remember all the courtesies I'm supposed to live by."

"Then don't bother," she agreed easily, secretly amazed at how great the gap was between the lord and the captain, liking the captain much better all the time. "We'll just be wench and Captain until we get back to England."

Immediately, Brett's face changed, his eyes growing darker. "No, sweetheart. You can't stay on in Port Royal. It's just impossible. There are some honest planters on the island, but most of the men . . . well, they're barely better than buccaneers, Cerissa, than pirates. The law they live by is very rough. I'm used to it and they respect me, but it's no place for you."

Cerissa's chin went up stubbornly, but she held her tongue. She had come this far; she had no intention of reaching the Indies only to be shipped back home. But she had plenty of time to think of a way around that. Perhaps, if she were really with child as she'd begun to suspect, Brett would allow her to stay until the child was born at least. That would give her until the spring anyway.

Dinner passed easily, Cerissa asking a hundred questions about the ship and sailing, struggling with the new language of the sea. Brett coaxed her to tell him more about her experience as a stowaway, laughing at her recollection of fearing the sailors would drop the crate, astonished that the girl had never learned to swim and promising to remedy that upon first landfall.

But when the dinner was over and the lantern extinguished, the tension grew again, both stubbornly waiting for the other to suggest the obvious. But neither did, nor would. So at last, they squirmed and tossed sleeplessly in the narrow bunk.

Captain Lindsey's humor was less benevolent the next day, and Cerissa watched him cautiously, afraid to precipitate a quarrel. He was always a restless sleeper, but the hard lines of his jaw and the shadows ringing his emerald eyes indicated a sleepless night. He growled at Mate Oates when he brought the coffee in, and had glared wordlessly at Cerissa when she'd asked permission to go above deck for a breath of air. Finally, he had dressed and gone above to take the helm, leaving the uneasy girl staring at the small cabin walls.

Cerissa sighed, brushing her heavy hair with long, swinging strokes, Brett's borrowed sterling brush pleasantly familiar in her hand. Maybe she shouldn't have started this confrontation . . . maybe Brett's pride was too stubborn. He might never come to her. And yet to give in now would be unconditional surrender. It would force no change in their relationship. And worse, she would have cast away the only chance she would probably ever have to catch him in such an isolated situation . . . No, she couldn't give in yet. She would simply have to use every woman's trick she knew to coax him to her arms. She had learned so many in her few months in London—tricks she'd scorned to try before, trusting in the obvious potency of his usual passionate response to her, but now . . .

Obediently, Cerissa remained below in the cabin though she was thoroughly bored with the narrow room and longed to see the open sea and enjoy the sunshine of the warming day. Perhaps when Brett returned for lunch . . .

"Here's some grub, missy," Oates leathery face appeared at the door, his old eyes speculative as he glanced at the girl. The Captain's humor had been touchy enough before the girl had appeared on the ship. Then, for a few short hours, it had improved. But now, Jesus! The whole crew'd been walking on eggshells all morning, afraid of incurring his wrath . . . and with it, the cat o' nine tails or a cold trip overboard into the strong running seas. As the glowering Captain stepped in, the wary mate backed out and fled, glad to be out of harm's way for a while.

Cerissa watched the tall lord stalk to the table, heave a chair back so forcefully that it nearly overturned, then with a muttered oath, he slumped in the protesting leather and started to eat. The girl smiled faintly, a bit amused at his obvious ill-temper. Good, she thought in satisfaction, the strain is telling on him already. In pretended innocence, she circled to the front of the table and leaned across to take a plate, deliberately allowing her loose-laced borrowed shirt to fall away from her body, exposing her high, pointed breasts. Brett's face tightened, his eyes burning into her body a moment before he half-choked on his food and averted his eyes. Cerissa pretended not to notice and she carried her platter over to sit beside him, letting her knee fall to rest against his leg as she ate. In a moment, she felt his thigh begin to tremble and he quickly moved away, his jaw muscles twitching nervously.

"What's the matter, love? You seem edgy today," she questioned innocently.

Brett stared at her incredulously, his eyes quickly growing angry. "What's the matter?" he echoed impatiently, laying his knife and fork on the pewter plate with exaggerated slowness. "I'll tell you what's the matter! I didn't get two hours sleep all night, wench! That bunk isn't designed to fit two people—at least not lying side by side with a half acre of no man's land in between! So since that's what you evidently intend to continue . . ."

"Brett, that's unfair," she protested hastily, despising herself for making him suffer this way, "It's not what I intend at all. But all you have to do is ask . . ."

"I told you before I don't intend to grovel!" he snapped, his mouth taut and grim in frustration and fury.

"You don't have to grovel, Brett, just make a little effort for once," Cerissa replied calmly though her heart was hammering, her face flaming. "I'm not just a body to be enjoyed at your whim. I'm a person with feelings, who . . ."

"Oh, hell," Brett slammed his chair back, getting to his feet, his eyes flashing. "I'm going back above. Just stay out of my sight."

Cerissa fought tears back as he left, every line of his body bespeaking his nearly ungovernable fury. Oh damn! She thought in bitter frustration. Damn him and damn me and damn everything. The whole scheme was careening wildly out of control. God only knew what Brett was liable to do next.

She ate dinner alone. Evidently the Captain had chosen to eat with the other officers of the ship in their cabin. She was really too upset to be sleepy, but for lack of anything else to do, she climbed into the bunk and laid down. Hours later, Captain Lindsey finally came in, his handsome face stormy, his breath reeking of too much brandy. Without a word, he undressed and literally threw himself into the bunk, lying on his side, turned away from her. For long minutes, he thrashed and tossed, muttering angrily under his breath. Finally, he bolted upright, turning to stare at the girl accusingly. "God damn it, move over! How the hell do you expect me to sleep celibate when you're all over me whenever I move?"

"I'm sorry, Brett. I'm against the wall already, I can't move any farther..."

"Then get out!" he snarled, his emerald eyes glittering unpleasantly as he stepped from the bunk, holding the blankets up and pointing to the door.

Cerissa looked at him, not believing he meant what he said, her breath caught in her throat. "But Brett..." she murmured at last, her blue eyes wide, "But...then where shall I go?"

"Go back to your crate," he sneered, his black brows drawn together over flashing eyes. "I'll call down the hatchway when we reach the Indies."

Cerissa stared a moment longer at Brett's face, sure she would see him deny that order. But he didn't. He merely stood there, tall and strong and grim, every muscle tight beneath the sun-browned skin of his body, his gaze relentless. Cold with shock and sudden fear, the girl climbed reluctantly out of the bunk. With deliberate slowness, hoping desperately for a reprieve, she bent to pull her shoes on, and fumbled with the clasp on the fur lined hooded cloak. He couldn't actually mean to send her back there...with the rats...and no food...and the leering crewmen...

"Oh hell, take your cloak off," Brett sighed at last, frowning still at the trembling girl. "We both know you can't go back there. Why every one of those sixty sailors would have climbed on you before dawn..."

Cerissa closed her eyes thankfully, sending a silent prayer up to heaven, her knees too weak with relief to allow her to move again yet. "Well, where then shall I..." she murmured at last, unable still to meet his gaze.

"You take the bunk. I'll try to get some sleep on one of these chairs," he replied, eying the seat with little eagerness. Damn but the girl would have gone back there to that hold if he hadn't backed -off...Damn her for her stubborn contrariness...

"No, Brett, you take the bunk. You have to work very hard again tommorrow, you need some sleep."

He stared at the girl's solemn face in wry surprise. She was so damned concerned for his welfare but she wouldn't give in on the one thing she knew he really needed from her . . . "That's hardly a gallant way for a Captain to act, Cerissa. Even at sea, there are a few niceties we observe."

"Well, I won't take the bunk with you sitting up all night."

"Oh hell, then, we'll both take the bunk," Brett snapped impatiently. This whole situation was getting ridiculous.

Satisfied, Cerissa climbed back into the bed, laying all the way over, her shoulder touching the wall to give him room. In a moment, Brett followed her, laying silent in the darkness, puzzled and thoroughly frustrated, unable to figure out any way to solve the dilemma short of acquiescing—which his pride cried out against staunchly. The girl moved on the mattress and he turned to see her face near his, pale and shadowed by the soft moonlight from the windows. Hopefully, he returned her searching gaze, a faint smile lifting the corners of his mouth, his eyes warm, his body already responding.

"Goodnight, love," Cerissa whispered at last, bending to lay a gentle kiss on his lips. "Sleep well."

The dark haired lord stared after her as she curled back up to the wall, disappointed and frustrated again. "Oh, God damn you to hell," he mumbled finally, bunching the pillow up beneath his head with angry fists. And as he fell asleep, too exhausted to spend another night awake, his brain was working desperately, trying to discover an honorable way out of this damn, stupid situation. He couldn't stand the strain of many more days like this—living with the wench, even sleeping with her, his body clamoring without cease for some release, some satisfaction, for the physical fulfillment of burying himself deep within her, tasting the familiar sweetness of her mouth, her soft, taut breasts beneath his hand.

Chapter Seven

When morning dawned, the dark haired lord rolled over lazily to stretch, yawning and rubbing his face with one hand in relief. Sometime during the night, the solution had finally come to him—so obvious, so simple and even enjoyable that he was amazed at the difficulty he'd had finding it. He would seduce the girl of course. He'd done it once already with Cerissa, that first night in Bainwater, though she had been ready enough to come to him anyway. So she might resist a little longer tonight, perhaps, but then he knew her better now too. Knew just where to caress her to light her own passions, just how to kiss her sweet, soft lips . . . And hell, he admitted ruefully in a flash of honesty, so what if his seducing her meant he was giving in? It wasn't the same as actually having to ask her in so many words . . . Besides, he thought he might enjoy the novelty of the challenge involved. He'd always had his women so easily and so often, he'd never bothered to work for one. Might it not make the loving even that much sweeter?

"Good morning, princess," he called lazily to Cerissa as she stood washing her face by the shallow iron basin. The girl turned quickly, surprise at his good humor showing in her blue eyes.

Hesitantly, she smiled back, wondering why he seemed in such fine temper. Was it only a better night's sleep?

A soft knock heralded the mate's arrival with coffee and biscuits. Warily, Oates glanced at his captain, expecting the usual morning curses. "A fair morning, Captain," he murmured at last, "It promises sunshine and a good wind."

"Good," Brett smiled, reaching hungrily for a hot bun and smearing it liberally with sweet strawberry jam.

The grizzled mate looked quickly at the mystified girl, but she seemed to be as puzzled as the sailor. So it wasn't that which had improved the man's temper...

Cautiously, Cerissa cleared her throat, catching Brett's eye. "Since it's supposed to be so nice today, could I come upstairs...above deck, rather, for just a little while?"

Captain Lindsey frowned a moment, cocking his dark head to one side as he considered her request. It really was asking for trouble from the crew to parade the girl in front of them and yet...if he expected success with his plans for the evening, he'd better humor her wishes for the day. "Well," he replied reluctantly, "I guess it's all right. But only on the quarterdeck with me—not on the main deck with the seamen. No use throwing matches at a powder keg."

Cerissa squealed with delight, running to throw her arms around Brett's neck, embarrassing both he and the mate instantly. Gruffly, Oates murmured excuses and withdrew, climbing up the hatchway to the helm.

Brett extricated himself from her embrace regretfully, his eyes gleaming. "You go ahead and eat, sweetheart, and get dressed. I'll be up on the quarterdeck. When you get ready, come on up...But throw a cloak around yourself and don't stop for a stroll. Come straight to me."

Cerissa nodded, her smile radiant. "I will, I promise!" Impulsively she leaned forward to kiss the top of his thick, black curling hair. Brett halfchoked and stood up hastily, taking his coffee with him as he left.

A half hour later, she was hauling herself up the steep steps of the hatchway, glad for once to be free of her burdensome petticoats and long, trailing skirts. At the top, she shielded her eyes from the bright, warming sunshine and glanced about, uncertain where to go.

Mate Oates jumped easily to the main deck, taking the girl's arm and pointing up to the quarterdeck. "There you go, missy," he grinned, turning to disappear into the open hatch. He had a whole list of orders from the Captain to get done before evening meal, and he was anxious to get them done—and done in style. At first, the Captain's good humor had puzzled him. But then, as he'd listened to Captain Lindsey's special menu for supper, seen the darkening gleam in the man's eye, he'd finally begun to understand. Fresh roast of beef, a fruit stuffed capon, sweet frosted buns, onions and peas in cream, a raspberry trifle...Cerissa's favorite dish, fresh strawberries drowned in thick sweet cream, was unfortunately unavailable. But other than that, the Falcon's galley would produce dishes worthy of Whitehall, he'd see to that. If the Captain planned a seduction he'd best be successful at it, or the whole crew would bear the brunt of his bad temper. Evidently, he guessed from all the trouble the Captain was going to, the wench had been playing coy. So the Captain was planning to way lay her tonight and that's why he'd been grinning all morning. The oysters he'd offered to drag anchor for had been chucklingly refused though. It had seemed a natural choice for everyone knew of their aphrodisiac potency. But the Captain had only laughed and shaken his dark head, swearing he'd explode if he even smelled one of the shellfish cooking. Oates had laughed then too, sure that his guess was correct. Plenty of wine for the lady, the Captain had repeated, his eyes gleaming in mirth. A bottle of brandy for himself, as usual, but several good bottles of Rhenish for the wench...

Cerissa climbed into the half-enclosed quarterdeck, timbered solid at the back, with the wood continuing around the corner to form partial walls, a canvas awning stretched taut over the structure. Brett was inside, standing close to the open helm block, enjoying the sun and the fair weather today. He smiled a greeting from where he stood. Cerissa looked out into the distant sea, enjoying the fresh, salt-tangy air and the warm breeze. She frowned wonderingly as she noticed his hand shifting a long oaken lever inside the wooden box, for as he moved it she could feel the ship change course slightly beneath her feet.

"That's that thing?" she asked at last, pointing to the lever.

"It's the helm," he smiled "It steers the ship."

Cerissa arched her brows in surprise "How does a little stick like that control this big boat?"

"It's not just a little stick. It connects to a rather complicated series of levers, that eventually attach to the rudder. Only the rudder itself is actually in the water, and depending on which way the rudder is turned, the bow changes direction."

"Why do you have to change direction?" she pursued. "Isn't it a fairly straight line from England to the Caribbean? Why don't you just go along..."

"You have to change direction according to the wind, sweetheart," Brett grinned indulgently. "Here. Want to try it?"

Cerissa paused, staring warily at the lever he held in his sun tanned hand. "Are you sure I can't hurt anything?"

Brett chuckled, shaking his dark head. "No, Cerissa. There's nothing around for miles to run into. Go ahead."

Cautiously, the girl stepped forward, seizing the oak in one hand, giving a swift gasp of surprise as it started to pull out of her grip. Hastily she grabbed it with her left hand as well, crying out for Brett to take it back. "Why does it pull so hard?" she panted at last, stepping well away from the unwieldy stick.

"Because it's fighting the force of the water and the wind, sweet. You have to keep the ship on an angle to the wind and that puts pressure on the rudder."

Cerissa nodded, hiding her confusion. "But don't you get tired of holding onto that all day?"

Captain Lindsey shrugged and pointed to two thick leather cords handing on either side of the rectangular opening. "If you get tired, you can lash the helm in place. The wind's steady now so that's no problem. But it was changeable this morning—as it usually is early in the day—so I left it free. Besides, Jake Oates is a good helmsman. I often give it over to him, even in bad weather. Several others on the crew can take it in a pinch as well."

Cerissa considered that information solemnly, nodding her chestnut head in understanding. "Doesn't the wind always come from the same direction Brett?"

He shook his head, eyes intent on the deck below where some sailors were changing a rigging. "No, sweetheart, the wind comes from all different directions, although each place has what they call a prevailing wind—the one that's normal for that place. Sometimes the wind comes in directly over the bow, for instance. Obviously you can't sail into it, so you tack, or zig-zag, sort-of, this way," he drew a diagram in the air with his finger, then continued, "When the wind comes from starboard—or your right—near the bow, we call it coming from the starboard quarter. And sometimes it hits directly amidships, too. None of those are very good. The best winds come from behind you or to the sides behind the mainmast. It's coming over my right shoulder today, which is one of my favorites."

"I would think the wind coming from behind you would be best.

That must be the fastest and you can go straight without hanging onto that stick." she announced seriously, surprised to see a faint smile on Brett's face.

"It is a good wind," he agreed with equal seriousness, though his green eyes danced merrily "Except that it's often too strong for the ship. And it may be gusty. Plus, it tends to shove the bow too deep into the water."

"Why does that matter?" she questioned intently, "Why doesn't a stronger wind just make the ship move faster? Why should . . ."

"Whoa, Cerissa," the dark haired lord grinned openly. "You ask more 'why's' than any three other women I've ever known!"

The girl fell silent, pouting a little. She was only trying to learn something about a subject that interested him. She herself could care less about helms and winds and . . .

"Okay," Brett sighed, noting her quivering lip. "I'll answer these, but no more 'why's' for a while then, agreed?" The girl nodded quickly, smiling again. "Every ship has a maximum velocity, sweet, what we sailors term the hull speed. You see the stronger the wind, the faster it pushes the ship forward, and the deeper the bow cuts into the ocean. So, at a certain point, the drag of the water on the hull reduces your speed. That's why an empty ship travels faster than one loaded with cargo—it sits higher out of the water."

Cerissa nodded and fell silent, wandering over to a small table littered with oddly marked maps, a compass and a strange, semi-circular movable globe laying atop them. "What are these?" she asked thoughtlessly, bending over to stare closely at them. Behind her, she heard Brett sigh again as he glanced over his shoulder to answer. "Don't think you're going to trade what's for why's," he warned with a grin. "I feel like a damned deacon already. Those are navigational maps showing the currents and the prevailing winds for our voyage. We're about midway in the ocean now. There's Jamaica marked below and the other maps show more of the islands in detail."

Cerissa made a face at him, laughing at his exaggerated protests. She knew he loved the sea and she knew he loved talking about it. But just for now, she was content to be silent, letting her mind wander over possible reasons for Brett's unexpected good mood today. She guessed that he had something secret planned for her. There was a certain, odd gleam—almost amusement, almost anticipation—in his green eyes. And he was obviously going out of his way to charm her. But to what end? Did he expect her to back down on her determination to force him to do the courting at last?

Was he hoping she would relent and ask him to her bed instead?

Suddenly, a loud voice on the deck below shouted. "Whales to port, Captain." and she turned eagerly, pleased to remember so easily which side of the ship port referred to. Brett lashed the helm in place quickly and came to stand alongside, drawing her to the edge of the deck and bracing her with an arm around her shoulders. He put his hand up to shield his eyes from the brightness of the sun on the water and looked out, scanning the sea for the huge mammals. Finally he pointed far out, showing her a barely visible group of the animals, diving and splashing with beautiful rhythm.

"Oh, they're so far away," Cerissa protested quickly, straining her eyes to see. "Can't we get closer?"

"Not this time, princess," he replied. "They're going the wrong way. But the ocean is full of them—as many as two thousand in a single herd. We'll see plenty more. If you're lucky, we'll hear them singing, or whatever that noise they make is supposed to be. You may even see one of the babies though it's late in the year for that."

Cerissa stood against him for a long moment, not looking at the whales any longer, just enjoying his touch, his nearness. At last, he dropped his arm and turned into the small house, nodding to Mate Oates as he jumped up to join them.

"Ready for relief?" the old seaman asked, already moving to the helm.

Brett nodded, stretching leisurely with the grace of a huge cat. "I think I'll lay down and enjoy the sunshine for a while," he announced "Call me if you need." Carelessly, he turned toward the starboard section of the open deck, drawing his white linen shirt over his head as he moved, tossing it onto a chair lashed within reach. Then, evidently remembering something, he leaned closer to the mate, the two men exchanged comments in voices too low for Cerissa to hear. At length, Brett laughed and slapped the seaman's shoulder good-naturedly before walking out into the golden light.

Cerissa dropped her eyes to the floor of the deck, afraid the men could tell her thoughts from the expression in her blue eyes. Seeing Brett standing there, so casually half-dressed, had brought memories flooding back. She had felt her face flame as she'd looked at his wide, sun-browned shoulders, dropping her gaze along the line of muscle that led to his flat, lean belly. Involuntarily her eyes dropped even lower, down to the massive golden clasp of his wide, brown leather belt. The breeches he wore here on shipboard were cut differently than those he had worn in London. These were tighter, fitted snugly around his hips and thighs, made of some nearly white bleached cloth. And they didn't rise as high into his waist as the ones in England either, but stopped below it at his hips, held in place by the leather belt looped through large cloth guards sewn onto the breeches themselves. A wave of moist warmth had surged through her loins as she'd found herself gazing at the place where his body bulged beneath the pants' buttons in front, the tightness of the cloth leaving little to the imagination. Guiltily, she had blushed and quickly looked away.

"I think I'll go back down...below," she said to the mate, walking over to give the captain a farewell kiss where he lay stretched on the deck, his dark head resting motionless on his brown, folded arms.

Oates grabbed the girl's arm, shaking his head and smiling. "Best leave the Captain be, missy. He's mean as a baited bear if he don't get his sleep. And he's liable to be busy tonight."

Cerissa smiled and nodded, wondering what the weathered seaman meant by that. The weather looked fair enough, why would Brett be busy? Perhaps the officers had a meeting...Yet the man's eye held a distinctly amused expression as he gazed at her—as though he knew a private joke but wouldn't tell her. "Good day, then," she answered pleasantly, throwing a last wistful glance over her shoulder to where Brett lay in the sun. She thought she'd go down and have a little nap herself—perhaps bathe and wash her hair as well. She was beginning to believe she couldn't hold out much longer against Brett...she might as well be as clean as possible, as pretty as possible, so she'd be ready when the time came.

She finished rinsing her hair in the small bucket, dunking her whole head in to wash the soap out. Fresh water was precious on board ship, it was not to be wasted. So she had managed to take a complete bath and wash her waist length hair all in one small bucket. It was growing late already. She could see the sun sinking into the crimson sea. She had slept later than she'd intended to, and she listened eagerly for Brett's footsteps in the gangway for he usually came down this time of day.

Finally she heard him. A moment later he sauntered into the room, his chest still bare, his white shirt swinging in his hand. He grinned as he saw her, his teeth flashing white and even, his brown face now reddish-brown across his nose and cheeks from new sun. "Helped yourself to my bedrobe, I see, you saucy wench."

Cerissa shrugged, glad he wasn't angry. She had just needed to feel feminine again and Brett's breeches hardly accomplished that. So when she'd come across this pale-blue silk kimono style robe in Brett's sea chest, she'd borrowed it for the evening. "You don't mind do you, Brett?" she smiled "Isn't it an improvement over baggy breeches?"

The dark haired lord laughed and nodded, reaching for the bucket to start his own bath. In a moment he returned, bathing and washing his own black hair, finishing with a shave. Cerissa sat on the edge of the bed, watching him, a half-smile on her lovely face as she brushed her chestnut hair dry with his bristle brush. She always loved to watch Brett shaving, or dressing, or doing any one of the thousand simple everyday things. For the moment, she ignored the reality of their relationship and watched him with a wife's eyes, pretending they were married. "I think I like you better as a Captain than as a Lord," she mused aloud, cocking her head to gaze teasingly at him.

Momentary surprise flickered across Brett's face before he grinned into the mirror, his eyes seeking hers in the polished reflection. "And I think I like you better as a cabin boy than as a London wench," he replied gallantly, his eyes gleaming with amusement as he concentrated again on shaving.

Cerissa swung her legs off the bed, going to the table to pick up a thick, triple sealed packet of parchment she had found in his chest. "What's this, Brett?" she murmured curiously, peering at the packet as she held it up to the fading light.

He glanced over his shoulder and frowned quickly. "Be careful with that, sweetheart. It's the only thing that keeps me from dancing on the gallows with the rest of the pirates."

Startled, the girl replaced the packet carefully in his iron bound leather sea chest, murmuring a hasty apology.

"It's all right. No harm done," Brett smiled. "That's my letter of marque from Charles. It makes me a privateer instead of a buccanneer. Of course, I remember you saying that we're all alike anyway," he teased.

Cerissa wrinkled her nose at him in an exaggerated pout, secretly pleased that he'd even remembered that conversation, now so long ago. "Why in the world would the king even bother with such nasty things? For all the trouble he gets into for it..."

"Charles needs the money, Cerissa. Privateering is only a shade less profitable than piracy. Of course, I have to split any prizes with the Crown..."

"You're teasing me, Brett," the girl protested quickly "How can a king need money?"

"Even a king has to eat," he laughed, wiping his face with a clean towel as he reached for fresh clothing. "Parliament granted Charles an income of only 800,000 pounds a year, sweet. And he only gets that when they meet, of course. Since he'd dismissed the Parliament, well . . . he's still got a hungry Court to feed and a government to run."

"You mean he doesn't have any money at all?" Cerissa asked astounded.

Brett laughed again at the concern on her face, shaking his head in wonder. "Jesus, Cerissa, are you sure you ever lived in England? Of course he's got some money. His wife's dowery brought him about 800,000 pounds, and he gets more from Louis of France for secret alliances. Plus, of course, the income from crown lands and shipping and all his other ventures."

Cerissa stared at the man, aghast at the figures he'd mentioned. Months of London living had convinced her that a pound sterling was not the fortune she had believed it in Bainwater, but still . . . 800,000 pounds! "And he needs more?"

Brett chuckled as he answered. "That's hardly a lot to have to run the government on, sweetheart. Think of the clerks to pay, his guards, army and the navy, maintaining buildings and roads and all the rest of it. Of course, Charles isn't known for his thriftiness either, but it doesn't really all go to splendor and mistresses. I've known the king to be so short of money personally that he's borrowed from me to pay a racing debt."

Cerissa continued to stare at him in amazement. At last, a tiny frown of concentration formed on her forehead and she gazed at Brett sharply. "You must be very rich to lend a king money," she decided at last.

"Yes indeed," he grinned. "Kings are notorious for not paying it back."

She pouted immediately and tried a different tack. "Be serious, Brett. How much money have you got?"

The dark haired lord was silent a moment, pulling his fresh breeches on and lacing his full-sleeved shirt. "Well, the Falcon cost about 6,000 pounds to build," he replied. "And I've got four other smaller ships without the guns . . . worth maybe 4,000 a piece. I've got 30,000 with the goldsmith Isaac Benjamin on Lombard Street, and about another 30,000 invested in land in Jamaica and a place called Carolina."

"Gemini!" Cerissa breathed, thoroughly awed. "That's over 80,000 pounds."

Brett laughed again, a teasing glint in his grey-green eyes. "Deciding whether I'd be a worthwhile catch, wench?"

Cerissa ignored him, still too overwhelmed to respond to his baiting. "Were you born that rich?"

He shook his head, shrugging his shoulders as if the subject embarrassed him. "No, sweet. About the only thing I inherited was the family home—a place called Whitross Manor up near Oxford. It was originally called White Rose, but during the War of the Roses, I guess it got changed to be more diplomatic in case the Lancasterians won. Most of the money I got doing just what I'm doing now—privateering."

"But, Lord!, Brett," Cerissa argued. "You have plenty of money now! Why keep on with this? Why take such risks and spend so much time away from England?"

Captain Lindsey shrugged, faintly frowning. The last thing he wanted right now was a quarrel. "Let's just say I have a restless streak in me, Cerissa. I got bored silly mincing around in Court velvet, playing cards and dice all day long. The islands are very different from England. People are more real, more basic, more honest. Honestly wicked sometimes but at least honest. I found myself comparing England to Jamaica when I went back, and found the homeland lacking. Not that I don't love England. I do. But I'm more comfortable now on the deck of a ship than I am in a drawing room."

Cerissa looked at his solemn face, noting the defensive, faintly angry shadows in his eyes. He acted as though he expected her to disapprove. "I've never seen the Indies, Brett but I think I agree with you a little bit. I like the Falcon better than London too." she said softly.

The dark haired lord stared at the girl a moment in obvious surprise. Slowly, a gentle smile formed on his lips and he turned away hastily, shrugging his wide shoulders. "Wait till you see Jamaica, sweetheart. It's beautiful. Orchids and morning glories grow wild, and the land is lush and green. Except for the hurricane season, it's usually sunny and always warm—about 80 degrees by the ocean, cooler up in the mountains. The water is clear as an aquamarine and the beaches are pure white. You can see the different fish without even going in the water. I'll take you swimming out to a coral reef when you learn how—show you some of the crazy colored little creatures that live out there. A lot of them are friendly as puppies, coming right up to your fingers."

Cerissa smiled radiantly, warmed by his obvious admiration for the island. She'd been right about Brett . . . he was a different person out here on the sea. And, though she'd never have believed it possible, she began to love him more than she had when she'd left London to follow him.

"Dinner's served, Captain," Mate Oates cheery voice interrupted the two, and Cerissa sprang to her feet, hurrying toward the table. It was just as well the seaman had come in when he had—the rush of warmth she had felt growing for Captain Lindsey was dangerous. In another moment, all resolutions to the contrary, she would have gone into his arms. Astounded, she stopped short, staring at the feast being laid before her. Brett kept a better than average table even for a Captain, but this . . .

"Here, sweetheart. The place of honor." Brett drew a chair back gallantly, standing tall and motionless behind it, his smile tentative, his grey-green eyes strangely calculating under their thick black lashes.

Cerissa smiled mechanically, moving to her chair. Something odd was afoot here, no doubt about it. First the mate's ill-disguised amusement this afternoon, and Brett's own exceptionally charming manner all day—now this extravagent supper and all this wine. She giggled aloud, her hand flying quickly to her mouth in an effort to smother the sound. Of course! What a dolt she had been! Brett was trying the oldest trick in the book . . . although, she reflected in wry amusement, it had worked well enough for him that night in Bainwater. So he intended to seduce her . . . the devious rascal. He'd go to all these pains rather than simply say he wanted her. Well, if he expected easy success, to get what he wanted without eventually putting his desire in words . . . But no use quarrelling yet. Just for now she would pretend ignorance and enjoy her seduction.

"Tell me more about the islands, love," she demanded sweetly, enjoying Brett's quick frown. He'd had enough talking. He wanted to eat and get on with it.

"Well, there really isn't much more to tell," he shrugged hopefully. But the girl just continued to smile, ignoring his reticence. With a silent curse, he continued. "The English took Jamaica from the Spanish in 1655. And the Dons have really lost most of their power in the islands since then. The Bermudas have been English a long time. St. Kitts and Barbados too."

"Then who are you privateering against?"

"Against the Spanish still. Although they've lost ground, they still control most of the metal-producing colonies. And gold, silver, even tin and iron are good booty."

"But we signed a peace with Spain," Cerissa protested indignantly.

"Yes, but . . ." Brett shrugged, unwilling to get involved in England's complicated foreign policy just now.

"But how can you attack Spanish ships if we've a treaty with them? That isn't fair," the girl continued stubbornly, casting a disapproving eye at the dark haired lord. "You ought to be . . ."

"Cerissa, please," he sighed impatiently, "Explaining this would take us hours, can't we just . . ."

"Well we have hours, don't we?" she inquired sweetly "You've nothing else in mind, do you?"

Trapped, Brett scowled and took a deep breath, cursing the girl's eternal curiosity. "Part of Charles' marriage agreement with the Queen was that he harry the Spanish—to keep them off the Portugese backs. Plus we have a long standing maritime rivalry with the Dutch—and it would please France to have us take a few of the Low Countries' ships. We have an alliance with the Dutch just now, but Charles has to keep in with Louis of France because he depends on Louis' money. But Charles really doesn't like France so well anymore—I think he probably prefers the Dutch actually, except that they are in such fierce competition with our own ships—so he wouldn't mind if we found a French ship to take, provided the booty was rich enough to be worth the trouble to soothe Louis' ruffled feathers. You see, Cerissa, we really don't have to be engaged in a declared war to privateer a bit. Everyone does it. And Charles is smart enough to realize that the English have to fight Dutch sea supremacy, capitalize on Spain's present weakness, and keep a wary eye on French ambitions on our colonies. Our navy, through lack of funds, has been reduced to a miserable state. Charles is anxious to increase our sea power, but, with no money to build his own ships, he's forced to rely on private investors instead. And the only way to lure private money into such a risky business is to promise potentially enormous profit—ergo privateering. You know," Brett added thoughtfully, "I believe Charles would be a good king if he only had some money to work with."

"He is a good king!" Cerissa protested stoutly, glaring at Brett.

He only laughed, spreading his hands in a gesture of apology. "All right, sweetheart. He'd be a better king if he had some money. He's right in thinking that France needs an alliance with a naval power—either us or the Dutch. And right now if those two combined against us, well," he shrugged expressively, his face

101

solemn, "we're going to come to blows with the French eventually, in spite of his care. Our interests conflict in the colonies. If he weren't dependent on Louis for money, Charles could cement a stronger alliance with the Dutch. Now that we've got New York from them..."

"Well, if he needs money, he could convene another Parliament," Cerissa interrupted tartly, remembering conversations she had overheard in London. "That would be the legal way."

Brett laughed indulgently, his eyes teasing. "Why, if you aren't a fanatic Whig at heart, princess!"

"I am not," Cerissa pouted, for the Whigs were, in her mind, traitorously anti-Stuart and she believed in the near-divine right of kings. "You know I'm loyal."

"Yes, of course," Brett nodded soothingly, reaching across the table to lift one of her tiny hands, placing a conciliatory kiss on her palm. "But that really is one of Charles' few potentially dangerous failings. He is absolutely bent on having his brother James succeed to the Crown, and Parliament is equally bent on excluding him in favor of a Protestant heir. I don't understand Charles' stubborness on that point. No one, even Charles, thinks James would be a good kind for England."

"Then why doesn't he declare Monmouth his heir? I've heard he is well-liked, and he's Protestant. I've even heard a rumor that he is legitimate—that the king married his mother by some rites."

Brett shook his dark head, a faint shadow of worry in his green eyes as he sighed. "I don't know, sweet. Perhaps Charles had doubts of the boy's courage, or his ability to rule. Monmouth is charming, and affable to the extreme. There's little doubt he's Charles' son. There's a certain physical resemblance—and the boy obviously inherited the Stuart lasciviousness—he was keeping a wench at 15. But perhaps Charles thinks he lacks the consistency, the ruthlessness... even the strength of his own conviction that a king needs to rule. James has those qualities in abundance, even in excess. He's stubborn, and fanatic, but hardly weak."

Cerissa studied the man, troubled at Brett's evident uneasiness. She'd never seen him so openly concerned about anything before. Obviously, the question of Charles' succession was a very serious matter. "What will happen then Brett?" she asked in a small voice, her blue eyes wide and solemn.

"I don't know, sweetheart," he answered, equally serious. "Trouble I'd guess. James will succeed and try to force Catholicism and absolutism back on this country. The kingdom will rebel—declaring for Monmouth or perhaps William and Mary of Orange—and we'll have civil war again. And maybe worse. James is ardently Pro-France. He'll support Louis' ambitions to swallow the Netherlands. That will leave us facing an enemy here in the colonies who'll have both land and naval supremacy. We'd be helpless to resist France then."

For a moment, the cabin was absolutely silent, burdened by fear of the future for England. Finally, with an effort, Brett smiled and shrugged off his melancholy. "But don't you worry, sweetheart. Charles is only in his fifties. He could live for years yet. Hell, as active as he is in bed, he might remarry yet and sire a legitimate son! Heaven knows he's got enough of the other kind."

Cerissa smiled, convinced that whatever came, Lord Lindsey would anticipate events and take care of his own. She was safe with him. "May I have some more trifle?" she asked happily, reaching for another glass of wine. She hadn't forgotten Brett's intention to seduce her—nor her determination to enjoy it. The dinner grew gay again, and Brett's eyes gleamed contentedly with the anticipation of fulfilled passion.

At last, with a bottle and a half of the Rhenish wine gone, and Cerissa's face flushed enticingly, Brett decided that the moment had come. With a last, sidelong glance at the girl, he stood up to his full six feet, stretching and feigning a yawn. "How about rubbing my back for a while, sweetheart? I must have pulled a muscle in it sometime today."

Cerissa nodded agreeably, concealing her amusement. "Why don't you lie down here on the floor? I can get a better . . ."

"No," Brett interrupted hastily, guiding her smoothly to the bunk "The mattress is more comfortable."

Cerissa walked with him to the bunk, trying to make a final decision. He still hadn't asked her to lie with him in so many words, and yet . . . the whole evening had been a request in a way. Suddenly she turned, gazing intently into Brett's darkly handsome face above her. She reached her hand up to touch his face gently, a faint smile curving her lips tenderly. "You're trying to seduce me, aren't you, Brett?"

The dark haired lord returned her gaze, and slowly, a rueful grin appeared on his face. "Yes, sweetheart," he shrugged, his eyes gentle and a touch chagrined "I guess I am."

Cerissa stood motionless, lost in the depthless green water of his eyes. Every instinct of her woman's soul said this was it, this was as far as Brett would go. She could give in to him—and, in a sense, to

103

her own equally passionate need for him—or she could continue to hold out, hoping she would eventually force him to accede to her demands. But, there was a kind of terrible inner strength in Brett. The kind of strength that would allow him to bend, but never to break. It was one of the things she loved in him so dearly. She had asked him to come to her this time, to consider her as a person instead of a toy. Hadn't he really done that this evening? Hadn't he made a genuine effort to please her? To court her? Were the words really as important as his actions had been?

Finally she tossed her head teasingly, a wide smile spreading on her face. "Well you handsome rascal, I guess you've succeeded."

Brett grinned his response and threw his dark head back, laughing as he pulled Cerissa against him. Quickly he bent his head down again, his mouth seeking hers, trembling with the intensity of long suppressed desire. His lips lingered against hers as if tasting the sweetest honey, his tongue plunged deep within her mouth, only to retreat and caress her lips gently, then, the force of passion overwhelming him, plunged deep again until Cerissa grew breathless and giddy in response. She touched his sun-darkened hand, guiding it to the sash of the blue kimono, urging him to unfasten it and release her body to his touch. In a moment, the silk fell away, the warm pressure of his fingers closing around her breast, his thumb caressing the taut nipple gently as she felt him grow hard against her belly. With a soft moan of answering passion, she reached her slender arms up around his neck, half lifting herself off the cabin floor to mold closer against him, her hips eagerly pressing against his. Suddenly, with a soft groan of almost animal need, Brett bent and lifted the girl into his arms, swinging her easily onto the bunk, dropping quickly beside her, his hands seeking her body, his dark head buried between the soft mounds of her breasts, his breath hot on her skin. Cerissa's arms encircled his shoulders, holding him desperately in her embrace, lifting her head to rain kisses on his black curls and forehead, opening her thighs to him in welcome. At last, he reached down pulling his breeches off and kicking them away, raising his shoulders to help Cerissa free him of his laced shirt, rolling back instantly to cover her body with his own, his skin feverishly hot with desire. Cerissa arched her back, drawing him deep within her as he entered, her soft cries mingling with his low ones. He rocked his hips violently within her, lost in mindless urgency, conscious only of her warmth and her moistness surrounding him. Again and again he penetrated her, his thighs moving to pin her legs ever farther apart, his lips caressing her breasts, her throat, her face, her closed eyes.

Cerissa writhed beneath him, her own loins stabbed with quivering flashes of need, her hands moving over his shoulders, his back, and down onto his hips, her fingers pulling him deeper within until at last she lay moaning in helpless passion, only aware of Brett thrusting himself inside her, burying himself in her, aware only of her insatiable craving for him to thrust again, to fill her again with the warm hardness of his masculinity, to give her release from this unbearable, ever mounting need.

At last, she felt her body exploding, swept away on irresistable tides of pleasure, only dimly aware of Brett's body arching beneath her hands, of his own cries of ecstasy blending with hers, and finally, the still, heavy weight of his exhausted body lying motionless on top of her.

In a kind of awed contentment, Cerissa lifted her hand to play gently with his raven curls, waiting patiently for him to return to her from the lazy nothingness which always claimed him after lovemaking. In a moment, he turned his head where it lay on her breast, saying nothing, only kissing her softly in unspoken thanks. She lifted her head to return his kiss, understanding only now how much he had, in his own way, been reaching out for her this evening. Had she let her pride overrule her love, she would have lost him forever. She knew clearly, very suddenly but very surely, that he would never have humbled himself for her loving if she hadn't offered it freely at last, as a gift of her boundless love for him, he would have drawn away from her, his cynicism strengthened, his budding love extinguished. In sudden gratitude of her own, realizing all at once what even this tentative attempt had cost him, Cerissa tightened her arms around him, lifting her chestnut head to whisper in his hear. "Don't you dare go to sleep just yet, my love. I intend to pay my passage to Jamaica in style..."

"Oh, Brett, I thought you said it was all green and luxurious!" Cerissa cried in quick disappointment. "This is like a desert!"

The dark haired captain laughed and threw the girl a teasingly affectionate glance over his shoulder from where he stood on the quarterdeck, his hand on the helm. "This is only the southern coast, sweetheart, don't judge the whole island by this view. For a few miles inland from the sea it is sand and cactus, but the mangroves and the palms aren't far behind. And in the sheltered harbours, only the beach itself is so desolate. You'll see when we reach Port Royal in a couple of hours."

"Port Royal?" Cerissa echoed "Why aren't we going to your plantation first?"

"Because my plantation is inland, sweet," Brett grinned patiently. "And damned difficult to sail into. Besides, I have to get our cargo unloaded and either sold or stored. And I have to find passage back to England for you. That won't be easy. It's past hurricane season now but near winter back home. Not many boats will be travelling north this time of year."

Cerissa stared at the dark haired captain in dismayed surprise. He hadn't mentioned her return to London for weeks now! She'd guessed he'd changed his mind. "Oh but Brett, I don't want to go back to England!" she pleaded, her lips quivering with disappointment. "I want to see your sugar plantation! And you promised to teach me to swim!"

Brett only shook his head, his eyes intent on a map of Jamaica's coastal waters. "Sorry sweetheart, but home you go—as soon as possible. I know I promised to teach you to swim, and I intend to keep that promise. I don't like the idea of your being aboard any ship again until you can at least paddle to a life boat in an emergency. We'll have to see about getting to the plantation. It isn't far from Port Royal, but I'm going to be busy the next few days."

Cerissa forced herself to remain silent though her chin raised stubbornly and her averted eyes burned with rebellion. She was not going back to England so soon! She wasn't! Brett didn't know about the baby she carried yet. Perhaps, if she told him in just the right way, caught him in just the right mood, he might be protective enough—curious enough—to let her stay. And if that news still didn't change his mind ... well, she would think of something then.

Port Royal was, as Brett had said, very different from the arid, desert-like land of the exposed southern shore. The city rose slightly as it drew away from the docks, and behind the buildings she could just see the edge of a dense, green forest stretching up into the foothills behind. The waterfront was crowded, the small bay dotted with ships—most of them smaller than the Falcon and with fewer guns showing through the gun ports. The flags flying were predominantly the red and blue and white of England, but there were some others scattered through as well. Of these only the blue and white fleur-de-lis of France were familiar to her.

Within an hour, the Falcon's sails were furled and the small launch boat had rowed the larger one up against her moorings. With rowdy eagerness the crew dropped the thick, tar coated ropes around the pilings and the Falcon lay secured.

Cerissa remained on deck, enjoying the warm breeze and marvelling at the sweet, gingery odor of the air as she waited patiently for Brett to take her ashore. The sun was high and hot already in the late morning sky, and it seemed to hang above the emerald island like a huge golden globe. Beneath the clear, perfectly blue water of the bay she could see tiny silver and white fish darting in and out of the shadows of the dock. No wonder Brett had been eager to return to these beautiful islands. Everything looked so clean, smelled so fresh compared to London.

At last, Brett turned toward her from the wide, timbered dock, waving the girl forward to join him. He'd gotten clearance from the governor's aide to dock and unload. Now he would get the girl settled and return to supervise the handling of the precious cargo.

Cerissa stumbled repeatedly on the short walk to the rooms Brett had arranged for, her eyes too busy taking in the strange, colorful sights of the colonial town to be watching where her feet were going. She would have liked to wander around the town awhile, but Brett seemed anxious to deposit her in the apartment and return to the Falcon. At last, she tripped and nearly fell on her face—only Brett's quick hand on her arm saving her.

"Still got your sea legs, sweetheart?" he smiled good-naturedly. He didn't blame the girl for her curiosity. He'd been the same way himself four years ago.

"Oh, my legs are all right," Cerissa laughed in return, her blue eyes deep and bright with wonder. "But I've just never seen anything... What's that place up the hill over there? With the wall around it?"

"The governor's mansion, sweet. It's walled for defensive purposes. Not long ago, all these islands were under nearly constant attack from some quarter... the Spanish, the French, the Dutch, the pirates... even us, I guess, though we tend to forgive ourselves more easily. This street here is the main road through the town. The government buildings are up there, clustered around the mansions except for that white stucco one right by the docks for clearances. The warehouses are up there, private living quarters over here, and the few general supply shops right along that crossroad."

"What are those down there?" Cerissa pointed back toward the docks at a busy, crowded section of the city Brett hadn't mentioned. Some of the tall, narrow buildings had what looked like tavern signs swinging in the breeze, but others...

"They wouldn't interest you, sweetheart," Brett laughed, his eyes sparkling with mischief. "They're the taverns and the whore houses. Much in favor with us lonely sailors, but hardly the haunt of young ladies like yourself. Stay clear of that section, sweet, or you'll be snapped up by some hungry pirate."

Cerissa made a face at him, not at all daunted by his warning.

She always felt completely safe with Brett. "I already got snapped up by some hungry pirate," she retorted teasingly, giving him a poke in the ribs. "So why should I worry about that?"

Brett only grinned and shook his head, refusing to rise to her bait. The voyage was safely completed now, the Falcon docked, the heavy responsibility for ship, crew, and cargo lifted off his shoulders for a while. He was going to relax tonight, get good and drunk and enjoy Cerissa's responding passions with undivided attention. Suddenly he laughed aloud, looking back down at the girl in realization.

"Jesus Christ, Cerissa!" he grinned "No wonder we're getting such strange looks! I'm so used to you in breeches that I almost forgot! People must think I'm being a mite over affectionate with my cabin boy."

Cerissa stopped dead on the street, open mouthed in embarrassment. She had forgotten too! Partly because she hadn't seen a single woman on the streets to remind her! "What will I do for clothes, Brett? Aren't there any women here?"

"Yes, there're plenty of women down there," he grinned, nodding his black curls toward the dockside taverns. "And a few honest types—Government wives or daughters, or planter's families—but not many. I'll stop on my way back to the ship and send a seamstress up to measure you. We have plenty of linen aboard ship and the islands produce pretty cotton cloths. You can pay me back for the dresses later tonight," he grinned, his eyes gleaming with ill-disguised anticipation.

"Will you be very late?" Cerissa asked, her eyes slanted up at the corners seductively "I mean, shall I eat before or after?"

Brett chuckled and shook his head in wonderment, "I've never seen a person your size eat so much, Cerissa! Why this last month or so, you've outeaten me at every meal!"

Cerissa only smiled, feeling smug in her secret knowledge, unwilling to share it yet with Brett. Her only hope was to wait until just before he shipped her home.

"By the way, sweet," Brett continued, his face growing sober. "I heard from the clerk that there is only one more ship scheduled to sail for England this season, the Mary Rose. She's a good ship and I know her captain in passing. I'll speak to him about making a berth for you." Immediately, seeing the rebellion burning in the girl's eyes, he shook his head firmly. "No arguments, Cerissa. You noticed the lack of women in town yourself. There's a reason for that and I'm not willing to be responsible for harm coming to you."

The girl merely shrugged, knowing a quarrel would only defeat her cause, and the couple walked the rest of the way in silence, Brett's eyes dark and faintly troubled. At last they reached the house where they would stay—a pretty, airy building with a stout brick facade. The landlord had been advised of the captain's coming via an earlier ship, and he was ready and waiting for the man to move in—the room clean, and freshly aired, the bed linens crisp and new. If he had misgivings or any disapproval of the fact that Lord Lindsey had brought a wench, he hid them well.

"The 'Sea Queen' sailed yesterday for Barbados, Lord Lindsey," the innkeeper announced after a polite greeting. "Captain Blackstone asked me to advise you so. They should only be a couple weeks."

Brett nodded, explaining to Cerissa that Blackstone was captain on one of his smaller boats, a sloop, named Sea Queen. "Any bad hurricanes this season so far?"

"Only one about a month ago and it passed well north of the island."

"Good," Brett replied, handing Cerissa the heavy, ornately wrought key to the rooms above. "I'm sending a seamstress over this afternoon, and we'll need a good meal tonight—in the room. Some fresh mullet, fish if there's any available, and a roast beef. Anything else the girl wants just charge it to me."

With a quick smile, Brett was gone and Cerissa turned to take the stairs. He was still acting like he had on the ship, but unwillingly she wondered whether that would last long now that they were on land again. Hearing the landlord call him 'Lord' again had been a shock. She had gotten accustomed to hearing Captain—even thinking about him as Captain. Would the cynical superficial 'Lord' now replace her beloved seagoing Brett? She sighed unconsciously, then hurried to smile at the startled innkeeper, assuring him that nothing was amiss. As he turned to go, she called out after him, requesting a bath and a bite of lunch. Regardless of how Brett acted on land, there was no use starving to death.

The hot, golden days had flown by swiftly, punctuated occasionally by a sudden evening or morning cloudburst, the sun shining the rest of the time, the moon huge and dripping silver on the calm seas at night. Brett had been busy through the day, disposing of the cargo and catching up on the fortunes of his other ships. He had told her the voyage had made 8,000 pounds profit, and she had celebrated happily with him, glad of Ardsley's sure delight in his investment, proud of Brett for his success. A bit to her surprise—and delight—he had returned every night to her at supper time, staying there with her until morning came. And despite the fact that he still insisted she return to England, Cerissa was beginning to hope he wouldn't pursue it. Why should he when he obviously was so content with her? Oh, the dangers he talked about, of course, but she was sure he exaggerated them. More and more she had begun to believe that her revelation of the child coming would induce him to keep her in Jamaica. If only she could find the right time to disclose the news.

"Hello, sweetheart," Brett's return in mid-day startled her and she jumped guiltily, afraid he would guess her thoughts. He, amazingly, had not changed at all toward her since landfall four days ago, and she hoped now that it was only London and the Court which affected him so strongly. Still, every time he came in the room, she wondered whether today would be the day he'd return to his courtly manner.

"You're home early," the girl said, forcing a quick smile, "nothing wrong, I hope."

"No, I'm all done for a while," he smiled, walking over to drop a light kiss on her chestnut hair. "Still want to learn how to swim?"

Cerissa's reaction was one of mingled delight and apprehension. If Brett was still anxious to teach her to swim, it meant he still intended to send her home on the Mary Rose when it left Saturday—only three days away counting today. Still, to spend the day outside in the sunshine, with Brett . . . "Promise you won't let me drown?"

The dark haired lord's only reply was an easy laugh as he walked over to the small table where the remains of her lunch lay, pausing to grab a hunk of bread and a thick slice of cold beef.

"When do you want to go?" Cerissa asked, cocking her head in question, admiring the fine strength of his face, the leashed power of his tall frame for the hundredth time.

"Right now," he replied, drawing his pistol from his belt to check the priming. In London, he had only worn his rapier—a thin, straight sword designed for a gentleman's requirements of fencing and duelling. On board the Falcon, Cerissa had noticed the addition of a loaded pistol, carried barrel down, thrust through the wide leather belt of his breeches. The other officers had carried thicker, curved blade swords and pistols. Brett had explained that their swords were called cutlasses, and were more popular among seamen and the islanders than the rapier since they were designed

110

for slashing rather than thrusting—requiring a less developed skill than the finer rapier. In addition, a cutlass could be used against the dense undergrowth of the tropical rain forests where a rapier was almost useless. Brett was one of the few men who still preferred to carry the lighter sword, admitting frankly to Cerissa that he was too used to the weapon to change. Mate Oates had added later that Captain Lindsey was an astounding swordsman, and that the rapier suited his quick movements and lightning reflexes. He could do far more damage with the rapier—the cutlass would only slow him down in a hand-to-hand fight. Cerissa had been glad of the knowledge, understanding now the fear on men's faces when Brett had drawn sword against them.

Evidently aboard ship the chance of mutiny was great enough to warrant the officers' carrying a pistol as well. And Brett had not abandoned the weapon upon reaching Port Royal. The town was obviously a rough one, where violence was expected and anticipated. Despite herself, Cerissa shuddered.

"Where will we swim, Brett? I mean...is it safe for just the two..."

"Yes, sweet, I'm just checking the pistol to be safe. There's a small cove about a half hour walk from here—too shallow for boats, but it should be perfect for our requirements."

Cerissa hurried to pull her shoes on, throwing a brush through her hair and grabbing a fluffy cotton towel. "Oh...what do you wear to swim in?"

Brett grinned, a wicked gleam in his eye. "Well, I swim nude sweetheart, but I wouldn't suggest it for you. Just in case anyone should happen to see you, well, a lovely, naked water nymph would be irresistible. I'll lend you one of my shirts to wear."

Cerissa nodded, blushing a bit at the idea of their being so disrobed out in the sunlight. She was accustomed to Brett's nakedness in the privacy of their room, but outside...and she had no illusions about the likely outcome of such naked sport. It would be surprising if she even got a swimming lesson first.

But Cerissa was wrong about that. Brett was all business as they walked to the edge of the tiny beach, stopping to stare intently out into the quiet aquamarine water. She stood silently for several minutes, then her curiosity forced a question. "What are you looking for, Brett?"

"A couple things, sweetheart. They have a kind of poisonous bubble fish in these warm waters—they float in on the wind and the tide sometimes, and we call them Portugese men-of-war as a kind of

111

joke. And there are scorpion fish in some waters—also poisonous. But mostly I want to check for sharks."

Cerissa blanched, her eyes going wide. "Sharks?" She had heard horrible gruesome stories from the Falcon officers about those loathesome creatures eating men alive. She wasn't sure she really wanted to swim anymore.

"They usually don't come in this shallow—at least the bigger ones—but it doesn't hurt to check." Brett's voice was carelessly unworried and the girl took heart. Although she didn't think she even cared to meet a small one. "All right, in you go!"

Immediately, Cerissa retreated, casting a wary eye on the water. "You go first, Brett."

He shrugged and smiled, stripping his clothes off quickly, and laying them in the white sand, his pistol on top of them. He pulled a small dagger out and stuck it hilt up in the hard sand near the tide's edge, then ran easily into the breaking waves, diving under one as he got deeper. At last, he turned and swam toward her, grinning at the girl's obvious unease. "No more excuses, Cerissa. Come on."

Reluctantly, she threw a last hasty glance around the small cove and proceeded to pull her own clothes off, reaching quickly for Brett's long shirt to cover herself. Then, much more timidly than he, she stepped into the blue sea, pleasantly surprised at its warmth.

"Well, sweetheart, where shall we start? Can you swim at all? Even float?" Brett's tanned face loomed above her and she stepped closer to him for security, only shaking her head dismally for answer. Brett nodded, apparently undisturbed by her total ignorance, "Take a deep breath then and go under the water—get you whole head wet. We'll start on a float."

Cerissa obeyed and tried to follow his orders in the water. But no matter how hard she tried, she couldn't float for a minute. As soon as Brett took his arms out from under her body, she panicked and tried to sit up—succeeding only in dunking herself time and time again. Amazingly, he remained patient, only his green eyes bright with merriment as he encouraged her to keep trying. At last, she managed to stay above water for a few seconds, though she was rigid as an oak board, and he nodded his dark head approvingly.

"Good, sweet. Only you'll have to relax more," he smiled.

"How can I relax when I'm petrified with terror?" she spluttered, wiping the water out of her face disgustedly, embarrassed by her lack of success.

"You'll get used to the water," he grinned. "Then you'll be all right. You've got the basic idea anyway."

Cerissa nodded though her face reflected disbelief at his words.

Glad the ordeal was over, she turned towards the beach.

"Whoa girl," Brett cautioned, grabbing her arm "The lesson isn't over yet."

Cerissa turned back to him, her eyes distressed. "But you said . . ."

"For the float, yes, but you still don't know how to swim. Here watch me and then you give it a try."

Cerissa watched his brown shoulders cut through the water effortlessly as he did a strange, smoothe, over-arm stroke, his head coming out of the water only to breathe. Slowly he turned and circled back to her, passing her once more to demonstrate the method. She knew she couldn't match that but she tried obediently anyway. Finally, even Brett acknowledged that it was too difficult to learn so quickly and he showed her an easier stroke, where her arms went out in front and then pulled to her sides. She liked that better for it kept her head above the water, and she practiced with more effort. At last, she was feeling more at ease in the water, and she encouraged Brett to stand farther away as she swam to his outstretched arms. When she had managed to cover about 25 feet without stopping, she grinned at him in childish delight, immensely pleased with herself, proud of his answering grin.

"You're a natural mermaid, sweetheart," he chuckled in approval, reaching out to pull the girl to him for a kiss.

Cerissa laughed in return, feeling clever and a little wicked as she pressed closer to him in the water, looping her arms around his neck. "Lessons over?" she teased.

"All but one," he murmured promptly, his voice growing husky as his body pressed against hers. Swiftly he bent under the water and scooped her up in his arms, carrying her easily through the water toward the beach. At the very edge of the sea, he stopped, laying her down on the hard packed sand, raising the hem of her shirt above her waist as he bent his head down to her exposed belly, his head on her wet skin, her body responded immediately to his desire. Cerissa allowed her eyes to wander the length of his browned, naked torso, enjoying the silken ripples of his muscles under the sun-darkened skin, the lean lines of his back, his long, muscular legs, the blue-black of his raven hair glinting in the sun. She felt embarrassed, but also terribly, gloriously free to be lying in Brett's arms out in the open air, the sunlight bright and all revealing. And gradually, her embarrassment passed as passion took hold of her, its force as irresistible as the tides that washed her feet and thundered in her ear.

She forced her eyes to remain open, enjoying seeing as well as feeling his body react to hers, watching his strong, tanned hands cupping her white breast, his dark leg cover her pale one to part her thighs. Brett's kisses tasted sweetly of the salt of the ocean as he crushed her tender mouth under his, his tongue seeking hers impatiently, his head moving restlessly above hers as he dropped his lips to cover her breasts and throat, his tongue tickling her taut dark nipples, leaving them wet and glistening in the sun as he moved his head back to seek her lips again. She felt his knee pressing against her thigh and she spread her legs farther apart on the gritty sand, arching her hips to draw him within her, her own loins hot and greedy for union. She sighed as she felt his swollen body slide into her, plunging deeper as he thrust again, his hips coming down hard against her, rocking against her, until she clutched at him in mindless pleasure, her legs locking over his thighs to keep him deep inside. Brett's back was tight and trembling, his voice husky as he murmured his pleasure against her ear, his breath uneven, his chest heaving against hers. At last, Cerissa moaned her urgency, her body arching up against his to seek fulfillment. At once, with a soft answering moan of ecstasy, Brett drove deep inside her a last time, his arms holding her tight against him as she cried aloud in explosive satisfaction, hardly aware of the sun above her, the cove around her.

At last, after a seemingly endless period of floating in a sweet, dreamless, gentle sea, Cerissa opened her eyes, gazing lovingly down at Brett's dark curls, now touched with white where the salt water had dried. Almost reverently, she stroked his hair, smoothing it back from his forehead.

Brett lay silent, enjoying the warm afterglow of contentment that seemed to follow his lovemaking with Cerissa. Never before her had he found this blissful, all-tender feeling. And even after he had found it the first time with her, he had not succeeded in duplicating it with the other women he had taken to his bed. So it was somehow associated with her, he realized, perhaps an extension of his growing love for her—as if not only his body had reached fulfillment, but his soul as well. He turned his face up towards hers, his eyes soft with tenderness, knowing his love for her, wanting to tell her of it, knowing he couldn't.

With a quick smile, he rolled aside and got to his feet and headed for the ocean. Cerissa sat up, watching him go with a faint sense of frustration. Several times recently after their loving she had felt as though Brett was on the brink of revealing something to her, yet always he drew away, as though running from something. But what? she wondered silently. Did he believe himself falling in love and fear it so? Or was it more than that? Cerissa watched the dark haired lord covertly for long minutes after he'd come back from his swim, while he lay stretched full length on the hot sand, picking at an encrusted piece of metal he'd found with a sharp, broken shell, she answered his amiable chatter carelessly, enjoying the freedom of the islands. In England, the women guarded their pale skins jealously—for white or creamy colored skin was highly regarded for beauty, a sun-tanned face or hands bespoke a coarse, farm life. Here in Jamaica she could do the unthinkable. Sit out on a beach clad only in a wet, clinging man's shirt, enjoying the warmth of the afternoon sun.

"What do you want for supper, sweetheart?" Brett questioned lazily, his eyes intent on the silver disc he was picking at, lying propped up on his elbows belly down on the beach as casually as if he were fully dressed instead of stark naked.

Cerissa shrugged, cocking her head to think about it. "I don't really care except...I'd like some more of those yellow things...bananas you called them, in some sweet cream."

Brett chuckled, throwing a quick glance over his shoulder, then reaching to give the girl a gentle poke where her slightly rounded belly showed beneath the damp, clinging, linen of the shirt. "I think you've had enough bananas."

Cerissa caught his eye, smiling softly, and drawing a deep breath. If there was ever to be the perfect time..."It's not bananas, you dolt," she murmured tenderly, her eyes suddenly shy.

Brett frowned at her a moment in puzzlement, then sat up cross legged in the sand, scowling faintly and tossing the silver metal away impatiently. "Oh, Lord, sweetheart, I'm sorry. I should have been more careful. I guess."

Cerissa swallowed hard, trying to believe that Brett was only surprised, not angry, at her announcement. "I...don't be sorry Brett, I'm not," she whispered quietly, stroking his shoulder awkwardly.

He turned to force a smile, shaking his head. "I don't mean to be so grim Cerissa, I am pleased in a way, only...Well, it takes our choices away, sweetheart. You're a sweet girl, and a beauty besides. You deserve better than bearing somebody's bastards. I'd thought I'd be able to give you that choice when I left England, only..." he shrugged and looked away again, his green eyes frustrated and faintly angry.

Cerissa sat stunned by his reaction, not fully understanding his words. "Well, if it bothers you that it will be a bastard, you could . . ."

"No!" Brett's voice rang out sharp as a pistol crack, his eyes sharp and relentless as they met hers. "Don't say it, Cerissa, don't even think it. It's absolutely impossible and you know it."

Cerissa leapt to her feet, feeling the sunshine fade from her world to leave it dismal and dead. Brett's hand shot out to grasp her wrist, drawing her back to rest against him, his arm going tightly around her head, his lips touching the top of her head with infinite gentleness.

"Oh hell, sweetheart, don't misunderstand me, please. I care about you—honestly I do, more than I can ever even admit to you I think, but still . . . marriage is all political with us, you know that. No matter how I felt it wouldn't change that. I could never offer you . . ."

Cerissa lifted her head, her eyes swimming with tears but her heart thudding hopefully. Was Brett trying to tell her . . . ? "Brett," she whispered, holding his gaze with hers. "Do you love me? If you do, I'll wait forever for you . . . I know someday . . ."

Brett stared back at her, his whole soul pained. He'd known she would feel this way, she could never understand the utter, final ruthlessness of the aristocracy. If he ever admitted his love, he doomed her to an endless, futile lifetime of hoping. He swallowed hard, clenching his jaw with the effort of returning her pleading gaze. "No," he finally murmured, almost choking on the lie that dimmed the beautiful light in her eyes, "I don't love you." Hastily, he looked away, unable to stand the hurt in her eyes.

Cerissa stared wordlessly at his averted face, confused and immensely disappointed, but gradually understanding. Brett's face was as pale as ash, his jaw clenched and his jaw muscles twitching spasmodically. Obviously the scene was as painful for him as it was for her, but why unless he did love her? Was he still unwilling to commit himself to her love? Or was it that he still understood her so little? Did he believe she could stop loving him if he refused encouragement? Didn't he understand that her love was endless, timeless, as uncontrollable as the seasons or the tide he sailed on? It was not within her control or his to alter it . . . "Brett, I love you. I always shall . . . I'm not afraid to bear your babies, legitimate or otherwise. You're the only man I ever loved. The only man I ever will. Whatever you're willing to share of yourself, that will be enough," she whispered, touching the side of his face gently. Wordlessly, he turned his head, laying a tender kiss on her fingers as

116

they passed his lips. Finally, he drew away, drawing her up from the sand to stand beside him, handing her her discarded cotton gown, reaching for his own clothes.

"Come on, sweetheart. We'd better get back to town. You leave in two days, you'd best get organized."

Cerissa walked beside him, holding his hand, not really surprised at his decision. If he had worried about the dangers before, knowing about the child would only increase his concern. In a sense, she was pleased that he was being so protective—for now she knew beyond any doubt that, for his own selfish reasons, he would keep her with him here in Jamaica. Of course, it didn't change her own decision either. She was still every bit as determined to stay in the islands with him. The only question now was how.

Chapter Eight

Cerissa gathered the food together and tied the corners of the blanket around it, checking one last time out the casement window to be sure Brett was still down at the dock. It would ruin everything for him to see her leave the small house and head for the forest. As a last thought, she grabbed one of Brett's heavy, hooded sea-cloaks. The wind was getting stronger and the sky getting grey and threatening. If it started to rain, she might need the extra warmth. It was late Friday already—in 24 hours she could return safely, for the Mary Rose would be gone tomorrow at first light. Brett might be frantic with worry but he would probably guess her game and know she was only hiding. Even so he would be furious with her again. With a last, deep sigh, she walked down the stairs, nodding an absent greeting to the landlord's son as she passed. The forest was only an hour's walk away. Once she got there, she would be safe.

Brett hurried into the doorway of the house, swearing at the foul weather brewing. He hurried up the stairs, anxious to shed his wet cloak and clothes and have a good hot cup of coffee or chocolate to erase the storm's chill. Opening the door, he stopped in surprise, Cerissa was not there. He frowned, then shrugged. She'd probably gone to see the shops or purchase another book or play to read. She'd be back soon with the weather so threatening.

He pulled his shirt off and bent over to remove his boots, turning toward the bed to throw himself down. He stopped, frowning, aware of something strange but unable to place it. At last he nodded, his green eyes puzzled. The blanket of the bed was missing. The linens themselves were neatly made up as usual, for it was one of the girl's idiosyncrasies—she never left without dressing the bed. He often teased her about that, had she been around during the great fire of London in 1666, she'd have burnt to a crisp, staying behind to make all the beds before fleeing the flaming city. Even on shipboard, she had kept to her habit, struggling every morning with the narrow bunk, tucking the sheets carefully down in the crack between the mattress and wall. So the bed was made, but the blanket missing. Why would she have taken that off? Puzzled, now a shade uneasy, he turned to sweep the room slowly with a searching gaze. Nothing else seemed strange—except that the lunch platters were absolutely cleared of food. Cerissa's pregnancy had made her ravenous, and she always ordered huge quantities of food for each meal. But usually, she got too full to come close to finishing the meal. Evidently, today, she had managed to eat every . . . No. The sheer quantity of dishes was too great. No person could have so cleanly polished off . . .

Brett shook his dark head in frustration. What was the girl up to now? If they were home in London, he'd guess she'd gone picnicking in St. James Park, but here . . .

He swore softly and hurried to the door, meeting the landlord halfway down the stairs. "Have you seen Cerissa?" he asked impatiently.

The man returned a blank gaze, saying nothing, his surprise obvious.

"She's not in the room, and the weather is growing bad," Brett explained.

"I haven't seen her but I'll check with the others downstairs," the innkeeper offered, turning away.

With a quick nod of satisfaction, the dark haired lord hurried back to the room, silently cursing the landlord for his stupidity. He stopped himself, his face grimacing in self-disgust. It wasn't the

119

landlord who was a stupid son of a bitch, it was him. He should have been prepared for such a move on the girl's part, but her apparent docility about leaving had fooled him. Of course, looking back, he realized now that she had never once actually agreed to leave on the Mary Rose. Damn! How stupid could he be? He, of all people in the world, knew how stubborn the girl could be, how willful and devious. He should have bound and gagged her and locked her in a trunk, then sat on the lid until she was safely on board the outbound ship. With a last vicious oath, he grabbed his shirt, throwing it angrily back over his head, pulling his nearly knee high boots on again and bending to fasten spurs on them. Then he rebuckled his sword belt, shoved his pistol through his belt, and reached for a cloak. He frowned again, looking at the wardrobe. Cerissa had borrowed one of his heavy, hooded cloaks as well. So she was planning to be gone long enough to need some food, perhaps to sleep on the blanket overnight, long enough to take a cloak for warmth but not long enough to need a change of clothes. No doubt about it. She was determined to miss the sailing of the Mary Rose. And she was out there somewhere in a gathering hurricane, wandering around alone in one of the most dangerous cities in the world. Damn the wench!

Brett slammed the door behind him, almost running into the nervous landlord who had just come up. "No luck yet, but I haven't talked to everyone," the man shrugged.

Brett nodded, his face dark and scowling, "Keep checking—and saddle me your best horse. I'll be back in a few minutes."

In a moment, he stood outside in the gusty, cold wind, raising his hood against the hard, slashing rain. The storm was getting worse by the minute, he'd better find the girl quickly. Perhaps she'd walked down to the docks.

Brett hunched his shoulder into the wet wind, feeling thoroughly frustrated and foolish. Suddenly he stopped, staring down the street, then cupping his hands around his mouth to call out. "Jake! Jake Oates! Over here!"

In a moment, the grizzled old seaman had hurried over. "What's up, Captain? You already fixed the Falcon for . . ."

"It's the girl, Cerissa. Have you seen her?"

Oates responded with the same vague stare the landlord had given him, only this time Brett would have sworn a gleam of merriment crept into the man's eyes as well.

"Given you the slip has she?" the sailor asked, his mouth jerking with the effort to repress a grin.

Brett scowled, his eyes sparking with temper. "It's not funny," he snapped. "A girl wandering alone in this town . . . with a hurricane likely brewing."

The grey-haired mate sobered immediately, promising to search the waterfront area for her.

"If you find her, bring her back to my rooms, and lock her in! Or better than that, tie her to the bed first and then lock her in. She's going on the Mary Rose tomorrow if I have to . . ." the dark haired lord shook his head, and turned impatiently away, scowling a goodbye to the older man. He stood for a long minute, shielding his eyes from the driving rain, staring out into the misty greyness of the bay. The Falcon's sails were furled, a half-dozen storm anchors out and well caught, her bow pointed into the wind and waves. It was all he could do for the ship now except to pray the storm was a small one, or, failing that, that at least it didn't come directly at them. He shrugged, his eyes shadowed with concern as he turned back to the inn. The wench would pick this hellish weather to go chasing off.

Brett lost his temper and slapped the skittish gelding hard again on his lathered neck, swearing at the nervous animal to behave, as they climbed a street already muddy and slippery from rain. The landlord had declared him the best animal in the barn, but perhaps the man was unwilling to risk a better one in this storm. At least he had found some information about the girl. His son had remembered seeing her, his attention drawn by the blanket bundle she had slung over one arm, and he was sure he had seen her head up the hill toward the governor's mansion. Brett had already passed that. No one there had seen her, but one man thought he might have seen a girl trudging up towards the forest. On the strength of the man's vague, half remembered guess, he'd spurred the horse forward. When the English had taken the island from the Spanish, the Don's slaves had escaped into the wild forests and mountains inland. Groups of these half wild men still roamed the island, fighting to retain their freedom, often ambushing an isolated plantation for supplies and revenge against the hated Europeans. Usually the ex-slaves stayed farther away from the towns than this, but the chance of a band of hunters venturing closer could not be ignored.

The bay gelding shied again at the edge of the forest, sweating and snorting at a swinging palm branch. Mercilessly, Brett dug his spurs in again, wrenching at the bit to keep the animal from whirling and bolting for home. He understood the horse's fear of being out in the storm, and he hated to be cruel to the beast, but Cerissa's safety took precedence just now. Half a dozen times he had been tempted to turn back out of the wet and slashing, gusty chill of the weather, sure that Oates had found her and was even now awaiting his return, but he always forced himself a little farther on, into the dense mangrove woods. If he didn't find her soon, he was turning back. It was miles now back to Port Royal and growing dark. He had no desire to be wandering lost in the blackness of the jungle.

Suddenly, the gelding shied again, jumping to the right, nearly off the path and into a thorny bush. Impatiently, Brett swore and slammed him again, forcing him back on the trail, hardly wondering what had caused the animal's nervousness. The wind was ripping now at the tops of the trees, sending weak limbs and occasionally whole trees crashing down. And, although the forest offered some protection from the slashing rain, the falling branches were even more dangerous. With a frustrated sigh, he started to turn the gelding back to town, then pulled him to a quick halt. There, piled neatly under the edge of a small, waxy-looking bush were three banana skins. The horse's sharper eyes had noticed what he had not. Evidently Cerissa had stopped here to eat. No animal would leave the skins so tidy. And she couldn't gone much farther either. The horse covered the distance three or four times as fast as she possibly could.

Anxiously, he forced the gelding onward at a brisk trot, searching the path ahead for any sign of Cerissa. Suddenly, barely audible over the wind's dismal howling and the loud rain spatters drumming on the tree tops above, he heard her screaming, and a moment later, heard the answering shouts of undeniably male voices. Damn! She had blundered into a group of the mountain men. Swiftly but with deliberate stealth, he kneed the horse forward, staying close to the concealing edge of the forest. At last, he could see the group ahead, and he halted the horse instantly, drawing his pistol out of his belt and loosening the rapier. There were five men and a younger boy surrounding Cerissa, who was already gagged, wrists tied. The men were prodding her to run forward, shouting and shoving her brutally as her heels caught in the hem of her long dress, tripping her time and time again, sending her sprawling on her face helplessly. Brett's eyes flashed and his jaw clenched white in fury, controlling his temper only with great effort. He couldn't afford to go charging in there blindly, he was too badly outnumbered.

Drawing a deep breath, he forced himself to study the group. Two of the men held cutlasses, two more spears and the fifth had a bow and a quiver of arrows slung over his shoulder. Of the weapons, the swords were probably the most dangerous—providing he could surprise them and get away without giving the bowman time to fire.

One of the cutlass carrying men walked over to the girl as she fell again, aiming a vicious kick at her ribs. Instantly, Brett drew his sword and aimed his pistol as he thundered forward, forcing the horse to divide the men on either side of the narrow path. His pistol shot took the closest swordsman full in the face blowing his features into bloody ruin as he bent and grabbed Cerissa around the waist with that arm, hauling her up to the gelding's withers. A few feet beyond the shouting men, he whirled the horse hard on his hind legs and spurred him back toward the group facing him. For once he wished he had a cutlass instead of his rapier, for the lighter sword was virtually useless for such a slashing attack, and, of course, he didn't have time to stop and reload the pistol. Anyway, he had to hang on to the helpless girl with one arm or she would fall. So the rapier, ideal or not, would have to suffice. Drawing the trembling girl closer to him and hunching his shoulder forward to protect her as much as possible, Brett raised the rapier and spurred the gelding again to a full gallop, heading him directly toward the two men on the side of the trail—one holding a spear, the other the bow. The two other men jumped forward, one raising his cutlass in a menacing gesture of defiance. At the last moment, Brett pulled the horse to the left, surprising the men and forcing the swordsman to take a hasty jump out of his way or be trampled. He leaned sideways, whistling the fine rapier through the air at their throats, intent on keeping the cutlass back. He was helpless to defend himself on the other side, for Cerissa's body was between his sword and the men there. All he could do was move as fast as possible, and hope they would miss.

They didn't. As the gelding pounded by in headlong flight, he felt a swift, searing stab of pain in his right thigh, and instinctively sensed that the spear had gored him. But the main danger was past now, the man with the cutlass too far away to use the weapon. Brett glanced quickly over his shoulder, seeing the dark bowman kneel to fire an arrow. He tightened his grip around Cerissa's waist and bent low over her, hearing the missile whistle harmlessly by above his lowered head. Just to be safe, he stayed in the awkward position for another hundred yards, then as the path bent sharply to the right again, he sat up, relieved to have escaped so lightly.

Darkness was falling at last as they came to a fork in the forest path. The right hand trail led back towards Port Royal, the left—with a few detours—to his own plantation. Frowning in indecision, he halted the lathered horse, listening again to the sounds of the storm raging. At last, he became aware of Cerissa's demanding sounds and realized she was still gagged and bound. In spite of his anger, he grinned down at her frustrated face. "You know, wench, I think I'll keep you like this," he chuckled, enjoying her furious expression. "You'd be ever so much more controllable."

Reluctantly, at length, he drew his dagger and cut her wrist-rope, then untied the filthy rag from around her face. As soon as it was out, the girl coughed and choked, trying to spit out the lingering dirt in her mouth, the anger in her eyes fading as she began to tremble.

Brett sat still, looking down at her face quietly, amazed that his fury at the girl seemed to have evaporated, leaving only relief that he had found her in time. "You all right?" he asked, softly.

Cerissa felt her eyes fill with tears. She had been ready for his anger, not his sympathy. Hastily she nodded, wiping her tears away with the back of one hand. "I thought you'd be mad at me for running away." she sniffed still unable to meet his eyes.

Brett sighed, the horse moving restlessly beneath him. "I should be. I swear I don't know what's the matter with me anymore."

Cerissa smiled guiltily, still amazed at his strange mood. "I'm glad you're not, Brett," she murmured, leaning her head thankfully against his broad chest. "I'm all right now, we can go back to town."

The dark haired lord shook his head, staring keenly down the trail into the growing darkness. "I don't think so, sweet," he said at length, "The storm sounds worse down that way. And besides, those men we met up with are liable to double back here and try to ambush us. That one man was dead for sure, and they can be fiendish for revenge in such cases. My plantation lies down this way. I think we'll try for that instead."

Cerissa stared at him in surprise, feeling the fear start to reclaim her at the idea of meeting those half-savages again. "How far is your plantation, Brett?" she questioned softly, repressing a shudder.

"Fourteen—maybe sixteen miles, I guess. But Port is about ten this way, so it wouldn't be a much longer ride. The only real problem is going to be the storm and the lack of light . . . there won't even be a moon out tonight."

The girl said nothing, content with whatever he decided.

Carefully, she turned a bit on her perch in front of the saddle and reached to pull her skirts back in place. She leaned down, staring at the dark, spreading stains on Brett's breech-leg, touching them with a hesitant fingertip. Immediately, she whirled to face him, her eyes dismayed. "You're hurt, Brett, there's blood on your leg."

He nodded absentmindedly, still intent on his alternatives. "I know, sweetheart. The spear grazed it I think."

Cerissa bent her head again to peer at his wound, holding her heavy chestnut hair away with one hand, her face pale with guilt and worry. "Oh Brett, I'm so sorry, I really am. I cause you nothing but trouble and I never mean to. I only wanted to hide in the forest until..." her voice trailed off, her throat closed in sorrow. "Oh Brett, please don't hate me. I know you have every right to, but..."

"Hush, Cerissa," Brett interrupted. He had enough trouble without soothing a hysterical woman. "I don't hate you. At least right now I don't hate you. Now just try to stay calm. I may need your help more than your tears before we reach safety." Immediately, he turned the horse to the left fork and urged him forward, swearing softly as the renewed motion set his leg to throbbing again. He really ought to stop and see how bad it was, bandage it to reduce the bleeding, but there wasn't time. If this was a hurricane, and if it came right at the island, the woods were twice as dangerous a place to be.

On through the pitch black jungle they rode, trusting the gelding's eyes to see the path, missing a needed turn once and returning to search for it. Despite the tree cover, both Cerissa and Brett were thoroughly soaked, she shivering with cold when they finally came to an open field covered with tall, reed-like stalks. The girl heard Brett heave a weary sigh of relief behind her and she turned eagerly, shouting to be heard above the roar of the wind. "Is this it, Brett?" The dark haired lord nodded, too exhausted to waste words. The wound in his leg was still oozing blood and his whole body ached with fatigue and cold. He forced off his dizziness, and searched the darkness for the house lights. It had been almost a year since he had been here and his memory was vague. Coming off the main road, the house lay to the right, but which field was this? And what direction did the manor lie from here?

Cerissa pulled at his sleeve, pointing toward a faint, set of lights. Thankfully he nodded and set the horse forward again, gritting his jaw at the now nearly unbearable, tearing agony that burned in his whole leg. Free of the forest cover, the two lay nearly flat on the horse's back, Brett's arm aching and stiff from holding onto the girl as the wind tugged to pull her away. The rain fell in slashing sheets, diagonally from the force of the gale, stinging their bodies like slivers of glass. For all his earlier anger, Brett now felt only gratitude for the game little beast that plowed courageously ahead, his hooves sinking deep in the muck of the fields, his head hanging low and spiritless as he fought his way against the merciless winds, the tops of the tall suger cane whipping in the storm to slash his body and legs bloody. At last they stood in the dark stableyard of the plantation, staring wordlessly at the astonished Negro groom who peered at them from the shelter of the barn, his eyes wide and white in the dimness.

Brett drew a deep breath, summoning the last of his strength as he slid Cerissa gently to the ground. He gathered the reins in one hand to follow her down, kicking his feet free of the stirrups, bracing himself for the pain that moving his leg would bring. At last he swung free of the saddle and dropped heavily to the ground, moaning involuntarily as shooting pain flamed up his right leg, feeling it start to collapse beneath him.

Cerissa threw her weight against his side, her arms around him, struggling to brace him up before he fell. Brett tried to walk and stumbled again, going nearly to his knees before she managed to haul him back upright. In desperation she screamed at the motionless groom to help her, Brett's weight growing heavier every second, knowing she couldn't support him much longer. At last, the startled Nego leapt forward in recognition of the man, grasping him beneath his shoulders as he slid out of Cerissa's arms toward the wet ground.

"Go dat way, miss, into de house. I bring de master here." The man shouted above the storm, nodding his head toward the white stucco building lying on her right. Thankfully, Cerissa turned and stumbled forward, the few hundred feet feeling like a thousand miles to the exhausted girl. None too soon, she reached the door and hammered frantically on the heavy brass knocker for admittance. The door swung open suddenly and she fell in, too weary to even care.

Cerissa opened her eyes to see a round, black face leaning over her. Involuntarily, remembering the savages in the woods, she jumped, her eyes opening wide with fear.

The woman chuckled, her low voice as deep as a man's. "Don't fret, child, I ain't going to bite you. I'm Liza, Captain Brett's housekeeper here, and de best one in de whole island. Sit up now and drink dis hot chocolate. It make you feel better."

Obediently, the girl drank the whole cup, feeling its warmth deep in her bones. At the end she set the cup down and sighed gratefully, smiling at the woman. "Hello Liza, I'm Cerissa."

The housekeeper nodded, murmuring her name with evident approval, her shrewd eyes flickering over the girl's slightly swollen belly. "You Captain Brett's wife?"

Cerissa flushed, shaking her head in denial. "Where is Brett? Is he all right?"

Liza nodded, smiling brightly, anxious to make amends for her tactlessness. "Oh, he's a little under de weather now, chile, but he be fine soon. He lost some blood and got hisself a touch of fever in his leg, but I seen plenty worse. How you two come to be riding around in this devil weather anyway?"

Cerissa described the events of the day and circumstances leading to her flight while the woman listened in growing amazement, finally whistling with surprise.

"Dem Maroons grabbed you, chile? You lucky girl to have Captain Brett rescue you! They all bad. Course, they was slaves and they hates white folk—especially English white folk."

"Maroons?" Cerissa echoed in confusion. "Why do you call them that?"

"Dat's what dey called, honey," Liza replied simply. "'Cause dey ain't really black and dey ain't white neither." The woman paused and glanced shrewdly at the girl. "You love the Captain pretty good to be wanting to stay so bad. Dis island ain't healthy for pretty girls. Dere's pirates and ruffians, and sharks in the waters, and fevers in the jungle. You best go back to England like Captain Brett says."

Cerissa's eyes filled with tears and she shook her head rebelliously. "He told me about the dangers, and I don't care, Liza! I love him so much—I only want to be with him. I don't care what may happen to me. I won't go back, I won't!"

The rotund housekeeper patted the girl's hand soothingly, her eyes troubled. "All right, honey, don't fret!" She sat silent for several moments, deep in thought. "De Captain must be mighty much in love with you too, chile, to go chasing after you in the middle of this hurricane—risking his life to grab you away from dem Maroons. That his baby you carrying?"

Cerissa nodded, her blue eyes intent on the woman's face. She had no idea how much influence Liza might have on Brett, but any help at all...

"I sho would like to see one of Captain Brett's little-uns," the

127

woman murmured, her eyes sparkling with mischief. "When did you say dat ship—Mary Rose—was leaving?"

"Saturday morning—this morning," Cerissa stammered, her heart pounding in sudden hope. "Oh please, can't you help me Liza? I love him so much and I won't be any trouble, I swear I won't."

The woman chuckled, her smile broad. "Now I can't do too much for you, honey, I daren't go against de Captain's direct orders. If he says you go, den you go. But, de more I thinks about it, I think he be sicker than I reckoned at first. Maybe I make him a nice sleeping potion. Won't hurt him none to have a couple days nap. Take care of dat fever maybe, and his leg be hurting him bad if he was awake."

Cerissa squealed with joy, throwing her arms around the woman's round shoulders. "Just give me a day, Liza, that's all I ask."

"One day won't do you no good, honey," the housekeeper chuckled. "Ain't no ship crazy enough to leave in a hurricane. But captains be powerful attached to keeping on schedule. If the weather clears, dat ship will go, maybe today, maybe tomorrow. I can't leave Captain Brett sleeping forever, but I give you two days, chile."

Cerissa nodded, praying that the Mary Rose would be long gone by then. "Can I see Brett before..."

"Hell, yes honey. You gonna take care of the man, I's too busy for that. You give him a little of this potion I give you every four hours. And give him some watered wine and some soup broth too. He may wake up now and den but he ain't like to make much sense if he do. Just keep him covered good and he'll drift off again soon enough."

Cerissa threw her head back and laughed out loud, thinking that life had never seemed so perfect. She loved Liza and she loved Jamaica and she loved Brett beyond all reason and she was carrying his child—his son, she was sure—and the Mary Rose, would sail for England and leave her to enjoy at least the whole winter with her handsome, black-haired captain who was finally beginning to love her too! Oh yes, the world was a marvelous place!

It was late morning when Cerissa awoke, and she held her breath, listening to the sounds of the storm outside. Was it wishful thinking or did the wind sound just a little less fearful, the rain a shade softer? She lifted her head and glanced over to the bed where Brett lay sleeping, his handsome face shadowed in the faint light, his black hair spilling forward onto his forehead in places, the ends curling gently in half circles. The girl glanced quickly at the ebony-framed clock on the bureau, noting that it was time for another dose of Liza's herb potion. Brett didn't even stir as she dribbled the dark liquid into his mouth, holding his head up on the crook of her arm to help him swallow easier. Once the medicine was down, she reached for some well-watered burgundy, then spooned down a half cup of the soup a negro girl brought in. That done, she rested content. He would sleep now another four hours. Bless Liza!

By late afternoon, the storm was almost over. Even the light, grey drizzle faded finally, leaving only scattered wisps of clouds to streak the blueness. By sunset, the island sky was mostly clear again, and the dying sun left hazy red lines along the horizon. Brett had indeed, true to the housekeeper's word, slept the day away, though his sleep had been restless and he'd mumbled incoherent phrases occasionally. Even the faint flush of fever had disappeared now from his cheekbones, and the nasty gash on his thigh had ceased bleeding.

Sure that she was safe now and that the Mary Rose had surely sailed already or would leave early the following morning, Cerissa slept more soundly than she'd intended to, waking with a nervous start to see gray dawn seeping through the cracks of the shuttered window. Instantly, she leapt to her feet, grabbing the medicine bottle and silver spoon, not needing the clock to tell her that Brett's dose was long overdue. Her heart hammering, she tip toed cautiously to the bedside, breathing a silent sigh of relief to see him still asleep. Hastily, she pulled the stopper from the bottle, and started to pour the inky liquid out.

"Hello, sweetheart."

Brett's mumbled greeting startled her and she jumped, nearly dropping the spoon, feeling her heart plunge in despair. Nervously, she forced a smile, trying to edge nearer his head, putting her body between him and the window. If he noticed the dawning sun... "Feeling better, Brett?" she whispered at last, her voice tremulous.

He grunted for answer. Whether that meant yes or no she couldn't tell, but his eyelids kept drifting shut as though he had to struggle to stay awake. Maybe if she could get another dose in him soon enough...

Brett frowned, forcing his heavy eyelids open, focusing upon the girl with difficulty. "What time is it?" he murmured thickly, trying to turn his head on the pillow to see out the window behind her.

"It's early yet," she lied. "Still night. Do you ... Does your leg still hurt very much?" she questioned, trying to distract his attention from the window.

"Like bloody hell," he grunted, moving a hand down to touch it gingerly, then grimacing as he tried to move. He relaxed back into the pillows, his eyes closing slowly again.

Cerissa held her breath, hoping he would fall back asleep, but he didn't. In another moment, he frowned, forcing his eyelids to open again. Without waiting for him to speak again, she poured the medicine into the spoon, trying to keep her shaking fingers still enough to keep from spilling the liquid on the floor. "Here, love. This will help the pain." She shoved the spoon at his mouth, but he grimaced and turned his head quickly away.

"What the hell is that?" he mumbled. "Smells like turpentine."

"I don't know what's in it," she answered truthfully. "But Liza said to give it to you every few hours. She said it would help the fever and the pain both." For a long breathless second she stood motionless, sure that Brett would refuse to take it. But at last, he sighed and turned his head, opening his mouth obediently to swallow the bitter drug. Only after she had seen him finish the second spoonful did Cerissa dare to breathe easier. If she could only keep him distracted now until he fell asleep again. "Can you eat something, Brett? It would do you good," she coaxed, reaching for the custard Liza had delivered the evening before. The soup was too cold now, but the rich, egg pudding would do fine. With forced calm, the girl spooned the yellow pudding into Brett's mouth, noticing with ever increasing hope that he paused longer each time between mouthfuls, his eyes closing for longer periods of time before he forced them to reopen. At last, as she waited breathlessly, his dark head fell sideways against the pillow, his lips parting in sleep. She laid the custard bowl on the tray and leaned back herself, heaving a deep, thankful sigh of relief. The rest of the day she watched the clock anxiously, never missing another dosage until after midnight when Liza came in. The housekeeper had chuckled at her sleeping master, nodding her black head in satisfaction. "He doing just fine," she murmured in approval, winking at the girl mischievously "He bout ready to stop needing his medicine."

Cerissa grinned conspiratorially at the woman, nodding agreement. "I'm sure the Mary Rose has sailed already," she whispered "Or it will first thing this morning. When shall I stop then?"

Liza cocked her bandana covered head to one side, her black eyes thoughtful. "You give him another dose about dawn, chile, then let him be. He sleep that one off and wake up maybe lunchtime. It be too late fer him to catch that ship I think. Now remember, when he wake up he liable to have a bad headache and be grumpy as a old man. And when he realizes you missed dat ship, he gonna be even madder. Far as I knows, I never heard nothin bout no Mary Rose, honey. I just give him stuff to take the fever away."

Cerissa nodded, hating the thought of how angry Brett would be at her but knowing it would be unfair to direct any of his fury at the housekeeper. "Would he whip you, Liza?" she questioned softly, frowning at the idea. She had been surprised to encounter the practice of slavery when she'd gotten to the islands. And she wasn't at all sure she approved of it, regardless of economics.

The housekeeper threw her a startled glance, shaking her head quickly. "Captain Brett don't held with them ideas, honey. He don't usually need to either. We ain't slaves here at Sweetwater."

Cerissa stared her surprise at the woman's face. She merely assumed, seeing the servants color, that...

"Captain Brett don't hold with slavery," the woman explained proudly, her gaze fond as she looked at the sleeping lord. "He buy a slave, he make up indenture papers right off. We work good, treat him honest, for ten years and then we free. Only I free already, cause I pulled him through a bad bout of island fever when he first come here four years ago. I stays on cause I wants to, and Captain Brett pay me good wages to do so."

Cerissa smiled, terribly proud of him. In a sense she should have anticipated such a system. He'd said often enough that none of his ships were, or ever would be, slavers. And he hated any restrictions on his own freedom with such a fierceness... "I'm so glad," she murmured at last, rising to give the black woman an affectionate hug. "Thank you for telling me."

After a while, Liza had waddled quietly out, giving the girl a last wink of encouragement.

Cerissa sat up in a chair, her eyes intent on the sweeping hands of the ebony clock, refusing to sleep until she gave Brett the last at five o'clock. Then, knowing she would wake to his anger, she laid down to sleep at last.

Brett's restlessness roused her near noon, and she saw at once that the day was beautiful and sunny. She leaned over and stroked the dark haired lord's frowning forehead gently, whispering his name. Finally he sighed and opened his eyes, turning his head toward her.

"Good morning, love," she murmured softly, brushing the black hair away from his eyes.

To her surprise, he smiled sweetly, though still a touch drowsily, and stretched slowly, his eyes clear and emerald green under the thick ebony lashes. "I'm ravenous," he announced at last, pushing himself to a sitting position on the bed, his gaze flickering to the window. He frowned and stared past Cerissa to the clock, then glared accusingly at the trembling girl. "God damn it, wench! It's high morning already. I've got to get you back to Port Royal." Instantly, he swung his long legs off the bed, stumbling as the pain in his wounded leg hit him, fresh crimson already spotting the white bandage.

"No, Brett," Cerissa cried urgently trying to push him back onto the bed "Ged back in bed, you've reopened your . . ."

Liza's anxious face appeared at the door and she bustled into the room, clearly agitated, shaking a stern finger at the staggering lord. "What you doing out of dat bed, boy? You get back in dere and stay put afore I sit on your head. You got no business even thinking bout going nowhere."

Brett scowled at the woman, shaking his head. "Cerissa has a ship to catch, Liza. It's supposed to leave this morning and . . ."

"Den one of de boys can take her into town. You ain't budging. Now git in dat bed."

Helplessly, Brett sank back onto the mattress, his face ashen from pain and anger. "I just hope that storm delayed her sailing Cerissa, or by God! wench you'll regret your stubborness. Why didn't you tell someone you had to be back to town by Saturday morning? Did you think . . ." He broke off, staring crossly at the housekeeper's face. "Now what the hell is the matter with you, Liza?"

The woman answered slowly, shrugging her huge shoulders apologetically. "I's awful sorry to be the one telling you, Captain Brett, but this ain't Saturday morning. Saturday morning be long gone. Dis Monday morning. You slept for two days after you come in from de storm."

Brett stared at the woman, astonishment slowly changing to frustrated anger as he took in her words. "When did the storm break?"

"Broke yesterday morning. Guess it changed it's mind and gone further south."

With a groan, Brett shook his dark head, dropping it into his hands for a moment. When he raised it again, he was glaring at Cerissa in cold fury, his jaw tight and his mouth grim. "Send a boy into town right away, Liza. Tell him to find the captain of the Mary Rose if by some miracle she hasn't left yet. Tell him it's worth an extra 100 pounds if he'll stop by the spit and send a launch boat in for the girl."

The housekeeper nodded solemnly and turned to go, shrugging helplessly at Cerissa as she moved, "Wait a minute, Liza. Take this stubborn wench with you. If she's to stay, then, by God, she'll earn her keep. Find a bed for her in the servants quarters and find some work for her to do."

Cerissa gazed pleadingly a moment into Brett's cold eyes, but his expression never softened. At last she nodded and walked to the door. He was even angrier than she'd guessed he'd be, but, if the Mary Rose had sailed, then it was all worth it. Pray God the ship had cleared Port Royal when the boy got there . . .

A week had gone by, and still Cerissa slept alone in a narrow cot, sharing a small room with a maid named Taney. She had seen Brett only three times in twice as many days even though his leg had healed well enough to let him move around freely. Each time he had ignored her greeting, hardly looking at her, as cold and impersonal as if she were no more than a piece of furniture in the house. So she had forced herself to be patient, polishing the silver and helping in the kitchen as willingly as if she'd been born to do it. She actually enjoyed preparing the meals for she was fascinated by the exotic fruits and vegetables of the islands and she was happy to learn how to cook them. Surely Brett would relent soon, forgive her for missing the Mary Rose. It couldn't take much longer.

But it was nearly two weeks before Brett appeared in her room one night, startling both girls as he flung the door open with a crash, interrupting their chatter about household affairs.

Cerissa jumped to her feet, surprise turning slowly to fear as she smelled the brandy on his breath from across the room. Brett scowled blackly at the quivering Taney, ordering her from the room. In terror, the girl hitched up her skirts and fled without a backward glance. Cerissa clasped her hands tightly together to stop their trembling, drawing a deep breath as she forced herself to meet Brett's angry eyes unflinchingly. "What do you want Brett?" she questioned quietly.

"You know damn well what I want," he snarled, his words slightly slurred as his green eyes glittered dangerously. "Since you're devil bent on staying here, I've decided to make use of your stubborness."

Cerissa stared at Brett's flashing eyes, her face draining slowly of color as she shook her chestnut head in wordless denial. No, not like this, she wanted to cry, don't defile our love like this... But no words would come and she could only plead with her eyes. Suddenly, she found her voice and she cried out, turning to run away. But Brett moved faster, his strong hand fastening around her wrist in a cruel grip. Terrified she swung around, balling her free hand into a fist instinctively, swinging it at his face with all her might.

Brett grunted and stumbled as her arm caught him just above his ear, but he kept his grip on her wrist, his eyes dark and sparking cold fury as he ripped at the bodice of her dress, the light cotton gingham tearing easily under his fingers. Cerissa writhed in his grip, flailing at him futilely with her fist, crying incoherent words of terror and pleading. He ripped apart the waist band of the gown, and then the long full skirt and she felt Brett's arm reach behind her back, pulling her against him so viciously that her head snapped backwards nearly stunning her. In the next instant, he threw her to the floor, following her down before she could recover her senses to move, pinioning her body beneath his as he penetrated her brutally, taking her with a savage violence that left the girl moaning in pain, twisting helplessly beneath the punishing weight of his body as he thrust ruthlessly inside her, uncaring of her terror or her agony. Mercifully, he climaxed quickly, the ending brutal as well as swift, and Cerissa moaned quietly like a wounded animal, turning her head aside to let the tears fall onto the hardwood floor. After a moment she felt Brett roll away from her to lie propped on his elbows stretched out beside her, his head dropped between his muscled forearms, almost resting on the floor as he shook it slowly. She closed her eyes and swallowed to still the nausea rising in her throat, one hand going down to rest on top of her swollen belly, hoping against hope that the baby within it was unharmed by his father's violence. After another moment, she heard Brett say "Oh my god" in a voice of anguished horror, and heard him getting slowly up to kneel above her. When his hand touched her shoulder, her eyes flew wide in renewed terror and she shrank away from his touch, anxious to escape a repetition of his earlier brutality. But his hands followed her, his arms going under her shoulders and legs to lift her up against his chest. Despite herself, Cerissa whimpered in terror, feeling her body trembling. Then she felt the mattress under her as Brett laid her on the bed and stood silently over her. She opened her eyes at last, pleading with him for mercy, shaking her head slowly in a kind of stunned denial, but he continued to stand tall and silent and powerful, towering over her, his own gaze filled with a strange expression. He shuddered violently, closing his eyes abruptly, one hand reaching up to cover them as he turned away. At the doorway, he turned back again to stare at her, horror and stunned astonishment etched deeply on his face. Then he was gone and Cerissa cried wracking sobs, her arms folded around her aching belly, hardly even aware of time passing until Liza suddenly hovered over her, her queerly accented, deep voice kind and comforting as she held the hysterical girl in her huge arms, rocking her as if she were a child.

Afternoon came and Cerissa opened her eyes, surprised to realize she had slept, finding the black housekeeper still sitting silently beside her. The girl's hands moved quickly to her belly, and Liza smiled gentle reassurance.

"De bab's all right, honey, I thought you might lose him at first, but it's all right now. Don't you worry no more."

Cerissa felt swift tears of relief sting her eyes and she nodded slowly. "And Brett..." involuntarily she shuddered, remembering too clearly the horror of the night before. "Where is he?"

Lisa's mouth grew grim as she shook her head. "I don't know, chile. After he... after he done what he done to you last night, he knocked at my door and asked me to see to you. Then he got on a big black horse of his and rode out like de Devil was chasing him. I don't know where he went and he ain't back yet. But I not gonna let him hurt you no more, honey, so don't you even wonder bout him. You drink this medicine I made up for you now, and you sleep some more. Dat's de best thing for you just now. No thinking and no remembering honey, just sleeping."

Cerissa drank the housekeeper's potion and drifted gratefully into sleep, not waking until the sun was nearly setting. Then, her growling hunger forced her from sleep, and she smiled drowsily at Liza's anxious face as she murmured her hunger.

"I done figured dat baby be hungry by now, honey, so I got your dinner here. And I got something else for you too when you're done eating."

Cerissa frowned at the woman in confusion but ate her meal obediently. What could Liza be talking about? A special dessert? Or another dose of the bitter herb brew perhaps? At last, she was finished and the housekeeper handed her a wrapped package without comment. Cerissa untied the satin ribbon slowly, her heart suddenly hammering again, her fingers clumsy. Finally the paper

135

was off and she opened the leather box, catching her breath in surprise at the sparkling, green emerald ring lying on the white velvet cushion. She had expected the gift to be a small token from Liza or perhaps from Taney, regretting her cowardly flight, but this...something of this magnificence could only be from Brett. Her hand trembled as she slid the ring on her finger, looking up at the housekeeper in wordless expectation.

"Yes, honey, it's from Captain Brett. He come back from Port Royal with it this afternoon. He asked me to give you this note along with it."

Cerissa opened the folded parchment slowly, almost afraid of what it might say. If he thought to simply buy her forgiveness...

> *I bought this for you in Port Royal, sweetheart. I don't intend for it to erase the horror and shame I caused you last night, but nothing can do that except time. If you'll give me that time, I'll try to make it up to you, Cerissa. You've always loved me enough to forgive me before. I pray you love me enough still.*
>
> *B.*

Cerissa read the note several times, her eyes bright with unshed tears. He wouldn't say he loved her, yet he would buy her a stone that signified that. Love and fidelity were always associated with an emerald. In fact, legend decreed that, given from a lover to his beloved, the stone would stay clear and whole only so long as their love remained the same. If either one of them faltered, the emerald would grow cloudy and shatter...

"He wants to see you, chile," Liza murmured at last. "He feels awful bad bout what he done."

Cerissa sighed, trying to make her decision. The housekeeper watched her anxiously with round black eyes, finally speaking to the troubled girl. "Long as I known him, Captain Brett's had all his feelings locked up so tight inside himself that I think he done forgot he even had any. You trying to unlock dat box to let the love out, chile, all dem other feelings got to come out too. Person can't love unless he can hate too."

Cerissa met the woman's eyes for a long minute, then silently nodded. Liza smiled happily and nodded in return. "I never said I'd make it too easy on the Captain, honey. He best learn a lesson from this dat won't need repeating."

136

The girl smiled in complete agreement, her heart feeling whole again at last. She would forgive Brett, of course, her love demanded it. But she would make him worry a while anyway. When he walked in at last, she met him with cold eyes, her face solemn and unforgiving. Seeing him again brought the horror of the evening past back stronger anyway, so it wasn't totally feigned coolness she greeted him with.

"Hello, sweetheart," he murmured softly at last, standing a few feet away from her his face equally solemn and his smile touched with sorrow. Cerissa only nodded, unwilling to speak. At length he spoke again, every word an obvious effort, his voice low and uncertain, his grey-green eyes shadowed by trouble and fatigue.

"I don't need to tell you how sorry I am about...about last night, Cerissa. If you don't want to stay here, I'll understand. I can send you home on one of my ships though I don't advise it. The crossing's dangerous this late in the year. But I could probably find a place for you to stay with one of the other planters." He hesitated, his eyes searching the girl's face intently. It remained closed and cold as stone and he continued with a hopeless shrug. "I can only say if you'll forgive me and stay here with me, Cerissa, that I won't...I won't hurt you again like that—I swear it."

Cerissa remained silent, though her eyes were swimming with tears. She knew what an apology like this cost the proud lord, and she ached for him, wanting to ease his own regret but reluctant to forgive him too easily. At last, he sighed and spoke again. "I hope...is the baby all right? You didn't lose it did you?"

At last, she cleared her throat and replied, "No," she said simply. "Though Liza thought I might at first." She watched Brett's face as she spoke, seeing him wince and grow even more ashen at her answer. It was the first time he had indicated any feeling about the child at all. If it had taken nearly losing it to make him recognize it's preciousness, perhaps it was partially worth it.

Brett stood for several minutes, his eyes on her face, his gaze searching and full of sorrow at her apparent relentlessness. At last, he shrugged his broad shoulders and turned away, murmuring another apology and a promise to seek room for her at another plantation at once.

Cerissa allowed him to get almost to the door before she called his name, softly, reaching a trembling hand toward him, a faint smile forming on her lips. He stared at her a moment, color flooding back into his ashen face as he shuddered slightly, and drew a deep breath of relief. His green eyes grew warm and loving as he smiled at last, coming quickly across the floor to take her in his strong arms.

"You won't regret it sweetheart, I promise you, you won't regret it." As his dark head bent to kiss her hair with infinite tenderness, Cerissa leaned her head against his chest, kissing him and stroking him gently to soothe the wild trembling of his body. And she knew, just as he promised, that she would not regret forgiving him, just as she would never regret loving him. In great contentment, she lay quiet against him until the sun disappeared at last, bringing sweet night.

Chapter Nine

In the months that followed, Cerissa was proved correct. No husband could have been more loving, more attentive, more tender than Brett was. He had moved her into his large master suite with him, commissioned seamstresses from Port Royal to make her a gorgeous, lavish wardrobe, then assigned a servant girl to be her personal attendant. He had bought her a lovely, fine-boned bay mare and encouraged her to improve her riding skills so she could accompany him around the plantation, and occasionally, go visiting the other planter's women. Unlike England, many of the aristocratic men who owned the huge sugar, cacao or indigo works lived openly with women of inferior social status. Sometimes the lord's wives remained at home in England, preferring, no doubt, the merriment and sophistication of the Court to the lazy, warm simplicity of island life. Consequently, most of these men maintained Jamaican families, their mistresses usually much younger and better suited to the tropics. Some of the women were

English like Cerissa, some Negro from Africa, others a blend of the two. Her favorite friend, an Octaroon named Stacy, lived at the neighboring plantation with Lord Freemond, and often, for her sake, Brett would invite the couple over to Sweetwater for dinner and cards. Cerissa had learned the game so quickly and so well that she occasionally even beat Brett, and her enjoyment of the game was endless. As her belly had grown larger, however, the dark haired lord had cast an increasingly uneasy eye at her riding about. Finally he had found a small carriage for sale, and paid an outrageous fee to obtain it for her. Even with that, he had urged her to invite her friends to Sweetwater more often, preferring to see the peace of the plantation unsettled by a troop of chattering females than to risk Cerissa's travel on the island's rutted roads and narrow jungle paths. When he was forced to leave her, as he was a couple weeks out of the month, he always brought outrageously extravagant gifts home from the sea journeys—everything from rich jewelry, to bolts of fine cloth, to new books to feed Cerissa's voracious appetite for reading. And though she missed him when he left, and hated to see him sail again, the stories he brought back of the other islands were so fascinating that she soon forgave his absence. He spoke of a place called Barbados where the sea was sometimes warmer than the air, and made her giggle with disbelief as he recounted how he'd gone in the water to warm up, then sat in the shade under a palm tree to get cool again. And following one of his longer trips, he told her of the jungle coasts of Spanish Florida, and the luxurious hardwood forests of Carolina above. The Bermudas, he swore, had pink sand on the beaches and huge, 500-pound fish known as groupers who were friendly, though shy, and he recounted legends of their affection for man—how they might rescue a ship-wrecked sailor, how they would play like children if one tossed a ball into the sea for them.

He still took her swimming with him and she gradually improved, though that sport came nowhere as easily to her as horseback riding. And he taught her to fish as well, standing knee deep in the warm surf to cast the line out beyond the breaking waves. Once she had hooked a small shark and he had laughed to see her dismay, assuring her that it was far too small to be any menace but agreeing to reel it in for her regardless.

And, for the first time in their relationship, Cerissa knew beyond all doubt that Brett was absolutely and completely faithful to her. She shared him with neither the whores of the Port Royal brothels, nor the willing, even eager, servant girls of Sweetwater. When she was too tired, or her back ached, or her stomach rebelled at the burden carried beneath it, Brett still slept next to her, holding her against his chest as she fell asleep, his fingers stroking her hair gently.

Now, with Christmas only ten days away, Cerissa's world lacked only one thing to make it perfect. For, though Brett's every action indicated it, his every tender smile confirmed it, he still had never said he loved her. Cerissa chided herself for allowing such a small thing to mar such perfect bliss, but the fact remained that it did. And though she had contrived a dozen conversations designed to force the words from him, Brett always managed to turn the schemes aside, changing the subject or teasing the girl away from it.

Now, as they stood in the parlor together putting Christmas candles on the pine tree and Brett hanging what passed for holly here in the Indies, Cerissa shook her head in disbelief. "It just doesn't seem possible that it could be Christmas so soon Brett—especially with this weather. Why we were swimming yesterday! Who ever heard of eighty-degree weather for Yule? It should be cold and snowy."

Brett chuckled patiently, still intent on tacking the waxy green plant along the mantel. Jamaican winters were a far cry from England's. The air was only a few degrees cooler during the day, though the nights were definitely chillier, but in contrast to the home island . . . "It'll seem like Christmas when you see all your presents wrapped under the tree," he teased. "By the way, do you want anything special from me?"

Cerissa shrugged and started to reply. She really had more than enough of everything under the sun. But suddenly, she cocked her chestnut head, fixing Brett with a hopeful stare. "I want you to love me." she replied softly, holding her breath for his reply.

Brett only smiled, not even turning his head to meet her eyes. "Ask for something harder to get," he answered.

Cerissa pouted, a frustrated frown marring the usual serenity of her face. "Oh, Brett, why won't you say it?" she blurted suddenly stamping one foot in temper. "You say it in so many ways, every day, but you just won't put it into words."

At last Brett sighed, turning to face her. "Sweetheart, I know you better than you think I do. I know you spend half your time plotting and scheming to make me say what you want to hear. And if you ever succeeded . . . what would you think about then? You'd work on making me marry you next. You'd dream up a thousand different plans to lead me into asking you that final question—and

141

none of them would ever work. Where you were raised, love and marriage went together, Cerissa and you'll just never accept how different it is for us. So once you get a declaration of love you'd only intensify your efforts to win a wedding ring. And that's something that would eventually break your heart, princess, because it's the one thing I can never give you."

Cerissa ran forward to catch at his hand, her blue eyes pleading, "It isn't that, Brett, you're wrong. Knowing you loved me . . . well, it wouldn't make me dream about marrying you any more than I already do. But until I actually hear those words from you, I'll never really be sure! Oh, don't you see Brett? No matter how much your actions say, a little part of my brain is always whispering—if he did love you, he'd say it, Cerissa. Please, please, Brett just say it once for me! It would give me the strength I need to live at times without you, when you're away. The strength to bear your children, and raise them and love them whether they're legitimate or not."

For a long minute, Brett remained motionless, staring down at the girl's flushed face, his eyes gentle. Cerissa held her breath, waiting for his reply, feeling sure that finally, this time she had succeeded. Suddenly the dark haired lord shook his head, beginning to turn away again. Cerissa grabbed his arms with trembling desperation. "Please Brett, answer me! Do you love me?"

Finally shaking his head slowly and sighing, Brett turned back to stare down at her, his gaze tender, his faint smile touched with sorrow. "No, sweetheart," he whispered at last, pulling the trembling girl against his chest in a tender embrace, his lips brushing the top wisps of her dark brown hair. "No."

Cerissa closed her eyes, feeling hot tears of wordless frustration squeezing through to drop onto her cheeks and trickle to touch her mouth with their salt. Why should he be so stubborn? Every fiber of her soul knew from the sound of his voice and the sorrow haunting his eyes that he had meant yes while saying no. The warmth of his arms, the gentleness of his kiss, all screamed yes, Cerissa I love you. Everything but the word itself . . . no. At last, she wiped her tears against Brett's laced shirt, and drew back to smile tremulously up into his troubled grey-green eyes. "I won't give up, you know," she warned him softly, her chin rising in fresh determination.

At last, Brett smiled faintly in response, his eyes locked with hers. "I didn't think you would, sweetheart," he murmured. "I didn't think you would."

Christmas day dawned hot and cloudless, and Cerissa laughed again to be feeling too warm on the usually too cold holiday. She

142

drew her new dressing gown on eagerly, for, at six months pregnant, her swollen belly had finally out-grown the old one. Brett reached down to take her arm as she descended the stairs, and he seemed as eager as she to commence the festivities.

Liza brought in a huge tray of sweet rolls and fruit and, inevitably, a steaming pot of rich coffee for Brett. Cerissa had taken to drinking warmed chocolate instead of tea in the mornings, and today, as usual, she added several spoonfuls of Brett's coffee to her cup. She was still trying unsuccessfully to acquire a taste for the inky brew he loved so passionately. She had finally gotten used to the faint taste of it mixed with her chocolate, and even enjoyed that, but drinking it by itself . . . well, its bitterness still repelled her.

Brett waited patiently, grinning, as he watched her finish her breakfast. Her appetite had grown ravenous and he seemed to enjoy providing whatever her whim of the moment required. Once he had detoured a ship via Barbados to bring a crate of sweet pineapple home for her. Now, at last, she licked the last traces of sweet jam from her fingers, and nodded in satisfaction. Brett threw his dark head back in laughter, his green eyes dancing. "Not fully already?" he teased "After only four buns?"

Cerissa made a mocking face, not at all offended by his amusement. She knew she basked in his undivided attention just now. Even though the girl was sure the child she carried could not be Brett's first—a man of twenty-eight years, with his compelling good looks, well, he had surely sired other children though he never admitted as much. Still, from his undisguised delight and pride, it might as well be. Cerissa knew that the Court ladies of London were sophisticated and quite cool about bearing their lovers' children. If their precautions to avoid pregnancy failed, they thought little of drinking the secret herb potions prepared by the witchwomen to flush the baby from their wombs. So, probably, none of Brett's many court amours had borne him children. But what of the others? The countless other wenches and servant girls who had shared his bed in the past? But she never asked, not really caring to know, grateful to him for pretending at least that the event was as unique a delight to him as it was to her. Every time she squealed to feel the baby move within her and caught at his big, sun-browned hand to have him feel it too, Brett smilingly obliged her, marvelling with her at the strength and quickness of the child's actions, agreeing endlessly that yes, he too thought it must be a fine healthy boy, and yes, of course, he was sure he would have his grey green eyes as well.

"Here Liza, these are for you," Brett began the gift giving at last, handing the round Negro housekeeper a huge stack of red papered boxes, then proceeding on around the circle of the gathered household servants. No one at Sweetwater that Christmas, from lord to lowest field hand, went without a gift. And the exchanging and the unwrapping continued almost to noon. At last, only Brett's and Cerissa's presents for each other remained and the servants slipped tactfully away, murmuring final thank you's.

Cerissa insisted he open his first, pleased to see his genuine delight. She had bought him an emerald ring to wear on his small finger, a match to the one he had given her months ago, and a fine new pair of riding boots, and a gorgeous lightweight velvet formal jacket she had cut and sewn herself, adding a fine trim of gold piping along the sleeves and cuffs to accent the white lace he would sport at wrist and throat.

Brett handed three gifts to her, two large boxes and one small one. Inside the first of the bigger boxes was a beautiful lace blanket for the baby's christening, and her eyes filled with happy tears that he had thought of the child. Brett grinned at her pleasure, silently blessing Liza for suggesting such a plan, and urged her to open the next. In there was a gorgeous silk gown, the bodice cut high and the skirts full to accomodate her pregnancy, the sleeves cut wide open and then gathered over the white under sleeves in a half dozen places with small sapphire pins. It was, except for the waistline, the very height of style and rich enough for the King's own drawing rooms at Whitehall. She beamed and held it up full length against her, the blue of the silk catching the blue of her huge eyes to make them seem even larger. The small box she unwrapped slowly, savoring the anticipation. At last, the lid opened to reveal a sparkling, clear white diamond pendant cut in the shape of a heart. On the heavy gold clasp were two hearts intertwined, the initial 'C' in one and 'B' in the other. She smiled faintly, touching the stone with a gentle fingertip. Another symbol to take the place of the words he would not say.

"I have one more present for you too, sweetheart. Not a gift really—more of a surprise," he grinned mysteriously. "But you have to wait to see that one until we get to Port Royal."

And all Cerissa's pleading could not persuade him to divulge the secret, though her coaxing kisses did serve to delay the visit an hour or so. At last, still totally mystified, the girl followed Brett down the long wharf where the Falcon lay moored. Finally they reached the ship and the dark haired lord grinned, pointing wordlessly up to the ship's bow as it rolled and dipped in the calm motion of the harbor waters. Cerissa's gaze followed his arm, her eyes puzzled. Suddenly she stared at the prow of the ship, raising her hand to shield her eyes from the reflected glare of the sea. When the Falcon had left London, the bow had been plain, unadorned by any figure. Now, like most of the other vessels in the harbor, the Falcon boasted a figurehead—a larger than life sized carved wood statue of Cerissa, brightly painted to match the reddish brown of her thick hair, the cornflower blue of her eyes. The figure was dressed in a full sleeved, low cut, white peasant blouse, a black bodice laced over it, a full blue-grey gathered skirt billowing beneath. With a start, Cerissa realized it was the exact outfit she had been wearing when she'd first seen Brett—standing ankle deep in mud that long ago afternoon, her apron pockets full of seed peas. Later that night, minus the apron, it was what she had worn to Mrs. Tyler's, what she had left on the floor of the bed the first time she had lain in his arms. Astounded and deeply touched that he had remembered, she began to turn back toward him, then noticed a new nameboard, the letters ornately carved, and touched with gilt paint. "Cerissa" the sign proclaimed, and the girl gazed at the dark haired lord in amazed pleasure. She knew what a ship meant to it's captain. For Brett to rename the Falcon in her honor...

Brett grinned down at her, shrugging a touch self-consciously at the radiance of her eyes. "You can't be jealous now of my loving my ship, sweetheart." Cerissa wiped the welling tears out of her eyes, then reached up to throw her arms around his neck in an exuberant hug. At last, laughing, Brett drew back, disentangling himself reluctantly. "No more of that, sweet, or we'll give the good people of Port Royal one hell of a public display. I promised Jake Oates we'd meet him for supper in town. He's anxious to see you again."

The girl nodded and, linking her arm proudly through his, walked back up the dock. She had never had such a marvelous Christmas—never had such a marvelous year. And this spring she would give birth to Brett's son, and somehow, someway she would coax an "I love you" from him too. Oh yes, the next year promised to be even better than this one!

By the middle of March, though, Cerissa was having some doubts. Her belly had grown so large and awkward that she could no longer even get in and out of the soft feather mattress without Brett's help. She couldn't see the ground beneath her feet and her breasts were swollen and aching. Even Brett's most imaginative lovemaking had failed at last—her body was just too overburdened for any position to be practical any longer. Liza clucked and scolded at her every move inside the house, and Brett had forbidden her to stir outside it, except for short walks around the manor itself.

Finally, after a night of mild cramps her belly dropped and preparation for the birth began in earnest. Brett reluctantly sent the newly rechristened "Cerissa" to St. Kitts without him, and even Cerissa realized that that, more than anything else, signalled that the child's coming was imminent. Only the dark haired lord's unfailing affection and patience had maintained her spirits these last few weeks. He had remained as faithful to her as before though he teased her often now about the inconvenience his son was causing him. Each night, with a faint smile and a gleam of laughter lighting his green eyes, he helped her into bed and held her gently until she slept, then gallantly helped her crawl back out again the half dozen or so times a night she needed to.

Cerissa stirred drowsily, opening her eyes with a weary sigh, twisting around in the bed to try to ease her aching back. Another faint pain like the one that had first awoken her crept across her belly again, turning it rigid as rock beneath her fingers. She frowned in the darkness, a little apprehensive, but it soon passed and she closed her eyes again to sleep, moving her head to nestle against Brett's outstretched forearm. Suddenly she gasped as another cramp seized her, stronger and of longer duration this time. Instinctively she knew what was happening and she drew a deep breath to quiet her hammering heart, peering through the darkness to see the clock on the bureau. It seemed to her straining eyes that the gold filigree hands on the dial spelled four o'clock and she chewed her lip, hating to wake Brett at such an hour. Liza had warned her that first babies often took days to appear after the pains had begun, and she hated to raise the alarm too soon. Another pain stabbed her belly, and she brought her legs up instinctively to ease it, biting her lip to keep from crying out.

"What is it, sweetheart? What's the matter?" Brett's drowsy whisper sounded in her ear and she felt her eyes fill with quick tears of relief. She didn't care any more if she was being a baby herself, she was afraid and she was glad he had woken up.

"I . . . I'm not sure, Brett, but I think maybe the baby's coming," she murmured back, tightening her fingers around the hand he reached toward her. She was astonished to hear Brett's low chuckle in the darkness.

"Damn if Liza didn't call it right on the nose. All right, sweet, you just relax. I'll get everybody going."

146

With a quick kiss and a final reassuring squeeze of his hand, Brett was gone, only pausing to light the lantern on his way out and to throw a dressing robe around his tall, naked sun tanned body. Cerissa pulled the pillows up behind her, wiping the perspiration of her palms on the bed linens. If it was going to be days yet before she actually birthed the baby, she was going to remain calm, remain composed and not panic like a half-witted child.

But it wasn't days, it was only hours later that the birth actually began. And for hours after that she screamed and writhed helplessly as the pains got more tortuous, less relenting, clinging desperately to Brett's steadying hand, her fear growing greater with every second. It wasn't only the concern that haunted Brett's eyes even as he smiled and hastened to reassure her, nor was it Liza's anxious face as she pushed down of the girl's unyielding belly. It was something deeper than that, some primeval instinct that warned her. After this much time, with the pain so intense, the baby should be coming, but he wasn't. At last, nearly unconscious with agony and weariness, the girl felt Liza's greased hands slide into her, up into the womb, pulling at the child within. And finally, her insides screaming for release, the baby came at last, guided quickly by the housekeeper's sure hands.

In a misty, drowsy, almost dreaming state she saw Liza hold the squalling infant triumphantly up to Brett, saw his broad grin and undisguised relief on his face above her.

"We've got a gorgeous son, sweetheart, it's all over now," he murmured gently, bending down to kiss her wet forehead with proud gratitude, his hand still locked within her grip. "He was turned breach in there, so it took a while longer than usual, but everything's fine now. You go to sleep now and don't worry. Liza and I will take good care of him for you."

Cerissa gazed a moment longer up into his smiling green eyes, her whole soul warmed by the love in his gaze, then, unable to delay it any longer, she followed Brett's orders and drifted off into a sweet, dreamless sleep.

It was evening again when she awakened to find the bed linens changed beneath her, a new bed gown on herself, and Brett standing a few feet away, his large sun-tanned hands gently swinging the dark pine cradle set at the edge of the bed. He turned at her movement and smiled a greeting, moving over to sit on the bed beside her.

"Feeling better, sweet?" he questioned softly.

Cerissa nodded, moving her head to rest against his hand in deep contentment. "That was harder than I thought," she murmured, forcing a faint smile onto her lips.

Brett's grin broadened as he nodded agreement. "Why do you think I spoiled you rotten all these months?"

Cerissa wrinkled her nose at him in a pretended pout, then turned her gaze toward the cradle. "Can I see him, Brett? Is he sleeping?"

For answer, the dark haired lord swung his long legs off the bed and walked back to the cradle, stooping to pick up a small bundle wrapped in white cotton cloths, then carrying the baby awkwardly back to the eager girl. Cerissa reached up to take her son from his father, smiling at Brett's obvious unease with the infant, then peering down into the tiny, wrinkled face of her first born child. With a wondering finger, she touched the baby's little nose, the soft pout of his mouth. "He is beautiful," she whispered at last, amazed at the delicacy and perfection of his features. Even at only hours old, he was his father in miniature, even to the lock of raven dark hair on his head. She raised her eyes to meet Brett's in a warm glance of mutual congratulation, then dropped her gaze to the baby again, cooing softly at the sleeping infant, touching his forehead with her lips. "What shall we do for a nurse?" she questioned at last in a soft whisper, tearing her attention from the child with an effort.

"Liza's got that all arranged sweetheart, unless you'd rather do it yourself. I thought that decision would be up to you."

Cerissa thought a moment, then nodded her head slowly. "I'd like to nurse him myself, I think," she decided. 'You don't mind do you?"

Brett shook his head and shrugged, "The least I can do is lose a few night's sleep for such a fine son, sweetheart. No, I don't mind. I'd even offer to help but I'm afraid I'm not equipped for such tasks. What do you want to name him?"

Cerissa hesitated, wondering how to reply. She had thought she'd like to call the baby after Brett if he were indeed the son she was sure he'd be, but how would Brett react to that?

The dark haired lord chuckled, shaking his head slowly, his green eyes gleaming. "Oh no, sweetheart, not Bretegane please. I'm very flattered of course, but let's spare the child such a burden. I've been teased all my life about this damned name—or at least I was until I got good enough with a sword to put an end to it. Pick any other name you like and I'll agree." It wasn't only that which had made Brett eager to forestall the girl's obvious choice. The child would grow up as a bastard. That was a heavy enough burden to

148

bear without carrying such a distinctive name—one which would leave no doubt in anyone's mind of the boy's parentage. And for whatever reasons in a later time if it suited the child to keep his paternity a secret.

"I think I'd like to name him James then, after Lord Ardsley," Cerissa decided with a smile, "he was always so kind to me."

Brett grinned, obviously pleased with her choice. "All right, James he is then. And now, Jamey my boy, back in your cradle you go. Your mother has to eat yet before you do."

The baby was christened in April, with almost all of the couple's Jamaican friends in attendance. The congratulations were warm and genuine, the presents generous and Cerissa could not help but compare the child's reception here to the one he would have had in London. Of course, most of the children who attended with their parents were as illegitimate as Jamey, and perhaps that was a major reason for the greater tolerance, yet it went beyond that. The people here were almost a different breed. Less conforming to rules and regulations, less concerned with what a person was than how they felt about him. And Jamey was a happy, gurgling, charming infant as well as a handsome one. He seemed able to enchant even the most hardened anti-child members of the community. Proof of that lay in the solid silver porridge bowl Mate Oates had contributed. And Liza, who had taken to the child as if he were her own flesh, had given a tiny silver case with a crystal lid, one fine lock of the child's dark hair caught in a ribbon within it. Brett had bought a silver cup and a matching, gold handled sterling spoon, and other gifts included bells and rattles and precious velvet dresses and miniature brushes and combs and mirrors.

And despite the growing heat and humidity of the island as spring rolled into summer, Cerissa was thoroughly content. The first sign of an impending disruption of her idyllic Jamaican life came in the beginning of June when Brett returned from a sailing trip, frowning and uneasy at rumors he had heard in Port Royal of a fever outbreak on the south east end of the island.

Cerissa listened only half attentively as the dark haired lord told Liza which plantations were already affected, looking up at last to catch a strange look which passed between master and servant before both pairs of eyes turned in her direction. She sat silent for a long minute, suspicion growing deep within her, as she stared first at Brett, then at Liza, and eventually returned her gaze to Brett again, shaking her chestnut head in slow denial.

"Oh no, Brett Lindsey, I'm not leaving without you. If its safe enough for you to stay, it's safe enough for me."

He shook his dark head in grim disagreement. "That's not true, Cerissa. I've been here for years already. Most of the fevers I've already gotten, the others I'm not likely to catch after this long. It's senseless for you to take such a risk, sweetheart, I just won't..."

"No!" she declared loudly, dropping her head to stare down at Jamey's face where it rested against her breast, her face carved into lines of a stubborn pout. "We go together or not at all."

Over her head, Brett and Liza exchanged a slow silent glance of agreement, the dark haired lord nodding ever so slightly to the Negress before he shrugged and walked over to where the sullen girl sat, bending to drop a light kiss on the top of her hair. "There's no need to quarrel yet, sweet. Maybe the fever won't spread. If it does... well, we'll figure that out later."

Cerissa glanced up suspiciously but his face reflected nothing out of the ordinary and at last she relaxed, reaching a hand up to clasp his in contentment. Maybe Brett had finally learned how determined she was to be with him. And maybe too, he was as loath as she to think of parting. Anyway, she would keep a wary ear on reports of the sickness. She had no intention of being shipped back to England alone.

Brett and Liza stood silent above her needing no words to communicate their thoughts. Jamaican summers, following the rains of May and June, were always more dangerous for sickness than the winters, but for a major outbreak to be occuring already was unusual. And Cerissa, in her weakened state following childbirth, her body already taxed by the strain of nursing, would be a prime candidate for illness. And, of course, there was Jamey as well. Often enough, a healthy young body could survive the onslaught of a tropical fever but an infant... Very, few of them did.

Brett rode into Port Royal the next day, returning home before dusk. He said nothing more about the fever epidemic nor about sending Cerissa home to England so the girl began to breathe easier. Instead, he was especially attentive during the next few days, staying close to Sweetwater, pampering Cerissa's every whim, playing happily with the little boy, his lovemaking more intense than ever, more passionate than ever, his kisses sweet and lingering as if his lips longed to cling to hers forever. The days flew by in golden contentment, the tropical sun hot enough to force steam up from the rain forests on the northern hills, the seas calm and clear as a jewel. Mornings were spent on horseback as Brett took the girl for leisurely rides along the beach, dismounting to walk barefoot in the warm waves, stooping for a pretty shell occasionally. The more sultry afternoons he took her and the baby down to play in the water, keeping careful eye on what swam in it, laughing his deep, rich laugh as Jamey gurgled and chuckled in babyish delight as the waves tickled his tiny feet. Evenings, Brett and Liza seemed to take special pleasure in offering her all her favorties of the island's exotic dishes and she soon swore she'd be as fat as when she had carried a baby within her. Nights were full of magic only Brett could work on her soul.

Cerissa smiled drowsily and buried her head beneath the pillow, away from the bright light, remembering the sweet loving of the night before. Brett had made love not just once to her but twice. The second time a strangely unhurried loving—almost dreamlike in its gentleness and leisure. How long his lips had lingered on hers the faint taste of his brandy mingling with that of her wine, his black eyelashes brushing against her cheek, his green eyes dark and warm and filled with a strange sorrow. How slow his big, browned hands had moved on her body, stroking her breasts and belly and thighs, his fingers tangling in the thick masses of her hair, his body heavy and infinitely pleasureable above hers. How gentle his movements within her had been, how controlled the violent instincts of his masculinity, until she had reached that sweet pinnacle, her body answering his with waves of pleasure, exploding within her, carrying her away into dreamless peace. She didn't even remember falling asleep, though she had had the strangest dreams all night. She recollected being lifted from the bed in Brett's strong arms, the closed, quiet darkness of a carriage ride, then again being lifted in his embrace as he carried her somewhere terribly familiar . . . his ship, that was it. She remembered the soft lap-lap of the water slapping the sides of the oaken hull. Funny how dreams lingered. Just remembering brought the lulling rocking motion of the ship back so strongly . . .

Suddenly, with a small cry, Cerissa bolted upright, searching the unfamiliar small room with desperate eyes. This wasn't Sweet-water—this was a ship! And not the 'Cerissa' either but one she had never seen before. And where was Brett? What was she doing here?

Thoroughly frightened, she jumped from the bunk and raced for the narrow door, pausing only to grab for a cloak before realizing she was somehow already fully dressed. Wrenching the door open she burst into a narrow, low ceilinged gangway, almost running into a plain-faced older woman just outside. "Who are you?" Cerissa blurted helplessly. "And where am I?"

The woman smiled faintly, handing the distraught girl a sleeping

Jamey. "I am Mary Horne," she replied quietly. "My husband is Captain of this ship—Kensington Duchess. We're bound for London."

Cerissa shook her head in stunned disbelief, clutching her son against her mechanically. "No...no, you must be wrong," she whispered in growing horror. "Why would..."

"Here, child." Mrs. Horne handed the girl a thick folded parchment, her name written on the outside in Brett's familiar masculine writing, the edges sealed with wax. "Lord Lindsey asked me to give you this when you awakened. I assume it will answer many of your questions. It's half past five now and I'll send someone over with your supper in a few minutes. If you want any help, just knock on my door. We're the last cabin there."

Wordlessly, Cerissa nodded, taking the parchment with numb fingers, unable to force even simple courtesy from her frozen lips. Trembling and sick with fear she walked back into the narrow cabin, setting Jamey in the cradle by the bed, drawing a straight backed wooden chair over near the single window to use the light.

Drawing a deep breath, she opened the paper carefully, almost afraid to read what lay within, taking long minutes to loosen the seal and keep it intact on one edge of the parchment. At last, her hands shaking, she unfolded the note and smoothed it open on her lap.

> *Dear Cerissa,*
>
> *By the time you read this you will be safely out to sea, a hundred miles from Jamaica on your way back to England. I did not want your memories of the island troubled by a bitter quarrel, nor did I want to end our happiness here together on such a note. The fever I spoke of is a virulent one and was spreading rapidly. I could not risk losing you or the child—or both. Please try to understand. Since you have become so adept at thwarting my plans for you, I decided to do it this way...*
>
> *Captain Horne is a good man and a friend of mine. He is taking his own wife and family away from the island and agreed to take you as well. He will see you safely to England, and Ardsley will, hopefully, meet you and see you are settled. If James fails to get my earlier letter, or for some reason fails to arrive in time, Captain Horne will help you instead. He carries as well a letter to Isaac Benjamin, authorizing a draft on my account for 5,000 pounds in your name. I expect to*

*rejoin you in London before ice forms on the Thames, but in
the event of something unforeseen, this money should enable
you and Jamey to live comfortably for many years. Lord
Ardsley would, in addition, befriend you for my sake as well.*

    *Try not to be too angry at me, sweetheart, and think of me
kindly. Do not believe that it was any fault of yours, or any
dissatisfaction with you that moved me to send you home.
God knows if I loved you less, I would have kept you with me.*

B.

    With a small sob, Cerissa dropped her head into her hands, her
face wet with tears. After all this time, all these months of waiting,
and coaxing, and scheming to have him finally say those precious,
precious words only now ... when they made the parting only that
much more bitter. Hopelessly, she stood at last to press her face to
the window, straining to catch a last glimpse of the island behind
her, her vision blurred by tears. There on the horizon was a far away
speck of green amidst the blue, but whether it was Jamaica or
another of the countless islands, she could not tell. She stared at it
anyway, watching it blur in the heat distorted air, standing still as
carved stone until a sailor knocked with dinner.

Chapter Ten

The London summer was much as she remembered it from the year before. To escape the heat, she took Jamey out to the country for long visits, but she always grew uneasy and hurried back. If Brett should change his mind and sail home sooner than he'd planned, she wanted to be there to meet him. Ardsley had tried to ease her loneliness when he could, often escorting her to the bookstores she loved, or to the plays, or out for dinner—even including his young namesake on many daytime outings to St. James or Hyde Park for a carriage ride or picnic, sometimes a cool yacht cruise along the Thames, but nothing could replace the joy of Brett's company and Cerissa felt only half complete without him. Oh, her days were much fuller now, more varied and more interesting than the year before. She enjoyed the fashions and the gossip and the wonderful new books being published—especially a political treatise by a man named John Locke—and of course, Jamey took much of her time and filled much of her heart, but at six months old he was more Brett's replica than ever, his blue-eyes finally changing to his father's grey-green, and the girl longed to share the baby's accomplishments with Brett, longed to see his broad grin and the pride in his eyes when he saw the child again. Absently, she crossed another day off the calendar, September 24, and turned to pick up the lute she had learned to play.

A knock on the apartment door forestalled her, and she gathered her skirts to go answer it. "Ardsley!" she exclaimed in pleased surprise, "I didn't expect you so early. I thought you'd said seven..." she hesitated suddenly, uneasy at the odd expression in the lord's blue eyes, feeling the sick, cold hands of fear in her belly. "What is it, James? Is something wrong?"

"Let's sit down, sweetheart. I'm afraid I've got bad news for you." The blond lord closed the door behind him quietly and walked to the buffet, pouring two brandies into small glasses, keeping one for himself and handing the other to the girl.

Cerissa stared at him, her throat dry, her fingers trembling on the glass. "It's Brett... he's not coming home this fall... or... oh my God, he's not married is he, Ardsley?"

"No, sweet," the blond man shrugged, his eyes soft with pity. "I wish it were only that. I'm afraid he's dead, Cerissa, I only, got word myself this..."

"No." The glass slipped from the girl's trembling fingers to smash unnoticed on the floor, the liquor dyeing her skirts dark "No, you're joking..." Desperately, she searched the man's face, but the anguish in his own eyes stole her last hope. She shook her head, feeling sick and terribly dizzy. "How... when...?" she murmured at last, her fingers clenched white on the edge of the chair, her face bloodless.

The blond lord shrugged apologetically, dropping his gaze. "He was sailing with two others of his ships to Spanish Florida, and a pirate fleet attacked. They managed to beat them off but not without heavy damage... to his ship in particular, I guess. They said both the main and the mizzen masts were down and they think the ship was taking water... Anyway, a tropical squall came up suddenly and separated all three of them. The Sea Queen and the Brighton managed to find each other again, but though they searched as long as they dared, they never found any sign of the Cerissa..."

Cerissa swallowed hard, her eyes lighting with sudden hope. "That doesn't mean he'd dead, Ardsley," she pleaded aloud, her voice unnaturally loud in her ears. "They never found the wreckage, or his body then so he may have..."

"No, don't torture yourself with false hope, sweetheart. The

155

Cerissa was in no shape to ride out a storm...she went to the bottom with all hands."

Cerissa closed her eyes, a sob breaking free of her mouth at last as the tears started to fall. "No...oh, no it can't be true...it can't be true..." Helplessly she turned against Ardsley's comforting arm, her breaking heart bringing tears to his own eyes as he held the girl, rocking her endlessly, trying to ease her unbearable grief. At last, when she grew quiet again, he stayed to see her to bed, promising to help any way he could to lighten the blow Fate had dealt. But the girl seemed hardly to have heard him, her responses dry and mechanical. Time, he knew, was the only answer to Cerissa's sorrow. In time she would learn to live without her black haired lord.

Time did seem to help, as Ardsley had hoped, and by spring the girl was much her old self. If a touch of sorrow haunted her lovely eyes occasionally, well, that was understandable. But she laughed now too, and enjoyed life again, especially her year old son who was walking well, though a shade unsteadily and even beginning to talk. Ardsley had done what he could to fill her loneliness, though his own wife sneered contemptuously about lords becoming infatuated with country girls. And in a sense, he had grown to love Cerissa though not in the same sense his friend had. And of course, he didn't sleep with the girl. His initial advances in that area had been kindly, though firmly, rebuffed. But his fondness for the girl lay not in her obvious physical charms but in the warmth of her own returned affection, and partly in his memories of her association with Brett. One thing was certain, whenever he drove Cerissa and Jamey home from an afternoon's outing, he felt almost as though he'd been with his friend in a way. The boy's resemblance to his dead father was almost uncanny, even down to a certain expression on the child's face when he laughed. The only thing he had been unsuccessful at was in persuading Cerissa to allow other men to court her. Her looks, her sweetness—and her 5,000 pounds he admitted honestly—attracted many worthwhile suitors. One of them, Gerard Whitestone, was an acquaintance of his, Brett's too, a country squire who had been with the two of them that first day Cerissa had seen them. Of course, Gerard didn't remember seeing the girl and Ardsley was careful not to mention it. He always introduced Cerissa as the widow of a sea captain and let it go at that. No use making trouble for the girl or her illegitimate son if he could help it. Why if Cerissa were smart enough to marry the right man, Jamey could be adopted and lead a normal, more accepted life. If only the girl would stop watching the incoming ships with those haunted eyes, always watching for a man who lay at the bottom of the sea ... Gerard would be a perfect husband for her.

At last, Cerissa weakened under Lord Ardsley's relentless urging and she began seeing Squire Whitestone. The man was young enough and not ill-looking at all, and even she had to admit that he was uncommonly kind to her, apparently doting on her every word and every move. But the few tentative kisses she had allowed him left her soul untouched, her body cold. So she had refused his marriage proposals steadfastly up to now, hoping, always mindlessly, senselessly hoping that somehow, someway Lord Lindsey would magically reappear, raised from the dead to draw her into his strong arms again as he had so many times. Well over a year had passed now since she'd seen him last, and though she could still remember his face in certain poses, or more rarely the sound of his deep laugh, he had begun to slip away from her. Her love remained as great and undiminished as ever, yet her heart had locked it away. Remembering brought only unbearable grief at what she'd lost. More and more, Brett lay only in her dreams and she always awakened from those crying.

Perhaps Lord Ardsley was right in urging her to marry Gerard. Perhaps she would love him in time. Perhaps living with him would ease the pain of remembering Brett. If he hadn't shown such affection for Jamey, hadn't promised to adopt him as his own son—and more than that, as his heir to Gerard's land and his title—she would never really have considered the marriage. But as it was ... perhaps she should relent a little. Perhaps her instinctive revulsion of the man came only from comparing him to Brett. There was no other basis for it surely.

And yet, Cerissa could not refrain from stalling for ever a little more time, finding a thousand small excuses to delay Gerard without hurting his feelings. Even she could see the man adored her—she could not bring him the sorrow of knowing why she waited. Even to herself she barely admitted the truth. But when October came, and the weather chilled, she forced herself to a decision. She would marry Gerard when ice formed on the Thames. If word of Brett had not come to England by then, she would relinquish her foolish hope, acknowledge him gone forever to her, and do what she must to best protect their son.

The winter came early to England that year, and on October 25 Cerissa woke to her wedding day. Her gown was of pale blue, not

157

white since she was supposedly a widow and not a maid, and covered with tiny seed pearls. Joylessly she dressed in it, sitting patiently while her maid dressed her hair in long curls, fine ringlets around her face. She clasped a small sapphire pendant Gerard had given her around her neck and took her cloak from the servant, reaching for the door. Suddenly she paused, turning back toward her small jewelry chest. She had worn Gerard's sapphire instead of Brett's diamond heart for obvious reasons. Gerard had an almost effeminate interest in her jewelry and he examined every piece intently, holding the stones to the light, creasing the soft gold of the settings with a fingernail to check the purity of the metal. He had therefore, noticed the engraved hearts on the clasp of Brett's diamond, and she had admitted that it was a gift from her deceased "husband." Obviously, she could not wear such a thing to marry another man, much as she would have liked to, for the diamond was much finer and of far more exquisite workmanship than Gerard's sapphire. But she could wear the emerald ring Brett had given her. She had never told Gerard where it had come from so he could not object. And it might keep a tiny piece of Brett's love close to her during the wedding, giving her the strength she needed this afternoon. Gladly, she slipped the ring onto her finger and turned again for the door.

Ardsley met her at the doorway, taking her arm to guide her to the carriage, his eyes faintly sad though his mouth smiled. He had no illusions about Cerissa's feelings for the squire. He knew she didn't love him as she had Lord Lindsey, but hell . . . this marriage was the best thing for her. Regardless of her feelings, the man obviously adored her—almost to an overwhelming degree. Whitestone would provide a home for both she and the boy, give him a name as well, and he would make every effort to assure her happiness. It might not be the idyllic ending Cerissa's marriage to Brett would have been, but even if his friend had lived, that would never have happened anyway. And so the blond lord smiled and chatted with a great show of merriment, pretending he didn't notice the suspicious brightness of the bride's eyes, or the ashen pallor of her face.

At last, the carriage rolled to a jerky stop at the marble steps of the church. Ardsley jumped down and turned to help Cerissa, shivering in a sudden gust of cold wind. The girl stepped down carefully, holding her light skirts up out of the street dirt, hardly aware of the cold in the dizzying whirl of her emotions. Every instinct of her soul cried out against this marriage and she fought to

158

keep her body straight, walking slowly toward the open church door. At the top step she paused a moment, drawing a deep breath, then reaching down to move her cloak away from her feet. Suddenly, the emerald slipped from her finger falling in a kind of slow-motion before her horrified eyes, striking the edge of the cold marble step to shatter into a thousand fragments. With a stunned cry, she knelt down, heedless of the raw winter winds, collecting the gold setting and a few of the larger pieces in her trembling hand, her heart hammering sorrow, nearly mindless in despair. The legend of the emerald, she heard again in a far away echo deep in her soul, only clear and whole so long as love is true... love betrayed, the stones grows cloudy and breaks...

Helplessly, she put the pieces into the pocket of her cloak, putting her fist against her mouth to smother an involuntary sob. Oh no Brett, she wanted to cry to the heavens, you don't understand... I'm only doing this for Jamey... for your son...

"Cerissa, what's wrong?" Ardsley's voice was anxious as he stared at the girl's anguished face.

"The ring... Brett's emerald..." she choked at last, clutching the blond lord's arm, her eyes wild. "The legend says..."

Ardsley repressed a quick shudder and shook his golden head firmly, "That's nonsense, sweetheart, that's only a tale for children. The air is cold, that's all. It's not uncommon for rings to slip off in this weather. Especially since that was made for you in the tropics—and you were pregnant then too, your finger would have been swollen."

Forcing her heart to stop hammering, drawing a deep breath, Cerissa forced herself to nod agreement. Of course, Ardsley was right. It was only coincidence. It meant nothing. It was only a ring—an inanimate object. It must not deter her from her purpose. Jamey was real. Jamey was her son. She would provide for him. She would marry Gerard. At last, she smiled faintly at the blond lord, her face composed again. "All right then, James. I'm ready."

And Cerissa could not complain of Gerard's behavior toward her in any way. Their week long honeymoon at Brackton Spa was restful and serene, unmarred by quarrel or incident. Gerard seemed to view his newly acquired rights to enjoy his wife's body as a privilege, and he was always careful to sound out her wishes, acceding graciously when she demurred. Cerissa pretended for his sake to be more pleased by his lovemaking than she actually was, for still, though he was a considerate enough lover, his touch lit no hungry fires in her body. Usually when she sensed Gerard's eagerness she shared his bed willingly though, for he was unfailingly kind and almost obsequiously attentive.

Jamey, at a year and a half, was still somewhat shy of his new step-father when they returned from Brackton but Gerard seemed unperturbed. He still assured Cerissa that he intended to pursue the boy's adoption and even hired a lawyer to begin the work.

Cerissa ran the squire's modest household easily, drawing on the skills she had acquired under Liza's tutelage at Sweetwater. She saw Ardsley, though less frequently, and Gerard was always congenial in the extreme when the blond lord visited them. Of late, he had begun spending more evenings away from home, but Cerissa didn't complain. In truth she didn't actually care that much. Gerard's company at best was only mildly interesting to the girl, for he seemed more keen on court gossip and news of the quality than he was in the world outside of London, or political and economic issues. He had made an attempt, half hearted perhaps, to read John Locke's work for her sake, but found it horribly boring and soon quit. Cerissa took her pleasure in new plays and books, and in showing her young son maps of the world, reading him stories of the faraway islands he'd been born in—but cautiously, of course, for she didn't want Gerard to suspect the boy's true parentage nor her own past. He seemed so patently devoted that she doubted it would change him, but there was no use taking needless risks.

One evening in mid November, as Cerissa sat stitching a small jacket for the boy, she heard a faint knock on the outside door. She raised her head, thinking to call one of the two household servants to answer it, then changed her mind. Laying the fabric aside, she rose to her feet and went for the door. It was probably Gerard home, though it was early yet for him being only ten o'clock, but she would let him in personally. She often felt somewhat guilty about the fact that she didn't love him when he so obviously doted on her, and tried to conceal her lack by doing affectionate things.

Smiling faintly, she turned the brass handle on the door and opened it wide. "Ardsley!" she murmured in surprise, her smile deepening with surprised pleasure. "What a nice ..." Her eyes went over the blond lord's shoulder to the shadowed darkness behind, her words dying in her throat, her eyes wide and staring. There, just behind James, leaning one shoulder against the door post, a faint smile on his face, stood Brett.

Ardsley managed to catch the girl just before she dropped, and she felt herself lifted in his arms and carried over to the couch.

Darkness still swam before her eyes and she could not speak yet for the grief and anguish in her soul, couldn't even hear the words of murmured comfort the blond lord was saying as he held the shaking girl against his chest. Cerissa found her breath again, though her eyes were too full of tears to see yet, and she clutched the lord's shirt with desperate fingers. She had to tell Ardsley whom she'd seen standing there . . . he would never believe her of course, but still . . . oh God! How had she ever deluded herself into believing she could forget him . . . even his ghost held more power than any living man she knew.

Gradually, the roaring in her ears subsided and Cerissa could make out the words Ardsley was saying. She sobbed helplessly against him, trying to speak, realizing in a kind of vague horror that even the blond lord's voice sounded terribly like Brett's now. Cerissa sobbed again, tightening her grip on the man in desperation. She was losing her mind, going insane . . . she had to regain control of herself. Finally, with a last supreme effort, she forced her head away from his chest and stared up at him, her eyes wide and pleading for help. And suddenly, her heart lurched again, her breath choking in her throat. It wasn't Ardsley's face that bent above her. It wasn't Ardsley's arms that held her so gently. It was Brett's.

"I'm sorry, sweetheart, I should have known this would be a shock for you." His voice, deep and resonant and rich as she remembered, sounded softly in her ears. Hesitantly she reached an unbelieving hand up to touch his face, watching him turn to lay a gentle kiss on her fingertips.

"Oh, Brett . . . Brett it is you," she whispered helplessly, her eyes devouring every beloved feature of his handsome face. "I thought I'd lost my mind . . ."

The dark haired lord smiled faintly and shook his head. "No, sweet, I'm not a ghost."

Gradually, Cerissa began to believe it. He was real. He was alive. His arms were warm and strong and supporting her still, his eyes the strange grey green she remembered them. At last, with a cry of pure joy, she sat up, flinging her arms around him possessively, clutching his body against hers. "Oh thank God, Brett! You don't know how I've missed you. Now you're back and we can be together again and I'll never . . ."

Brett frowned faintly, disengaging her embrace with obvious reluctance. "No, sweetheart, that isn't possible. I don't think your husband would think very highly of such an idea."

The girl stared at him again in sick horror, feeling the color drain from her face. "Oh my God...I'd forgotten...Oh, Brett, I'm married now..."

"Yes, I know, Ardsley told me," Brett replied gently, remembering the initial pain Ardsley's announcement had caused him. He had been surprised, not that she'd married for he knew they would all have presumed him dead long since, but surprised at the husband. "Whitestone?" he had frowned at his friend uneasily "I never cared much for him. I didn't think you did either."

"Well, true," Ardsley had admitted reluctantly. "But he's totally devoted to the girl, Brett. And when he offered to adopt the boy...make him his heir...We were so sure you were dead, it just seemed too good an opportunity to let Cerissa ignore." A long silence had followed that while the dark haired lord had struggled to adjust to this new idea. Cerissa married, his son belonging to another man..."Does he still gamble?" he'd asked at last, his face revealing nothing of his thoughts.

Ardsley had grinned, raising one blond eyebrow in mocking surprise. "You have something against gamblers?" he questioned drily. "Seems to me I remember both of us doing plenty of that ourselves."

Brett had forced a quick grin and shrugged in rueful agreement. "Yes, but we were better at it than Whitestone. I always had the feeling he was losing more than he could afford."

"Well having a family ought to settle him down then," the blond had replied obviously intent on defending his choice for the girl. At last, Brett had shrugged again before turning to other subjects. Regardless of what his friend assured him, he was going to remember to check up on the squire.

"Brett," the girl was saying, tugging at his sleeve for his attention "Brett it doesn't matter. I'll get away from him somehow, divorce him if I can, then we can get married and..."

"No, Cerissa," Brett shook his head sadly, averting his eyes lest she see the pain in them. "Nothing's changed. You're really much better off this way...surely Jamey is. No, Gerard is a good husband for you. I won't come between the two of you."

Stunned, Cerissa stared at his face, hardly believing her ears. "But in the letter you sent...you didn't mean it? You only said your love for me ...?"

"No," he interrupted hastily. The pain in the girl's voice wrenched his heart unbearably. "Of course I meant it. I did love you, sweetheart...do love you still. My God, I think that's mostly what kept me alive all those months—thinking about you, wondering what you were doing, trying to picture your face in my mind...and Jamey's too...wondering how you both were, whether he'd be walking yet, or talking..."

"But you still wouldn't have married me?" she pressed incredulously. "Even though you love me?"

"No," he replied, not absolutely truthfully, he realized, but still... It was a question he had asked himself every day of the five week sailing home, but he'd never come up with an answer. Still, no use allowing the girl to guess that. The knowledge would only torture her for what might have been.

Cerissa drew a deep breath to ease the aching tightness of her chest. At least he said he loved her...if only she weren't married already... "I waited until ice formed on the Thames," she breathed helplessly at last, touching his hand with an apologetic finger.

"I know, sweetheart, we were terribly late but I was so anxious to get home. We docked at Plymouth instead. I'm not angry at you, Cerissa, for not waiting longer, I'm glad you..."

At last her control shattered, her brittle nerves cracking. "You're glad?" she cried accusingly, tearing herself away from his arms. "You're glad? Glad that someone else took care of your responsibility for you? Glad that someone else has the bother, the awesome inconvenience of me and raising your son?"

Brett stared at Cerissa's anger flushed face in shock, shaking his head as answering fury grew within him. "No, damn it, that's not what I said and not what I meant! You think its easy for me knowing you share another man's bed? Imagining his filthy hands on you? His body inside you? You think I'm glad to see my son lost to me..."

"Don't!" with a cry, Cerissa flung herself against Brett, locking her arms around his body in agonized remorse. The pain in his voice, in his eyes... "Please, please forgive me, Brett, I never meant to say such terrible things...Oh please, Brett, I'm sorry, so sorry..."

At last she felt his arms go around her again, his head dropping as he rested his cheek against the top of her hair, feeling his chest heave in a sigh. "I'll find a way to be able to meet you," she whispered. "Gerard is often out in the evening..."

"No, sweet, let's not torture ourselves. Your husband's no fool and men dislike being cuckolded...I won't be staying in London that long now anyway, and it's better if..."

Helplessly, the girl listened to Brett's voice, hearing reluctance, but also an odd firmness in it. It wasn't fair, she thought to herself over and over again, life simply wasn't fair... At last, Brett turned to go, reaching for his cloak. "No, you can't go yet!" she cried desperately. "How did you get back here? Where have you been all this time? And... and Jamey," she pleaded urgently. "Don't you want to see him? Oh Brett, you must! He's so handsome, you'll be so proud. Everyone thinks he looks just like you, except Gerard of course, he thinks..." she pressed a hand against her mouth, wishing she could bite off her tongue for uttering such stupid words. But at last, a faint smile on his face though a strange expression lingered in his eyes, Brett nodded and dropped his cloak again. "All right, sweetheart, I guess you are entitled to an explanation. But don't wake the boy, I'll just go in if I may. And I can't stay long. I want to be gone before your husband comes in... he knows me slightly already, Cerissa, and with the way Jamey looks... seeing me here would only make him suspicious. Even a fool could make that connection."

Grateful for any time at all, Cerissa nodded hastily, taking his hand to lead him to the child's room. "And you must tell me how Liza is, Brett, and Taney and Stacy and Lord Freemond too..."

Cerissa heard Gerard come in sometime after midnight and she pretended to be sleeping when he bent over to peer at her in the darkness. She practically held her breath, afraid to move until she heard his even breathing and realized he was asleep. She opened her eyes again in the darkness, remembering every word of Brett's, the look of his eyes, the line of his jaw, his rare smiles, the familiar scent of his body, the touch of his hand. How proud he had been of the boy. Even in the darkness she had seen the radiance of his eyes, the wondering, faint smile of his mouth. Indians, she repressed a quick shudder, and glanced fearfully at Gerard, praying she hadn't wakened him. Brett had explained about the battle with the pirates, how the Cerissa had taken most of the damage because she had done most of the fighting with her guns. When the storm had come up, Brett had left the sails up on the one remaining mast, letting the violence of the wind and sea run them headlong toward the Florida coastline, helpless to prevent it. A towering wave had raked the ship over a coral reef then hurled her high on a narrow beach. The swampy jungle inland was inhabited by Indians, he'd said. Tall, well favored people with black hair and eyes, a faint reddish tint to their brown skins. These Indians had treated them well at first, until one of the seamen had raped a young Indian woman. Then the tribe had fallen mercilessly upon them, executing that man with ingenious, fiendish tortures, enslaving the rest. For a year things had remained the same, many of the men dying of fever or from the bites of the many poisonous snakes that haunted the swamps. Finally, during the early summer, Brett had befriended the Chief's eldest son. The boy's canoe had tipped in the water, and a fearsome creature—a huge, scaled lizard with teeth like a shark's—had swum after the frightened boy. Brett had managed to rescue the child, fighting the lizard off with only a gnarled tree limb. In gratitude, the Chief had set the white men free, even helping to repair the badly mauled Cerissa so she could sail again. Finally, he had made Port Royal—just in time to prevent the sale of Sweetwater—and then careened the ship and set sail for England.

Cerissa sighed, turning restlessly in the bed. Brett had insisted he would not see her, would not take the chance of Gerard's discovery of the affair. And, though his eyes were soft and tender, his half-smile sad at the leaving, his jaw was firm and the girl knew he meant what he said. But how could she bear it? Knowing he was alive, knowing he was in England, without being able to be with him. Helpless tears trickled from her eyes to fall soundlessly into the pillow. What could she do? Oh God, what could she do?

Chapter Eleven

Christmas passed without word from Brett, though Jamey received so many presents from Lord Ardsley that Cerissa was sure some were actually from his father. Gerard spoke vaguely about unavoidable delays in processing Jamey's adoption, and though Cerissa began to believe he was not pressing the procedure as urgently as might be, she saw no reason to complain just yet. January was rolling by at last, bringing February's hope of better weather soon. The air was still bitter cold though the sun was bright and Cerissa, anxious for spring decided to go to the London Exchange for spring fabric and trim. Walking slowly around the cloth seller's section, she suddenly held her breath, her ears straining. Were those two women behind her talking about Brett? Was that actually the name she had heard? Starved for news of him, feeling a familiar tightening in her chest, she slowed her steps, pretending to be interested in a piece of velvet cloth.

"Yes, I wouldn't mind marrying Lord Lindsey," the slender

blond smiled to her red-haired friend. "He was certain...ah...qualifications to recommend him."

"Of course," the redhead smirked, "two in particular—he's handsome and terribly rich."

"Not only that," the blond laughed, "he has the most marvelous habit of sailing away to parts unknown! Just think, Marcia, how convenient for maintaining a diverse love life!"

The redhead laughed, fluttering her elaborately painted fan. "But has he asked you yet, Alicia?"

"No," the blond admitted with a sulky pout, throwing an unfriendly glance at her friend for asking the question, "but I'm sure he will. He plans to sail for the Indies again at first thaw, and he's invited me and some mutual friends up to spend a week or so at Whitross, the family manor, before he goes. With a week to work on him—plus, the idea of his sailing again so soon—of course he'll ask me this week."

"When are you leaving dear?"

"Tomorrow, I believe. We'll go by coach to Lichester and spend the night there. We'll get to Whitross the next evening."

"Well, good luck, Alicia." the redhead smirked. "I have a feeling you'll need it. Any man as good looking and wealthy as Brett Lindsey, if he hasn't married by now...my God, isn't he thirty by now? There must be some reason he's been so elusive."

Cerissa stood breathless, her heart hammering, as the two women drifted away out of earshot, chattering all the while. Brett, her Brett, marry that blond. Alicia? Never! Never while she drew breath would she let him go without a fight! And certainly not to someone like that—someone who was already planning her infidelities to him! But what had the women said about him leaving? Sailing for the Indies...oh, beloved Jamaica and the white marble columns of Sweetwater...It was January 22 already. First thaw would come soon, probably the first week of March. Winter had come so early—usually that heralded an early spring as well. She would have to see Brett somehow, even if that meant getting to Whitross. Brett had never taken her there, but he'd talked often enough about it, she knew where it was. But how could she get there? What could she tell Gerard?

She waited up for her husband that night, even though it was well past midnight before he appeared, slightly drunk but in a good enough humor. She forced her face to appear impassive, clasped her hands together to conceal their trembling, as she made casual mention that she'd like to take a visit to the country to visit her family, preferably before the spring planting began that would take all their time from dawn to dusk.

"When do you want to leave, Cerissa?" Gerard questioned carelessly, his blue eyes gleaming with frank desire as he ran his gaze up and down the girl's body, poorly concealed within her clinging bedrobe.

Cerissa shrugged, controlling the shudder that always followed Gerard's expression of desire. "As soon as possible, if you don't mind. Of course, I'll take Jamey too," she added hastily. If he had any suspicions about her sudden departure, that should end them. How many women would take their two-year-old son with them for an assignation?

To her surprise, Gerard agreed easily, almost indifferently and Cerissa glanced at him in amazement. For a man who acted so devoted, Gerard seemed strangely anxious to be free of her for the week. And in spite of all his protested eagerness, she had heard nothing further of his adopting Jamey either. Hastily, she shrugged, forcing such suspicions from her mind. Gerard was in love with her, she assured herself, and he loved Jamey too. In time, the adoption would come through. She was just so ignorant of legal proceedings.

"Why'd you wait up for me, lovey?" he smirked, moving heavily toward her. "Want a little from the old man, huh?"

Cerissa forced a smile as his lips came down on hers, ignoring the faint flash of nausea which always came with Gerard's initial touch. Passively, she yielded to his caresses, following him wordlessly into bed. It was only one night, she told herself over and over as she gave her body to him, by tomorrow I will be on my way to Brett.

The hired coach was musty and well worn inside, the ride bumpy on the rain-rutted roads. It had been pouring since the morning when she and Jamey had boarded the carriage at Lichester. Now, although well past supper time already, the rain continued unabated. She held the baby against her with one arm, cushioning his head in her lap as he slept, content but exhausted by the wonders of their travel. Cerissa stared anxiously out the single window into the darkness. They were entering an oak lined drive, flanked by stone pillars. Perhaps this was Whitross. Or, at least, perhaps they were getting close by now.

Suddenly, the coach lurched to a stop, almost unseating the girl. She scrambled back for her seat as the door opened, the driver announcing they had arrived at Lord Lindsey's manor. Cerissa took a deep breath, looking at the massive, double oak doors, ornately carved and polished to a gleaming sheen. Faint light shone out the windows on one side of the huge, rose-brick house. Someone was here then, she realized, for those wouldn't be servants' quarters there just off the hall. Gently, she eased the little boy off her lap to lay on the seat, and gathering her cloak around her, she stepped out into the rain, reaching for the brass knocker.

After long silent minutes, filled only with the over-loud pounding of her heart in her ears, one of the doors creaked ajar and a stern, unfamiliar man looked out. "May I help you?" The old butler's eyes were frankly sceptical as he stared at the rain-soaked, travel-worn girl.

Cerissa raised her chin, trying to appear as haughty as she guessed a noblewoman would. "Yes. I'd like to see Lord Lindsey, please."

The butler pursed his lips, obviously about to deny her request and slam the door. The girl looked like a country wench to him, pretty enough, but...perhaps one of his lord's casual amours thinking to trouble the man by following here.

"Please, I know Brett...Lord Lindsey is here with Alicia and some friends," Cerissa added hastily. "He's expecting me."

Finally, his lined face reflecting disbelief and faint disapproval, the butler nodded, swinging the door a bit wider. "I'll call him."

Cerissa waited uneasily at the edge of the door, trying to edge into the marble floored hall far enough to get out of the rain. Now that she was here, she almost wished she weren't. What would Brett think when he saw that she'd followed him out here? Mightn't he be angry at her presumptuousness? Maybe, with the blond Alicia for company, he would have no interest any longer in his simple Country girl.

"Someone at the door for you, Lord Lindsey," the butler bowed formally, his face reflecting nothing of his disapproval of the scene here in the drawing room. The room reeked of brandy fumes, wine from the ladies, of too-heavy perfume, and the table was littered with dirty plates and scattered cards. The lord was lying stretched on the sofa, his black head in the blond woman's satined lap, her painted face bending to kiss his ear—a disgusting display, in his opinion. This stuart age was simply too licentious.

Lord Lindsey turned his head carelessly, a bored half-smile on his face, "Who is it, Parker? Not some rain soaked peddlar I hope."

"No sir, not a peddlar. I don't know her name, but she said you were expecting her. I should have known better, my lord, she hardly

looked like someone you'd receive at Whitross. I'll send her away."
He bowed and turned to leave, halted by Lord Lindsey's reluctant
denial.

"Never mind, Parker. I'll go see for myself." Brett sighed and
swung his long legs off the sofa, ignoring Alicia's quick pout.

"Don't be long, Brett," she murmured sulkily, making sure her
pout was a pretty one.

"I won't Alicia," he replied drily. "Do try to survive a few
minutes without me." Without a backward glance, he walked out of
the elegant drawing room, shutting the door behind him, pausing
for a moment to lean back against it, inhaling slowly. He really
didn't care who was at the door, he was happy for the excuse to
leave his company for a while. Each time he left England, he found
it harder to return to the insipid, frivolous society of the London
gentry. He stretched leisurely, hating the confining snugness of his
formal brocade jacket, then turned again to open the main door.

"Cerissa?" Brett stared dumbfounded at the rain-soaked girl,
then grabbed her quickly to pull her out of the weather into the hall.
"Jesus Christ, Cerissa! What the hell . . . ?"

"Brett, please . . . please don't be angry," she blurted hastily. "I
had to come. I heard you were leaving again."

"Yes, but how . . ." Brett shook his head angrily, his green eyes
troubled "You shouldn't be here, Cerissa. How did you get here?
Where's Gerard?"

"Gerard's in London, Brett. I told him I was visiting family. He
wasn't suspicious—he even seemed anxious for me to go. And I
brought Jamey, we came by that coach out there."

"Jamey's with you?" For a moment, Brett fell silent, an
involuntary pleasure lighting his eyes. Cerissa watched him
hopefully, holding her breath. But finally, the dark haired lord
shook his head again, slowly this time, with obvious reluctance.
"Hell, sweetheart, you've got to go back."

Cerissa felt her face flush with rebellion. "I'm not going back,
Brett. I'm not going to let you marry Alicia without . . ."

"Marry Alicia?" he interrupted, surprise widening his eyes.
Reluctantly he chuckled, his gaze teasing. "Who said I was
marrying Alicia?"

Cerissa opened her mouth to reply, then stopped, hearing the
blond woman's voice calling from the salon. "Who is it Brett?
Hurry up, we're ready to play cards."

Lord Lindsey frowned. "I'll be there in a minute, Alicia," he
called back, the tight lines of his jaw indicating his impatience with

170

the woman. Cerissa noted his expression and felt her heart begin to beat more normally. He wasn't in love with the blond woman, thank God.

"Brett, please let me stay," she pleaded quietly, her blue eyes locked with his. "I can't bear it without you—knowing you're alive, knowing you're in England, but not being with you. Please, please, Brett. If you're leaving so soon, can't we have just a few days together? No one will ever know."

Slowly, as if drawn against his will, the lord moved toward her, his arms reaching out to catch the girl against his chest as she flew to him, her hands clutching his jacket. His head bent down to hers, his lips touching hers as a sound almost like a groan escaped his mouth. Beneath her fingers, Cerissa felt the muscles of Brett's back tighten and begin to tremble. "Oh Jesus. I've missed you," he murmured against her ear as he raised his head at last. "I know I should send you right home, sweetheart, but damned if I can do it."

Cerissa smiled despite the tears in her eyes. The pained reluctance in his eyes, the uneasiness written on his face meant nothing so long as she could stay. She could soothe the trouble out of his grey-green eyes, she knew it. As long as she had the time, she could do anything.

"I have company in here, sweet, you and Jamey will have to stay in the cottage for a couple days. It's small, but I don't want to chance anyone here seeing you. I'll think of some way to get rid of them, but it may take some time. I'll send servants out to light a fire and get you settled."

"Will you be able to come see us tonight, Brett?" she whispered hesitantly, glancing nervously toward the drawing room door.

"Yes, but it's liable to be quite late. You go to sleep if you want. I'll wake you."

Cerissa nodded, her happiness shining in her eyes as she drew her hood up and turned for the door, waiting while Brett gave low-voiced instructions to the dour butler. At last, with a final lingering kiss of promise, he left her. She stood for a moment, watching him go remembering so well the easy balance of his walk, on land or ship, the arrogant swing of his broad shoulders. Finally she turned to the door, throwing a quick smile at the obviously astonished butler before reentering the coach for the short drive to the summer cottage.

It was very late, after two Cerissa guessed, when she finally heard Lord Lindsey's light footsteps coming down the flag stoned path toward the cottage. A moment later, the door opened and

171

Brett walked in, tossing his cloak onto a chair, moving nearer the fire. "Sorry I'm so late, sweetheart, I . . . ah . . . didn't want to arouse Alicia's suspicions by coming earlier."

Cerissa smiled. "I don't mind, Brett," she murmured quietly, reaching one hand out to clasp his and bring it against her face. She knew he had just come from the blond woman's bed, but she was strangely not jealous. A faint smile lingered on her face as she looked at the dark haired lord standing beside her, his handsome profile shadowed by the dying fire's light, dressed only in velvet breeches and a lace edged formal shirt, minus the jacket and formal, knee length over vest. His white shirt was buttoned only a few inches up from the waist, the neck hanging wide open from the weight of the unfastened lace stock, the matching lace of the cuffs, also unbuttoned, hanging almost to the knuckles of his hands. He hadn't bothered with the more formal stockings and buckled shoes either, but had merely drawn on his high black riding boots instead. Cerissa smiled, remembering so well how much Brett preferred the simpler clothing of the islands to the high-fashion of Court. For Alicia, he would wear the required satins and stiff brocades, but to come to her he abandoned his pretense. How like a little boy he was at times.

"This is crazy, Cerissa, we both know this is a mistake. Let me put you on a carriage."

The girl shook her head firmly, holding his hand tighter. "You're wrong, Brett, this isn't a mistake. This is the most sensible thing I've done in months. I made a mistake marrying Gerard, but then, even I had begun to believe you dead by then. I shouldn't have. Some tiny part of my soul always knew you were alive, still, I think, but I ignored it and went on with the wedding anyway, knowing it was wrong. And I made another mistake waiting so long to come to you. I wasted all these months I could have seen you. But I'm not going back to London now, Brett, because that would be the third mistake. I love you and I'm staying here for however long you'll have me." Cerissa's voice was firm and her chin raised in characteristic stubbornness, her eyes slate colored with determination. Brett glanced at her sideways, chuckling at her expression.

"Seems to me I've seen that look on your face before, sweet, and it usually means I've lost the argument," he grinned. "I have to admit this is one I'd just as soon give in on anyway. So you stay. But out here, out of sight, until the others leave. Please, sweetheart, agree to that much caution at least."

Cerissa nodded, her smile content, waiting for Brett to come closer to her. It had been a year and a half since she had last laid in his arms, and the time hung heavy between them, making her shy. No matter, she thought, in his own time he will come. Just now, he was standing beside her, staring into the fire, his face solemn, his eyes still troubled. She knew he was struggling to justify his decision to let her stay, struggling to make himself believe they could have this time together without risking Gerard's discovery and subsequent fury. At last, Cerissa patted the padded arm of the huge, upholstered chair she had curled up in waiting for him, wordlessly inviting him to share her seat with her. Brett turned his head slowly and looked down at her, his eyes warm. After a long moment, he bent down over her, dropping his dark head to hers, sliding one arm behind her as his mouth covered hers. Cerissa melted against him, tears filling her eyes to feel the sweet trembling warmth of his lips, the soul-filling ecstasy of his touch. In a minute, he bent and lifted her off the chair, laying her down on the rug by the fire, his hands moving over her, seeking the belt of her bedrobe and then the buttons of his own breeches.

Cerissa yielded fearlessly to the almost desperate harshness of his loving, returning his hungry kisses, not flinching under the nearly painful pressure of his fingers on her breasts. Though he would not admit it, was perhaps not even consciously aware of it, she had guessed Brett was still slightly angry. His lovemaking had confirmed it. Angry perhaps at her for marrying another man, angry at the months of missing her, angry too, probably, at himself for wanting her so badly he had agreed to such a foolhardy risk as this. She returned his bruising kisses gently, her hands caressing his face and muscled shoulders with soothing slowness, murmuring soft words of love and pleasure against his ear. And gradually, she managed to gentle him, to quiet him as he lay above her. Though his breathing was no less ragged, nor his face less flushed, his lips grew softer against her, his tongue caressing instead of punishing as it filled her mouth and traced the outline of her lips. His hands moved over her more gently, his fingers kind and lingering on the taut nipples of her breasts, his touch slow and caressing as he slid his hand down over her belly and between her thighs. Still, she forced him to wait, forcing herself to wait as well while lightning tremors of heat stabbed her loins, demanding she fill her throbbing body with his maleness. At last, the pressure of his knee between her thighs grew coaxing instead of demanding, and she allowed him to spread her thighs apart, giving him welcome. With a moan, he penetrated her, plunging deep within her aching body, his mouth still fixed on hers, his arms possessive and tight around her as he moved within her, thrusting with barely controlled masculine power until she moaned and writhed beneath him in passionate response. Cerissa drew her legs up, flinging them over his to lock his hips closer against her, rocking her hips in harmony with his, whimpering in helpless ecstasy to feel him fill her completely with his hot body. Suddenly, she reached down, clutching him to her as her body exploded in brilliant throbbing waves of pleasure, leaving her nearly senseless, hardly aware of Brett's own shuddering ecstasy above her.

For long minutes she lay breathless beneath his weight, her eyes still closed, her arms wrapped around him. At last, she felt him draw a deep breath and raise his head from her chest to roll beside her. She smiled faintly and snuggled against him in total contentment, her head finding its usual place on his shoulder as easily as if it had been days instead of years since they'd been together. Cerissa lay silent for a little while, enjoying the soft caresses of his hand, breathing deeply of his dear, familiar smell. Even here in England he wore the lime cologne he had used in Jamaica. It did not seem possible that their time in the islands was now years behind them. "Have you missed me, Brett?" she murmured softly at last, moving her head to rest against his cheek.

"You should know you don't have to ask that question, you're only fishing for compliments."

Cerissa felt the muscles of his face move as he spoke and she knew he was smiling. With a sigh of contentment she nestled ever closer against him. "I know," she admitted. "I missed you too." She fell silent for a moment as a faint frown formed on her face. "Why do you have to leave England again so soon, Brett? Why don't you stay until summer at least?"

The lord shrugged, the faint smile fading from his mouth. "England offers little to hold me here, anymore, sweetheart."

Cerissa bit her lip in a fresh agony of remorse. Damn Gerard! Why had she ever married that...

"When are you leaving, Brett? And where are you going this time? Back to Sweetwater?"

Brett smiled faintly again to hear the wistfulness in the girl's voice. He turned his head to touch her hair with his lips. "Maybe, although I'd like to see more of that new colony, Carolina, while I'm away this time. They say it's beautiful, and the land very rich. If it is, I'll probably buy some additional property there. As to when I'll be sailing, well . . . that depends on the weather. As soon as I can get the

Sea Queen and Brighton out of the Thames, we'll go. The Cerissa is anchored at Portsmouth, so she's no problem."

"How long is that then, Brett?" she questioned softly, "A month or so?"

"Yes, probably."

"And how long can we be here together, Brett?"

"Only a week, sweetheart, maybe ten days."

"Make it ten days!" she pleaded instantly turning her face to his. Brett smiled and nodded. "Ten days then, but no more. I promised King Charles I'd be back at Whitehall by February 4, at the latest, to talk to him about the political and economic state of the Indies. Then I have to select cargo to take back to Jamaica, and hire a crew, and visit Isaac Benjamin, the goldsmith, as well." Brett frowned quickly in the half light, remembering the reason for that errand. While he'd been in London, he had carefully, though unobtrusively, checked up on Cerissa's husband. From what he had heard, it appeared that Squire Whitestone was back to his old habits. Many of the evenings which Cerissa had mentioned spending alone, Gerard had evidently spent gambling. Before Brett left England again, he would check with the goldsmith to find out how much of Cerissa's five thousand pounds remained. He didn't like Whitestone, and he didn't trust him. Ardsley should have picked a better man for the girl. Brett turned his head to ask Cerissa how Jamey's adoption was progressing, then smiled and remained silent. The girl was sound asleep, her face the picture of contentment. Perhaps he'd better not mention his suspicions of Gerard to the girl. It would only upset her needlessly. He'd just check with Benjamin, and caution Ardsley to keep an eye on Cerissa and Jamey for him while he was gone. That would be sufficient.

Cerissa woke with the feeling that someone was staring at her. She opened her eyes, smiling drowsily to see Brett's face above hers.

"I have to go back in now, sweetheart." he murmured quietly, touching her face with a gentle hand.

Cerissa nodded, not complaining. She could see the first rose and orange of dawn lighting the sky. He was right, it was time for him to get back. "Tonight again, love?" she asked reaching down to draw the blanket Brett had covered them with last night up higher over her shoulders.

"If I can sweetheart," he nodded. "Why don't you go in to bed? You'd be more comfortable there."

She only shook her head slightly and settled it back into the pillow which still bore a faint scent of Brett's lime cologne, smiling happily. With a last, reluctant kiss he left her to seek his own bed up in the manor. Cerissa watched him until the door shut quietly behind him, then settled back to sleep. She knew Brett would come back again tonight, even if it were late again. He could not more resist the pull of her soul on his than she could his on hers.

So Cerissa waited patiently, spending the next two days inside the small cottage with Jamey and a servant girl she had instantly named "Aunt Mary." With Jamey the age he was, she could not expect him to understand the necessary secrecy of their visit to Whitross. So she had done what she could, calling the servant by her aunt's name, referring to the cottage as Bainwater. The little boy accepted it all in stride, apparently as delighted as his mother by the adventure.

The third night, Brett came in even later than before, wearing a weary grin of satisfaction as he walked in. He returned Cerissa's greeting kiss then stepped away, shaking his dark head and laughing as he threw himself full length on the blue velvet couch. "Sorry sweetheart, not tonight," he grinned, his eyes teasing but genuinely tired. "I guess my old age is showing but I can't keep up with both you and Alicia."

Cerissa laughed back, tossing her head haughtily. "Then you'll have to get rid of Alicia," she retorted. "I don't intend to be treated so shabbily!" She dropped to her knees beside the sofa, reaching her hand up to take the hand Brett offered.

"That's just what I did," he mumbled, his eyes already closed though his mouth still grinned. "The whole stupid bunch of them are leaving for Bath tomorrow, about noon. You and Jamey can move up to the house as soon as they're gone."

Cerissa laughed in wicked delight. "Oh Brett, what in the world did you tell them? Poor Alicia must be furious that she never got that marriage proposal from you she was counting on."

"Told them I had business affairs here . . . and mentioned that I was not feeling too well. Of course, I didn't tell them my ill health was due to keeping a demanding mistress here in the summer house."

Cerissa only smiled, knowing Brett too well to take his teasing seriously. She leaned her head against his hand, tired herself. In a moment, she felt the muscles of Brett's hand relax and she looked up to see him already sleeping. With a fond smile, she replaced his hand carefully on the couch and reached for a knitted blanket to cover him, brushing a stray strand of ebony hair back from his forehead. He was thirty one now, as of November past, nearly three years older than when she had first met him. Except for the slight deepening of the smile lines at the corners of his wide set eyes, he looked much the same, his raven hair still full and thick and untouched by silver. With a last kiss, Cerissa turned away, covering a yawn with the back of her hand. Tomorrow afternoon she would coax Brett into having a winter picnic with she and Jamey. Eight whole blissful days of being together lay ahead of them now, a virtual eternity . . .

Brett was grinning when he walked in after bidding his guests goodbye. Alicia's poorly concealed frustration had amused him, obviously Cerissa had been right when she'd said the blond had expected a marriage proposal. Yet their parting had been pleasant enough. Perhaps she yet had hopes that she would snare him before he sailed. He sant into a chair, resting his long booted legs on top of Cerissa's packed trunk, chuckling at her obvious eagerness to move into the main house. She was always that way, like a child sometimes, so easily excited about things.

"Not ready to move already?" he drawled teasingly as she hurried in, holding a squirming two year old in her arms.

"Oh . . . Brett," Cerissa's surprise showed on her face. "Are they gone?"

"Yes, sweet, all gone. Who's that I see?" he asked grinning at the wide eyed boy.

"Say hello, Jamey," Cerissa urged the shy child gently.

"Who that?" the child lipped, pointing directly at his father.

Brett grinned at Cerissa, delighted to hear the boy talk so clearly. They were the first words he'd ever heard his son say. "Well, who am I?"

Cerissa shrugged apologetically, wishing with all her heart she could tell the child the truth but knowing she couldn't. "How about Uncle Wat?"

Brett grimaced, but nodded. "There are people I'd rather be, but . . . Uncle Wat I shall be for a week. Come here, Jamey, and tell me what you'd like to do best of all this afternoon."

The child smiled quickly, breaking away from his mother to climb on the lord's knee. "We going picnic?" he asked, his grey-green eyes staring up innocently into his father's matching ones.

"Yes, Jamey, whatever you like," Brett promised, his gaze tender and proud as he looked at his son's beautiful face. "Whatever you like."

177

The eight days that had seemed so endless to Cerissa passed with terrible swiftness. And suddenly, it was time to return to London—to Gerard, to her life as his wife, to long, lonely nights without the man she adored.

Despite her pleadings and her tears Brett refused to continue their clandestine affair in London. He would not risk the scandal of discovery, nor would he accept the half-joy of sharing Cerissa with another man. He still had not mentioned Gerard's excessive gambling to Cerissa, nor did he mean to even now. Instead, he would check on the squire's behavior a bit closer upon returning to London. Then, if his suspicions were proved correct, he might drop word of it in the king's ear and suggest a divorce proceeding. He was sure Cerissa would be delighted to be free of her husband, and he himself could imagine no other solution to their dilemma. Jamey might lose his chance to be adopted and hence gain legitimacy, yet that was a small price to pay for a long, happy future with his own father able to claim him once again.

Of course, he didn't dare mention a word of such plans to the girl. If, as well it might, any one of a hundred things disrupted the scheme, Brett would bear the disappointment alone. To raise Cerissa's hopes, then have to dash them, would be needlessly cruel. Better for the girl to believe their affair must simply be suspended for a time.

Lord Lindsey nodded wordlessly to James, Duke of York, Charles' brother and, it appeared now, imminent heir to the throne of England. It still seemed incredible. Two days before he had spent hours out riding with the king, explaining the slave trade, the French dangers, the crops, the weather, the spirit of the Indies, and once, a fairly casual observation about a certain squire's indiscretions. Then yesterday, for another hour, he had elaborated on economics and politics before Charles' council while the king had listened avidly, in perfect health. Charles had spoken so passionately of the sailing ships, the need for a greater navy, that one of the lords had finally joked about it, remarking that the Duchess of Portsmouth and Castlemaine, Duchess of Cleveland would be put into a frenzy if they ever discovered the king's favored mistress, the main beneficiary of his generosity, was a sea going lady and not themselves. They had all laughed heartily, Charles loudest of all, ruefully admitting the truth of the jest.

Yet now in the space of less than a single day, the king lay dying. No doctors or prayers could help any longer. The merry monarch of

England was on his death bed, stricken by a massive stroke.

Brett shifted his shoulders against the uncomfortable wood back of the chair wondering again why Charles had sent for him. He had been here almost two hours now while the king had issued last instructions to a dozen officers of the government. Now only he and James and the physician were left in the sumptuous room. Even the doctor now was gathering his instruments, admitting defeat and preparing to go.

"Doctor," Charles' voice was remarkably strong as he raised a commanding hand at the man. "Do me a favor please. Apologize for me to my courtiers outside. Tell them I'm sorry to be taking such an unconscionable time to die."

Despite himself, Brett frowned, his grey-green eyes angry as he stared down at his clenched fist. Damn, he thought disgustedly, is nothing, not even death respected any longer in the abysmal superficiality of this Court?

"What are you scowling at Lindsey?" the king chuckled suddenly, staring in obvious amusement at the dark haired lord.

Brett shook his head, shrugging. "You shouldn't do that, Charles, it's not right," he replied, meeting the king's questioning stare with serious eyes.

"Shouldn't do what, my noble sea captain?" Charles chuckled. "Shouldn't die or shouldn't take so long to do it?"

Brett grinned in spite of himself, a bit ruefully. Charles' merriment, even on his death bed, was infectious. How many times had he heard the man criticized for being too affable, too witty for a king? "You shouldn't apologize for it, damn it," he smiled his eyes still troubled. "Does your cynicism never end, Charles?"

"Never," the king replied promptly. "You know that, Lindsey. Besides, since when are you a rosy eyed romantic? A couple of years ago you were as bad even worse, than I. What turned you into such an idealist?"

Brett chuckled softly, embarrassed, spreading his hands in a gesture of helpless apology. "I fell in love with a country wench," he answered at last, grinning at the king's expression of exaggerated horror.

"Od's blood," Charles shuddered with a laugh. "What a miserable fate!" He met the dark lord's eyes for a long moment, his gaze fond but a touch unbelieving. Finally he spoke again. "Why shouldn't I apologize to the Court, Lindsey? You know they're all standing out there, milling about like cattle. They don't think they ought to dance, or sing, or play cards while I'm in here passing away, so they're all bored silly. I never liked to bore anyone."

Brett shrugged again, his face serious once more. "Nothing I say will change either you or them, Charles," he admitted candidly. "So let's just say such superficiality at such a time as this is . . . well, it's just uncomfortable for me. What can I do for you, Charles, why did you call me in here?"

"I thought, if you didn't mind, I'd ask you to tell me a few good sailing stories while I wait for . . . while I wait," the king smiled. "You know I love the sea and I love to hear of it, and I've been so damn busy most of my life I haven't indulged my passion to the fullest. So, since I happen to have some time just now, if you oblige me . . ."

Brett nodded, moving to the bed. He spoke at length of seamen legends, great feats of navigation or courage, the feel of the helm in a tropical storm, the taste of the air in the spice islands. The king listened, his eyes wistful, his face even more pale against the bleached linen pillow. "Next to being king, I'd have been a captain," he murmured at last, smiling faintly. "Thank you, Lindsey. Just hearing of such things . . ." Charles turned his head with an effort, gesturing to his brother James.

"James, if you'll step away a moment, I have something private to say to Lord Lindsey."

Brett frowned slightly, caught off guard by the king's words, waiting uneasily for the Duke of York to move to the other end of the room. What did Charles have to say? There had been no time to mention his problem concerning Cerissa and Squire Whitestone, so what?

"Lindsey, a very special request . . ." the king's voice was growing more labored already. The end could not be far off now . . . "Monmouth . . . the Duke of Monmouth, my son. He's in the Netherlands, Lindsey, and I worry . . . I have told him so many times but I know he still has hopes of becoming king. He mustn't try, Lindsey, he can't possibly succeed, I'm sure of it. But Argyll will try to encourage him, others too, for their own reasons. Go for me to the Netherlands. Tell him I spoke to you. Convince him to be content with what he is, what he has, not to attempt a rebellion. Please, Lindsey, there are so few I could trust with such a mission, and your ship is anchored at Plymouth, free to go."

Brett stood silent a moment, knowing the dangers inherent in such a scheme. Reluctant too, to leave London just now with Cerissa still ignorant of his plans, the girl and his son dependent on a man he'd grown to dislike and distrust more and more as he'd investigated him further. Yet, how could he refuse the king who had always been uncommonly good to him, uncommonly kind, who now lay dying?

Finally, still filled with misgivings, Brett nodded slowly, forcing a half-smile to belie his troubled thoughts. The Duke of York started to make his way back toward the royal sick-bed, sensing the audience was at an end.

Brett bowed and said the required formal farewell due a king, then paused a minute more, staring down at the dying man. Impulsively, he held out his hand, gripping the king's in fond sorrow. "Goodbye, Charles." he murmured at last, forcing a broader smile. "Keep an eye on my ships from up there."

The king chuckled, nodding. "Yes, I never believed God would damn a man for enjoying life's pleasures, Lindsey. I'll try to arrange a good wind and calm seas for you." Charles watched the dark haired lord as he strode quickly from the room. He'd known the man's mother quite well in his younger days when the court had lived in exile in Brede. Often when he spoke to him, he wondered whether Brett might possibly be his own son. He was the only child Abby Lindsey had ever conceived in her twenty year marriage to Brett's father. Strange that it had coincided so closely with their own affair.

"You know the problem of the colonies?" he questioned his brother finally. "They'll drain our best men away from us, James. Look at Lord Lindsey, one of the few truly strong, intelligent men sitting today in the House of Lords. But he'll leave us for the islands, or Virginia perhaps, one of these days. Damned shame." Charles fell silent again, pleased with the notion that he might be Lord Lindsey's true father. There would be a son to take pride in...."A country wench," he chuckled softly to himself, his eyes gleaming with merriment. "Od's blood!"

Brett caught sight of Ardsley as he left the king's room and walked quickly toward him, hating the day, hating the court, suddenly eager to be free of England and back to sea. A man caught up his arm as he passed and held it until he turned.

"Is he dead yet?" the man queried petulantly. "This interminable waiting is driving me mad!"

Brett stared at the man in incredulous fury, finally swearing viciously and beginning to draw his rapier out of the hilt. Ardsley pushed through the crowd to grab his friend's arm, whispering hastily to him and pulling him toward the open garden door.

Behind the two men, the people buzzed loudly, astonished and amused at Lord Lindsey's show of temper. The man he had nearly drawn sword against, managed a nervous, deprecating laugh. "Od's lud, but he's prickly as a thornbush, isn't he? You'd think I'd insulted him the way he acted..."

Gerard's announcement of King Charles' death shocked Cerissa and she stared at her husband in speechless dismay, remembering suddenly Brett's uneasiness about the king's possible heirs. The squire explained the day's events slowly, obviously relishing his own self-importance as the bearer of such monumental news, elaborating on the king's collapse, the subsequent details of a frantic organization to prepare to pass the throne to James, Duke of York, now, though uncrowned, king of England, the hush and the weeping when the death itself was announced.

Cerissa listened, still half dazed, feeling unexpected sorrow at Charles' passing. Brett had spoken kindly of him, even affectionately at times, of his innate kindness, his generosity, his easy, merry laugh. The brother, James, was reputed, by contrast, grim and stubborn. How would England adjust to such a radical change?

"Another strange thing, Cerissa, Lord Lindsey nearly killed Martin Bickley right there in Whitehall this afternoon. He'd just come out of the king's apartments, and looked black as thunder. All Martin did was ask whether Charles was dead yet! He was as tired of standing around, waiting and waiting, as the rest of us. But when he said something, Lindsey whirled around on the poor man, pulling that wicked rapier of his nearly free of the sheath. Luckily, Lord Ardsley managed to grab his arm and get him outside before any blood was spilt."

Cerissa stared at her husband, feeling faintly nauseous. "You mean Bickley actually said he was bored?" she asked incredulously, not believing she could have understood Gerard's explanation correctly. Surely, not even the Court was that callous.

"Why, yes, of course," Gerard snapped petulantly. "Why not?"

"But...that's horrible, Gerard, to think he...didn't he even care about the king?"

"Well of course he cared, we all loved Charles," he replied sullenly, half turning away from her accusing stare. "But that doesn't mean we felt like standing there doing nothing all day long. Oh, it was exciting enough at first, but later..."

Cerissa swallowed hard, feeling her lip curl in an involuntary grimace of utter loathing and disgust, as if she had just found something unpleasant under a wet rock. She saw Gerard stare at her, a frown forming on his face and she hastily forced a strained smile, pretending agreement. "So what did Lord Lindsey do, darling?" she asked as casually as she could, nervously aware of the sudden color rising up her neck.

Gerard sulked a minute more, then relented, enjoying Cerissa's attention. Usually she showed little interest in Court gossip. "Well, King Charles had called him in, no one knows why, perhaps Lindsey wanted some money or some land or something. My guess is he was turned down for whatever he wanted, because he was obviously in a terrible humor when he walked out. I tell you," he repeated, carefully, nodding his head for emphasis, "if Lord Ardsley hadn't deterred him, there would have been a duel right there in the drawing room. I used to know Lord Lindsey quite well," he bragged. "Quite well. He used to be some fun, very amusing at times, he could be. But even then he walked around with one hand on his sword all the time. A habit, I assumed from living so long among the pirates and ruffians in the colonies. But he's been fearfully unpleasant to almost everyone this past winter. I don't know how Lord Ardsley stands him."

Cerissa pretended to concentrate on her knitting though her mind was miles away, her thoughts whirling. She knew why Brett had turned on Martin Bickley and she was glad he had, proud of him for it. Of course, Gerard would never understand, very few of the Court would. The scene had obviously appalled Brett, disgusted him as it had her. It had nothing to do with a petition not granted. Brett needed nothing from King Charles. He had probably only gone out of friendship, for he had been strangely close to the Stuart king.

Suddenly, Cerissa frowned slightly, throwing her husband a studying glance from under her lowered lashes. Strange that Gerard—who had loved her passionately enough to marry her despite the difference in their social stations, who professed to love his stepson so strongly that he was willing to adopt the child—strange that he could be so callous, so totally superficial in all other regards. She jumped in startled surprise, pricking her finger with the long needle, as realization hit her. She really wasn't sure of Gerard's love at all. Oh, he told her—told anyone who would listen in fact—how deeply he adored her, how precious the child Jamey was...but did he actually mean it? With a sense of surprise, Cerissa realized that she had begun to have misgivings about her husband months ago, but she had never dared admit them to herself. Certainly Gerard worked hard enough at convincing her, and Lord Ardsley, their friends, even the servants . . . when anyone was around, he practically fawned on her, rather making a fool of himself actually. Yet, Cerissa realized looking back, when they were alone, he rarely was so attentive. In fact, they did not even share that sense of easy contentment that she and Brett had when they were in the same room. Oh, and all last week, hadn't she spent the time assuring Brett of Gerard's undoubted devotion, thinking to ease his troubled thoughts about keeping her at Whitross? Hadn't Brett merely stared at her strangely those times, never agreeing, but never disagreeing either? Did he doubt Gerard's sincerity too? Did he wonder too, whether the man's protestations were fact or sham? Probably so . . . Brett alone then, of all their friends, shared her misgivings. Lord Ardsley, she knew, was completely deceived. He often congratulated himself on being such a successful watchmaker. But what would Gerard have to gain by marrying her? He had a title, though not a grand one, lands, and even a manor somewhere northeast of London. Why should he pretend to love her so conscientiously, then? What could she offer him but herself?

Thoroughly uneasy, Cerissa glanced again at her husband. She had to talk to Brett before he sailed again this spring, she simply had to. Gerard, like many of the lesser gentry, was an obsessive social climber. He always pushed her to pursue her friendship with Ardsley, fawning over the lord when he came to visit, almost pathetically courting the man's friendship. Perhaps she could use that . . . "Lady Ardsley had asked me to visit her tomorrow," she lied casually. "But I suppose, with Charles' death . . ."

"No, no," Gerard turned, shaking his head, his eyes bright and sharp as a weasel's. "That won't matter, go ahead. I like to see you enjoy your lady friends, it does you good."

Cerissa hid a small smile. He was really so easily fooled. "I'll go then, I guess. May I use the carriage?"

"Of course, love," he replied magnanimously. "You can't very well visit the wife of a future Earl in a rented coach. And wear that new satin gown, the lilac one. You look especially lovely in that."

Cerissa nodded, pretending indifference, as she resumed her knitting. Pray God Brett would be at Ardsley's, or that the blond lord would know where to find him. She was growing surer and surer that there was something odd afoot. Brett would know what to do.

184

"I'm sorry, Mrs. Whitestone, but Lord Lindsey left for Portsmouth his morning, very early."

Cerissa smiled, thanking the woman as she tried to conceal her disappointment. "And Lord Ardsley, is he here?"

"Sorry, ma'am, he's gone to Whitehall for the day. With King Charles gone, and King James yet to be crowned, I don't doubt there's plenty to do. Will you leave a message?"

The girl considered a moment, then shook her head. What message could she leave for Ardsley? That she had begun to doubt Gerard's sincerity and affection? She had no real complaint about him other than that . . . he was still the model husband. "No, I guess not," she replied at last. "Thank you. Just tell Lord Ardsley I stopped."

Chapter Twelve

Gerard answered the door personally when he noticed Lord Ardsley's carriage pull up to the curb outside. The fine, warm sunshine of the April morning promised a good day for hunting. Perhaps he could manuever the blond lord into inviting him along for a day's sport.

"Good morning, Squire," Ardsley nodded as he walked in. "Is Cerissa at home?"

"No," Gerard lied easily. "She's out shopping already. You know how women are when spring arrives. All the winter gowns are immediately passé. Of course, I know I spoil her terribly, but . . ." he laughed and shrugged.

The blond lord chuckled in reply, turning back to the door. "When she comes in, will you give her a message from me? My father has taken very ill and I'm leaving at once to go to the family manor. If she has need of me, she can send a message there to Marlham." Already half out of the house, Ardsley didn't notice the way the squire's eyes narrowed unpleasantly, an odd expression flickering in them for a moment. "How long will you be gone?" Gerard asked, pretending only casual interest.

"I really don't know. It might only be a couple weeks, but it might be a couple months, too."

"It must be nice in the country this time of year."

Lord Ardsley glanced over his shoulder at the squire, a faint smile on his lips. "Well, you and Cerissa are welcome to come visit if we plan to stay very long. Just send a note up first." He waved and walked hastily away. Gerard's constant importuning, hardly even subtle, had begun to wear on his nerves. If it weren't for Cerissa and the boy, he would avoid the fellow altogether. But, he had promised Brett before his friend had left so suddenly for Portsmouth that he would keep careful eye on the girl in his absence. Of course, Brett's dislike of the squire was probably rooted in possessive jealousy, yet maybe not. Lindsey was usually a fairly accurate judge of character. It was unfortunate he hadn't caught the girl at home, but surely her husband would relay the message. It was only a few days travel to Marlham where he would be. If the girl did have any reason to reach him, she could do so easily.

Cerissa thought Gerard's eyes shone with peculiar expression when she came down the stairs, but he turned quickly to smile pleasantly as he greeted her, and she shrugged her uneasiness away.

"Going shopping, love?" he questioned, holding her cloak up around her shoulders.

"Yes, Gerard, to the Exchange. Can I get anything for you?"

"No, not a thing. I think I'll go out a while myself today. You just go ahead and enjoy yourself. Buy something for Jamey if you like."

Cerissa smiled, regretting her earlier suspicions of the man. Gerard had been more considerate, more devoted than ever recently. "I would like to get the boy out of skirts," she agreed, "since he's two already, he should be in breeches now and jackets. Maybe I'll buy some lightweight satins or velvets for his summer clothes."

"Good idea, love," he agreed lightly, holding the door for her, "see you this evening."

Cerissa spent most of the day at the Exchange, choosing the fabrics for Jamey with eagerness and care. It was quite late, nearly dusk by the time she returned home and she hurried up the stairs, hoping to share dinner with her son since Gerard was not yet home. She found the baby still sleeping—evidently his afternoon nap had been late today—and a roast capon dinner was laid out on a tray in her sitting room. A scrawny kitten Jamey had dragged in two days before was circling the table hungrily, mewing its hunger, its huge golden eyes pleading for food. As she took up the knife to begin carving the chicken, she heard Jamey shuffling out, his small, round face still flushed from sleep, his small hands rubbing at his eyes.

"Me hungry, mama," he lisped softly, bending down to pat the kitten with the flat of one hand, grabbing for the cat's tail as it tried to scurry away from the child's overzealous attention.

"In a minute, Jamey. Kitty asked first," Cerissa smiled, laying several slices of the fowl on a plate and placing it on the rug. "Now, I'll cut some for you and I."

She took up the knife again, slicing deeply into the succulent, browned breast, her mouth watering. Suddenly, she heard Jamey give a soft cry of puzzled frustration, and she turned to see him pulling one leg of the motionless kitten angrily, urging the cat to stop sleeping and get up. Cerissa frowned, reaching down for the kitten, feeling its skinny body still and lifeless under her fingertips. She stared at the animal in disbelief, touching the matted fur gently. What in the world . . . ?

"What wrong with Kitty?" Jamey questioned imperatively, staring at the cat.

"She's . . . she's sleeping, sweetheart," she answered hesitantly. "Put the chicken back on Kitty's plate, Jamey, that's dirty, Kitty licked it."

"No, me hungry," he answered rebelliously, putting the meat to his lips.

Cerissa reached over and snatched the food away from the child, scolding him for his disobedience. "Now you be a good boy, Jamey. Mommy's going to put the Kitty away while she's sleeping." She bent and started to reach for the dead cat, repressing her innate sense of distaste, then suddenly halted, sniffing closely at her fingers where they'd held the chicken. There was a peculiar odor clinging to them, a bitter smell . . . "Oh my God!" she choked, stumbling back to her feet, staring at the dead animal in sick fascination. The chicken was poisoned . . . that was the smell . . . that was what had killed the kitten . . . But who . . . why . . . ?

The scrape of a plate behind her brought the girl whirling around, her heart in her throat. "No, Jamey," she cried, making a lunge for the child's hand.

He darted away, one fist full of the meat, his green eyes defiant. "Me hungry!" he squealed. "Me eat! Me do it!"

Cerissa stood helpless for a breathless moment, meeting the boy's willful gaze. If she tried to grab it he would only run again and shove the chicken into his mouth all the faster.

"Please, darling," she coaxed, her voice cracking in her terror. "Please wait for Mama. See, this is your plate. Let's set the table. You put your chicken here on your plate and I'll put this chicken on mine, see?" She paused hopefully, but the child hadn't budged. She drew a deep breath and tried again. "Remember how we had a picnic together—you, and, Uncle Wat and I? Wasn't that fun? Let's do that again."

The child smiled, looking toward the door. "Uncle Wat coming?"

"Yes, sweet, in a few minutes," she lied quickly, thanking God for the inspiration. Jamey had taken so to Brett in only that one week—much more than to Gerard though he had lived with him for months. "Now you want to be a good boy for Uncle Wat, don't you?"

The child nodded eagerly, running to the table to hurl his chicken on the plate. Instantly, Cerissa grabbed his arm, wiping his hand clean with a linen napkin, clasping the boy tightly against her as she ran into her bedroom, locking the door behind her. Jamey wailed indignantly at the deception, but she ignored his temper, concentrating on the horrifying revelations of the past hour. The chicken had been poisoned, deliberately poisoned—then set out for she and Jamey to consume for supper. Who could have done such a thing? Who would want to? They only had two servants in the house, and both had seemed friendly and loyal, obviously fond of the baby. Neither of them would have anything to gain, either, by her death. And who else but Gerard . . . ?

Cerissa's face turned ashen as she sank slowly onto the bed in growing horror, her stomach churning, her hands shaking. Gerard. He had found out about her meeting Brett at Whitross. He must have. But to murder her . . . Jamey too . . . She shuddered violently, remembering the kitten's open, sightless eyes, her stiff legs. She had to get out of the house before Gerard came back and discovered his plan had failed. She could go to Ardsley's—he would protect her.

Hastily, almost clumsy in her fearfulness, listening with breathless terror for the sounds of her husband returning, Cerissa grabbed a change of clothing and a hooded cloak, fumbling at the catch of her jewelry box. As it sprung open with a snap, she gasped again, staring at the nearly empty chest. All her jewelry was gone already. All but the gemless gold setting left from Brett's shattered emerald ring. Without daring to pause for tears, she grabbed that and threw it into her purse, reaching for the boy's hand to run into his room, collecting his clothes as well.

At last she bent and picked the squirming child up and hushed him, carrying him out to the hall. She stood a long second listening for sounds in the house below. Nothing. She took a deep breath to bolster her courage and stepped forward, moving silently down the first step, then the second, and then the third.

Suddenly the front door flew open and Gerard stood silhouetted, staring up at her, the surprise on his face gradually replaced by an evil amusement. Cerissa returned his stare helplessly, unable to move or make a sound, aware only of the incredible loudness of her beating heart, the absolute silence of the rest of the house.

"Not hungry tonight, love?" Gerard sneered lightly at last. "What a pity, I thought stuffed capon was your favorite dish..." Slowly, holding her motionless with his gaze, as cold and hypnotic as a snake preparing to strike, he came toward her, finally reaching one hand out to grasp the banister.

At last, Cerissa managed to collect her wits, holding the baby close against her, retreating carefully back up the stairs. Jamey had ceased his squirming and clung to her silently now, his arms wrapped around her neck, his legs tight around her waist, his eyes wide and solemn, sensing her fear. Cerissa struggled to find her voice, even while she knew it was useless to try to excuse herself for betraying him with Brett, seeing death in Gerard's glittering eyes regardless of what she said...but, perhaps, for Jamey at least... "How long have you known?" she breathed at last, her voice a hissing whisper in the perfect silence of the house. "How did you find out?"

Incredibly, Gerard laughed, cold and mirthlessly, slightly hysterically. "Oh really, Cerissa, I'm much cleverer than you ever gave me credit for being. I knew before I married you. What a ridiculous, flimsy lie to try to pass off...married to a sea captain, so conveniently widowed, of course. Did you really believe I would give my name to that illegitimate brat of yours, Cerissa? Whose is he anyway? Lord Ardsley's perchance? Is that why he's always nosing around? Or someone else's? Maybe you don't even know, my dear! Were there, perhaps, so many different men involved that you can only guess at his father?" Gerard's face contorted in a loathesome sneer, his face slightly flushed and beaded with perspiration.

Cerissa stared back at him stupidly, her surprise overcoming her fear for an instant. So it wasn't Brett. Wasn't seeing him at Whitross that week . . . he'd never even guessed about him, or Jamey, or . . .

"It's a pity you didn't eat your lovely dinner I fixed especially for you, Cerissa," Gerard continued, moving up the stairs toward them once more. "But no matter. Perhaps you and your brat will take a midnight swim in the Thames." He chuckled as her face paled further, her eyes huge with terror. "Oh, and there's no use screaming or making a fuss, dear. The servants are both sound asleep in the kitchen. I gave them some special wine this evening, just in case."

Helplessly, the girl retreated before her advancing husband, her heart hammering, her palms damp with fear. She felt her legs bump into the oak desk at the wall behind her, heard the silver candelabra rocking from the blow. At last, her brain began to function as Gerard, climbed nearly to the top step, his hand already reaching out toward them like a monstrous claw. Instantly, she grabbed behind herself for the massive ornament, ironically a gift from Brett—worked with dolphins and mermaids to remind her of him—and hurled it sidearm at Gerard's contorted face. At the same moment, she whirled, turning for the hallway, racing for the back stairs. Out of the corner of her eye she saw Gerard's forearm go up to shield his face from the candelabra, saw it strike his arm and riccochet into the wooden banister. Saw him topple backwards, his balance upset by the unexpected blow. Without pausing to watch more, she darted through the narrow door and leapt desperately down the stairs, flying through the kitchen to the pantry door. Gerard had been truthful, at least about the servants. Both were sitting slumped in their chairs, mouths open as they snored away their drugged sleep. Cerissa fumbled frantically with the bolt, her fingers clumsy from fear. At last, the door swung open and, clutching Jamey against her, she bolted into the black, London night and ran for the main street, searching the narrow streets desperately for a carriage, expecting any moment to feel Gerard's murderous hand fasten on her shoulder.

Finally, she heard the clippety-clop of a horse, then saw a battered coach rolling toward her, bouncing over the cobblestoned street. She ran toward it, waving her whole arm at the driver, praying to God the coach was not already occupied. Her luck held. The coach was empty. Thankfully, with a last fearful glance over her shoulder, she scrambled inside, calling to the driver the first address that came into her mind—the small inn where she had stayed with Brett upon first arriving in London nearly three years ago. The hostelry was a good one, the rooms clean and the food wholesome—and she remembered the landlord and his wife as a kindly couple. Gerard would never think to look for her there. She would be safe until she got to Lord Ardsley's tomorrow. She relaxed at last into the cracked leather seats, exhaling a long, shuddering sigh, feeling her legs begin to tremble and her body grow weak in dizzying relief. Jamey stirred against her, and she stared down at him in the darkness, seeing his eyes wide with confusion and fear. She drew his small head against her breast, folding her arms protectively around him as she covered his hair with kisses, unmindful of the tears that wetted his black curls. "It's all right, now, darling we're safe now. Mama's here, she won't let anything happen to you." The child huddled against her, clutching the bodice of her gown. Gradually, his tiny fingers relaxed and he reached his hand up to touch his mother's face anxiously.

"Why mama crying? Mama no feel good?" he questioned fearfully.

"No, darling, mama feels fine. Mama's just . . .," she sniffed with an apologetic smile, "just happy to be leaving that house."

The child nodded solemnly, nestling against her contentedly. "Me happy too," he announced seriously. "Squire scare me. Me no like him, anymore."

Cerissa kissed his hair again and stared over the child's head at the buildings rolling by. How strange, she mused silently, her eyes thoughtful, how strange that it should have been Brett's candelabra that saved us—that gave us the moment we needed to make an escape. Even with him leagues away, in God knew what foreign land, his love protected us from Gerard. Pray God it will protect us still until I get to Ardsley's tomorrow. Pray God Gerard won't find us tonight.

She reached over to draw the blanket higher over Jamey's shoulder, making sure the child was sleeping soundly, then stood up from the bed, walking over to a cushioned chair by the shuttered window. She opened the shutters to let the moonlight in, curling up in the chair to collect her thoughts.

She'd had twelve pounds with her when she'd fled the house from Gerard, now six pounds eight shillings were left. Room and board for she and Jamey had cost five pounds for the week, payable in advance, and she had given the coach driver a generous tip as well. Six pounds, eight wasn't very much money, but it should last the two of them well enough the few days they would need it. Once she got to Ardsley's house, he would provide for her until Brett returned. He could even go to Isaac Benjamin's and withdraw money for her from the five thousand pounds Brett had given her. Unless...she frowned suddenly in the darkness, shifting her legs uneasily on the chair. If Gerard had never been deceived...had never loved her...then he had married her for the money. How clever indeed he had been, making such a show of devotion. He had intended to murder her all the time evidently, yet he had concealed that design so well...Suppose he had succeeded. Suppose she and Jamey were dead by now. Who would ever have suspected the adoring husband? And Gerard would doubtless have pretended to be prostrate with grief. Even Ardsley would have sympathized with the murderer, pitying Gerard's loss. The servants would have testified to his unfailing devotion, their friends as well. Perhaps Brett would have guessed when he returned, but what proof would have remained by then? But knowing Brett, she decided, he would have killed Gerard anyway, on the strength of his suspicions. Oh God! If only Brett were here in England to help her now...She frowned again, puzzled by a new thought. Why now? Why tonight? Why not two months ago, or three? Or why not wait until the summer when a boating accident in the country could have so easily been arranged?

Cerissa shrugged at last, still wondering. But it didn't matter, she decided tiredly, moving toward the bed to sleep, the nightmare was over now. It didn't matter any more what schemes and evil machinations Gerard had designed. Lord Ardsley's house was only a few miles away. She would go there first thing in the morning.

But, in the morning, the light of dawn brought new suspicions to Cerissa's mind. Wouldn't Gerard be expecting her to do just that—bolt thoughtlessly for Lord Ardsley's protection. Hadn't he even mentioned something about the blond lord nosing around? Of course, he would be awaiting her there, looking for her, sitting in a carriage like a great black spider, while he waited for her to walk into his trap. Well, no matter. She would wait for a few days to visit the lord, throw Gerard off the scent. Wait until he would believe she'd fled for the country. Wait until he left London himself to pursue her there.

So, the girl waited for three days, staying close in her room, passing the time playing with Jamey or talking to the landlady while she helped out in the kitchen. Mrs. Bryant was a good-hearted soul, fond of children though she had none herself. She talked at length to Cerissa about her sister who lived outside of London, how she took in children to raise, how much she enjoyed her visits there surrounded by the happy youngsters. Cerissa listened carefully to the woman's chatter, considering such an idea for Jamey himself. He was old enough now to enjoy the company of other children. Perhaps she should talk to Ardsley about taking the boy into his own household nursery for a while. The blond lord had two boys of his own—one four, the other a few months younger than Jamey. It would be the ideal solution.

At last, on the fourth day, Cerissa decided it would be safe to seek Lord Ardsley. Leaving Jamey with Mrs. Bryant, she hired a carriage and drove to the brick residence, peering anxiously around the street for signs of Gerard. Deciding finally that it appeared safe, she signalled the driver to continue. But a few seconds later, the coach stopped again.

"Sorry, ma'am, I can't take you in there," the driver called. "The gates are locked."

"Locked?" Cerissa's gasped in puzzled dismay. "But why? Where's Lord Ardsley?" She leaned out the window to stare at the house herself, her eyes disbelieving. The driver was telling the truth. The wrought-iron gates were swung closed over the gravel drive, a thick chain securing them shut. The house beyond was silent, windows shuttered, no sign of life. In sick frustration, she hit the side of the door with her fist, struggling to hold back her tears. How dare Ardsley do this to her—go away without warning! He'd mentioned nothing of any plans to travel when she'd spoken to him last! Where was he? What in the world was she going to do now? Another carriage appeared at the end of the street, rolling slowly toward them. Cerissa jumped back into the coach and shouted to the driver to return to Bryant's. There was little chance that the coach contained her husband within it, but she was taking no chances.

The days passed swiftly. The note she had sent to Ardsley's had been returned by the boy unopened. The house was still deserted. Helplessly, Cerissa paid another five pounds to the landlord, leaving her nearly penniless. If Ardsley didn't return soon she would have to go to the goldsmith's herself, though she was desperately afraid of meeting Gerard there. She cursed her husband again, hating him as she'd never believed she could hate any living creature. Obviously, Gerard had been aware of Lord Ardsley's plans to leave London. That's why he'd moved when he did. He'd known the blond lord would be safely away. But where? Cerissa asked herself frantically. Where? And when would he return?

At last, the second week drew near a close and she forced herself to go to Lombard Street. Holding tightly onto Jamey's hand she stepped from the carriage into Isaac Benjamin's small offices, clearing her throat self-consciously. She wasn't sure women were supposed to do this sort of thing themselves, and yet, who else...?

"Yes, madame. May I be of service?" a small, greying man nodded kindly toward her, his hands busy amidst the papers on his desk.

Cerissa smiled, grateful for his kindness. "Yes...at least I think so," she stammered. "I have some money here, I believe, and I need it."

A little smile touched the old man's face as he came toward her from behind the desk. "And whose name is this money in, dear? I don't believe I know you."

Cerissa blushed, embarrassed at her forgetfulness. "Oh, I,m sorry, I didn't think. I'm Cerissa Hammond, Cerissa Whitestone now," she added with a small, involuntary shiver of distate, "Lord Lindsey said he'd left..."

"Mrs. Whitestone?" the man interrupted in surprise, his gaze suddenly sharpening beneath the yellow skull cap he wore. "Oh, I didn't realize, forgive me...Let me apologize, madame, and offer you my consolations."

Cerissa returned his gaze blankly. "Consolations for what?" she asked in confusion, her heart suddenly hammering with budding fear. Oh God! Something hadn't happened to Brett...not again...

Isaac Benjamin stared at the girl in obvious shock. "For the loss of your husband, of course, child. Didn't you know?"

Cerissa stood motionless, dumb in surprise, feeling her head grow suddenly dizzy, her knees weak with relief. She fumbled for a chair and managed to slide into it, still staring open-mouthed at the goldsmith.

"Forgive me, forgive me," the man apologized hastily, fetching a glass of water for the girl. "I shouldn't have been so blunt...that was terribly stupid of me, please forgive me, dear. You didn't know? You've been away?" he questioned nervously, afraid the woman would faint dead away any minute, never for an instant guessing her pallor to be relief instead of grief.

"Yes, yes..." Cerissa managed to stammer at last. "In the country," she lied. "Please, what happened?"

The goldsmith shrugged uneasily, unable to meet her eyes. "A robbery, they believe. He was found lying at the bottom of his stairs, his neck broken...by a fall, I gather. A...a silver

195

candelabra was found on the stairs, near the top, and it seemed the bedrooms upstairs had been gone through as well. The two servants were held for a few days, then released. They swear they never heard anything, but perhaps... the constable had no evidence though against them, no money or jewels at least."

Cerissa swallowed, trying to regain her composure. "Have they any other suspects?" she asked carefully, ignoring the pounding of her heart. Oh God! She had killed him when she'd thrown the candelabra at him! Killed him! She had murdered her husband.

Benjamin shrugged again helplessly. "I really don't know madame. I believe there was some confusion about the whole affair—something sinister about a dead cat and poisoned food. But don't you worry," he added hastily noticing her sudden pallor. "You just go to the constable. Explain that you were away. I'm sure whoever did it will be apprehended soon."

Cerissa nodded, her mouth uncomfortably dry. "Yes... yes of course," she agreed softly, struggling to smile. "Now, about the money..."

The goldsmith winced guiltily as he stared at the girl. "There isn't any left, I'm afraid dear."

Cerissa stared at him again, stunned. "But... there must be. I had five thousand pounds only a few months ago, and..."

"Yes, child, I know. Believe me, I'm terribly sorry. But your... oh... deceased husband was quite a spender. He'd reduced your account to below 2,000 pounds by the end of January. Lord Lindsey authorized me to take it back up to 5,000 pounds before he left, but..."

"But he spent that too?" she breathed incredulously. How? On what, her brain screamed? They had lived fairly modestly.

"It appears he gambled heavily, my dear," the man apologized with his eyes. "When his death became known... well, I was literally overrun by creditors. Even the five thousand pounds didn't quite cover all his debts. I believe his country house is up for sale now. Hopefully, that will cover the remaining money owed, because..."

"Because, if not, I'm liable for his debts," she finished numbly, feeling lightheaded again. She had no way to pay any debts. She had less than a pound left to her name. Failing to pay meant Newgate—the debtor's prison. If, of course, she weren't hanged for murder first.

The goldsmith smiled pityingly at the girl, patting her shoulder. "Child, if I were you I'd lie low until you see how the estate finishes up. Unless you have friends to help out. Newgate is not a pleasant experience—especially for a child his age. I'll advance you fifty pounds, that should help you live until..." he fell silent, a bit surprised at his own generosity. Fifty pounds was a healthy sum to be letting out with no collateral. But, then, there was obviously some link between the girl and the wealthy Lord Lindsey... and seeing her little boy, there wasn't much question what. Lord Lindsey was a good customer. He would be pleased at his generosity. Pleased enough, hopefully, to make good the loan.

Cerissa got to her feet slowly, her whole body slumped in weary defeat. Gerard dead, the police probably searching for her... huge, unpayable debts. Brett out to sea, half a world away, and Ardsley... heaven knows where... "Thank you," she managed to murmur to Isaac Benjamin as he handed her a small, heavy pouch. "May I leave a note in your care for Lord Lindsey? One for Lord Ardsley as well?"

"Of course, dear" he promised compassionately. "I'll keep them until I see the gentlemen again."

Cerissa nodded, writing briefly of her predicament to both, urging them to contact her through the Bryant's as soon as they returned.

At last, she returned to the inn, counting out forty pounds to the landlady. At least Jamey would be safe. She would send him to the country with Mrs. Bryant's sister, Mrs. Lawson. He would be well-cared for, surrounded by other children, safe for a year regardless of what happened to her. He would miss her, and she him, but it was the only solution. And she, with only the ten pounds left, a fugitive from the constable, would have to disappear into the London crowd change her name and find a means to support herself. Hopefully, Ardsley would return soon, or Brett would sail home before the winter ice closed the Thames. And hopefully, she could avoid being hanged as a murderess or imprisoned for her debts until then.

Chapter Thirteen

The life—more accurately the existence—of London's countless lower classes was filled with filth, squalor, poverty and disease. St. James Park and the airy apartments of the quality were far removed from the dirty, rat-infested, tenements that most Londoners lived in, and Cerissa realized for the first time since seeing the city why Brett had been so concerned about her surviving there. Her life at Bainwater had been poor and hard, but the country offered a wholesome kind of poverty unavailable in London. Here, with so many thousands of the poor piled on top of each other, even a window that let in fresh air was a luxury, not affordable to Cerissa any longer. She had given up her apartment at Mrs. Bryant's of necessity—her mere ten pounds would hardly allow such extravagance. Her room now cost one shilling a week, and she ate what the tavern guests left on their plates for another three shillings a week. Her total salary as tavern maid amounted to fourteen shillings a month, so she was unable to save any money at all for new dresses or shoes—even her weekly bath ran her over her income. But, she reminded herself grimly, she was lucky to have even what she did. Jobs were scarce in the overcrowded city. She had been lucky to find anything at all. Her roommate, Janey, supplemented her meager income by prostitution, sometimes forcing Cerissa to make her bed outside, in the dark narrow hallway, but so far, at least, Cerissa had been able to avoid that degradation. And seeing some of the filthy, stinking men that Janey shared her cot with had doubled her disgust and revulsion.

Wearily, Cerissa wiped the tables down in the commons room, sweeping the floor free of garbage and debris before turning for the stairs. Gerard had been killed only two and a half weeks ago yet that life of a respectable country squire's wife seemed eons past. She had worked here only thirteen days, yet the stench of the place, the inadequate food, the lack of fresh air and sunshine was already undermining her health. She would be only nineteen next month, yet her reflection showed an older image now, her chestnut hair stringy and limp, her face colorless, her blue eyes shadowed. If Ardsley did not return to London soon...

"Going to be, missy?" the inn-keeper, her landlord and employer, materialized suddenly out of the shadows of the first landing.

Cerissa jumped, startled, and forced a small smile as she nodded and started to edge past him. Of late, he had looked at her too intently for her pleasure, with a lustful glitter in his small dark eyes.

"Whoa, girlie, not so fast," he leaned toward her, his breath stinking of ale and rotting teeth as his hand fastened around her arm. "I've a mind for you to share my bed tonight. Come along."

Cerissa snatched her arm out of his grasp, her face white with revulsion. "You forget yourself, sir," she replied icily, pushing past the man in the narrow hall. "You pay me for services in the tavern, not for my bed."

"That comes with the job, missy," he chuckled, grabbing her more forcefully, his face obscene with anticipation. "I been letting you take your time, of course, cause I could see you was a cool one, but the waiting's over. I'll give you an extra couple pennies fer it if that's what's troubling you."

Cerissa wrenched herself away from him, slapping at the burly hand that reached for her breast, running for the stairs. The inn-keeper stood in the darkness behind her, his face ugly with frustrated desire as he cursed after her.

"You get out of here then, girlie, miss high and mighty! You be

199

too good for me, you thinks, then go elsewheres, see who else'll be giving you a job and food to eat! You'll come back begging me to take you for nothing, then, begging me to let you fondle me body for your job."

Cerissa flew to her room without turning back, her stomach churning with nausea. She didn't care how she'd live for the next months, she'd manage somehow—she still had seven pounds, six shillings left. Surely that would be enough.

"Ye Gods, Cissy! Ye look like death," Janey blurted as the girl ran into the airless room and slammed the door "What in creation?"

"The inn-keeper tried to make me sleep with him," Cerissa stammered, shuddering as she reached beneath her mattress for her hidden money.

"So what?" the other girl answered with a careless shrug, staring in confusion at Cerissa's obvious agitation. "He ain't bad . . . at least he don't beat ye or nothing like some blokes do."

Cerissa stood up, her small pouch tight in her hand, merely shaking her head for answer. How could she ever explain to Janey how different her life had been until now? Her roommate had grown up in the squalor, begging as a child, selling her virginity for a shilling at eleven-years old. How could she understand Brett, or Sweetwater, or even her life with Gerard? "Goodbye, Janey, good luck." She reached for the door, struggling against her fear that the innkeeper might be standing outside it, waiting to take her whether she would or nay.

"Oh hey! Wait a minute," Janey cried suddenly, jumping from her bed. "This note came for ye earlier—ye were busy in the kitchen and I forgot it 'til just now."

Cerissa reached for the paper, her hands trembling with hope, but the writing was unfamiliar, neither Ardsley's nor Brett's. Quickly she scanned the short note. It was from the goldsmith, Isaac Benjamin. He said neither of the two lords had been in to visit him yet, but another client had mentioned that Ardsley's father lay dying in Marlham, and that the family was gathered there. Cerissa heaved a thankful sigh. It wasn't much, but at least she knew where Ardsley was now. Perhaps, for seven pounds, she could hire a coach to drive her out there. Perhaps she could break free of this poisonous city existence right away. "Thanks, Janey. Take care now," she called softly as she slipped into the hallway, clutching her purse and her one spare gown. "You can have my bath tomorrow. I've already ordered and paid for it." Shutting the door, Cerissa missed the quick look of astonishment that crossed the girl's dirty face. Baths! No sir! Everyone knew they caused disease...

Cerissa curled up happily in the seat of the battered carriage. It hadn't been easy locating a driver who would go all the way to Marlham—a three day trip even straight through—for only seven pounds. At last she had found this one, who had agreed providing the seven pounds was paid in advance. She hoped to be able to tip him generously when she got to Ardsley's but she hadn't mentioned that. The man would surely think her lying if she, in her faded gown and frayed cloak, were to claim association with a lord. One more day and part of a third, she calculated happily. They had left London this morning late, and had driven most of the day. It was dark right now. She would sleep in the back of the coach for a few hours and...

Suddenly, the carriage lurched to a stop and she sat up slowly, peering out the window in confusion. Why were they stopping? Especially here in the midst of these woods?

"Sorry, ma'am, you'll have to get out here," the coach driver announced cheerily opening the small door.

Cerissa stared at him in total bewilderment, not moving. What in the world was he talking about? Why should she have to get out here? Was something wrong with the carriage?

"C'mon, miss, get moving," the man urged, giving her hand a tug.

Cerissa obeyed reluctantly, stopping at the edge of the door to stare down at the driver. "Why am I getting out?" she questioned at last, frowning her puzzlement. "I don't understand what..."

The man chuckled as he hoisted her to the ground, raising one hand to scratch his lice ridden hair. "Well, I'll tell ye, dearie. This is as far as I go for seven pounds. Marlham is that way," he pointed down the dark, rutted road. "I figure you ought to get there by Friday."

"By Friday?" she echoed in total astonishment. "What are you talking about? This is only Monday! I hired you to take me to Marlham by..."

"Aye, ma'am," the man grinned again, turning away to jump up into the driver's seat, taking up the reins of the shaggy, half-starved looking horses, "But see, I already got your seven pounds, don't I? So I don't need to be taking you no where now."

Cerissa stared open mouthed, starting to realize what the man meant. "Why you're a thief," she cried in sudden fury. "You agreed to take seven pounds for the whole trip. How dare you dump me out here in the middle of nowhere? How do you expect me to get to Marlham on my own? Those seven pounds were all I had left in the world! I don't even have money left to eat or purchase lodging, much less hire another..."

"Sorry about that, dearie," the coachman called, chuckling. "Here's a half crown then to ease your way."

Cerissa caught the small gold coin instinctively as he flipped it to her. She stared at the man in helpless rage, knowing she could do nothing to prevent his leaving, damning herself for being such a fool as to have paid him in advance.

"Good luck, ma'am," the driver chuckled as he turned the coach and headed back toward London. The wind took the sounds of his faint laugh back to the girl's ears as he rolled away. Soon, a sharp bend in the road hid the coach from view and Cerissa stamped her foot in uncontrollable, useless fury.

She couldn't possibly walk to Marlham. It was simply too far. She would have to return to London—if she could even make it that far on a pitiful half crown! Damn! Damn! Damn! She thought in silent fury. So much for trusting people! Now all her money was gone. The Bryants were too poor themselves to help her, what could she do? Go to Isaac Benjamin and beg another loan perhaps?

Wearily, she hitched her skirts up and started to trudge back to the city, all the while cursing the dishonest coachman to hell. As she turned the corner of the road she froze in her tracks, staring at the scene illuminated by the silver moonlight. The carriage was stopped, the driver pinned motionless to the side of the coach by a bright, gleaming silver sword held at his throat. Around the carriage, three mounted men in long black capes that circled their dark horses. Highwaymen! She realized with a start of fear. Robbers! Instinctively, she bit her lip to repress the cry of fear that sprung to her lips. They were too far away to hear distinct words, but the murmur of their conversation drifted toward her, the voices angry. She could see the coachman pleading, his arms gesturing wildly back up the road. Suddenly, with a gasp, she hitched her skirts to her knees and darted for the edge of the forest. He was probably explaining that he'd left his passenger up here—the highwaymen would be riding to search for her soon! Above the hammering of her heart, she heard the sound of rapid hoofbeats approaching, glancing over her shoulder to see a man in pursuit already. Her sudden movement must have caught his eye. Panicked, she flew for the trees and the concealment of the forest shadows, but she could not force her fear frozen feet to move swiftly enough. In an instant, she felt a strong, male arm catch her around the waist, swinging her off her feet and high up onto the horse's withers.

Cerissa screamed and kicked in helpless rage and fear, writhing in the man's grip. "Put me down!" she screamed, trying to twist around in the man's arm to hit him with her flailing arms. "Put me down!" Despite her desperate efforts, she couldn't even begin to free herself and she swore and hissed in fury, cursing the man with words she'd never spoken before, words she'd overheard Brett and Ardsley use when they thought she wasn't listening, words she'd never thought to use.

Suddenly, she stopped, astonished. The highwayman was chuckling, he was laughing at her! "Oh damn you!" she sobbed suddenly, drooping helplessly in his grip. The frustrations and terror of the evening overcame her at last, and she was hardly even aware of the horse moving deeper into the forest, or the other men who gathered behind her captor. Finally, even her tears ran dry and she sat, exhausted, numb, in his arm.

"Feeling better, darlin?" a deep, strangely lilting voice whispered against her ear.

Cerissa lifted her hand to wipe her wet face dry. "What do you want with me?" she sniffed. "I don't have any money or jewelry. I gave that rotten, thieving coachman every last penny I had."

He chuckled, "C'mon, lady love, you curse like only the gentry know how to curse. You may be down on your luck just now but you're no working girl, either. What's your name, darlin?"

"Cerissa Whitestone," she mumbled. There was no need to lie about her identity at least. He was as much an outlaw as she—he couldn't turn her over to the London police.

"Cerissa?" he repeated. "T'is a pretty name, Cerissa."

She shrugged, "What do you want with me?" she repeated stubbornly.

"I'm thinking to do you a favor, darlin'. The coachman told me he'd pulled a pretty trick on you. I hated to see you wearing out your feet trying to walk all the way to Marlham. It's a far piece. Happens I'm going that way myself and I figured, perhaps, we could arrange a bargain to benefit us both."

Cerissa was silent a moment, considering his words. She had no doubt what he was offering—nor what price he was asking. But, what choice did she really have? Even if she could have walked back to London, what awaited her there? Sharing a room with Janey again, and her bed with the loathesome tavern owner? Anyway, the man who rode behind her was an outlaw. What would stop him from taking what he wanted if she tried to refuse? "You'd take me to Marlham?" she asked cautiously, twisting around to try to peer up into his masked face.

He grinned, showing white teeth in the moonlight. "Aye, darlin'. Close to your door step as I dared."

"And what if I . . . declined your offer?"

He laughed softly, his eyes behind the mask dancing with amusement. "I'd have it anyway, Cerissa, but I wouldn't take you to Marlham."

She turned around to stare ahead. "That's what I thought," she sighed dejectedly.

"Here now. T'isn't so bad as that," he consoled with a grin, his arm squeezing her waist. "I won't hurt you anyway, darlin', and I may do better than that. I've loves a plenty back in Ireland, but I'm lonely in this England of yours. Won't you give a traveler a kind welcome?"

Cerissa bit her lip to hide an unwonted smile. Ireland . . . that explained the strange accent in his deep, musical voice. He did seem honest enough in his own fashion, even good-natured. And what she could see of his face below his mask looked young, and not at all unattractive. And Brett . . . would he understand if she . . . what would his advice be if he could know of her choice? Wouldn't he understand this as well, even better maybe, than her selling herself to Gerard for Jamey's sake? Wouldn't he want her to do what she could to ease her way . . . so long as it was unavoidable anyway? Her only real choice was whether she would let her captor help her reach Marlham—not whether she would give herself to him. "What's your name?" she questioned at last.

"Sean," he replied. "Or Johnny, to you English."

"Just Johnny? No last name?"

"No last name needed," he chuckled, not unkindly. "I only asked you to sweeten a few lonely nights, darlin', not to marry me."

Despite herself, Cerissa laughed ruefully, "That seems to be the story of my life," she admitted, shaking her head. "The only man I want to marry won't agree, the ones who do agree aren't ones worth marrying."

He laughed, kicking his horse into a canter as they came to a small path. "Sounds like a story there, darlin'," he murmured, "We've a couple hours yet before we camp and no more work to do tonight. How about entertaining me with your history?"

So she complied, not really unwilling to talk the whole confused scene out for once, not needing to fear the stranger's opinion. She mentioned no names, at least not Brett's or Ardsley's—she feared the highwayman might try to hold her for ransom if she did—but she explained her marriage to Gerard and her subsequent flight. He listened attentively, obviously shocked and revolted by the squire's schemes, laughing with her as she realized how funny her predicament with the coach driver had actually been.

By the time they reached a spot to camp, Cerissa had relaxed with the roguish highwayman, and was content with her decision to submit graciously to his demands on her. Supper was cold beef and bread, with cheese wedges and apples for dessert—not a feast, she admitted but infinitely more wholesome than what she had eaten lately at the filthy tavern kitchen. At last, the men spread blankets on the ground, leaving a discreet distance between their leader and themselves. Cerissa turned away in embarrassment, but Sean did not press her immediately, merely leaned against a tree trunk, staring at the dying fire with a faint smile on his lips. Cerissa studied the man from beneath lowered lashes. He was tall, but somewhat shorter than Brett's six feet, his hair tawny gold, eyes a warm brown. His face was handsome and masculine, not spectacular looks perhaps, but certainly better than average. His shoulders were broad, but his build chunkier and more massive than Brett's lean, graceful frame. He really looked very like Lord Lindsey except for a certain strength to the jaw line, a certain male stubborness perhaps. Yet Cerissa couldn't deny a strange attraction to the man—although his evident good nature and easy charm might account for most of that. "Do you mind if I call you Sean?" she asked, turning her head slightly to meet his glance.

"No, darlin'," he smiled, not moving except to fold his arms across his chest, "Whatever you like."

Cerissa continued to study the man as he returned his gaze to the red and black embers of the dying fire. She frowned and cocked her head to one side. "You're not born to robbery, Sean. Why are you doing this? How did you become a highwayman?" She stared at his face intently, watching as a swift smile flashed across his averted face. The lines of his features, the fineness there bespoke quality, not common birth. But what would a nobleman—an Irish nobleman no less—be doing here in England, pretending to be a common outlaw?

"Darlin'," he answered softly at last, his eyes kind. "People pretend to be what they're not for any number of reasons. Mine are of interest to me, but hardly to anyone else. T'is right you are that

I'm not a highwayman by trade, but..." he shrugged, smiling faintly. "You told me your story—or part of it, at least. Perhaps I'll tell you mine before we part at Marlham." He pushed himself away from the tree and brushed the dirt off his breeches as he walked toward her.

Cerissa stood quietly, waiting for him, yielding passively as he slid his arms around her, his golden head bending over hers, his mouth surprisingly sweet against hers. With a sigh, she allowed her body to respond to his loving, not protesting when he led her to the spread blankets, nor when he unfastened the snaps of her gown, to slide his hands within her bodice to caress her breasts. Perhaps her soul didn't sing with joy as it did at Brett's loving, but at least it did not cringe and shudder in revulsion as it had at Gerard's. She moved closer against him of her own will, her mouth opening to receive his kisses, her hands enjoying the tremble of his back muscles under their touch. In a moment, Sean covered her body with his own, moving her legs apart with a gentle knee, his body obviously eager for hers but waiting, considerately, for her own readiness to match his. At last, she arched her hips upwards, inviting his entrance. He moved at once, sliding deep within her, his hips gentle at first, then more violent as his passion increased, his lips crushing hers, his fingers pressing on her breasts, soft on her taut, throbbing nipples. Moaning, Cerissa answered his mounting desire with her own, her hands clutching at his buttocks to draw him deeper and closer against her as he thrust again and again, his breath ragged in her ear. Finally, she felt her body exploding with pleasure and she lay content against Sean as he rolled away.

"Whoever your lord lover be, he's a lucky man, darlin'," he murmured at last, just before sleeping. "I could be taking you to Scotland, and still have the best of the bargain."

Cerissa smiled in the darkness, returning Sean's goodnight caress. She was glad she had pleased him, glad he had pleasured her as well. There could be no real harm in this, she assured herself. Brett need never know, and even if he did, would he protest? When he knew he had her absolute and undivided love, would he care whom she'd shared her body with for a few nights? Yes, a small voice in her heart replied. He would care. Involuntarily, she shivered and Sean stirred drowsily against her, reaching an arm out to draw her closer to him. I need Brett to marry me, she decided solemnly at last. I need the protection of a husband's name, the commitment to a future. No matter how sweet a lover Sean is, I would rather be with Brett... or sleeping alone. Surely, when he returns this time to find Gerard dead, when he hears what I've been through—surely, then, he will marry me. Surely then.

They broke camp late the next day and rode farther west, away from London. Sean offered an extra horse as Cerissa's mount and she accepted gratefully, even though she had to ride astride. The men were surprisingly good company, their language decent, their songs and stories not obscene as she would have expected from a group of outlaws. Sean sang "Barbary Allen" and a melancholy Gailic song, the language strange and hauntingly so beautiful to her ears, the melody tinged with sadness. Cerissa congratulated him on his surprisingly good voice, remembering with a twinge of loneliness how sweet Brett's baritone was on the rare occasions she could coax him to sing as she played the lute accompaniment. Brett's favorite was the haunting "Greensleeves" and he sang it so beautifully it brought tears to her eyes.

The days passed pleasantly enough, Cerissa growing increasingly fond of her charming captor. Most evenings the men haunted the carriage lanes, stopping occasional coaches on the lonely, dark roads. But the girl grew increasingly puzzled, too, watching the four men at work. The whole atmosphere of the group was odd—wrong for supposed tough criminals. The men's attitude was markedly deferential toward Sean, more like servants to a master or soldiers to their captain, than like rowdy outlaws to their chief. His orders were never questioned, the surprising lack of booty not remarked on, and they ate better than Cerissa guessed real highwaymen would. She had learned in her few weeks amidst London's teeming poor that highwaymen were the elite, the nobility of the underworld; the richest, the most daring, the most respected. Even so, Sean's broadcloth breeches were too well cut, his laces too fine. He and his men even bathed when they could in the cold forest streams, a sure sign of quality, for bathing was held among the lower classes to be a sure road to ill health and even death. And the coaches Sean picked to stop...often a fine one would roll by unmolested, the voices of its occupants trilling merrily in the night air. And then, as a battered old carriage came along, Sean would signal the men with a silent hand and they would burst out of the woods at a headlong gallop to intercept it. Often enough, it seemed to Cerissa watching from the shadows, that Sean was more interested in talking to the passengers of these coaches than he was in actually robbing them.

Finally, Cerissa could keep silent no longer, and she turned in Sean's outstretched arms that night, moving closer against his muscled body under the blankets, lifting her head off his shoulder to stare down at his handsome face in the fading firelight, drowsy and content from their earlier lovemaking. "Sean," she murmured, cocking her head quizzically. "Why are you really stopping these coaches? You're no highwayman—why you haven't even taken enough loot this week to pay for the fine meals you eat. And your men—they never even protest when you allow rich prizes to roll by."

"Darlin'," he chuckled, opening one eye to wink at her. "You're a clever girl. And ye've been a good companion this week, too, so if ye can keep a secret, I'll tell you."

Cerissa promised solemnly, her blue eyes wondering.

"Ireland had a pretty good time of it under King Charles, darlin'. There's some at home who wonder how well we'll fare under brother James. He's Catholic you know, Cerissa, as is much of Ireland. But some of the country—the north especially—is Protestant, as I am. I think James will soft peddle his Catholicism here in England, at least for a while, until he's more firmly set on the throne, but in Ireland... I'm a nobleman at home, darlin' and I don't wish to be losing my lands if I can prevent it. Thought I'd come over and see what was brewing here in the Court. The people I've stopped have been couriers of Duke Ormonde, part of his spy system. Some of us in Ireland are wondering whether we'd be better to support young Monmouth's claims on the throne if he presses them. He's Protestant at least even if he isn't legitimate."

Cerissa nodded, remembering Brett's countless explanations of British civil affairs, glad of them. "Yes," she murmured thoughtfully, "Brett's often wondered about how good a king James will be."

"Brett?" Sean echoed, opening both eyes to stare at her in surprise. "It wouldn't be Bretegane Lindsey you're speaking of?"

Cerissa stared back at the man, silent too long as she wondered whether it would endanger Brett in any way if she said yes.

"So, t'is Bretegane Lindsey you've lost yer heart to, darlin'," he chuckled finally. "Ye picked a good man, anyway. I've been wondering whether I should invite ye to come back to Ireland with me. Wondering, since I've gotten uncommonly fond of you, whether I should be leaving you here all on your own. But since ye've picked the man you have..."

"You know Brett?" she questioned breathlessly, clutching his muscled forearm with unaware intensity.

Sean chuckled again, shrugging slightly. "Darlin', I can't say I

208

know him. I won't say I don't either. Let's just say I might know a man by that name. So, you won't be wanting to come to Ireland with me? You're still thinking to wait for your lover?"

Cerissa smiled faintly, touching Sean's face with an apologetic finger. "You've been sweet to me, Sean, and," she smiled, teasing. "I've grown uncommon fond of you too, but Brett . . . well, I think he may finally marry me when he returns this time. I know he loves me, Sean, and he knows I love . . ."

"Wait, darlin'," Sean interrupted frowning, his brown eyes troubled and compassionate. "Ye mustn't pin yer hopes on marriage. Believe me, love, I hate to sadden you but . . . Lord Lindsey might love you till the stars fall out of the night sky, but he can't marry ye darlin', he just can't. Don't ye know that marriages of the quality have all got to be approved by the king, Cerissa? Usually, it's just a formality left over from the middle ages, but in this case . . ."

Cerissa merely stared at the man, trying to understand. "You mean the king would care who Brett married? He wouldn't approve of me?"

"Not you, personally darlin'," Sean smiled faintly "No man would disapprove of you for yourself. But nobility is supposed to marry nobility—to keep the lands intact, the whole system going. If we started marrying commoners, well . . . Listen darlin', try to understand. King Charles might have approved it, he was more casual about such things, but James . . . he's of the old school, very definite about the blood royal, and noble as opposed to commoner. No, darlin', he'd never approve of a lord of Lindsey's stature marrying out of the pedigreed lines."

Cerissa searched Sean's face intently, feeling her heart sink to see only truth, and a touch of sorrow perhaps for her, written there. "What could the king do if Brett defied him—married me anyway?" she asked in a soft voice.

Sean shrugged his ignorance. "I don't know darlin', except he could banish him from the Court, even trump up some nonsense to confiscate his estate. If ye love the man, don't ask it, Cerissa, ye might get away with it, but ye might ruin the man too."

Cerissa laid her head back down on Sean's broad shoulder, taking silent comfort from the strength of his arm around her. At last she understood. It wasn't only stubborness that forced Brett's reluctance, wasn't any lack of love that he refused her a wedding ring, refused her son his name. Brett's wealth, his influence, his position in the kingdom, all lay against her. How could she ever combat these kinds of odds? Could she even ask him to take such a chance? But damn! It was so unfair! she thought. A man had a chance of rising into the nobility if he were clever enough, necessary enough to the king. How could a woman gain a title? Only by marriage ... and only then by marrying someone so unimportant, so far removed from the running of the kingdom that King James wouldn't care who such a man married. And then, she would have a title but she would also have a husband again. . . . So she couldn't marry Brett then anyway . . .

Finally, she forced her mind from the dilemma of her insolvable problem and raised her face to find Sean's brown eyes still upon her, his gaze solemn.

"I'm sorry, darlin', but at least now you know," he murmured. "And one more thing. Had I known whom ye belonged to at the first, I wouldn't have taken advantage of the situation I found ye in. Not that I can undo that now. But I would have respected his claims on ye, Cerissa, and now I'm sorry for our bargain. Anyway, I'll not be telling Lord Lindsey about us. If you choose to bespeak it, then fine. But as for me, I found you walking on a country road and escorted you to Marlham for gallantry only. All right?"

Cerissa smiled her understanding, feeling a faint rush of warmth for the Irish lord. "Since you said we'd be reaching Marlham tomorrow, Sean, it's a bit too late for either of us to be regretting our bargain. Besides, I could have done far worse in the situation I was in. Don't blame yourself. I don't. Even though I won't go to Ireland with you, I do thank you for your offer ... and your kindness. I'll remember you fondly ... the most unsuccessful highwayman I ever knew," she teased gently, touching his tawny hair with a caressing hand. He smiled back and tightened his arms around her body, drawing her down against him, his lips sweet and soft and tender as he kissed her. Cerissa gave herself to him without bitterness, a little sad to be saying farewell, a little glad to be so near to Ardsley's protection. So the loving was bittersweet for both, every touch and every kiss slow with the knowledge of finality. And, when it was over at last, and Sean's face was sleeping and still beneath the silver moonlight, she studied him for a long moment before she slept as well, wishing to remember him.

Cerissa waited for Lord Ardsley in Marlham's single small tavern, trying to ignore the overly interested glances from several of the men in the room. Sean had left her there, paying the stableboy to deliver a message to the manor, then had ridden back into the forest shadows, pausing at the edge to look back a last time as she stood waving, tears filling her eyes. He had raised a big hand in fond farewell, blowing her a kiss before turning to disappear among the trees. She had stood a moment longer, her smile thoughtful and a touch regretful, then taken a deep breath and turned for the inn. Sean was a darling, and he had been good to her in his fashion, and yet . . . she wasn't altogether sorry to see him go. Their bodies had enjoyed each other, but her soul had remained untouched. Seeing Ardsley again would bring Brett one step closer to her. Whatever Sean had said about the chances of marriage, she would never give the idea up. Somehow, someday, she would marry Bretegane and see her son Jamey succeed to the baronetcy. Now that Gerard was dead, leaving her a respectable widow of a country squire, she would somehow contrive to reach even higher. She would never rest content until she and Brett were man and wife. Too, she knew in the depths of her soul, Brett would never be truly content with less than that either. So for both their sakes, she would find a way for the marriage to take place.

"Here, miss, mind if I sit down here?" one of the men startled her from her musing, and she glanced up to see him edging closer, an unpleasant expression in his glittering eyes. She shrugged and turned slightly away, trying to ignore him.

Undaunted, the man sat on the bench beside her, unnecessarily close, his bearded face leaning too near hers. "Permit me to introduce myself, little lady," the man continued, throwing a smug smile at his watching companions before sliding even closer to the uneasy girl. "I'm Sir William Heathman," he announced with an obvious expectation to impress her. "A knight."

Cerissa continued to ignore him, shifting away from him on the bench.

"I'm free for the evening and looking for some company," he confided, reaching one hand out to touch her knee. "Perhaps you'd . . ."

Cerissa smacked his hand off her leg indignantly, rising immediately to her feet, her face flaming. The man frowned, his mouth growing ugly as he grabbed for her arm, uncomfortably aware of his companions' amusement. "Here miss, don't go putting on airs with me. Don't take much to see what you are and what you're sitting here for in a tavern room. Now be more pleasant or you'll lose my business."

Cerissa whirled to face him, her blue eyes flashing fury as she gasped, struggling to free herself from his grasp as the man tried to pull her against him, his eyes hungry.

"Hey, you damn fool!"

211

The knight flew suddenly backwards, as a man's hand fastened hard on his shoulder, then swung around angrily to the source of the interference.

"Ardsley!" Cerissa cried in relieved delight, running to throw her arms around the lord's neck.

"Now see here, Lord Ardsley," Heathman protested, stepping forward "I found the chit first and I . . ."

"Shut up, you ass," the blond lord scowled. "This is Brett Lindsey's wench, understand? You want to tangle with his rapier when he gets back to England? Why he'd cut your guts out for blood sausage if he knew you'd even laid a hand on her."

The knight paled visibly, muttering a hasty apology to the girl before sauntering away with what nonchalance he could muster. Cerissa hid her smile of amusement and turned eagerly to the lord. "Oh, Ardsley, I can't believe I finally found you. Wait till you hear . . ." suddenly, her voice broke and she leaned into her friend's arm, feeling her tears begin. She was always that way, she realized ruefully, sobbing helplessly against Ardsley's comforting chest, unable to find voice to explain away the astonished confusion in his mystified blue eyes just yet. She could be strong only until the crisis had passed and she had someone stronger to lean on, then the emotions she had suppressed came flooding forth.

"Damned if I can make head or tail of this whole thing, sweetheart," the lord muttered as he led her toward his waiting carriage. "All of a sudden there's a note delivered saying you're here out in Marlham Tavern, no word of how or why, and you look like you've been weeks getting here besides. Best start from the beginning, princess. Where's Jamey? Is he all right? And where's your husband? And where's your baggage and your coach? Why didn't you send me a little notice you were coming out for a visit? I'd never have left you sitting in a taproom if I'd known . . ."

Marlham Manor was in view before she'd finished her story. Lord Ardsley had listened wordlessly, his face reflecting only mounting astonishment and worry, his jaw growing white and his blue eyes icy as he heard about Gerard's attempt to murder the two. "Damn, princess, that's my fault, all my fault. I should have told you myself where I was going but it never occurred to me. Don't worry, though, I'll get the whole mess straightened out immediately. And you'll be staying here under my eyes the rest of the summer as well. Jesus . . . Brett would've had my head if I'd let something happen to you or that boy after he'd warned me about Gerard . . ."

212

A warm bath, and a new gown lent reluctantly by Lady Ardsley, refreshed Cerissa's spirits and she explained the events of the spring in greater detail after supper. The blond lord apologized again for being of such little help and the girl accepted his offer to send a carriage at once to collect her son and bring him to Marlham to share the nursery with his own two boys. Even Lady Ardsley was kinder than usual, her normal haughty formality mellowed into a sort of astonished interest in the girl's tale. When, at last, she retired, Ardsley himself stayed up a few minutes more, telling Cerissa of Brett's anger and disgust toward the Court as Charles had lay dying, explaining that the dark haired lord had left almost immediately for Portsmouth. Though still too early in the spring to attempt an ocean crossing, Brett had seemed strangely anxious to careen the Cerissa and set immediate sail for parts unknown.

"But then, when will he be back?" Cerissa asked the inevitable question, gazing at the lord sharply. Was she imagining it or was he actually hiding something about Brett's activities?

Ardsley shrugged, flashing a quick smile, "You know Brett . . . Any day or any year. I never know any more than you do."

Cerissa studied him a moment more, then shrugged also. If Ardsley were hiding something, it would be useless to press him.

"I never congratulated you on gaining the Earldom, James," she said. "Although I'm sorry about your father's loss . . ."

"Yes, I was rather fond of him," the blond lord agreed, his eyes shadowed for a fleeting instant with faint sadness. "But now . . . I shall enjoy pulling rank on that baron you're so damned fond of . . . perhaps I'll even make him give me his chair and take this hat off in my presence."

Cerissa laughed, knowing Ardsley too well to believe he would adhere to such foolish etiquette. "Oh, James, I'm tired," she yawned at last, getting to her feet. "It feels so good to actually be here, be safe, at last. Do you really think we shall spend the whole summer?"

"I don't know, sweet, but we may. It's only the middle of May yet, so there's plenty of time to decide."

Cerissa gave the blond lord a sisterly kiss goodnight and went to her room. Sleep came to her almost instantly and it was nearly noon before she wakened again, joining the lord and his wife for luncheon. Ardsley mentioned that he had to travel into town that evening and Cerissa volunteered to accompany him. Shortly after supper, as the hazy red sun dipped below the horizon, they set off down the tree-lined, wheel-rutted track toward Marlham. Several miles from the manor, Cerissa felt the coach lurch to a sudden stop and heard the sound of shouting male voices outside. Sean, she thought instantly, her lips curling in a half-smile, checking up on me.

The carriage door opened and a masked man leaned within, his mouth parting in a familiar, mischievous grin as he saw the girl.

"Outside please," he requested in his odd, lilting accent, offering his arm to the girl to help her down.

Cerissa glanced quickly at Lord Ardsley noticing his thoughtful frown. Had he guessed already that this was the highwayman she had spoken of, or should she caution him? She didn't want him believing they were in any real danger—he might make some risky attempt to rescue her which could get either her or Sean badly hurt... "It's all right, James," she whispered softly. "It's Sean."

The blond lord nodded, apparently as unconcerned about their misadventure as she. Cerissa frowned quizzically as Sean led her farther away from the coach. Ardsley, she reflected, had hardly even seemed surprised when the coach had halted. She knew he'd carried a pistol for she'd seen the butt of it protruding from his sword sash, yet he'd never made an attempt to reach for it. Now what...

"Surprised to see me, darlin'?" the Irishman grinned down at her in the darkness, his brown eyes twinkling behind the black cloth mask.

Cerissa laughed softly, shaking her head, "No, when the coach stopped, I sort of suspected it might be you."

"Well, I have what I came for and I've got to be heading home for Ireland now. I just wanted to be sure you were safely settled before I left."

The girl smiled, reaching her hand out to squeeze his fondly. "Lord Ardsley's sent for my son already, and he's drafted a letter to send to his lawyers in London to clear up any lingering problems about Gerard's death. I'm all right now, Sean, thank you. I'll be staying with him until Lord Lindsey returns." Sean nodded once, apparently pleased with her answer and she smiled up at his handsome face, liking him greatly. Her love for Brett was special and unique. No other emotion could approach the intensity of her need for him. Yet, she loved Lord Ardsley like an older brother, depending on his strength and his protection. And, she realized suddenly, she loved the Irish highwayman as she might a younger brother. He might be five or six years older than her nineteen years, yet she had so filled her last few years with experiences that they

214

might count for nearer a dozen. "Be careful, Sean," she whispered softly her blue eyes solemn. "And God watch over you."

"I'll be careful, darlin," he grinned, apparently amused by her seriousness. "And don't look so sorrowful. T'isn't goodbye we're saying, but only adieu. I'll be hearing of ye back in Ireland, perhaps, or even seeing ye there now and again." He glanced swiftly over the girl's head to where Lord Ardsley stood some distance away, his back toward them. Wordlessly, he slipped an arm behind Cerissa's shoulders, drawing her against him as his mouth came down on hers for a quick kiss. "There now, love, that shall keep me warm until I get back to my girls at home."

Cerissa flashed him a laughing smile, noticing the mischievous merriment in his eyes as he walked her back. A few yards from the coach, though, he stopped again, his face growing serious as he whispered in her ear.

"If you should happen to see Brett Lindsey before I do, ye might pass this along to him. Tell him to be wary of getting involved in any rebellion against the king just now. T'is a sad fact for us Irish, I believe but the country just won't support an uprising now."

The girl nodded, returning the brief squeeze of his big hand as he lifted her back into the carriage before turning away. She heard his low voice murmuring something to Lord Ardsley and then the blond lord entered the coach as well, signalling the driver to start moving again. Cerissa gave a quick glance out the window but the highwaymen had disappeared, melting back into the forest shadows. She waved anyway, to the darkness.

"So that was your rescuer," Ardsley murmured with a faint smile. "I think you have more luck than a leprechaun sweetheart. You're right, I'd bet, on his being quality. And he is certainly Irish."

Cerissa nodded, studying Ardsley's thoughtful face. "Did you expect to meet him out here? I heard you two talking..."

"Yes, he had a message for me from Brett, no less. He warned me to stay away from the southwest of England during the month of June. Asked me to be sure you and Jamey were away from there too."

"How strange," she mused aloud. "He gave me a message for Brett as well. That the time was wrong for a rebellion, whatever that meant. What's going on Ardsley? Where is Brett and what is he doing?"

The blond lord shrugged uneasily, looking away. "I don't know for sure, Cerissa, but I'd guess—strictly between you and me—that young Monmouth is planning something. Argyll's rebellion in

Scotland failed miserably in April, but that may not have discouraged Monmouth from trying. I hope he doesn't. From all I've heard, such an effort would be unsuccessful."

"Do you think Brett is involved with Monmouth?" she questioned breathlessly. Treason, her heart was hammering, death on the scaffold or lifelong exile if . . .

"No, sweet," Ardsley was shaking his golden head. "I can't imagine so—not that Brett is enthusiastic about James, few of us are. If he's involved at all, I'd guess he was working to dissuade the man from such a disaster. But I don't really know, I can only guess so . . ."

That uncertainty cast a cloud of anxiety over what would otherwise have been idyllic days for Cerissa. Jamey arrived in wonderful spirits, having obviously enjoyed excellent care at his temporary home. And the spring was a beautiful one, the greens vibrant and lush, the wildflowers splashing color across the rolling land.

It was the end of May now, and Cerissa had left her window open to coax the cooling breeze inside as she curled up in a chair, reading by the light of the glass paned lantern. A knock at the door interrupted her reading and she stretched her legs out straight a moment, tying her robe sash more securely around her waist before going to the door. Lord Ardsley was waiting in the doorway, a huge grin on his sun tanned face. "Someone to see you downstairs, Cerissa."

She stared at the blond lord for a long breathless moment of surprise. She had heard hoofbeats on the drive below a few minutes past, but she had assumed it was only a courier's mount. Suddenly, with a little cry, she ran for the stairs, hitching her skirts up high, her bare feet taking the oak stairs two at a time. That grin on Ardsley's face could mean only one person . . .

Breathlessly, she threw the parlor door open wide and stood in motionless joy on the threshold. A man was standing across the room, staring out the window into the moonless night, his broad back turned to her. At the sound of the door, he glanced around, his sun darkened face breaking into an answering smile as he held his arms out to catch her headlong flight to him.

"Oh, Brett," she murmured, locking her arms fiercely around him, feeling her eyes fill with joyful tears. "Lord, how I missed you . . . When did you get here? Was that your horse I heard a few minutes ago . . .?"

Brett silenced her breathless questions with a long kiss. When he

216

drew away again, his eyes were gleaming and he laughed softly at his own emotions. "I never expected to find you here, sweetheart, I guess I'm a shade over eager," he smiled ruefully, stepping regretfully away. "Is Gerard here?"

Cerissa's smile faded and she stared at his puzzled face a long moment in shocked surprise. "I...I had forgotten...you wouldn't have known," she stammered at last.

"Known what?" Brett questioned, frowning. "Ardsley said you had quite a story to tell me but..."

Ardsley's knock on the door silenced him and he drew farther away as the blond lord entered. "Thought I'd better knock first," he announced cheerfully. "I never know with you two..."

"What's going on here?" Brett interrupted, staring first at his friend and then at the white-faced girl in confusion.

Ardsley stopped immediately, glancing over to Cerissa. "You may as well do the telling, sweet, it's your story."

The girl took a deep breath, loath to recall the horrifying events another time but knowing she had to. She took Brett's hand to pull him down on the sofa beside her, feeling the involuntary tightening of his hand in fury as he listened to her tale. "That bloodless son of a whore..." he murmured at last, his jaw clenched white with helpless rage. "But you're all right? Jamey too? He didn't hurt you before..."

"No, love," she assured him hastily. "And meeting up with Sean as I did on the road...I was really very lucky in a lot of ways...Isaac Benjamin lent me fifty pounds, and the Bryants were so kind to me...and, you know, it was the strangest thing, remember that silver candelabra you gave me, the one with the porpoises on it? That was what saved us, Jamey and I..."

"And what the hell were you doing all this time?" Brett fixed his friend with an accusing stare. "Why didn't..."

Ardsley shrugged apologetically, his face admitting his guilt and his chagrin. "I know, Brett, I'm sorry. Most of it was my fault because I had to leave in such a damned hurry...and I never thought Gerard would keep my message from the girl. I'm sorry, I really am, I..."

Brett shook his dark head quickly, flashing his friend a strained smile. "Oh hell, Ardsley, I don't mean to get mad at you. Cerissa and Jamey aren't your responsibility, they're mine. I was the one who took off when I shouldn't have...Damn," he swore in bitter anger. "I knew in my gut that the son of a bitch had something..."

Cerissa stroked his clenched fist soothingly, her eyes anxious as

217

they met his. "You know, I had the feeling Sean knew you . . . the highwayman I spoke of," she explained, trying to distract Brett from useless regrets. "He wouldn't admit as much, but he knew you had ships and he gave me a message for you."

Brett frowned in surprise, returning her gaze. "An Irishman, you said? A lord?" At length he nodded, a half smile forming on his dark face. "Nearly as tall as I am? With light brown hair?" When she nodded, he smiled again. "Sean St. Michael, I'd guess. He is a lord—owns a manor near a port in Northern Ireland . . . You sure you didn't fall in love with the rogue, sweet?" he teased. "He usually has all the girls swarming around him whenever he turns on that Irish charm."

Cerissa laughed, shaking her chestnut head carelessly, glad of Sean's promise to keep their intimacy secret. "He even admitted I'd picked a good man to love," she smiled, squeezing his hand.

"I've met him a couple times in Ireland, when I've put into port there. You are lucky he was the one who found you . . ." Brett's smile faded slowly as he shook his head. "Don't worry, sweetheart, that will never happen again. I'll send a letter to the goldsmith authorizing a permanent draw on my accounts for you. And any further husbands are to be approved only by me," he ordered, his eyes growing warm. "And I shall, no doubt, be impossible to satisfy, egotist that I am," he chuckled teasingly, laying a light kiss on her forehead. "I think no one but myself is good enough for you."

Lord Ardsley took the hint and grinningly excused himself from the reunion, leaving the two to walk along together back to Cerissa's room. She forced herself to control her giddy joy long enough to relay Sean's message and hear Brett's explanation.

"So that's the way it ended, I'm afraid," he sighed his green eyes troubled. "Monmouth chose to listen to the hotheads and not to more sober opinion. I think he'll land in June sometime—at Portsmouth perhaps, but maybe in Dorset. He hasn't a chance of succeeding."

"Would he be a better king than James?"

"I don't know, sweetheart, maybe, maybe not. He's got no outstanding talent for the position, except that he's Protestant. But James is old now, and childless. I think we're best to let the succession take its natural course. Eventually it will bring James' daughter Mary to the throne, and her husband, William of Orange, is a fairly able leader. If Monmouth got the crown at his age, well . . . he might rule years and heaven knows what damage his ineptitude might cause. But I felt I owed it to King Charles to try to counsel his son Monmouth if I could help at all. Charles was fond of the boy I know. But..." he shrugged, his face reflecting his frustrations as he stared thoughtfully out of the bedroom window into the night.

Cerissa stood a moment, watching his face in the dim light, feeling her heart swell with joy and pride at the sight of him. "I think we've discussed enough business for the night," she murmured gently at last, moving forward to pull his riding cloak from his broad shoulders, then bending to unbuckle his sword belt from his waist. She felt his hands come down on her shoulders and she lifted her head, her eyes shining welcome as he bent his black head over hers, covering her mouth hungrily with his own.

An unexpected knock at their door startled them, and Cerissa jumped guiltily almost expecting Gerard to be standing there behind the door, but it was only a couple of manservants, carrying a large copper bath tub and several steaming kettles of water.

"My lord ordered you up a bath, sir," one explained. "Thinking you might enjoy one after such a ride, he said."

Brett glanced sideways at Cerissa and shrugged, a faint smile forming on his face. She laughed softly and beckoned the men inside, pointing toward the now empty fireplace. "If you'd light a fire, as well," she requested. "The night air grows cool for bathing." In a moment, the tub was filled, an extra kettle hung above the fire, and the servants tactfully vanished.

Brett shed his fawn colored broadcloth breeches and his soiled white shirt, and stepped forward into the bath, grimacing as he felt the heat of the steaming water. "Jesus," he swore, "Ardsley'll have me looking like those Florida Indians if I sit long in this."

Cerissa laughed, the total contentment filling her soul and needing to spill forth. "There's cold water in that extra pail," she pointed. "Honestly, Brett Lindsey, for a man who's traveled half the world, you're helpless as a babe at times."

"Only with you," he retorted grinning as he added cooler water. "Because I've always got my mind on other things."

She smiled and nodded, accepting his backhanded compliment, then sat on the edge of the feather down bed to watch him bathe. First he ducked his whole head under the water, lathering his ebony hair briskly with the herbscented soap, then ducked under again to rinse it clean. He began to lather his chest next, rubbing the foam well into the thick mat of black hair that covered his upper torso. Cerissa watched quietly from the shadows of the bed, feeling a familiar rush of heat through her body to see the muscles of his broad shoulders ripple smoothly beneath his sun browned skin. Impulsively, she rose to her feet and drew the dressing gown over her head, leaving only the short, clinging chemise on as she walked quietly toward the copper tub. With one hand she reached up, pulling the long pins from her hair to let it cascade wantonly down her back and across her shoulders, framing her face in it's chestnut curls.

Brett glanced toward her, sensing rather than seeing her movement, and he smiled slowly, his green eyes growing dark as ocean water. Cerissa smiled back, not displeased to realize that the nipples of her breasts were showing clearly beneath the thin silken shift. Brett's eyes dropped from her face to rest on her breasts, then dropped further to take in her whole body before swinging back to her face.

"Want me to scrub your back for you, love?" she offered, pretending not to notice the hunger in his eyes. She was enjoying this reaffirmation of her ability to inflame his passions, and there was no reason not to prolong it a bit.

Wordlessly, Brett nodded and held the sponge up out of the water for her to take, his eyes still rivetted on the edge of the chemise bodice, where her breasts swelled up out of the fabric, straining the satin laces. She reached forward for the soap, allowing her breast to brush against his shoulder as she moved, feeling her body renew its pleasurable throbbing at the touch, smiling secretly to see Brett's arm muscles tighten involuntarily in reaction. She lathered the sponge against the sweet smelling soap and washed his back and shoulders, scrubbing hard the way she knew he liked, pausing to rub the taut cords of his neck with the palm and fingers of one hand. She worked leisurely, enjoying his touch, enjoying the quiet closeness of the moment, and it was long minutes before she dropped the sponge back into the water to rinse it. Brett sighed contentedly, leaning back to rest his head against the back of the copper bath, stretching his arms forward to rest on the edges of the tub. His eyes were closed, a faint smile turning the corners of his mouth upwards. "Thanks, sweet," he murmured softly. "Why not join me in here? You're nearly dressed for the occasion anyway," he added teasingly, glancing quickly at her from beneath half raised lashes.

Cerissa smiled back, meeting his gaze and holding it, hoping to coax him out of the bath and into the bed. She leaned slightly forward, pressing her breasts against his forearm, deliberately exposing herself to Brett's eyes. His half smile broadened into a full one, his eyes gleaming as he lifted one tanned hand to touch her lips gently.

"You're all mine again Cerissa. I don't have to share you with anyone else. There's no need to hurry anything," he whispered, his voice soft and husky. He moved his dark head to lay a single kiss on her breast, then leaned back again against the tub, letting his head rest against the edge.

Cerissa hesitated for another moment, letting his words echo in her soul. He was right, they belonged only to each other again at last. They could spend a week on a single loving—no one would say them nay. With a soft sigh she stared down at his face for a minute, feeling her body redouble its yearning as she traced each perfectly handsome feature, admitted the undeniable, rugged masculinity of his sun-bronzed, well-muscled body. His black hair was beginning to dry already from the fire's heat, and the dampness made it curl more than usual, leaving the edges fringing his forehead and neck with tiny half-moon curves. Among the raven now was a rare silver gleam, proof that more than three years had passed since that March day in Bainwater. Thirty-one, he was now, she calculated musingly, touching a silver strand gently. Time passed so swiftly.

Quickly, she rose and unlaced the bodice of her shift, slipping the shoulder straps to let it fall around her ankles. She took the heated kettle and added a little fresh water, then stepped carefully into the bath. Although this one was bigger than the one she usually bathed in, it was still far from spacious and Cerissa settled herself cautiously between Brett's legs, drawing her knees nearly to her chin to fit in.

The dark haired lord smiled lazily at her, and reached a hand out to rest on her leg. Cerissa felt a nearly irresistible wave of urgency sweep her body and she shuddered slightly as it passed. Never had her senses seemed so vividly acute, her body so throbbingly sensitive. She felt her heart hammering wildly in her breast, realized her lungs were panting for controlled breath, her breasts tingling and aching for the touch of Brett's fingers against them. Daringly, she leaned forward, reaching one trembling hand out to his chest, letting her fingers drop down through the soapy water to find his manhood, enfolding it coaxingly with her hand, stroking him gently as she felt him responding, growing rigid and swollen under her touch. With a soft moan he leaned forward, drawing her head closer with one hand behind her neck, the other sliding up her thigh beneath the sweet smelling water, seeking her. Cerissa moaned and pressed against him, pressing her breasts hard against his lean chest,

221

her lips parting beneath his possessive kisses, accepting his tongue deep within her mouth, writhing and twisting within his embrace to move closer to him, seeking the gratification her every instinct now demanded. She gasped and felt her head fall helplessly to his shoulder in blinding pleasure as she felt his hand upon her, his fingers seeking deep within her, pressing, stroking, caressing her with maddening slowness. Almost mindless now in her desperate need for him, she forced her body to move, lifting her hips to cover his, her thighs straddling his beneath the water.

At last, Brett's own control broke and he locked his arms behind her, pulling her down against him, groaning with ecstasy as he penetrated her quickly, plunging up inside her. Cerissa moved her hips awkwardly upon him, every sweet sensation exploding into starbursting ecstasy. She wrapped her arms around Brett's neck, crushing his head against her breasts, every touch of his tongue, the soft nibbles of his teeth on her taut nipples, driving her to ever more frenzied heights.

At last, with a murmured oath, his green eyes emerald and flashing with passion, Brett tore away from her grip, lifting her off his lap and up into his arms in one move. In the next instant, he stepped out of the tub to lay her down on the thick cotton towels before the fire, following her down to pinion her motionless beneath the weight of his body. With one arm, he held her still while he slid his body lower over hers, his mouth lifting from her breasts to kiss the soft, dark triangle between her thighs. Cerissa'a eyes flew open in surprise as she felt his lips on her, his tongue caressing her where he had never kissed her before. Involuntarily, she moaned, trying to draw her legs together, almost afraid of the lightning flashes of aching, throbbing desire his every touch aroused. Suddenly, helpless to control her body any longer, Cerissa felt her thighs spreading wider of their own accord, opening her innermost mysteries to him, coaxing another touch of his lips and then another until her hips arched upwards against his mouth, demanding relief. She cried suddenly aloud, shuddering beneath him as her body found the ultimate ecstasy, unaware of her hands reaching down to entangle her fingers in his ebony curls, holding his head still against her.

A moment later she opened her eyes again, astonished to feel another wave of desire building in her loins. Brett had bent his dark head back to her again, tasting her sweetness with his tongue, his hair brushing her belly and the top of her thighs with angel soft touches. Cerissa moaned, helpless to withstand the resuming

222

onslaught of passion, only reaching down to touch Brett's face, urging him mutely to come up to her, to let her taste his mouth again, to taste his lips. Brett lifted his head and moved upwards over her, sliding his arms around her back, pressing his lips hungrily against her swollen breasts, her pulsing throat, then up to possess her mouth. His body was heavy and warm above her and Cerissa panted under him. Feeling Brett's sudden trembling, hearing his soft moans of urgency, she opened her legs to him, drawing him deep inside. He buried his head against her neck, rocking his hips violently against hers, plunging full inside her and retreating to thrust again, every muscle of his lean, powerful body tightened and quivering with all consuming arousal. Cerissa felt her own body answering his need, letting him take her on a wild flight of ecstasy until the heavens themselves seemed to be whirling in response. At last she cried aloud, raking his back with her nails in helpless ecstasy, feeling Brett shudder and groan in simultaneous pleasure.

It seemed a long time before the world stopped reeling drunkenly, and Cerissa opened her eyes to find Brett's gazing down at her, one side of his mouth quirked upwards in a lazy, satisfied smile.

She returned his smile, reaching up to touch his tousled raven hair where the silver moonlight dappled it. "You're marvelous," she whispered, her eyes drowsy with contentment.

"You inspire me," he grinned in return, laying back into the pillows.

"It seems like heaven to me, Brett, to be with you again like this. Will we stay the summer here? There's the most beautiful little pond just . . ."

"Sorry, love, but there won't be time I'm afraid. I've decided . . ."

"Brett!" she cried, sitting up to stare at him with anxious eyes. "You're not leaving England so soon!"

"No, sweet," he chuckled, knocking her chin teasingly. "I guess I'm getting old or I've just traveled too hard these last few years. I want nothing more right now than to spend a lazy summer at Whitross with you and Jamey. Do some hunting, some falconing and maybe a little fishing. I'd like to buy a pony for the baby and teach him to ride."

Cerissa sighed and snuggled closer in great contentment. "That sounds wonderful, love. But why are you in such a hurry to leave here? Why not visit with Ardsley a while?"

"Monmouth's last plans involved landing somewhere in the

southwest of England—probably in June. Marlham is a shade too close to the scene of possible fighting. I'd rather be closer to London at Whitross."

Cerissa nodded agreeably. "Shouldn't we invite Ardsley to join us there then?"

"I already have love, but he's not too concerned yet. He said if Monmouth gets close, he'll come then."

Cerissa smiled tenderly in the dim light, turning her head to lay a gentle kiss on Brett's shoulder. His last words had been mumbled, his eyes were already closed. There was so much she wanted to say to him. So much love in her heart to spill forth. But now there was time. He'd ridden hard and he'd loved hard tonight—leave him sleep.

Chapter Fourteen

Monmouth's landing at Lyme Regis, Dorset, on June 11 seemed oddly unreal, incredibly faraway from the blissful serenity of Whitross. It was reported that he had disembarked with less than a hundred followers, expecting the people of England to rise quickly to swell his pitiful army. And though the country folk of southern England welcomed him heartily, they could offer little substantial aid against the trained armies of the king. James Scott, Duke of Monmouth, was cheerfully hailed as the "Protestant Duke" and several thousands did flock to his banner, but the nobility held aloof from the rebellion—dooming it to die by withholding their wealth and their weapons. Even Brett, who was obviously fond of the young bastard duke, withheld his support, hoping that Monmouth would finally admit the inevitable and retreat to the Netherlands while his head still sat upon his shoulders.

Cerissa knew occasionally—when her lover's green eyes grew troubled and he gazed silently out to the western horizon—that

Brett was uneasy about the rebellion, probably demanding of himself for the hundredth time whether he owed allegiance to the affable young Duke only five years older than himself, or to the dour, older James who wore the crown lawfully. Always though, in a few minutes Brett would turn back to Cerissa and Jamey again, forcing a smile, grabbing the boy up to ride on his wide shoulders or tumble somersaults on the summer grass.

Cerissa leaned against a tree trunk, watching the men where they sat near the small, still lake, the baby wading happily in the shallow water by the shore, Brett sitting nearby, laughing and talking to the boy as he graciously accepted the child's gifts of smooth stones and dandelion flowers. With one leg bent under him and the other drawn up to rest his forearms upon, Brett looked surprisingly like a youngster himself, his laced shirt pulled wide open at the neck, his cuffs pushed back nearly to his elbows, exposing his sun-darkened skin. He threw his head back to laugh at the boy's antics, his black hair ruffling in the warm June breeze, his white teeth flashing in his tanned face. Cerissa smiled as the low, rich sound of his laughter reached her, thinking she'd never in her life been so blissfully, totally happy. Pray God Monmouth's rebellion would not reach far enough east to touch them, they were . . .

Brett jumped suddenly into the lake water, reaching down with one hand to haul the boy high in the air before leaping back to the shore to let him down. Cerissa hurried toward them, her bare feet tickled by the long grass.

"What is it, Brett?" she called anxiously.

"Nothing, sweet. Just a snake, in the water." The dark haired lord smiled reassurance as he led the child up the hill toward her.

"Poisonous?" she asked with a shudder, glancing distastefully at the calm pond.

"Probably not," he grinned, noting her expression. "But I didn't want to take any chances. You know little boys like snakes, sweetheart, he might have have tried to grab it."

"Little boys like worms too, and spiders and mud and lots of other awful things," she grimaced, looking at her son's dirty face. "And you encourage him in everything, Brett. A fine influence you turned out to be."

"Oh hell," he laughed, obviously not the least intimidated by her displeasure. "That's what we fathers are for—to make sure you women don't make fops out of our sons. You don't want to grow up wearing ribbons and petticoats, do you, Jamey?"

"No, Father," the boy answered instantly, returning his father's conspiratorial smile. "Me want a pony and a sword too, Mother. Me want to have a ship and..."

"All right," Cerissa conceded with a laugh. "I'll have my daughter someday and then I'll raise her to be a fine lady. She won't care for snakes and roughhousing like you two seem so..."

"Hello, down there!" Lord Ardsley's deep voice sounded from the top of the hill as he waved his arm in greeting. "We finally accepted your invitation, or rather I did," he explained, walking toward them. "Marian took the boys back to London. Said she was bored silly with the country."

Cerissa gave him a quick kiss and the baby squealed delighted pleasure at his Uncle James' sudden appearance. He launched into an excited, and somewhat garbled, account of the snake in the water and finally Brett hushed him, sending him along to run back toward where his nurse sat waiting.

"Well, James, what is it?" the dark haired lord asked at last as they themselves neared the manor. "Is Monmouth moving closer toward us?"

Lord Ardsley nodded and shrugged slightly, glancing toward Cerissa. "I don't think we need to concerned at all yet, but country life doesn't agree with my wife so well as it does our Bainwater princess here, so... between the two... Monmouth's already taken Taunton and I heard he intends to take Bath and Bristol before turning east. He got a rousing reception in Taunton. Soon proclaimed himself the rightful king and issued some silly charges about James poisoning his brother Charles."

Brett frowned, linking Cerissa's offered arm through his own absently. "The damn fool," he sighed. "Bath and Bristol won't support him. He'd have done better to come straight across. Still... maybe King James will be forgiving of his charming nephew. I'd hate to see Monmouth hanged for being naive enough to pursue this nonsense."

"James is feeling far from forgiving from what I've heard. He's always been a touch nervous anyway—ever since the Popish Plot started the Catholic issue burning again. Heads are going to roll for this rebellion, I'm sure. I only hope they're the right ones."

Having Ardsley with them made the days seem even more delightful, for the blond lord was much like a chameleon. Away from the Court and the demands of his haughty wife, he fell easily into the merry informality of their country existence. Though he swore at first that Brett looked as disreputable as an outlaw with his

227

wind tousled black hair and his wide open shirt and broadcloth breeches, within days he was looking much the same. The lake bass were luting well and the falconing excellent this time of year. True to his word, Brett had bought a small, shaggy black pony for his son and all four of them rode out together for picnics—the child's pony led by a halter rope yet, for his two year old legs lacked the length yet to truly control the animal. At night, the adults played cards, Cerissa having learned the game well enough to hold her own even against the two veterans. The threat of Monmouth's uprising which had seemed real and suddenly, chillingly close upon Ardsley's first arrival now withdrew again and faded away like a frightening dream. Midsummer night was celebrated merrily and now June was fading to July. Lord Ardsley was leaving for London the first of the month, and though he promised to return with his own two boys later in the summer, Cerissa had an eerie feeling that their blissful weeks at Whitross were drawing to a close. But having no reason for her feelings, she tried to ignore them, putting such dark thoughts resolutely from her mind in the dawning sunshine of each summer day, only to have them descend upon her again in the midnight silence of each dark night. Brett too seemed wordlessly uneasy, though he would admit to no concern. More and more often he would start guiltily when she or Jamey repeated a question or touched his sleeve for attention. It was as though his thoughts were ranging far outside his body, and came back only with an effort.

"Brett's getting restless too, I think, though he won't admit it," Cerissa's teasing smile was touched with sadness as she kissed Lord Ardsley farewell at the door.

Brett shrugged guiltily and forced a laugh at his friend's quick surprise. "Not restless, actually," he assured the two hastily. "Maybe a shade..." he broke off to frown out into the bright sunlight, one hand covering his eyes. "I didn't know you planned to ride with your cousin Martin into town."

The blond lord swung around to follow his friend's gaze. "I didn't plan to," he shrugged in displeased surprise. "You know there's no love lost between us. In fact, I think he hates me only a hair less than he hates you, Brett. Damn! I should have left yesterday and I would have missed him."

Instinctively, without conscious thought, Cerissa melted closer against Brett's protective shoulder, remembering with unexpected clarity the horrors Lord Martin caused her more than three years ago on the road from Bainwater. First, he had expected Lord Lindsey to share his booty freely. Then, the ugly scene in the tent

228

over the card game when Brett had nearly drawn his dagger. And later, outside when he'd grabbed her and almost raped her before Ardsley and Brett had come running to her aid. . . . Brett had very nearly killed him that night, she remembered with a sudden shudder. And something in the man's cold blue eyes as he dismounted now at the doorway told her he hadn't forgotten—nor forgiven—the humiliation of that night.

"What are you doing here?" the blond lord asked bluntly, not bothering to hide his distaste for the man.

"I have a message for Lord Lindsey," the man replied with a ferret-like smile, "I didn't expect to find you as well, dear cousin."

"Don't expect me to say it's my pleasure," Ardsley scowled. "You're like a bad penny, Harry, you're always turning up."

"What message?" Brett interrupted, meeting the smaller man's glittering gaze impatiently. "And who are those men with you?"

Lord Martin snickered slightly before he replied, pretending to turn away to follow the dark haired lord's gesture. "Oh them . . ." he drawled slowly, obviously enjoying Lord Lindsey's impatience. "Don't you recognize the king's guards? Perhaps you'd be more familiar with bastard Monmouth's."

Cerissa felt a sudden weight of icy dread grip her stomach. King's guards? Monmouth? Did King James believe . . . ?

"You've been a naughty boy, Lindsey," Lord Martin smirked, his pale eyes gleaming with malicious glee. "The king is very unhappy with you. He's asked me to deliver a royal summons to you on his behalf. Seems he's found out you were in the Netherlands talking to his rebellious nephew most of the spring—very foolish, Lindsey, very foolish of you indeed to incite a rebellion."

Cerissa felt Brett's arm clench beneath her fingers and she held on to it firmly, almost breathless in her own horror. Of course Brett was innocent the man was only baiting him to force an angry reaction, but with his temper . . .

"Hold on, Brett," Ardsley moved between the two men, his own face red with rage. "Don't do anything foolish. James knows better than to believe you're actually involved in this mess. Harry's just trying to force your hand. He'd like nothing better than to take you on now with his two guards backing him up. Don't give him that pleasure."

Brett stared a long minute at the grinning lord, his green eyes cold and glittering with menace. Finally, he forced a deep breath and shifted his gaze toward the guards, seeking the captain of the two. "Is what he says the truth?" he asked coldly, indicating Lord

Martin by a disdainful nod of his dark head.

Uneasily, the two guards exchanged quick glances. "Yes, Lord Lindsey he does carry a royal summons," the senior officer admitted at length. "But I have orders to escort you to London, not to arrest you. You may remain armed as well, and you're welcome to take time to pack your things if you wish." The captain frowned at Lord Martin, dislike of the man evident in his expression.

Cerissa began to breathe easier, and she felt Brett relax under her hand. It wasn't as bad as she'd first thought at least. Brett wasn't already judged guilty of treason by the king.

Lord Lindsey stared a moment longer at Ardsley's cousin, his jaw clenced and white. "I have no doubt you've festered this whole ridiculous situation, Harry, and I thank you," he drawled softly, his eyes hard as steel. "I've disliked you for a long time without actually having a good enough reason to kill you. When I've cleared myself with King James, you'd best take care."

"Threats, my good lord?" Martin sneered laughingly. "Tsk! Tsk! Duelling's forbidden in England you know . . . it won't please the king to hear you've been threatening his loyal courier. Besides, I plan to be there whole and hearty to see you kick on the scaffold, for treason."

"If he does, I'll kill you," Ardsley smiled pleasantly as though the thought was a happy one. "So don't be too merry, Harry."

"I'll go pack," Brett murmured softly, squeezing the girl's hand briefly to reassure her. "Watch the son of a bitch while my back is turned."

Ardsley nodded, pulling Cerissa inside as Brett left. "It's all right, sweetheart, don't worry. There's an old rumor, you know, that Brett was actually King Charles' son. Brett's mother was having an affair with Charles about the right time . . . but Lord Lindsey accepted the boy as his own, and Lady Lindsey concurred. And Brett took after his mother's side of the family in looks, she had the black hair and the green eyes as well, so nothing much was ever said further. Whether he's actually Charles' or not is a moot point. Some people may think he is, including King James. I'm sure the King only wants Brett in London where he can keep an eye on him. With Monmouth on the loose, another unhappy nephew would be inconvenient. Especially one as powerful and respected as Brett. If he swung his support to Monmouth out of brotherly affection . . . well, anyway, don't worry. I'll make sure nothing comes of this."

Cerissa nodded hastily, her brain whirling with this new

information. Brett Charles' son? The thought was astounding and yet ... hadn't even Brett admitted to a strange closeness with the King? Much like the instinctive affection Jamey had shown to his father from the first? And in looks ... she'd seen the king once at the theatre. Brett's face was not terribly like his. It was, as Ardsley had said, more Scottish ... very rugged, and composed of strong, clean, lines ... but the black hair, and the tall, powerful frame ... the love of the sea ... even, perhaps, the magical Stuart magnetism for women ...

"Take care of Cerissa for me while I'm gone, Ardsley," Brett's deep voice startled her as he stepped up to them, and she clutched him fearfully for a second as he bent to kiss her. "Perhaps you might bring her to London if all ..."

"Oh no, excuse me, Lord Lindsey," Harry's oily voice interrupted, "I can't agree to that. Why heaven only knows whether you've embroiled my cousin already in your treasonous schemes. I can't leave a lovely innocent girl in the hands of a possible traitor. Oh no, I'm afraid I'd best take charge of her." Quick as a snake, he reached across to snatch her wrist and pull her toward him, Cerissa had a swift impression of the man's pale eyes above her, of his hot breath against her cheek, of his cruel grip, his alien smell. Instinctively, she threw her weight backwards trying to break his grip, her free arm swinging wildly to strike his face with all her strength. With a startled curse, he let her arm slip and she stumbled away from him, brushing against Brett as he moved forward.

"You filthy son of a bitch," he breathed, his green eyes flashing dangerous fire, his right hand already fastened on the jewelled hilt of his rapier, drawing it free. One suntanned hand reached out to grasp Cerissa's wrist, pulling her behind him.

With a muffled oath, Lord Ardsley jumped forward to separate the two men, using his broad shoulders to force Brett back a step. Lord Martin laughed suddenly, his merriment cruelly vindictive.

"Guards!" he cried, raising a beckoning arm. "Disarm Lord Lindsey at once. He's resisting the royal summons."

Hesitantly, the two soldiers came forward, staring uneasily from one to another of the hostile barons. Ardsley swore viciously as he turned toward them.

"It's not the summons he's resisting, it's Martin's obscenity with the girl. I've offered to take charge of her—there's no reason to subject her to this lecher's company all the way back to London."

The captain frowned as he glanced at Cerissa, then glanced up at Lord Lindsey's darkly furious face. There was murder in the lord's eyes, no question of that. He personally had formed no fondness for Lord Martin on this expedition, and yet...

"Lord Ardsley, I'm sorry," he began, choosing to speak to what seemed the more controlled of the two. "Lord Martin is in command here. He has rank, I dare not disobey his orders. If he says the girl is included in the summons..."

"You misunderstand, Captain," Lord Martin smiled evilly, meeting Brett's flashing eyes with cool mockery, his lip lifted in a malicious sneer. "I'm not accompanying you back to London—though the experience would doubtless be a memorable one. Bretegane Lindsey, at my command... I have business further north to attend to yet. I merely have decided to offer the girl the protection of the crown lest some hot-headed rebels seek to corrupt her loyalty to King James."

"For Christ's sake, Martin, you've had your fun today. This is no ordinary wench you're talking about," Ardsley scowled. "This girl is Brett's mistress—the mother of his son. Now, back off before..."

"No, you back off, cousin," he snapped. "Before your loyalty to the King comes into question too."

"My lords, please," the captain interrupted uncomfortably. "If I may suggest an acceptable solution. Leave the girl in Lord Ardsley's care. Surely that would prove..."

"No, Captain," Lord Martin smirked openly, enjoying Brett's helpless rage. "Even though Lord Ardsley is my cousin, I cannot vouch for his loyalty any longer. You've seen for yourself how partisan he is to this suspected traitor. The girl comes with me. If Lord Lindsey is adjudged guiltless of treason I shall return her to him later. I might even be able to get her with child by then, Brett, wouldn't you welcome an addition to your happy family?"

Brett's face turned ashen and he lunged at the smaller man with a vicious oath. Ardsley and Cerissa leapt to wrestle him backwards, while Lord Martin laughed in high-pitched glee. Finally, Brett seemed to regain his control and he stood motionless for a long moment, his eyes blazing and his lips drawn tight and colorless in grim fury. Cerissa shuddered as she glanced up into his face. The cold, murderous hatred written there sent an icy chill into her very soul. "It's all right, Brett, I'll go with him," she whispered numbly, turning to go. Better to play whore to the vindictive lord than see Brett lying dead at her feet in a puddle of blood. But Brett didn't answer her. Indeed, his expression didn't even change and she began to speak again, thinking he hadn't heard her.

"Captain," Brett called clearly, his deep voice steady and

232

relatively normal. "I've accepted the summons and am prepared to accompany you to London. But I'm not prepared to see the girl misused by Lord Martin. Can you offer her your protection?"

"No, my lord, regrettably, I cannot. My orders are to escort you and you alone to London. And I'm under Lord Martin's command in all else." The soldier spoke stiffly, hating his commander thoroughly. The man was obviously the worst kind of scum. To retaliate against a man by abusing his woman...

"I'll tell you only once more, Lindsey, before I order the guards to take Cerissa by force. Hand over the wench and go get on your saddled horse, now. Before my patience runs out."

Cerissa turned to go to Lord Martin, trying to ignore the dryness of her throat and the terrified hammering of her heart. Instantly she felt Brett's hand on her wrist, keeping her still.

"Now, I will tell you something, Martin," Brett announced almost casually, though the icy fire of his emerald eyes belied ease. "While I draw breath, you'll not lay one filthy hand on this girl. Now, make your choice."

Lord Martin laughed mockingly and beckoned the guards closer. "You're ready to fight three to one for your whore, Lindsey? Oh, how gallant you are!"

"If there's a fight, Harry, it will be three to *two*, not one," Ardsley warned hotly, freeing his own rapier from the sheath.

Cerissa glanced helplessly from one man to another, seeing only the cruel bloodlust of imminent fighting on their faces. Despite her fear, she shivered violently. This was a side of Brett—of Ardsley too—she had never seen. Aren't they fighting for her and her honor? She should be frightened but not ashamed or disgusted by them. She wasn't sure she liked it. It reminded her of vicious jungle cats, of ruthless, animal predators in a primitive age.

"Guards, I require your assistance," Lord Martin chuckled eagerly, drawing his own sword. He intended to let the two professional soldiers take the brunt of the fighting. Later, when Lindsey was worn down, possibly wounded, then...

"I'm sorry, Lord Martin," the captain replied stiffly, remaining motionless. "My orders are only to enforce Lord Lindsey's acceptance of the summons. He's already said he accepted such. If you gentlemen choose to quarrel over a private matter, that's your affair."

Lord Martin sneered angrily at the soldier then faced Brett again, his face contorted with loathing. For a long moment he was still, fear of Lord Lindsey's well-respected swordsmanship making him pause. Cerissa held her breath, hoping desperately that the captain's unwillingness to aid the man would decide the issue.

Without warning, Lord Martin lunged for the girl, dragging her away from Brett's protecting arm to clutch her in front of his own body as a shield. In the next instant, his sword was in his hand, glittering evilly in the golden sunlight. "I mean to have her, Lindsey, fight or no. I want to know you're trapped in London while I sport with your whore. I want you to feel it in your guts every time I climb on her, and know there's not one damn thing you can do to stop me."

Brett's answering rapier rasped free of its sheath. "Let her go, Martin, this instant, or I swear you're a dead man."

"How well will you fight this way with her in your way?" Lord Martin hissed and spat jeeringly, keeping Cerissa tight against him. "Will you take a chance on sticking her with your sword, Lindsey? Would you ever forgive yourself if it were your own thrust that found her heart?"

"Please, my lords," the captain held a warning hand out, his jaw muscles twitching nervously. "I beg you to remember that duels are expressly forbidden by the King. Lord Lindsey, consider," he urged the dark lord quickly. "I've given my word that I won't interfere with any arrangements you wish to make for the girl. I despise the man's actions as much as any gentleman would, but . . ."

"Step back, Captain," Brett interrupted impatiently. "I'm perfectly aware of the laws regarding duelling. What choice does he leave me in the matter? Do you honestly suggest I turn my back and let this whoreson have her?"

The soldier scowled and shook his head in frustrated anger. The man was right . . . what other choice was there? "Lord Martin, I do, as a gentleman and officer of His Majesty's guards, protest your conduct in this affair. I intend to make a full report to my superior in that regard—vouching for Lord Lindsey's reluctance to break the king's law despite the extreme provocation of your insults." He stopped and bowed to the dark haired lord, frank approval on his face. He'd heard incredible rumors of the man's ability with weapons but could even he overcome such an obstacle as now laid against him? Could the man even defend himself without fearing to strike the wench? "Man to man, my lord, may I offer a suggestion? As soldier for His Majesty, I am obliged to arrest you for duelling—not to mention the possibility of treason. If you prove successful in this fight, I'll go this far. Take your horse and an hour's start. I'll pursue you then as I would any other outlaw. If you can manage to elude us and leave England, I will be honored to plead your case to the king should you need a witness. No man could judge your actions anything less than honorable if the story's told true."

Brett smiled faintly and nodded his thanks to the guard. "Ardsley, keep Cerissa with you when I go. And no more marriages," he added dryly.

"I'll straighten this whole mess out with the king," the blond lord promised, also stepping away from the armed men. "Don't worry about anything but killing that son of a bitch."

Lord Martin tightened his arm around Cerissa's throat, pinning her helplessly to his chest. As ignorant as the girl was of fighting, she realized the risk Brett was taking. Never for a second did she fear for her own life. She knew Brett would never chance hitting her with his sword. Suddenly, she gasped as Lord Martin lunged forward, dragging her with him, his rapier slashing toward Brett's chest.

The dark haired lord leapt back easily, and the thrust passed harmlessly. He kept his own sword at the ready, but moved it when Martin struck at him, aiming then for his outstretched arm. Cerissa writhed and kicked in the man's grip, struggling to break free and allow Brett an unobstructed aim. But Martin only tightened his hold, shutting off her breath in her throat, until she gagged for air, the world growing dark before her wide open eyes. She heard, as if from an incredible distance, Brett calling to her to cease her struggling before the man strangled her. Obediently, she relaxed, going limp and motionless.

Lord Martin cursed as he leaned to thrust again at the circling Lindsey, his every movement hampered by the girl. Again, Lord Lindsey only slashed at his sword arm before turning to avoid the blade. But by this time, the strain and the hot summer sun were taking a toll on the lord and Martin's blade nicked his forearm as it passed.

With an eager laugh, Martin lunged again, seeking to follow his success with a more telling blow. Astoundingly, Brett lunged towards him this time, taking the tip of the rapier in his shoulder as he reached for Cerissa's wrist, hauling her out of the surprised man's grasp to swing her toward Ardsley.

The blond lord caught the astonished girl against him and immediately drew his own sword to protect her from recapture. "Got her, Brett," he called calmly, "Go ahead."

Cerissa turned in Lord Ardsley's arm to watch the fight with horrified eyes. The men all seemed so coolly controlled, as if they watched a lawn bowling meet, even commenting occasionally on an especially good move by one or the other swordsman. Brett, she knew, was by far the better fencer, but the blood of his deliberately taken shoulder wound was already soaking his white shirt with scarlet blood. Plus, Lord Martin was relatively fresh compared to Brett. He had remained in one place while he'd held Cerissa as a shield, while Brett had been moving constantly.

She gasped helplessly as Lord Martin lunged forward, his sword aimed for a wicked thrust, then breathed again as Brett parried the stroke easily and turned it aside, forcing Martin backward by a swift flurry of his own. The sword seemed almost a living creature in Brett's dark hand, like a glittering silver snake as it whirled and struck and whirled again, the tip moving so fast that her eye couldn't follow its course. Brett stumbled once, blinded for a moment by the sunlight slanting light, but recovered quickly. And gradually, it seemed to Cerissa that it was Lord Martin who looked most weary, his low forehead shiny with sweat, his narrow eyes beginning to show fear. Brett seemed tireless, calm and patient, though his left sleeve dripped blood on the stone drive and his green eyes clouded with occasional pain when he moved that arm. Still, clearly, it was becoming Brett's option when to end the duel and even the kind Ardsley's face wore a faint, merciless smile.

Finally, even Lord Martin seemed to realize the desperation of his plight. He licked his lips nervously and parried Brett's thrusts with an almost frantic haste, trying to edge backwards towards the watching guards. With a faint smile, Brett forced him the opposite way, using his glittering rapier now as a sort of guide, toying with his sweating opponent until he'd moved him back against the ivy covered wall of the manor. Lord Martin, feeling the brick behind him and realizing the trap, made a last desperate effort to fight free but Brett held him easily at bay. With a choking cry, Martin threw his sword out onto the drive and dropped to his knees, grovelling in the grass for his life.

Cerissa closed her eyes, looking hastily away. However much the man deserved it, she didn't want to watch Brett slaughter him. Astoundingly, she heard words instead of screams of agony and she whirled back to stare at the two men as Brett stood over the fallen lord, his sword tip steady, perhaps a hair away from the man's throat. For a breathless moment, the tableau seemed etched in motionless silence, then Ardsley spoke again.

"Finish him if you want, Brett. God knows he's given you just cause."

Lord Martin stared up at Brett wordlessly, his pale eyes bulging, his ashen face a mask of abject fear. Even to save himself, no words would come from his terror-frozen lips. Finally, with a shudder of disgust, Brett shook his dark head and drew away. "Get up out of the dirt and get out of here before I change my mind," he muttered, turning to walk back towards the waiting girl. "Ardsley, how scum like that was produced by your aunt I'll never..."

"Behind you!" The captain's voice broke the silence like a pistol crack and all eyes flew back to Martin's prostrate figure.

Not content with his life, the lord had drawn a small pistol from somewhere under his coat and now drew the flint lever back to cock it, the barrel pointed at Brett's unprotected back only a few feet away. Cerissa screamed as Brett leapt to one side, his upraised rapier flashing silver before it plunged down towards Lord Martin's chest. Even as he moved she heard the explosive crack of the pistol and she gasped and she started to run for Brett. Ardsley moved with her, reaching the dark haired lord in time to see Lord Martin's death throes, the blood-flecked saliva running from the corner of his slackened mouth.

"Jesus, Brett are you all right?" the blond lord grabbed anxiously for his friend as he stumbled and nearly fell, steadying him with his arm.

Cerissa reached up to touch the blood beginning to ooze from Brett's forehead, forcing his own questioning hand away from the shallow wound. "It's only grazed, Brett," she murmured in relief, beginning to tremble in belated terror. "Help me get him into the house, Ardsley."

"No, sweetheart, there's no time. I'll get it tended later," Brett mumbled, staggering again as he turned for the drive.

"Get your wounds treated and bound," the captain advised, stepping forward to beckon the girl to them. "I said I'd give you an hour for the duel, but take your time my lord. It's rare to see such a display of swordsmanship—rarer still to see such dishonorable filth as that dispatched from the earth. I'm in your debt."

Brett nodded and smiled wearily as he turned for the house, leaning slightly on Cerissa's shoulder as he walked, Ardsley close behind. It was still well before noon when he came back out to take the reins of his saddled stallion, and bent to give Cerissa a farewell kiss. She forced a smile though her blue eyes were still dark with concern. The pistol wound was fairly shallow and had not even required a bandage once the bleeding had stopped. But the shoulder wound from the rapier was deep and, though Brett refused to admit

237

as much, she knew it must be causing him searing pain. He needed to be in bed with a strong dose of brandy, not out riding the countryside, fleeing the kingdom.

"I'll be all right, little mother," he murmured teasingly to the girl, his smile warm if slightly strained. "I don't know how long I'll be gone, though. But the goldsmith has my draft for you and Ardsley will keep you posted. Say goodbye to Jamey for me. Tell him I'll bring him that toy sword he's been begging for when I return."

She nodded, struggling to keep her brimming tears from spilling down her cheeks. Why couldn't Fate just leave them in peace? They'd only asked for a lazy summer together, watching their son grow, maybe making another one. She lifted her face for another, final kiss and then he was gone, raising his hand in friendly salute to the guards as he cantered past. Ardsley, drew her under his arm, and led her toward the house. "Don't worry, sweet, we'll leave for London at once. King James won't stay mad at Brett very long. He'll be home before the summer ends."

Chapter Fifteen

Cerissa sighed blissfully, enjoying the cool country air that blew in the open window. London had been as hot and airless as ever this summer while she'd waited for the outcome of Brett's case. He had been cleared of treason, as both she and Ardsley had guessed he would, but the king was yet unrelenting about his duel with Lord Martin. Monmouth's rebellion had ended already, with the young duke on the scaffold. She'd been saddened to see him die like that and she knew, wherever Brett was, that he would be saddened as well.

Coming out here to the spa had been a wonderful idea, vastly pleased with her decision. It would be nice to meet some new people, hear some different talk, breathe sweet air and even swim in one of the nearby lakes. When she was done with her bath, she would go downstairs to the dining room for her supper instead of ordering it up. Ardsley had insisted she take a maid servant along so she wouldn't be totally alone, and besides, she would enjoy meeting the inn's other guests.

Cerissa took another bite of the fruit that had been delivered as a first course, cocking her chestnut head slightly to better overhear the conversation at the next table. The men there were talking about Brett's now famous duel with Lord Martin and she hid a secret smile. In the telling and the retelling of the event, fact had long since disappeared. Pretended eye-witnesses—of which there seemed virtually hundreds—had portrayed Lord Lindsey as a kind of invincible super being, doing everything from back somersaults to swinging from tree limbs as he dispatched his wicked foe. Cerissa had never fully realized before how popular a figure the dashing, dark haired lord was to the common people of England. More than one young boy she had spoken to in the country had professed his heart's desire to be on one of Brett's ships. Perhaps that was the real reason King James still refused to call the lord back to England.

"I tell ye, my brother-in-law's brother-in-law is the captain which saw the whole thing," the man insisted to his wide eyed companions. "Wounded near to death he was, but he never even slowed his pace."

Cerissa smiled, staring at her fruit. Brett's wounds had been painful, no doubt, and they had sapped his strength, but he was far from nearly dead of them. His last kiss had been proof enough of that.

"Aw, go on, George," another hooted. "If he be such a wonderful swordsman—how'd he get wounded so bad?"

"T'was getting the girl," the first speaker explained haughtily. "Surely you know that much. Gad! The man has no fear, Billie, let me tell you. He couldn't strike back, of course, for fear of hitting the wench Martin held. So his first concern was to be freeing the girl afore harm come to her. With his cool eye, he waits, ye see, and waits some more. He can't take Martin's sword in his right arm and still fight, and he can't take it in his belly for it'd killed him. So he waits for a thrust to the heart and jumps into it, see, sticking the sword in his shoulder long enough to be getting the wench out of danger. Then, calm as you please, he sets about destroying the villain what had grabbed her."

"You know what I'd like to see, George," one man wished aloud. "The wench they was fighting over. She must be something to have the man be taking sword pokes for her."

"Ah," George whispered confidentially. "The captain swore she were the most beautiful girl in England. Flaming red hair and black gypsy eyes, and a figure..." The man drew a vastly exaggerated picture in the air and all the men sighed as one. Soon their talk shifted to other matters, and Cerissa stopped listening. Flaming red hair and gypsy eyes indeed, she laughed to herself. What would those men say if I were to walk over and introduce myself? They'd never believe the story I told of the fight—it'd be way too tame for them.

"Excuse me, madam, but may we sit down here to share your table?"

Cerissa looked up to see two older gentlemen standing beside her and she nodded graciously, introducing herself and her maid Patsy. She made some polite small talk with the men for a few minutes then returned her attention to the servant, hardly conscious of the strangers' conversation until one comment caught her ear.

"Yes, by the time I've returned to London I'll be taken to Newgate," the older man sighed helplessly. "I'm in debt of 2,800 pounds and no way to pay it."

"Nonsense, Edward," his companion argued. "Marry a country heiress. You're an earl. Surely your title alone would be worth something."

"To a wealthy young girl who could have her pick of suitors? Hardly. I'm sixty-one this month and in failing health. Who's going to marry such a specimen? I'm not worried, though, my heart is too bad to last long in debtor's prison. I'll not be suffering very long."

"Excuse me, gentlemen, but I couldn't help overhearing your conversation." Cerissa forced a casual smile though her heart hammered in sudden awareness. A baron...an old, dying, baron who might give her the title she needed to marry Brett..."Are you really in such dreadful straits, my lord?"

"Unfortunately, yes, my dear," the man named Edward replied with a small smile. "But don't let the troubles of strangers upset your dinner. I am an old man. I'm resigned to my fate."

Cerissa smiled fleetingly and returned to her meal, her face composed though her brain was working furiously. Having Brett at Whitross for those few months had nearly dissipated her determination for marriage. After Sean's explanation of the obstacles to such a state, she had almost given up hope. But this might be a heaven sent opportunity if only she were wise enough to seize it. Brett was still in exile and might be for several years yet...if the old man was as sick as he said...Of course, Brett's initial reaction would probably be negative, but in time he would understand the wisdom of her choice. The duel with Lord Martin, for example, which had forced his fleeing the country. If she had been married to Brett, been Lady Lindsey—with the protection of his name shielding her—even Martin could not have dared to seize her. Brett could adopt Jamey then and make the boy his heir.

As the two men finished their meal and rose to leave, Cerissa leaned breathlessly over to the old earl to pluck at his sleeve. "If you are truly desirous of seeking a way out of imprisonment, come to my rooms after dark. I may be able to offer a solution."

The man looked at her with astonished eyes but quickly recovered, shrugging his shoulders and nodding his head. "About eight?" he asked in a low voice.

Cerissa nodded and told him the room number, watching him as he rejoined his companion and left the room. Her heart was still beating fearfully fast, her supper lay cooling on the plate before her. She had no intentions this time of selling her body as the price of marriage. She had done that once with Gerard and refused to do so again. But Edward was very old, perhaps he wouldn't care. And Brett would be less likely to disapprove as well if he were assured of her fidelity to him. That had been his major reason for hating Gerard—the knowledge that he shared the girl's body with another man.

Up in her room, Cerissa watched the door impatiently, trying to make a final decision. If only she had time to talk to Ardsley—to solicit his opinion of the match. It would do her no good at all to purchase the marriage and hence a title, with Brett's money if it so maddened the dark haired lord that he ceased to love her. But on the other hand, what a perfect life she and Brett could have together eventually as man and wife. This might be her only chance to secure such a future.

"Good evening, madam," the old earl bowed formally as he entered the room, a strained smile on his weathered face. He was clearly embarrassed by the meeting and Cerissa hastened to present her offer, trying to force her voice to sound strong and careless though her lips were dry as dust.

"Madame Whitestone," the earl frowned, "Am I correct that you are offering to give me the 3,000 pounds for my debts if I will marry you?"

Cerissa nodded, wondering desperately whether she was making the right decision. Damn Brett! She swore silently in a moment of irrational anger. The man was never around when she needed him!

"I feel it's only fair to caution you on a . . . a delicate matter, my dear," Edward stammered, flushing red, "I cannot offer you the . . . the ah . . . usual benefits a man offers his wife in the conjugal bed. For several years now, I have been unable to ... to perform in that way."

Cerissa gaped at him wordlessly, hardly believing her good fortune. There would be no need then to warn him about her own reluctance. Suddenly a daring plan came into her mind and she spoke with forced slowness. "Well, Lord Ramond, a young woman has certain ... ah needs. Would I be permitted to seek gratification of those elsewhere ... provided I was most discreet, of course, and not wanton in my choices?"

The earl frowned, but nodded reluctantly. Oh the best of all worlds! She could even continue to enjoy Brett while she waited for her freedom! "I have some small skill in dressmaking," she offered eagerly. "I shall open a shop in London. It may not make us wealthy, but it should provide enough to live upon."

The old lord studied the girl for a long moment, obviously tempted. "May I ask why a girl of your means, with such a lovely face and figure, should seek marriage with such as I?"

Cerissa smiled hesitantly, then shook her head slowly. Lord Lindsey was too well known in the country, too wealthy as well. Would the baron be content with the 3,000 pounds if he were aware of her connection with the dark haired lord? "I'm sorry, Edward, but no. Suffice to say, I am not with child now and looking for a name for him. I have a two year old son already, but you needn't offer your name to him either."

With a slow sigh, the old man nodded his acceptance of the conditions and turned to leave. "We shall be married then at your convenience, and begin the journey back to London whenever you wish. Until, tomorrow, then, goodnight dear child ... and thank you."

Cerissa watched him go with a faint sense of foreboding. Please God! She'd made the right decision ... Please God, Brett would understand and accept the situation when he eventually returned. Please God she hadn't made the same mistake she had in marrying Gerard.

Brett threw his dark head back and laughed as he shut the carriage door after his two companions. "No, Philip, it's too lovely a night to waste closed up in a coach. I'll walk back to my lodgings—they're only a few blocks."

"Well, keep a wary eye out for ruffians, Brett. The streets are dangerous so late at night."

"Now, who would dare attack a swordsman of such international repute?" the other man laughed teasingly. Stories of Brett's duel with Lord Martin were known even here in France.

Brett laughed and made a mocking grimace at his friends words, then waved carelessly as the carriage rolled away into the darkness of the night.

He took a deep breath, enjoying the warm sweetness of the balmy fall evening, his head spinning pleasantly from one too many brandies inside the gaming house. A girl's voice called down invitingly from one of the windows high above him, and he glanced up smiling at her offer. For a moment he was tempted. Her hair hung loose and thick over her creamy shoulders and down over her half revealed breasts, and the color of it was only a shade or two lighter than Cerissa's. But he shook his dark head finally in answer, replying in French that he was flattered by her offer but most regrettably disinclined.

Brett's black brows drew close over his eyes as he walked on. More and more over these last years he had found his passion linked specifically to Cerissa. Even now, when he had been without a woman since he'd left the girl at Whitross, he had no inclination to seek another in her place. He did not want merely any woman under him, he wanted Cerissa. The very thought of her slim arms locked around his neck, her full breasts pressed close to his chest, sent throbbing waves of hot urgency stabbing through his loins. Suddenly, he stopped still, laughing aloud in inspiration. How stupid he had been all these months, how blind! If it was Cerissa that he wanted, it was Cerissa he would have! Just because he could not go to her in England didn't mean she wouldn't come to him in France! So long as King James remained unforgiving, England was closed to him. But he could—no, he corrected himself with an eager grin—he *would* send a ship tomorrow morning for Cerissa and the baby. There was no reason why not, even if he couldn't enter England, she could surely leave it. Within a week she could be filling his arms again. He would provision the "Cerissa" for a long voyage and take she and the boy to the Bermudas, to winter in a milder climate. He laughed aloud again, quickening his stride as he walked through the dark deserted street. Jesus, what a dolt he had been! He could have sent for her long ago.

Suddenly, he stopped again, cocking his head to listen intently to the night sounds around him. Had he actually heard footsteps behind him, or had he imagined them? He turned and searched the dark alley carefully, seeing nothing. At length, he turned again to walk on, taking the precaution of loosening his rapier in it's sheath, leaving his right hand rest lightly on it's jewelled hilt as he quickened his pace. Up ahead was a major street, marked by an occasional lantern light. Perhaps he'd better stay on the more travelled roads this late at night.

Suddenly, his sixth sense screamed danger and he leapt forward toward the street light, drawing his sword as he whirled to face three assailants.

"No need to be testy, gov'nor," a rough Cockney voice warned jeeringly. "We're after yer wallet, not yer hide."

"I don't doubt, having one that you'd not be overly concerned for the other though," Brett replied drily, keeping his back to the pole and his sword at guard.

"Unless you figure to take on all three of us at once, you'd best be real nice," the ruffian growled menacingly, urging his equally filthy looking comrades to step forward out of the shadows.

Brett remained motionless, his gaze flickering swiftly over the other two men. One held a club, another a sword. The leader brandished a wicked looking broad-bladed sword—long and curved at the tip, like a moslem piece. Still, the club would be of little use while he held his sword still. So it depended on how well the would-be thieves could use their weapons.

Without warning, the man on his right sprang forward, thrusting clumsily with his rapier. Brett flicked his wrist quickly and drew a bloody line across the man's chest, sending him screaming backwards.

The burly leader of the gang stared intently at Brett's face, his eyes narrowed in consideration. "Pretty nice, gov'nor," he conceded admiringly. "But it won't do you much good against the sword I've got. I can take you down without even getting in range of yer little sticker there."

Brett smiled thinly, shrugging his disbelief. "You can try," he admitted casually, watching for the man's first move, his whole body tensed to spring. Behind him he heard the increasing clatter of carriage wheels on the cobblestoned street but he dared not look around to see it. If he took his eyes off the man for a moment he would be on him.

The ruffians heard the coach approaching as well and their faces grew worried. Both men charged at once, the leader swinging the long sword in a vicious too-handed stroke aimed for the throat. Brett jumped backwards to avoid the weapon and twisted like a cat to thrust at the man with the club. With a gurgling howl, the man went down, his weapon rolling out into the street. The leader took another step forwards, seeking to catch the lord off-balance from the last attack, and Brett leapt sideways again, slashing simultaneously at the robber's wrist.

"Ici! What's going on here!" a masculine voice demanded in French from the halted carriage, the coach door opening immediately.

Brett had a swift impression of an older man, well-dressed and bewigged, hurrying to his side, his sword drawn. At the same instant, the burly robber threw his sword aside and reached beneath his ragged coat, pulling a pistol. With a warning cry to his would-be rescuer, Brett leapt toward the ruffian, his rapier slashing down to force the pistol from the man's hand before he could aim to fire. But the older gentleman reacted on his own instincts, disregarding Brett's warning to spring between the two men, his shoulder catching Brett's to force the sword wild. Helplessly, the dark haired lord swore and stumbled against the outstretched body of one of his attackers, trying desperately to turn and strike again at the pistol-man. Before the rapier could find it's mark, the gun cracked loudly and the older man groaned, staggering backwards, his hand clutching at a spreading red stain on his velvet waistcoat. Brett plunged his sword deep in the robbers chest, feeling a sudden jar in his wrist as the man crumpled instantly, dead on his feet. Then he turned to kneel at the wounded man's side, calling urgently to the carriage driver for assistance.

"Help me get him in the coach," Brett ordered the frightened servant. "And drive to a surgeon—the closest one."

"Aye, my lord," the man replied, moving to help the dark haired Englishman lift his wounded master. In a moment, the two men had carried the wounded Frenchman inside the coach, laying him gently on the velvet covered bench within.

"All haste," Brett muttered to the driver as the man leapt back to the ground. Damn! he swore bitterly, what a rotten end to the evening. The man's wound was obviously a mortal one. His breath was choking already in his lungs as they filled with blood from the pistol shot. And the damndest thing of all was that it was totally unnecessary. He'd had the situation well enough in hand. Why hadn't the man regarded his warning? Why had he jumped forward, knocking Brett's sword thrust wild so the ruffian had time to fire? Damn! Why didn't he just stay out of the way?

"Am I dying?" the man's eyelids fluttered open unexpectedly and he fixed Lord Lindsey with a searching stare.

Brett returned his gaze helplessly, unwilling to state the obvious.

"I'm sorry, my lord. Don't speak, we're on the way to the surgeon's now."

"I don't need a surgeon, young man," the older man tried to force a smile but it ended in a pitiful grimace as he began to cough bright blood. "Are you a lord?" he asked at last in a breathless whisper.

Brett frowned in surprise, then nodded slowly. "Yes, an English baron. Bretegane, Lord Lindsey. I'm only visiting..."

"Good," the man rasped, reaching out to clasp one of Brett's hands with one of his own now wet and sticky with his life blood. "Then promise me you'll marry my daughter. She has no one else. My brother-in-law would stop at nothing to gain my title and money. She must have a husband to aid her. Promise me."

Brett stared in stunned silence into the man's pleading eyes. "I...my lord, I...surely your daughter has other courters more suitable for a match than..."

"No," the dying lord gasped. "None, she's a good girl, I swear it. She's been gently reared—in the convent school till now. She won't dishonor your name. She'll be a good wife to you, a good mother for your heirs..."

Helplessly, Brett shook his dark head. "True my lord, I do owe you a debt, but..."

The man's gaze grew almost fanatic and he grasped Brett's hand in a painful grip. "You owe me your life, Lord Lindsey. That ruffian's pistol was aimed at your heart, not mine when I jumped forward. You cannot honorably deny my request!"

Brett shrugged helplessly, unwilling to make the man's death utterly meaningless by admitting the truth. Still, he did owe the dying lord something for his aid. He could not marry the woman he loved anyway—if Cerissa would understand the circumstances—and if the girl would be content with his name only..."My lord, in fairness to your daughter, I must tell you this much. I love another woman. I have a son by her and I..."

"For God's sake man, what has love to do with this? I'm asking for your protection. I don't give a damn what you do with your heart—that's your own affair. Elizabeth?"

"Yes, father," a woman's voice answered from the shadows behind him, and Brett glanced around in astonished surprise. He had never even realized that a girl was in the carriage. She'd never made a sound...

"I want your promise to marry Lord Lindsey at once," he demanded, his voice rasping in his throat. "And yours, Lord

247

Lindsey. Your sworn word."

Brett dropped his head for a long moment, torn between honor and his own desires. He didn't want any woman except Cerissa. If he could not have her to wife, he wanted no other. But you do owe this man, another voice in his brain insisted, your duty commands you accept his death wish to protect his daughter. "All right, I swear it," he whispered at last, his eyes dark with bitter frustration.

As if he had forced himself to live only to hear that promise, the old lord gave a final gasping sigh and then laid still. His daughter flung herself, sobbing, over the man's motionless form, murmuring inaudible words as she clasped his hand.

Brett leaned wearily out the window, signalling the driver to turn for home instead, then sank back into the seat, staring at the still mumbling Elizabeth. Prayers, he realized at last, frowning slightly, Catholic prayers. The girl was Catholic of course. He was Anglican, Church of England. Would the girl perhaps prefer to marry within her own faith? No, matter, he decided heavily, she had promised her father. That would decide the question in her mind.

Finally, the coach rolled to a slow stop at the front of a large house. Brett climbed out of the carriage and offered his arm to the white faced girl. His wife, he thought numbly, staring down at her stranger's face. Dear God. Cerissa my only love, will you ever forgive me? Almost absently, he walked the distraught girl to the open door and handed her in, seeing her through oddly impersonal eyes. A slight girl, perhaps twenty or so, light brown hair, a reasonably well-favored face, not much of a figure. What a strange gown she wore, all dusty grey, high at the collar and loose through the bodice and waist, unrelieved by any accent of colorful silk or lace.

In a kind of stunned daze, he heard himself explaining the evening's events to the sorrowing housekeeper, heard himself agree to a wedding three days hence, heard Elizabeth's murmured farewell and made the appropriate responses. Soon, he was back at his own lodgings, delivered by Elizabeth's coach driver. He walked in, remembering to nod to the landlord as he passed, his heart still leaden and sick in his breast.

"A message for you, my lord," the innkeeper offered him a folded parchment.

Wordlessly, he took it, too drained to even feel excitement as he recognized Ardsley's scrawled hand. Inside was a simple message. "Welcome home!" Involuntarily, a low groan escaped from his lips and he crumpled the paper in his fist, bitterly.

Oh damn fate! he thought in helpless rage. If that message had only come yesterday, even earlier tonight. Now was too late. Too damn late. He'd sworn himself to marry a woman he didn't love, sworn to protect a stranger's interests from other unknown, grasping strangers...all when Cerissa had been within his reach again. White-faced in bitter fury, he tossed the parchment into the fire and watched it burn, a black scowl contorting his handsome face. Three days to the funeral—wedding day. Three days more he'd give to establish the girl's inheritance. Then, honor be damned, he was heading for home. Heading for England, heading for Cerissa. His new wife would simply have to accept that fact.

The funeral took all morning and they left directly from there to travel to the small church Elizabeth had selected for the wedding ceremony, attended only by close friends and family. The marriage mass took another couple hours and it was nearing sunset by the time it was completed. Brett forced a faint smile to his bride as he lifted his head from the obligatory kiss and offered his arm for the return trip down the narrow aisle. At the door, Elizabeth halted, looking over her shoulder toward a grey stone chapel. "May I beg your indulgence, my lord?" she murmured hesitantly, "I would like to say goodbye to the nuns. This is where I've lived for seven years now, since my mother died."

Brett nodded and released her arm, moving wordlessly into the dying sunlight to rest against a stone pillar. He was grateful for a moment to collect his own thoughts. And he was not impatient to begin the wedding night rituals. A wife, he thought numbly, watching the girl's slight figure disappear into the shadows, the last gleam of sunlight glinting off the gold wedding ring on her finger. That stranger is now my wife...For better or worse, until death...That woman will bear my children, her son will be my heir—not my darling Jamey now, however much I wish it...

Elizabeth clutched the nun's hand, her grey eyes full of tears. "I can't bear it," she choked. "Oh, Mother Kathleen, God forgive me, but I can't..."

The nun drew the sobbing girl gently down onto a narrow wooden bench and touched her hair consolingly. "You will, my child, because you must. Bow your head for a moment and seek strength from the Blessed Madonna. Pray for her aid in this new event in your life." She waited a minute while the girl lowered her head in obedience, then rose to move silently around the room, her own thoughts dark and troubled. She did not blame the girl for her misery, Elizabeth would have made a wonderful sister here. Suddenly, she stopped, peering out the grating into the grey granite courtyard. The girl's husband was standing there in thoughtful silence, his own face far from radiantly happy. Shrewdly she studied the man's face, safe in her concealment behind the grates. It was a strong face, a handsome one. Perhaps the jaw line was a shade too strong... was there a hint of ruthlessness bespoken in it? Involuntarily she shuddered. Suddenly Brett sighed softly and turned, raising his gaze to the stained glass window above her head, and the abbess caught her breath in surprise and relief. The face was very hard but the eyes were kind. And, meeting them for just the barest instant, she had sensed something sorrowful in them. Though neither his manner nor his face betrayed such, the man was greatly saddened by something.

She turned back to the still praying girl and touched her hair gently. "He is very handsome Elizabeth, and his eyes are kind. He will be a good husband."

"I wanted no husband but God," the girl whispered brokenly. "You know that. I wanted only to be one of the sisters here, to give my life's service to the Holy Church."

Despite herself, the nun's eyes filled with tears and she blinked them hastily away. "I know, my child, and you would have been welcome here with us. But you must resign yourself to God's plan for you. Pray for obedience to His will. Remember He works in mysterious ways. Your husband is not of our faith but he allowed you to choose this church for the wedding anyway. I don't believe he will prevent you from following your religion. Be comforted, my dear. Remember you do not leave God behind as you leave us today. God will come with you, He will live in your heart."

Elizabeth nodded, her lips still trembling with grief.

"One more thing, child, before you go. As I glanced into your husband's eyes I saw sorrow there. Do you know what has caused it?"

The girl's eyes widened in guilty surprise and she dropped her head again in shame at her own selfishness. She had been so overcome with her own grief she had not spared thought for his reaction to the marriage. "I..." she stammered, frowning in thought. "Forgive me, Mother, I have been so selfish. I didn't notice his sadness. Perhaps... I remember he told my father it was unfair of him to marry me—because he loved another woman. I believe he said he had a son by her..."

The abbess turned away swiftly, one hand clasping the crucifix as she struggled to conceal her horror and shock. "That is a mortal sin, Elizabeth, for him to lay with a woman out of wedlock. For his soul's sake, you must take care to end such an affair. He is your husband now, he must cleave only to you and no other."

The girl nodded again, wiping her tears from her face as best she could, then turning to leave. But at the doorway, as she clung helplessly to the nun. "No, I can't do it, not lay with him tonight. Oh, Mother Kathleen, help me, please, I beg of you."

The nun drew gently away, forcing the girl from her. "You must, Elizabeth, it is your duty now to do so. Take heart, child, I do not believe he will be unkind to you. Now go. We have pressed his patience long enough." With a last tearful kiss, the girl was gone and the nun watched as she reentered the light outside. Lord Lindsey turned and offered his arm to the distraught girl for the short walk to the coach. The abbess turned slowly away from the window, taking her rosary in her hand. Some instinct in her soul gave comfort to her for the girl's loss. She knew in some mysterious way that it would not be long before she returned to them—to live with God as she truly longed to do. Smiling faintly, she began to pray for the girl's good fortune in her new marriage, for the strength for her to endure what she would have to tonight.

The wedding supper was a solemn affair and the usual bawdy jesting not in evidence. The women, as customary, led Elizabeth up to the bridal chamber and prepared her for the bedding. The men escorted Brett up shortly thereafter.

As he stepped into the room, the girl's face drained bloodless and one of the maids reached to pinch her cheeks before leaving. In a moment, the door closed and they were alone. Brett moved slowly to extinguish all but one of the candles before sitting to undress, stripping himself first of the stiff formal brocade coat and waistcoat, then the finely woven high necked shirt and stock. He glanced quickly at the girl—his wife, he forced himself to say silently—but she was looking away, her eyes closed, her lips moving as if in prayer. He removed his hose and shoes and finally his satin breeches and walked toward the bed, his body quiet, almost reluctant. No bridegroom urgency hastened his pace or sent welling desire into his loins. This was a duty to be performed, nothing else. Oh God! Why couldn't it be Cerissa in the marriage bed awaiting him? Why this timid, quaking child instead?

Elizabeth felt the bed sag under her husband's weight and

251

clasped the gold cross hanging around her neck with fearful hands. She felt his breath loud in her ear, felt his warm, dry lips press against her throat, his hands seeking her body. With trembling effort, she forced herself to endure his caresses, even the wine taste of his mouth as his tongue thrust into hers. Soon she felt his weight above her, crushing the breath from her lungs and she clenched her jaw against her rising horror. As his knee moved her legs apart, she moaned helplessly, biting her lips to smother any other sounds, reminding herself of Mother Kathleen's words. It is your duty to lay with him...his rights...Suddenly, she screamed and arched backwards away from the searing pain in her belly as he entered her. Sobbing wildly, she beat at his back with her fists, writhing beneath his tormenting touch. At last, she felt him shudder slightly in her arms and he drew away, turning to stare at her tear stained face in troubled silence.

"I'm sorry, Elizabeth, I could not avoid hurting you," he murmured at last, frowning slightly in the moon dappled darkness. "Next time, it will not be so..."

The girl turned her head away, letting her silent tears fall on the linen pillowcase. Next time, she heard in horror...Oh God, give me strength. There will be a lifetime of such experiences. "Forgive my tears," she whispered at last. "I know you tried to be kind with me."

After a long silence, Brett shrugged and turned away to his own side of the bed, his eyes dark and frustrated as he stared sightlessly out the curtained window. Never in his life had he felt such a total lack of response from a woman. Not all had been as passionate as Cerissa perhaps, but never, ever...The girl had laid under him like a wooden creature, coming to life only when he'd finally given up trying to arouse her and simply decided to get the job done. Then she'd screamed and fought. And held onto that crucifix all the time...He shuddered suddenly, reaching out to raise the covers higher on his bare body. It degraded the act so to have her hold the cross so desperately. He'd felt as if he were raping a nun. Was that it perhaps? Had the girl decided, in her seven years at the convent school, that she wished to become a nun? Oh Jesus! he thought in bitter frustration. What a mess! What a bloody, God-forsaken mess.

Chapter Sixteen

"This is a lovely home, Edward," Cerissa smiled fondly at her older husband. "How nice of your friends to invite us."

"They're having quite a large crowd," the earl replied, glad of his young wife's pleasure. "Most of the London quality will be here."

Cerissa nodded, reaching absently down to smooth the skirt of her satin gown. They'd only reached London the day before—been married only two weeks. She hadn't had a chance to visit Lord Ardsley yet—to explain to him what had happened at the spa and how she had come to be married again. Her heart rose in sudden hope. If all the nobles were supposed to be here, perhaps Ardsley would be as well. It would be a perfect opportunity to introduce him to her husband and check what news there was of Brett as well.

"Lord and Lady Ramond," the servant bowed them through into the formal gardens, already crowded with richly dressed people, and she saw their hosts hurrying toward them to begin the round of introductions.

A whirl of names and faces, of gorgeous satins and sumptuous laces began. Cerissa greeted each new person graciously, struggling desperately to remember which lady went with which lord, who was Lord Bradford and who was Lord Bainford until her brain seemed hopelessly confused. She looked eagerly for Lord Ardsley but could see no sign of the blond haired lord or his wife amidst the milling crowd.

As she turned in response to her hostess' call, she felt her heart leap, then plummet with a sickening jar. Just ahead of her, a tall, broad-shouldered black haired lord with his back to her... it couldn't be Brett she reassured herself frantically as Edward's arm drew her inexorably closer to the man. Please God, not like this... without a word of explanation.

"Excuse me," the smiling hostess reached over to tap the man lightly on the shoulder and he began to glance around. "Lord Lindsey, may I introduce Lord and Lady Ramond."

Cerissa felt her face go bloodless and she swayed helplessly against her husband, unable to utter a single word, unable to tear her eyes away from Brett's turned face. He too stood silent, as if thunderstruck, staring at the white faced girl, his eyes filling with incredulous rage.

The silence grew longer and the host and hostess exchanged quick nervous glances, aware of the tension charging the air. "Lord Lindsey," the hostess faltered apprehensively at last. "Is something amiss?"

Finally, Brett managed to tear his eyes away from Cerissa's ashen face to stare numbly at her husband. He shook his dark head slowly, as if trying to clear it of a daze from a sharp blow, or the vagueness of long illness. Finally, he made a half-bow to Lord Ramond, muttering an apology for his rudeness in staring at the man's wife. "I ... I once knew a girl who looked very much like her," he murmured, his lips still grim and white, his jaw muscles clenched.

"No apology required, Lord Lindsey," Edward smiled kindly, though his eyes flickered from the dark lord to his wife in mute confusion. "She is a beautiful woman. Men often stare at her."

Brett bowed again and muttered a response to Lord Ramond's pleasantries. At last, Cerissa heard her husband's voice, as if from an incredible distance, asking if she'd like some punch. She could not even force a reply to him, just stared still at Brett's dark face in stricken horror.

"Cerissa, my dear, I asked if you'd care for some punch. They have it in a lovely fountain arrangement over there," Edward repeated kindly, pulling gently on the girl's arm.

At last Cerissa pulled her staring eyes away from Lord Lindsey's face. "Yes, Edward," she managed to say in a hoarse whisper, her wooden lips nearly too stiff to move at all, "I would appreciate some."

"Good evening, then, Lord Lindsey. I hope to meet you again sometime," her husband turned and began to move away, pulling Cerissa with him.

Helplessly, the girl flung one last look of urgent pleading over her shoulder toward Brett. But he was already turning away also, his beloved grey-green eyes catching hers for only the barest instant before they moved on. That instant had been enough for Cerissa however. Enough to see the shock and anger, the bitterness and the deep, incredulous hurt within them. She drew a sobbing, deep breath and fought back welling tears. What must he think seeing her like this? Could any explanation now possibly offset the pain she had caused him? How could he have been here? When had he gotten back? If Brett were here, surely Ardsley was as well. She would have to find the blond lord and explain it all to him. Perhaps, with his aid, she could at least coax Brett to listen to an explanation. She knew by the look in his eyes that Brett would not even do that much now. How could fate play such a cruel trick on her? To hurt the man so deeply when she only sought his joy.

"Your punch, child," Edward was saying as he handed her the cup, "Shall we go take a seat there? My old legs are nearly worn out."

Wordlessly, Cerissa went with him, her brain still too distraught to force conversation. Worst of all, she realized in a kind of stunned horror that she would have to smile and talk and dance and chatter all the rest of the evening as though nothing were amiss. The night would be endless.

The growing dark was forcing the guests inside when Cerissa finally caught sight of Lord Ardsley standing by the garden pool. She glanced quickly at her husband, some yards away talking to another older lord, then hastily excused herself from her companion to hurry over. She realized the woman was staring after her, frowning at her rudeness, but she didn't care. Nothing mattered any more except Brett! She had to talk to Ardsley!

Cerissa caught up to him just as he was turning to go in, and the blond lord glanced around in surprise, feeling her hand on his sleeve. Cerissa gasped as she met his eyes, their blue cold and contemptuous as frozen snow. She drew her hand away, her blue eyes answering hurt surprise at his look.

255

"Lady Ramond, is it not?" Ardsley smiled coolly and made a mocking bow. "Excuse me, I was on my way inside."

With a small cry, Cerissa grabbed for his arm as he shouldered by her and clung stubbornly until he stopped. "No, Ardsley, don't you be this way too!" she pleaded frantically, her eyes wide and beseeching. "You don't understand! I only married Edward for Brett's sake! He was in debt, I met him at the spa, he was going to Newgate and I offered to give him the money he needed. We can be married now, someday, Brett and I. I'll have a title. Edward's sixty-one and his heart is very bad and . . ."

"Spare me, Cerissa," Ardsley growled, his face closed and hard against her. "It's hardly a praiseworthy act—waiting around for the old goat to be laid out so you can run to your lover's bed. I'd thought better of you."

Cerissa stared a moment in wordless surprise, feeling a slow flush of embarrassment creep up her neck. It did sound horribly ghoulish the callous way Ardsley phrased it, but she didn't think of it in such morbid terms.

"One item of interest to me, Cerissa—or, excuse me, Lady Ramond—where did you find money for your husband's debts?"

The girl swallowed hard, lowering her eyes guiltily. "I used Brett's money, James, I had to . . ." she whispered. "No! Don't turn away, Ardsley, please, you must understand . . ." she cried pleadingly.

"Oh, I do understand," Ardsley laughed, a cold, cruel, mirthless laugh that chilled the girl's soul. "You saw a good thing so you snatched it up. All happiness to you and your elderly bridegroom, my lady." He jerked his arm out of Cerissa's grasp and strode hastily away, not looking back.

Cerissa watched him go with a feeling of sick hopelessness. Would no one even listen to her? Give her a chance to explain? Oh my God, she realized in numbing horror, if Ardsley hates me so much, what must Brett be feeling? I had counted on Ardsley to help smooth things over.

"There you are, darling," Edward's voice sounded in her ear as he took her limp arm in his. "Let's go in, now. They're beginning the dancing."

Cerissa was amazed at how well her outer shell managed to smile, chatter, even dance through the evening while her heart felt cold and heavy as lead, her soul more than partially dead. She saw Ardsley from a distance several times more, and Brett once, with a strange, plainly dressed woman she didn't remember meeting. Her husband had been the pillar of kind strength, tirelessly at her elbow, his old eyes troubled and oddly compassionate when they met hers. But thankfully, he asked no question about her strange behavior earlier in the evening and, with midnight drawing near, Cerissa began to breathe a shade easier. They could leave soon without insulting the host and hostess. Perhaps, in the quiet privacy of her own bedroom tonight, she could think of a way to untangle this snarl.

She sighed wearily and shifted in her straight backed chair, then suddenly froze. Almost within touching distance, on the dance floor, was Brett. He was swinging the blond Alicia in his arm, his dark head bent down to her ear, his lips curved in a faint smile at what ever it was she was saying. Cerissa's heart gave a sick lurch and she felt her throat close in nauseous fear. Alicia . . . that haughty blond beauty. She had made no secret of the fact that she had set her cap for Bretegane Lindsey. Now, with Brett believing she'd betrayed him, would he marry the woman? She pushed herself hastily to her feet, her forehead cold and damp, her knees barely holding her. "I don't feel well, Edward, I'm going to the ladies' room," she choked.

Lord Ramond glanced up, his eyes concerned. "Shall I have someone go with you, child? I really don't . . ."

"No," she hastily assured him, turning for the hallway, "Please. I'll be all right."

Brett danced again with Alicia, enjoying her obvious interest, using her whispered offers of assignation to assuage the bitter pain of Cerissa's falseness. But finally, with a smiling bow, he disengaged himself from her, watching as she collected one of her friends and hurried laughing toward the powder room. Then he walked back to the corner where his wife sat chatting quietly with several older ladies. He offered her a glass of wine he'd picked up from one of the servant's silver trays, and heard her murmured thanks as she set it to one side of her chair. Sensing his gaze, Elizabeth glanced again up to catch his eye then hastily looked away, her lip twitching nervously.

Brett continued to stare at her, having had too many brandies through the evening to care much for her discomfort. Damn, timid, little church mouse, he thought, in amused mockery, always looking at me with the eyes of a hunted animal. "I'm going outside," he drawled lazily at last, still watching her face. She smiled quickly, relief evident in her grey eyes. Giving way to a sudden cruel impulse, he leaned forward, sliding a hand behind her head to hold it while he pressed his mouth to hers. Instantly, Elizabeth's face drained of color, and her hands began to tremble in her lap. At last, he released her, his eyes dark with bitterness, his mouth drawn and grim. He turned quickly and walked into the darkness of the gardens, hating her and hating himself even more. It was the only pleasure he seemed to derive from their marriage—the pleasure of tormenting the girl. It was a rotten, ugly fact but more and more he was unable to resist such cruelty. Her fear of him, her revulsion in their bed, her constant pious mumblings and that infernal crucifix she clutched just now when she'd shown her gladness at his announcement to walk outside. Brett shook his head disgustedly as he moved toward the promised serenity of the dark garden house. And tonight . . . the added shock of seeing Cerissa introduced as Lady Ramond. All women were whores. He'd been a fool to ever believe otherwise.

Cerissa sat silently in the darkest corner of the ladies room, resting on the cushioned bench while a dozen women came and left. In all her life, she could never remember such a feeling of limitless despair. When Brett had meant to sail for the Indies without her, tried to send her home on the Mary Rose, when she'd thought him dead . . . a half dozen times she'd despaired before, but now . . . Tears started again in her eyes and she blinked them hastily away, forcing herself to draw a deep breath and gather her skirts to go. Sitting here brooding would help nothing.

She hesitated, drawing into the shadow again as two new women chattered their way inside the room. Alicia! her mind recognized numbly, the blood pounding overloud in her ears. Brett had been dancing with her all evening. Would Brett now offer to marry the blond? Feeling almost nauseous, she held her breath, straining her ears to hear the murmured conversation.

"I thought she was very nice," the one defended an unknown woman. "Rather an odd match for him perhaps, but nevertheless . . ."

"Odd?" Alicia laughed mockingly. "I'll say! They all call her the church-mouse you know when *he* isn't around. And no wonder . . . always dressing in that unflattering grey. I'll lay you a hundred pounds I have him back in my bed within a week. No timid little rosary mumbler's going to keep him interested very long. Not with his eye for women."

"And theirs for him," the other smirked. "I'm sure it set you back on your heels when Millford's introduced a Lady Lindsey."

Cerissa missed Alicia's retort as her brain seemed to explode

258

within her head and she fought dizzying nausea, gasping for breath. Lady Lindsey! Oh my God! She nearly fainted, clutching helplessly at the wall for support, the world spinning in front of her eyes. I couldn't have heard right! Brett couldn't have married someone else... before he'd even known about Edward.

"She's Lady Lindsey because her father was stupid enough to get himself uselessly killed. Of all the men I know, who but Bretegane Lindsey would have felt compelled to accede to such a ridiculous request?" Alicia snapped.

"Well, darling, I don't want to quarrel about it, but you must admit one thing. For a man coerced into marriage, he surely does fawn on the girl. He's always hovering around her, fetching her drinks, why, I swear I saw him kissing her just before we came..."

"If you don't want to argue about it then drop it," Alicia whispered venomously. "I've offered you a wager. Now take it or not."

"All right, I'll take it," her companion snickered. "Though heaven knows how either of us are going to produce evidence of such a bet, won or lost."

"Oh, I'll produce your evidence," Alicia laughed, her humor improving. "Brett's never been exactly shy in admitting his pleasures. I'll hang him on my arm at Whitehall and have him tell you himself."

"Speaking of Whitehall, Alicia, did you hear about Lord Graver's latest exploit?"

"No, tell me."

"Well, I've sworn to secrecy, but since it's you, I heard..."

Cerissa forced her breath in and out, through a throat which seemed unbelievably constricted, waiting for Alicia and her friend to wander back into the main party. Brett... married! Her brain seemed unable to comprehend the words, simple as they seemed. Married. While he was in France? Or had he come home and not even made any effort to contact her? No, not after their happiness at Whitross. But then, in France? Why though? Why? And why then his black fury when she had been introduced as Lady Ramond? If he had fallen so desperately in love with another woman that he married her, why should he care any longer whether she married or not? And what had Alicia meant about the woman being Brett's wife because of her father being killed? Oh God, what a night... so many questions with no answers. And even Ardsley, the one man who might have explained the situation, who could have linked Brett and she together at least long enough to find out the truth of both sides, even he was cold and obviously too furious to help her.

Forcing herself to move, she pushed herself to her feet, still terribly aware of the sickness in her stomach, the dizzy whirling of her brain. She stopped at the doorway, staring out down the hallway toward the brightly lit ballroom, alive with laughter and brilliant colors and masses of strangers . . . not yet. She simply could not face the gaiety just now. With the instincts of a mortally wounded animal, she turned toward the quiet concealing darkness of the now deserted gardens. If she could have just a moment or two in peace, in the anonymous shadows, to collect herself . . . Unsteadily, she groped toward the open doors, not even conscious of her velvet shoes slipping on the night-wet grass, not stopping her steps until the lights of the mansion faded behind her and she stood alone in the soft silver of the half moon.

The cool, late September air did seem to refresh her finally and she drew deep gulps of it, waiting for the dizzying nausea to pass. Brett could not depart so completely from her life. Somehow, she would force him to listen to her story. Somehow, she'd solve the hurt she'd put in his grey-green eyes. Explain about Edward and hope he could explain about his marriage as well. She glanced over her shoulder, aware that she should return to the party, totally unable just yet to do so. I hate you all! she thought suddenly, surprising herself with the thought. But I really do, she reflected grimly. If it weren't to marry Bretegane, Lord Lindsey, I wouldn't have cared a fig for your company or your titles. Bitterly, she turned away from the glittering manor and moved deeper into the dark, quiet gardens. There, by the edge of the oak stand, was a small white painted garden house. She would go sit there for a few minutes—regain her composure before she returned to the forced gaiety of the crowd, to her husband's kind solicitude. No one would even miss her.

Inside the garden house, Cerissa clung gratefully to one of the slender columns, enjoying the absolute quiet and healing serenity of the place. Then, at the sound of footsteps approaching on the gravelled path, she raised her head wearily. Probably Edward, she thought with a faint smile. Poor, dear, kind, stupid Edward—concerned for my welfare, wondering at my absence. She began to step toward the doorway, forcing a feigned smile of reassurance, then suddenly froze at the familiar sound of a man's deep voice, murmuring apologies for having intruded on the lady's privacy, promising to leave at once. Cerissa took a half step forward into the faint moonlight, stretching her arms out to him. "Brett!" she cried, her heart hammering loud in the silence of the small house. "Wait!"

He turned slowly, the soft light shadowing the hard lines of his face. "Lady Ramond," he drawled. "What a pleasure."

There was some terrible coldness in his voice that chilled Cerissa's very soul but she refused to run from him. Instead she kept her arms outstretched invitingly, pleading mutely with him. Her breath catching in rising hope, she saw him smile faintly and begin to turn toward her. "Oh Brett, my darling, my love," she whispered desperately, tears of relief flooding her eyes. "Don't hate me, Brett, I can't bear it. You were in exile and I couldn't ask your advice, but it seemed such a perfect opportunity. I only married Edward for your sake, so we could honestly and truly be together some..." Suddenly, she gasped. Brett's hands had fastened on her wrists in a brutally painful grip. "Brett, you're hurting me," she protested softly, trying to step away.

"Am I, darling Cerissa?" His voice was soft but terrifying strange and the girl shuddered in swift fear, struggling harder against his bruising grip. "I intend to hurt you more, too, before I let you go to run back to your doting earl."

"No, Brett," she cried, choking on sudden tears. "You don't understand at all. You've got to listen. Why, you're married too, I heard..."

"I'm through listening, sweetheart," he murmured, his head bending over hers in a cruel kiss.

Cerissa moaned and hurled herself backwards with all her strength. "Please, Brett, don't do this. What if someone should..."

"I'll tell them I'm only collecting a debt, Lady Ramond," he replied mockingly, his eyes gleaming eerily in the soft light, "It was my 3,000 pounds you purchased your husband with, was it not?"

Cerissa froze motionless in horror, unable to even shake her chestnut head in denial. Brett started to move toward her again, and she gave a startled cry, turning to flee past him out of the garden house door, crying again and she felt his arm catch her violently around her waist. Helplessly, she kicked and clawed at him, blinded by tears and choking for breath. Suddenly, Brett let go of her and cursed viciously, raising his arm to strike her backhanded full across the face, sending her stumbling into the wall. By the time she could think again to move, he was beside her again, his hand reaching down into the low cut bodice of her satin gown to free her breasts, the other hand hauling her heavy full skirts up to her waist as she moaned and writhed against him. Helpless to stop him, she felt his fingers on her breasts, his lips burning her throat, his teeth nipping savagely at her soft skin. Then his mouth was covering hers, bruising her lips against her teeth until she tasted salty blood, his body trembling with the violence of his unleashed anger and growing passion. Suddenly, Cerissa moaned, feeling Brett press closer against her, astonished to feel answering desire begin in her own loins as he pulled her down to the garden house floor. Even with such violence, such bitterness behind it she could not resist his lovemaking. Her soul screamed shame, but she could not control her body's responses to its familiar, beloved lover, and she felt her hands unclench from fists into soft caresses, touching his neck, his thick black hair, his muscled shoulders beneath the satin coat. He fumbled a moment at his breeches, groaning softly as his lips lay against her full breast, his mouth strangely gentle as he touched the taut nipple with his tongue. In another moment, he had penetrated her, his hips arching against hers as he thrust deep within her, withdrawing to thrust again into her welcoming body, rocking hungrily within her as he moaned in helpless pleasure. Cerissa drew her legs up, struggling free of the restrictive underskirts that tangled them, her arms locked around Brett's neck, her mouth locked of his, tasting the brandy sweetness of his tongue, arching her back to force her throbbing breasts tighter to his chest. She cried suddenly aloud, as waves of ecstasy overwhelmed her, clutching Brett mindlessly closer yet, forgetting her shame momentarily, forgetting all anger in the total, all-consuming pleasure of the instant. In her arms, Brett stiffened, his moans growing louder and more urgent as he buried his dark head against her throat. Then he shuddered violently in her possessive embrace, his hips moving convulsively in answering ecstasy. For a long moment he lay still, his breath ragged, his chest heaving above hers. He lifted his head only once for a final kiss, his eyes already closing, exhausted to mindless weariness by the passing of such turbulent emotions. Wordlessly, he rolled away from her to lie full length on the floor, asleep before he'd even stopped moving.

Gradually, Cerissa drifted back from her dreamy half-awareness and opened her eyes slowly, focussing on the garden house's domed timber roof with difficulty. She licked her lips, tasting blood there still, and slowly forced herself to sit up, reaching a disbelieving hand up to her face, feeling the soreness of her jaw where Brett had struck her in his fury, feeling her left eye begin to swell already from the blow. She moaned, dropping her head into her hands as she struggled to her feet and staggered to lean against the wall. Oh God, what a whore she was at heart ... despite his violence, despite his marriage to another woman, she had opened her legs to him eagerly, glad to his use of her under any conditions. Still stunned, her heart heavy and sick with self disgust, she pulled her gown back into what order she could, wiping the dirt on the back of her dress off. She took a deep, shuddering breath, feeling tears of bitter anguish sting her eyes, then turned once more to glance down at the sleeping lord. How had they managed to make such a terrible tangle of their lives? How could the gentle bliss of their months at Whitross have soured so quickly...He married...she married...yet still tormented by the irresistible fire for each other, regardless of the hurt, the anger, the total shame of such an encounter. Even now her heart lurched in pitiful, all accepting devotion. With a trembling hand she reached to button his breeches, then forced her fingers away when they longed to remain and caress him. At least, whenever he awoke or if someone found him here before he did, there would be no evidence of their being together. She might know herself for a shameless whore, and have to live with that bitter truth, but no one else need know it.

She walked back to the manor house, the laughter and the lilting voices within seeming impossibly mocking. Had she been gone an hour or only minutes? Whatever, surely Edward would be looking for her. She halted suddenly as she caught sight of her reflection in a glass paned window, and shivered to see herself so. Her high-piled hair was impossibly askew, her face already bruising from Brett's hand. She couldn't go inside looking like this...even if people missed the horrified guilt written in her tear filled eyes, they would not miss the dirt and grass stains on her back, nor her love-tangled hair. She turned swiftly and walked around to the curved driveway, turning only at the carriage door to ask the driver to find her husband. "Tell my lord, I am still not feeling well," she murmured, "Ask him to make my farewells for me and excuse my rudeness to the hosts. I'll wait in here for him."

Only minutes later, Lord Ramond climbed into the coach, his face anxious. "You're not well, Cerissa? What is it?"

"Too much wine, I'm afraid," she replied, forcing an apologetic smile as she finished unpinning her long hair.

Edward smiled in apparent relief and squeezed her hand paternally. "No shame in that," he chuckled. "There's more than one of those inside—but without the good sense to leave before they make fools of themselves."

Cerissa returned his fond smile mechanically and leaned back against the cushion, closing her eyes. If Edward only knew, she mused bitterly, what a fool I did make of myself. Not ten minutes since I was grovelling in the dirt like a bitch in heat beneath a man who chose another woman over me. She shifted uneasily in the seat, feeling a warm wetness, sticky between her thighs. Tears brimmed her eyes again and she turned her face into the corner, feigning sleep when her husband spoke again.

Elizabeth hesitated in the darkness of the gardens, reluctant to seek her husband. It was almost an hour now since he'd gone outside, though, and most of the guests were leaving. She'd searched the gardens for him already, perhaps the tiny garden house.

She entered cautiously, scanning the small enclosure for Lord Lindsey. Ah! she sighed in recognition. He was here, sleeping on the floor, one arm thrown carelessly over his head in contentment. A pity she had to wake him, but no help for it. The girl knelt down, touching his arm with a timid hand. Perhaps he'd slept some of the brandy off . . . perhaps he'd be too tired to desire her tonight. He stirred slightly, a faint smile touching his lips, then was still. Elizabeth forced herself to touch him again, shaking him gently. The dark haired lord moved again, murmuring something inaudible, then reaching lazily to catch her hand in his, drawing it down to rest on his chest. "Not again just yet, Cerissa, I'm too damn tired . . ."

Elizabeth snatched her hand out of his, her eyes wide with shock as she gasped in surprise. Brett's eyes flew open and he frowned in confusion to see her face above his. He pushed himself upright, his eyes searching the dark house swiftly before returning to his wife's ashen face. "Oh Jesus, Elizabeth, I'm sorry. God knows . . ."

"Don't compound your filthy adultery with sacrilege," she cried accusingly, "You who never seek a church nor murmur a prayer have God's name forever on your lips!"

Brett stared silently at the girl for a long minute, shaking his head finally im grim wonder. "I think my swearing actually disturbs you more than my infidelity, Elizabeth."

The girl stared at him, astonished to hear him admit such a damning guilt so casually. She shuddered silently, her fingers seeking her cross. Suddenly she sobbed, huge tears filling her eyes to stream down her face. Brett reached to hold her against him, his eyes soft with confusion and remorse.

"Oh Elizabeth, I am sorry, I know what those vows mean to you. Believe me, I didn't plan for this to happen," he whispered. "Forgive me please."

264

"I want to go back to France," she sobbed, struggling to free herself of his embrace. "I don't want to stay here any longer. You'll live in mortal sin and damn my soul along with your own."

Brett clenched his jaw against the anger rising within him, then firmly forced it away. The girl was his wife, she had a right to be upset about his infidelity. She wasn't the type who could accept her husband's adultery with a careless jest. But damn...damn! he swore silently, he didn't want to leave England again, especially now. He had begun the matter with Cerissa out of bitterness and hurt—a need to strike back at her for the stunning blow she'd dealt him by marrying again. Jesus! He hadn't even been three months gone before...But that didn't really matter. Despite what she'd done, he loved her still. Loved her as he could never love another woman, wife or no..."Yes, if we stay in England I'll see her again," he admitted quietly, frowning in the darkness as he remembered how brutal he had been in the beginning...he would see her again if she were willing...but would she be? Dear God, hadn't he struck her? And how would he tell her of his own marriage after reacting so jealously to hers?

"Then I insist we travel to France, my lord, I insist. I must seek guidance in this affair from the nuns of St. Jean."

Brett stared at her ashen face helplessly, seeing the stubborn, almost ugly set to her thin lips. "All right, Elizabeth, but a short visit only—two weeks at the most. And I can't leave immediately—I have too much business to catch up on after being away."

"Then you will not lay with your Jezabel again." the girl announced flatly, determination forcing her bravery.

Brett frowned another moment, withdrawing his arm from around his cold-eyed wife to rise slowly to his feet, still staring down at her. "I will not see her again until we return from France," he conceded grimly, his own eyes sparking now in frustrated anger. "But when we return, with or without your blessing, Elizabeth, then yes. Then if she'll still have me, then I will see her again."

Elizabeth rose to her feet without answering, her face white and set in the moonlight. "I will await you in our coach, Lord Lindsey. You may make my adieus for me."

Brett nodded and spun on his heel, stalking out of the garden house in growing fury. Vows or no vows, wife or no wife, he would have the woman he loved. If her aging husband objected, he'd kill him on the duelling grounds. If Cerissa objected, he'd lock her in a room at Whitross until she relented. He hadn't imagined her response to him tonight. She loved him still, at least he hoped she did, despite her marriage to another man. Suddenly, he halted,

265

drawing a deep breath of the cool night air to calm his temper. No, he wouldn't kill Cerissa's husband, Lord Ramond, even for her he couldn't coldly murder the man. And he couldn't wreak. his frustration upon Elizabeth either, that was equally unfair. But somehow, by God, he vowed silently to the stars above, somehow he would find a way to regain Cerissa. Whatever the cost, regardless of who—even the king himself—sought to keep them apart.

Chapter Seventeen

The chill of the late October winds promised a cold November and Cerissa hurried to close the door of the dress shop against the wind. She nodded hastily to the two girls working there, reaching for a cup of hot tea before she dared to speak.

"Feeling poorly again this morning, my lady?" one of the servants asked solicitously, pouring Cerissa a second cup.

She nodded, trying to force an easy smile. "Just a touch of the flu, Betsy." But as the girl turned back to her stitching, Cerissa bit her lip nervously. She was two weeks late for her monthly and she was usually like clockwork. Could it be possible that she . . . only that one disastrous night in the garden house at Millford's party when Brett . . .

"There's two fine ladies in today, Lady Ramond," Betsy confided nodding toward the front parlor. "Did you wish to be seeing them?"

Cerissa sighed, glancing wearily toward the peephole that

viewed the front room. Usually when potentially good customers patronized the shop, she made a special effort to see the women. She had a unique talent for sensing which style would best suit a particular figure, whether the gown's bodice should be ruffled, or laced, or merely cut revealingly low to let the woman's own charms serve as the accent. Colors too, were her special province. Depending on the hair color, the tint of the eyes, she could select the shade to make a plain woman look attractive, even pretty. But, of course, as Lady Ramond she could not reveal herself to the patrons. It was unthinkable for a person of quality to actually work for a living. She and Edward would be ostracized at once. For herself, she wouldn't have cared, but for her husband's sake she would play the foolish game. She frowned again, thinking of Edward. He had been so kind to her, so grandfatherly affectionate to Jamey whenever she brought him over from Ardsley's for a visit. Would Edward understand if she found herself pregnant now with Lord Lindsey's child? Or would even his fondness crack under such a strain?

And Brett, of course...No reason to tell him just yet when she was not even sure. She shivered slightly remembering their last violent meeting. Today again, as she had everyday for a month, she found herself wishing against herself—both hoping she would hear from him and hoping she wouldn't. Strange that she had had no word of him since the party—unless that basket of violets the next day had indeed been from him. The old woman who had knocked at her door to deliver the flowers had volunteered nothing. And with her husband standing right at her elbow, she had hardly been able to question the grinning crone, much as she would have liked to.

"Who are they from?" Edward had questioned rather petulantly, sniffing at the faint, sweet odor the violets exuded.

"There's no card," Cerissa had replied with feigned carelessness, setting the basket up on the dining table. Damn rotten luck, she'd thought in bitter frustration, Edward would have to be visiting me here in my rooms just when the old crone knocked. Brett had often picked the wild blue morning glories in the islands, offering them to her because they matched the color of her eyes. But violets...? Did he realize her right eye had swollen purple from his blow and sent these in apology...or mockery?

"My lady?" the girl prompted softly, still holding aside the curtain to reveal her tiny peephole.

"Oh...yes," Cerissa nodded, moving to the wall. Two ladies. Well, though plainly, dressed. In the wrong colors totally, of course, but she could easily...

"Left again for France, I heard," one remarked with a shrug. "Alicia was simply furious."

"Well, I can't be altogether sorry for her. After all, the way I heard it, there was a strong hint that the Lindseys left so abruptly because of that blond witch..."

"Because of Alicia?" the first woman laughed unkindly, shaking her head, "Oh no, dear, quite contraire. Alicia would not have been nearly so put out if that were so. No, it was someone else. I gather, no one knows quite whom. But Lady Lindsey refused to speak about the incident at all, of course. Only insisted Lord Lindsey return at once with her to France. And, like a devoted husband, he set sail almost at once."

Cerissa drew back with a gasp of shock. Brett in France again? At his wife's command? But how had she even found out...And what did that mean? Had he left England then forever? Could he value his wife so totally beyond her that he would avoid future temptations by staying hundreds of miles away? Could she have so totally misread his feelings that night at the party? Oh my God, she thought silently, if he loves his wife so much...Suddenly, she turned and ran from the shop, signalling a coach to stop for her. Perhaps in Brett's eyes, she had betrayed him. Perhaps he felt no explanations were due her. But at the least, she must speak with Ardsley, find out the truth. If Brett's love were indeed forever lost to her, she must know it for certain. That faint pitiful hope she had nursed since laying in his arms was more destructive, more unbearable, than the absolute despair of knowing could be. "Oh God, I beg of you," she whispered suddenly, sobbing helplessly against the dirty velvet cushions inside the hired coach. "Please dear God, don't let it be so...oh, please..."

Cerissa jumped up at the blond lord's approaching footsteps, whirling around to face him, her desperation plain in her tear filled eyes. "Ardsley...oh thank you for seeing me," she cried, running to fling her arms around his neck. "I had to talk to you...I had to find out..."

The blond lord frowned though he did not resist her embrace, but threw an answering arm around her quaking shoulders, his blue eyes darkening with concern. "You hardly left me much choice about talking to you," he muttered drily. "But for heaven's sake, sweetheart, you're shaking like a leaf. What in the world is the trouble?"

Cerissa's tears flowed faster at the note of compassion she heard in Lord Ardsley's voice. Knowing he at least, had forgiven her for her marriage only added another emotion to her already overburdened heart. When she managed to get her sobs under control again at last she still hesitated, suddenly fearing to ask her question, terrified that the blond lord's answer might eliminate the last tentative shreds of hope she clung to. Instead, she stalled for time, beginning a rambling explanation of what she'd done that morning from the time of her awakening, finally mentioning her outing to her small dress shop. "Two women were there that I didn't know, and I . . . I mean, one of them said that Brett . . ." Helplessly her voice faltered, her fear closing her throat and she dropped her gaze under Ardsley's questioning frown.

"A shop?" he echoed. "What kind of shop? A dress shop, you said? You needn't be doing that, sweetheart."

Cerissa shrugged and grimaced, not reluctant to pursue another topic just now. Every second of hope seemed suddenly precious. "We have to eat somehow, James, and Edward has no money."

"I wouldn't have let you starve, Cerissa, nor would Brett. In fact . . ."

"I felt I'd used enough of Brett's money already, especially under the circumstances," she murmured guiltily trying to force a faint smile. "And you are already keeping Jamey for me, and bearing the cost of his tutors and . . ."

"Brett takes care of Jamey's expenses, Cerissa. He insists on it, though I'd be happy to forget such a trivial matter. And Brett's account is still open to you, princess. I accompanied him down to Benjamin's last time when he withdrew some cash to take to France. I could see the draft still attached to his ledger, authorizing you free draw."

Cerissa stared at her friend in amazement, feeling hope's feeble wings stirring her soul again. "Then he isn't angry at me?" she breathed incredulously "He doesn't hate me?"

Ardsley grimaced and walked a few steps away before turning to study her face again. "Well . . . he's not terribly pleased, Cerissa, but . . . no, I'm sure he doesn't hate you. I think he wanted to at first, but found he couldn't."

The girl closed her eyes, heaving a deep shuddering sigh of relief. If Brett didn't hate her, then he couldn't have left England just to avoid her. Unless . . . unless his wife still came first in his affections.

"Tell, me, Cerissa," Ardsley demanded. "What in hell happened between you and Brett that night at Millford's party? My coach was behind Lindsey's in the drive, and just as I was preparing to leave, Elizabeth came walking up alone out of the gardens, white as a ghost, and looking like she could eat nails for dessert. Without a word to Marian or me, she climbed into the carriage and slammed the door. A little while later Brett came out from the manor, obviously apologizing to the Millford's for something. Next thing I heard, he and Elizabeth were going back to France for a ..."

"Elizabeth?" Cerissa's mouth was suddenly dry as ash again, her heart sinking in cold dread.

Ardsley's gaze was quizzical, his shrug uneasy. "Yes, of course, Elizabeth, Brett's wife."

A choking, gasping cry of denial broke from Cerissa's lips and she felt the earth tilting below her feet. Oh my God! her soul mourned wildly. It is true, he must love her. Elizabeth had found out he had been with me and forced him to choose between the two of us. And Brett had chosen her ...

"Jesus, Cerissa, are you all right?"

The girl opened her eyes and forced them to focus on the blond lord's face as it swam above her, his blue eyes wide with alarm. Woodenly, she forced herself to nod, trying to turn away from his eyes.

"But, then ..." Ardsley shook his head in angry confusion, holding her arm. "Jesus, Cerissa! What is it? You had to know he was married. Why else would you have attached yourself to Lord Ramond?"

Cerissa explained the lengthy story haltingly, feeling curiously numb and far removed from the events she described—as if she were telling a story about someone else. At last, she finished and Ardsley stared a long moment in stunned understanding, finally breaking the silence with a soft oath.

"Hell, sweetheart, I've got to apologize," he sighed, frowning faintly, his hands toying nervously with his belt. "I had it all wrong. I figured you must have heard of the marriage somehow and married Lord Ramond for spite. That's why I was so disgusted with you that day. I began to believe you were only a title hunter, and when Brett had been knocked out of the picture, you'd simply snatched the next available ..."

"Ardsley!" Cerissa's face drained of color and she stared at the blond lord in horrified disbelief. "You actually believed I would do ..."

"I know, girl," he interrupted hastily, his eyes pleading forgiveness, "The more I thought about it, the less I thought it was true. But then Brett was acting peculiar as hell and Elizabeth barely said good day before she was muttering Ave Maria's again, and ..."

"Why did he marry her, James? Does he love her so much?" Cerissa's voice broke as she whispered the question that seemed to tear her agonized heart apart. She dropped her head, unable to meet the lord's pitying gaze.

Ardsley reached over to pull the trembling girl against him, resting his cheek against the top of her shining, chestnut hair as he answered slowly, explaining Brett's unusual marriage, his words producing fresh pain in the girl's heart. Cerissa listened with mounting hope, and finally disbelief. "And she doesn't love him, either James?" she echoed softly. "I can't understand ... Brett was always every woman's ..."

"Yes, the rascal had that magic all right, but it's failed on Elizabeth, sweet, She's very pious, was nearly a nun, I believe, before the wedding. Hardly the right woman for an independent, reckless, old pirate like Lindsey. Now, you Cerissa, you always seemed to tame his tempers well enough but ..."

"No, Ardsley, please," she shook her head quickly at the fresh tears rising. "Don't joke about it, not yet at least. Elizabeth must have realized somehow that Brett had been with me at Millford's, James. Even if she doesn't love him, that would have been a disappointment to her. Is that why they left for France? Will they be living over there permanently now?"

"No, only a visit Brett said."

Cerissa nodded, drawing away from Ardsley's arm to turn for the door.

"Any message I should give Brett from you upon their return?" the blond lord asked gently.

Cerissa paused a moment, her emotions and thoughts too confused yet to have an answer. Could she continue to see Brett despite the dual marriages? Could she overcome her instinctive jealously and guilt at sharing even a small part of Brett with another woman? And what of the baby she believed she carried? Oh Lord ... what of that? And Edward ... ? Wordlessly, she shook her head, postponing any decision. Ardsley caught her arm at the door to kiss her fondly and she forced a faint smile for his sake, to lighten the trouble that shadowed his eyes. She paused again in the drive before reentering the coach to leave, glancing wistfully over her shoulder toward the nursery windows. She hated to leave without seeing the baby—dear God but she missed him so. Yet, no question but he was much better off living here with Ardsley's two fine boys, learning to speak and dress and behave the way a gentleman should. Perhaps tomorrow though, to lighten her own heart, she would,

272

steal him away for the afternoon. They could feed the ducks in the pond at St. James'. The boy might enjoy a pony ride as well. She smiled suddenly as she climbed into the carriage and waved the driver on. No matter what else Elizabeth might have of Brett's, she did not have his son. Yet even that smile faded slowly as the coach rattled on. Today, Elizabeth did not have his son. But what of next year? Or the year after that? Surely eventually in the lifetime she'd have as Brett's wife, eventually she would have his sons as well. Cerissa sobbed in sudden overwhelming bitterness pounding the velvet cushions with angry fists. "I hate her, I hate her," she whispered viciously, her heart nearly bursting with the force of her passion, her eyes blinded by hot tears. She had been such a fool, such a naive country child up to now, believing in love, believing in God's mercy, the essential goodness of the world. Once Brett had returned her love she'd thought the battle over and won, but she'd been wrong. Nothing in this crazy, twisted world was given freely by the cruel mistress of fate. If she still wanted Brett's love, and wanted to share her soul with him, she would have to surrender every other hope in her heart. Edward might die in a few years, but Elizabeth was a young woman. The fact of Brett's marriage, the fact that, whether he loved his wife or not, still he obviously felt an obligation to regard her wishes, these were things she would have to accept. She could never even dream now of being more than Brett's mistress. Never pretend that Jamey might become his heir. Never again know the completeness of his love that she had known those months at Whitross. To live forever a captive of helpless, futile love was her only future. Cerissa laughed softly as the coach rolled to a stop at her lodgings, the sound a chilling one, devoid of mirth, born of bitterness. Was it only three years ago a naive country girl had prayed starry-eyed for that love, denying the cruel truths both Brett and Ardsley had warned her of? Hadn't she, in her obsessive ignorance, drawn Brett into the trap as well? He, whom she loved more than life, hadn't it actually been she herself who'd doomed him to the same bitter misery she'd fled headlong into, ignoring all caution, ignoring all wisdom, believing that love would conquer all?

"Lady Ramond," the coachman leaned in, opening the narrow carriage door. "A woman here waiting to see you."

In cold self-possession, Cerissa stepped out into the bright October sunlight and then stopped, stunned and staring at the woman who waited. "Aunt Mary!" she gasped at last, her blue eyes huge with shocked astonishment. "Oh, Aunt Mary! How in..."

The woman smiled, reaching shyly for the girl's trembling hand to pull her toward the door. "I was sure it was you I saw leaving this morning! I'm in London to visit Annie. She married a deacon, you know, and lives a few blocks down. I was out for a walk and ... oh, child! Lordy, how I've missed you! Wondering what ever became of you, fearing for you ... and now, I hear you be married to an earl. Oh, I'm so happy for you! There's so much to be telling you I never had a chance to."

Cerissa listened numbly to the woman's story, resisting a growing impulse to simply throw her chestnut head back and scream and scream and never stop screaming ... All useless ... all wasted ... three and a half years of her life ... following Brett to the Indies, nearly murdered by Gerard, nearly imprisoned in Newgate for debts, all her schemes, all her plans, all for nothing. Three and a half years of chasing the impossible dream of marrying Lord Lindsey, when if she'd only known, if she'd ever even suspected ... they could have been married long ago ... avoided the terrible, irreversible tangle of their present lives.

"I couldn't believe my eyes when I saw ye this morning, child. All dressed so fine, and yer own coach ... And then when the maid here calls ye Lady Ramond! Well, I never ..." Aunt Mary shook her head in beaming amazement. "So ye married your young lord ye saw on the Bainwater road?"

Cerissa forced a faint smile, her heart curiously numb, her thoughts strangely collected. "No," she answered quietly with a slight shake of her head, "No ... another."

Aunt Mary nodded, her eyes still shining with happy satisfaction.

Cerissa stared down at her clasped hands a long moment, resisting the impulse to laugh at this supreme irony of fate. "But you're sure I am quality? Cerissa Lakeland is my real name?"

"Oh, aye! I've yer mother's papers and her wedding ring still to prove it. We ... Yer Uncle Wat and I ... we always meant to be telling ye on yer sixteenth birthday, but of course ..."

Cerissa smiled in mechanical response to the woman's expressive shrug. Of course. She had left with Brett before that day had come. Strange that she should feel so calm hearing such a story. Shouldn't she, by all rights, want to weep and storm with rage? "And Uncle Wat? He never told you ..."

"Wat's been dead over two years now, child. He died just after planting the spring after you left. My, but he were right frantic when you disappeared. Hunted all day for you he did, but never found a trace. Of course, I guess it all worked out for the best in the end.

274

Annie's been in London now half a year and she's give me my first grandchild—a sweet, pretty little girl. Her husband's the deacon down at..."

Cerissa pretended to listen, a polite smile fixed on her lips though her thoughts were years away. Uncle Wat had never told her adopted aunt about the beating he'd given her... had pretended instead he'd not found her at all. How different her aunt's conception of her leaving had been from the truth. Her flight from Bainwater had been far from the merry adventure she envisioned. But now? Was there any purpose now to revealing the truth to the woman?

"...of course, I still miss my Wat, Cerissa. He was a good man. Oh, he had his faults. I suppose, 'specially when his temper was up, but all men do. Yes, he was a darlin' good husband to me."

Cerissa opened her mouth, then quickly shut it again. It wasn't even Uncle Wat's fault, or Aunt Mary's, that her life had come to this pass. It wasn't her fault, nor Brett's, nor Edward's nor Elizabeth's nor anyone else's either. Fate had used them all as puppets in this bizarre little farce. Cruel, wicked, twisted Fate that she had believed in so confidently. Fate had betrayed her absolutely. "Thank you so much for stopping, Aunt Mary. I will go see Annie if I've time enough this next week."

"And yer papers, child? Ye'll be wanting them I suppose? I never thought to bring them with me! Lordy! Who'd have thought I'd ever have seen ye again in all this huge crowded place? But I've..."

"I may pick them up," Cerissa murmured, opening the door politely and then returning the woman's fond hug.

"Cerissa?" Lord Ardsley stood on the outer side of the opened door, looking curiously at the round, country-dressed woman just inside.

"Oh... Ardsley," the girl forced a faint smile and stepped back to let him in. "This is my Aunt Mary—from Bainwater. You've heard me speak of her."

The blond lord's surprise widened his blue eyes momentarily before he recovered his composure, dropping smoothly into a gallant bow. "My pleasure," he murmured. He stood for a moment, his brow furrowing slightly. "And your uncle, Cerissa? Is he here too? I'd like to meet that..."

"He's dead, James," the girl interrupted hastily, shaking her head in denial. "Aunt Mary said he went looking for me, but never found me. And then he died the following spring." Cerissa met the lord's astonished gaze for a long, breathless moment, then relaxed,

275

as he nodded and shrugged his willingness to maintain such a fiction if she wished. So many people had been hurt already in this game. She would cheat Fate out of Aunt Mary's...

"Is this yer husband, child?" the woman's kind eyes were sparkling in wonder, taking in Ardsley's handsome ruddy face, his fine satin coat and breeches.

"No, Aunt Mary. But an old, very dear friend," she answered quietly, remembering with sudden clarity the blond lord's reaction to the realization of Brett's and her love for each other. He had not been overjoyed. No, on the contrary, on that long ago spring day in Lichester Woods, his blue eyes had been troubled and haunted with a sorrow his words had been unable to belie. Had he guessed all along? she wondered silently, studying his familiar features with a sidelong gaze. Had Ardsley feared all along it would end in such grief for all concerned? "Aunt Mary was just telling me my true history, James. My parents were both quality—though disowned for their marriage. My real name is Cerissa Lakeland."

The blond lord's face drained slowly of color, his eyes rivetted to hers in helpless shock. "Oh my God..." he breathed at last, shaking his head slowly from side to side. "Then all this time..."

Cerissa forced a soft laugh, turning away to kiss her aunt goodbye again, watching the woman silently as she walked out into the fading light of the setting sun.

"Cerissa, what in hell is...?"

"No, James, please, not now," the girl murmured wearily, turning away from the intensity of his gaze. "It's been too much... the whole thing. I want to be left alone for a little while."

"But, sweetheart, I've got a very important message that I know you'll..."

"No!" Cerissa's whisper held the intensity of a scream and the blond lord stood hesitantly at the door, his eyes uneasy. "Please just go."

He stared at her set face for a long time, obviously unwilling to do as she asked. "Tomorrow then, princess? It is very important, and..."

"Tomorrow." she agreed wearily, already beginning to close the door on him. Tomorrow, she thought bitterly, if there's even to be a tomorrow. Who cares any longer? She whirled around and opened the door again, calling after the blond haired lord who stood at the end of the walk already, one hand on the coach door. "Ardsley! Promise me something!" she pleaded, her eyes solemn as they met his, "If something should happen to me ever... or to Brett... you'd look after Jamey for me wouldn't you?"

276

Ardsley frowned, not replying at once, his face still radiating concern. "Hell, Cerissa, what kind of question is that? What's going to happen to either of you? I don't like the sound of..."

"Please, James, don't question me. Not now. It's only...hearing about my uncle I guess," she lied, her eyes still demanding his promise.

At length, he shrugged and nodded, wrenching the coach door open to climb inside.

"Promise me!" she insisted as the door began to close.

"All right, sweetheart, I promise you," he agreed, trying to force a reassuring smile though his soul felt cold as death. "I'll be here tomorrow morning. Try to relax then and get some sleep. Everything will work out yet, I know it."

Cerissa nodded and held one hand up in farewell as the coach sped off. Then she turned, and walked calmly to her desk, taking a quill, and ink, and several sheets of parchment from the drawer. She owed Brett a letter surely, and Ardsley, of course, since she would not be there to speak with him in the morning. One to Edward, and one to her maid who had grown fond of her, one to the girls at the dress shop. And one, to be read much later, of course, to her son. Perhaps by the time the boy could read such a thing, he would be old enough to understand why she'd had to abandon him this way. At least, she owed him an explanation.

At last, the sun well gone and the moon hanging new and yellow above the sapphire horizon, Cerissa finished and sat back wearily in the straight back chair, rubbing her cramped fingers. Once the shock had passed for everyone, she believed they would understand. She could not continue living any more, the game was played to a finish. To live on now would only wreak more damage to all concerned. Perhaps with her gone, Brett could learn to love his new wife instead of being forever torn between the two. Perhaps, too, he could adopt Jamey. If not as his heir, then at least as a second or third son. Edward would be hardly touched unless there were scandal following her death. He was fond of her, but he had lost both wife and daughter long ago and he had survived. He would survive again. And the others, well...they too would survive. Ardsley would be, of all of them, perhaps the most grieved because he had seen her last, but even so...what other choice was there? To continue living now as Edward's wife, not even able to acknowledge her son's paternity, dying a thousand times a day to think of Brett, to think of how life should have been? And the baby she might carry inside her? Proof to the world of her adultery and shame? No, this was the coward's escape perhaps, but she no longer

277

cared. She would give Fate the final triumph of watching her destroy herself to flee the bitter, unbearable irony of it all.

Cerissa took her cloak and her muff and walked back to the front door, mumbling some thoughtless excuse to her maid in answer to the girl's surprise. Why not? she argued, her lips trembling in a mirthless smile, why shouldn't she walk by the river? She might even go by way of Ardsley's house, peek in the nursery window if Jamey were sleeping and have one last look at him. And then? If she were to fall from a bridge into the Thames in these heavy clothes...she could not possibly swim. So far as London would ever know, it would be only a regrettable accident.

"Promised what?" Brett frowned wearily, leaning forward from the chairback he'd rested on. Damn! he swore silently, this damn headache gets worse every time I...

"To care for Jamey," Ardsley answered, shrugging as he finished a brandy. "I know, Brett. It gave me the chills, but hell...after the shock she'd had today. First thinking you had abandoned her for Elizabeth, then learning, too late, about herself being quality. Hell, I don't blame her for wanting to be left alone. I thought if I told her then about you—about Elizabeth dying and your returning so soon—it would only have been one more shock for the girl. Even if this would have been a more pleasant one. After all, it hardly solves anything. She's still married to Lord Ramond."

"Yes, but didn't you say she'd told you he was impotent? If he is, then the marriage isn't consumated. I can have it annulled." Brett bent his head down into his hands, rubbing futily at the thudding ache behind his eyes. Hadn't Elizabeth complained of a headache the day before she...

"That'll create a scandal. Your wife dies and a bare week later you're agitating for..."

"I don't care!" Brett snapped, his head making his temper edgy. "I'm tired of living my life to please other people. It's a Goddamned blessing for both of us that Elizabeth did die! You should have seen her on her death bed, crying for joy to be going to her God, urging me to learn by her lesson and not let anything turn me aside from marrying the woman I loved. And by Jesus, I'm..."

"Hold on, Brett. I'm not criticizing you for God's sake. I know you too well to think you'd take advice even if I did disapprove—which I don't!" Ardsley hastened to soothe his friend's anger, frowning as he threw a quick sidelong glance at him. "I only wanted to point out the reality you'll be facing, Brett...that is if you're still on your feet tomorrow. You don't look well. Are you sure you're all right?"

The dark haired lord nodded slowly, trying to force the dulling ache out of his thoughts. He couldn't afford to sleep yet, there was something important..."Oh...Cerissa. She made you promise?" At Ardsley's nod, he frowned again, forcing himself to his feet. "I'm going to ride over there, James. Cerissa takes promises very seriously. She wouldn't have demanded one unless she was truly anxious..."

"Sit down. You look dead on your feet. I know you were itching to get home, but you could have stopped long enough for a night's sleep. I'll ride over and see what..."

"No, I'm going, Ardsley. No need for you..."

"I'm going too," the blond lord insisted, following his friend to the door. The way you look, you might fall off your horse. Hey! Aren't you going to take your cloak?"

"No, I'm so damned hot," Brett muttered, turning to walk to the stable area. "The air feels good."

Ardsley flung him another uneasy glance, wishing he could convince the man to go lie down. Hell, he'd never seen Brett look like this and he'd seen him after sleepless nights before. Besides, this wasn't July it was October, and damn near November. It wasn't pleasant out—it was cold. If the man had a fever...Jesus, wasn't that what the girl had died of in France? A fever? "Lindsey, for Christ sake, get back inside. I'll take care of Cerissa, I swear it."

"I know, Ardsley, but suppose she's not home. Then what you do? You wouldn't have any idea where else to look."

"Neither will you."

"Yes, I will. Cerissa and I...we have a kind of sixth sense about each other, crazy as it sounds. I have a much better chance of finding her."

Ardsley sighed, swearing silently to himself as he swung up into his saddle. No use arguing with Lindsey when he got that tone in his voice, he was hell bent to do what he wanted. At least he could offer what aid he could. Jesus, he hoped the man was wrong about Cerissa. She wasn't the type to pull a crazy, desperate stunt...he hoped not anyway.

But the girl was not at her house by the time they arrived there. And despite the maid's nervous resistance, Brett shouldered past into the living quarters to call for her.

"She's not here," Ardsley announced at last, staring down at the desk top with a quizzical frown. "But look here, Brett. She's written

279

a letter to you," he paused to thumb through the sealed and folded parchments, "and one to me as well."

"Open it," Brett ordered, reaching across to snatch his. "I don't like this whole affair."

Ardsley hesitated, feeling uneasy and intrusive. "Perhaps we shouldn't, Brett, they haven't actually been given..."

"Oh, hell on your fine scruples, James. Would you feel better if we delayed until she was dead or vanished?"

Ardsley frowned again but opened the parchment, his face draining bloodless as he began to read. Suddenly, Brett flung his to the floor with an angry curse and grabbed his friends arm, pulling him for the door. "Wait a second, Lindsey," he protested, hauling back on the other man's arm. "Let's take time to think for God's sake."

"We have no time to think," Brett snapped, pulling free to walk toward the wide eyed servant girl. "When did your mistress leave?"

"Not long ago," the nervous girl stammered, shrinking fearfully against a wall. "Perhaps a half hour, maybe a full one. She said she was going to walk by the river."

Brett cursed again, frowning at the girl as if he thought she was partly to blame. The girl cowered under the glare of his angry eyes, finally turning her head away with a frightened whimper. "If she comes back again, keep her here. Understand? Lock her in if you have to until I return. Take this ring, he paused and pulled at the emerald ring Cerissa had give him long ago, struggling to get it over his knuckle. "She'll know who it's from. Tell her I'll be back."

Scarcely had the girl nodded before he turned and hurried through the front door, grabbing at the reins of his tethered horse. With a start, Ardsley sprang after him, barely making the street in time to see the dark haired lord swing into the saddle. "Where to now?" he called anxiously, hauling his horse's head around viciously to follow Brett's lead.

"Your place maybe. I don't know." He replied frowning as he spurred the horse forward. "Just keep looking."

But the dark, cold October streets were empty that time of night, and the two men dismounted at Ardsley's house with a sense of growing desperation. The housekeeper denied having seen any visitors at all that evening, and Brett hurried down into the nursery with little hope. He paused only a moment to glance at his sleeping son, considering whether to wake him or not. If Cerissa heard the boy calling, she would surely answer from where ever she might conceal herself. On the other hand, if he found her too late... or not at all . . . best the boy stayed here in that case. Soft footfalls sounded behind him, and he turned, nodding to the governess who had appeared in the doorway. Quietly, he stepped out into the hall and shut the door.

"What is it, Lord Lindsey? Is the boy not sleeping?" the woman inquired softly.

"Yes, he's fine. It's his mother," Brett answered in a low voice, his thoughts racing ahead in frantic search of the girl. Where would she go now? Somewhere within walking distance—that limited her choice. By the river? But would she have told the girl the truth or given a deliberately false direction to mislead pursuit? And had she guessed she might be pursued? Or did she believe herself . . .

"It's strange, my lord, but I thought I heard someone outside in the gardens a while ago. That's why, when I heard someone come in here, I . . ."

"You what?" Brett's full attention snapped back to the governess and he stared at her intently. "How long ago?"

The flustered woman blushed under his scrutiny and shrugged. "Only 20 or 30 minutes ago at most," she stammered, wondering at the man's unnerving intensity. "Should I have alerted the guards do you think? I wasn't really positive it was anything other than the wind, so I . . ."

Brett turned away, leaving the astonished woman to stand silently in the dark hallway, gaping after him. Half hour . . . if it had been Cerissa, she would have had nearly enough time to get to the river already . . . but what part of the river? The Thames flowed through the city. If she meant to drown herself as the letters had intimated, would she search for a boat, or jump from a bridge, or simply wade in until her heavy clothes sank her? He hurried back to the drawing room where he had left Ardsley, trying to ignore the sick hammering of his heart that doubled the throbbing agony of his head. God damn! He hadn't been sick for years . . . of all the nights to be feeling feverish. "I think she was here, about a half hour ago, maybe less. We probably rode right by her on the street going over."

Ardsley stepped toward him, letting the full glare of the lantern light hit his eyes. Brett cursed and instinctively threw a hand up to block the light which sent new waves of stabbing pain into his head. The slight movement threw him off balance and he stumbled clumsily into a nearby chair.

"Jesus, Lindsey, what's wrong with you?" Ardsley's eyes were narrowed in searching concern as he stared at his friend. "You are

281

sick, don't tell me different. For God's sake go to bed before..."

"I can't, we both know that. Now shut up, old mother, and help me. You ride down to the Whitehall docks. They're the only ones that would still have boats for hire this time of year. I wouldn't expect her to go there with so many people about, but..." Brett shrugged, and forced himself to move for the front door, shutting the lead-limbed fatigue of his aching body out of his mind. "I'll ride up along the river toward the bridge by the Thrupence Tavern. On horseback, we may still have a chance to catch up with her."

"If I don't find her at the docks I'll meet you..."

"No, come back here. There's a small chance she might change her mind yet. If she does, she's liable to come here to see you or Jamey."

The blond lord nodded and took the horse's reins from the silent servant, mounting swiftly to avoid having to meet Lindsey's eyes. He didn't believe they would find the girl before it was too late. Cerissa was too stubborn, too determined once she set her mind on a course of action. And she was clever enough to outwit anyone eager to thwart her plans. She had proved that often enough in the past. But, hell, what else could they do? Retire to the drawing room with a warm brandy and discuss the situation? No, at least Brett was right about that. Action...even futile action...was better than sitting and waiting for the inevitable news.

Brett guided the lathered horse up the river road, his eyes searching the shadows carefully, looking for any trace, even a footprint on the muddy bank, a tatter of clothing, anything to guide his search. He shivered in the old autumn wind, feeling the fever sweat turn cold on his forehead. What could he expect even if he found her? After what had passed between them at Mill-ford's...she must not have realized his regret at the unfairness of his jealous anger, his shame at remembering how he had struck her. The fact that the savagery had ended in tenderness might not have been enough to convince her of his continued love. Might she not flee before him now? Try to avoid his attempt to aid her? Should he risk calling for her or would it only increase her desperation to hear his voice?

He reined in the tired horse, pulling him over into the shadow of a large oak. Was that a shadow or a person on the bridge? With a cloud covering the moon just now, he couldn't see...Yes! The silver streak of moonlight lit the dark bridge brighter now. It was Cerissa. Even at this distance in the poor light he could tell—not so much by

282

his eyesight as by the vibrancy of his soul. Brett gathered his reins and slid silently from the saddle, gritting his teeth to restrain a moan at the agony movement cost. Forcing his breath to come evenly, he tied the horse loosely to a low bough, then stepped forward onto the short path leading to the bridge. He moved cautiously, resisting an instinctive desire to run for her, still fearing the girl would flee if she noticed him. Yet, he was already on the bridge before she seemed to hear the creaking wood beneath his booted feet. Then without a word, she turned her head and looked directly at him, her eyes catching his for a brief second. Brett froze, willing her to be still, noticing only now with a sick shudder that she stood already on the outer edge of the wooden railing, leaning over the dark, rippling river water thirty feet below.

"Cerissa? Please, sweetheart, it's me, Brett," he called softly, edging forward again, his heart thudding loudly in his ears. He stopped still as she leaned farther over the empty air, praying she was not so distraught that she would not wait to listen to him. "Cerissa, I want..." his voice trailed off as she turned to face him again, her eyes soft and infinitely tender. Thank God! his heart sang. It's all right! I got here in time and she loves me still. Thank God. Eagerly, he smiled into her eyes and took a deep breath, letting his tense muscles relax in relief. With incredible swiftness, Cerissa looked away and jumped out into the air, her velvet cloak flying behind her as she plunged down toward the black water. With a cry of surprise, Brett leapt after her, too late to catch her clothing to stop her fall. Stunned, his green eyes dark in horrified disbelief, he watched for a seeming eternity as she fell to splash in the Thames. Finally, the sound of the water seemed to unlock his frozen limbs and he tore his coat off, unbuckling his sword belt and pulling his boots free with desperate strength, his eyes still locked intently on the moon-silvered river. He swung his legs over the railing, and took a deep breath, forcing himself to wait for some sight of her, refusing to remember that her jump had been deliberate, not accidental. She had seen him, recognized him, he knew it. Yet even so, even while her eyes spoke love for him, she had still chosen the water. At last, he saw a faint swirling movement in the river, over to the right and already ten yards from where she'd entered the river. The current would be strong tonight then, and swiftest in the center. He trained his eyes on the exact spot in the Thames and sprang out into the air, throwing his arms high above his head to carry him farther above the water, at last tucking to knife the icy water cleanly with his outstretched hands. The river was black as ink, impossible to see through and Brett groped helplessly along the bottom for several yards before swimming back to the surface for a breath, breaking the water's line with his eyes open, scanning the silver surface for any hint of where the girl might be, then kicking downstream in hopes he'd landed behind her. Another quick breath to ease his burning lungs and he dove again, his heart pounding frantically with growing terror. The chance of finding Cerissa in this inky, lightless water was nearly nonexistent, he knew that. Yet, impossible or not, he had to do it. Again he was forced to kick for the surface, his breath nearly bursting in his chest. Again the surface was clear, undisturbed by any movement and he felt the panic growing greater. Jesus God! Had he overswum her the last time? Was she down river or closer yet to the bridge? How much would her velvet gown and cloak weigh her down? Would they take her all the way to the bottom or hold her somewhere in between? Had the long cloak caught on a submerged branch and anchored her or was she drifting with the current yet? Helplessly, fighting against the fear that threatened to overwhelm him, Brett forced another gulp of air into his lungs and dove again. If he did not find her this time...she had been under water at least four or five minutes already. In another minute or two, whether he found her or not. Suddenly, feeling something brush his shoulder in the black water, Brett turned and arched backwards in the water, kicking hard, his fingers combing the current for whatever it had been, refusing to go to the surface as his tortured body demanded. At last, his fingers touched something soft... velvet, his mind insisted, and he clutched handfuls of it and kicked for the surface, dragging the cloth with him despite its leadening weight. He drew breath in a gasping sob, then ducked his head again to feel along the fabric for the girl. Yes! There! Her long hair was tangling around his fingers in the swift current and he tore at the cloak's snap to free it, hauling Cerissa herself back up to the air, hitting her hard on the back to force water from her lungs and force air in. At last, he heard her choking breath and reached down his leg for the dagger strapped to his calf. The river was so cold it was numbing. Already he felt his muscles cramping and growing sluggish from it. He could never make shore dragging her water soaked gown, it weighed them down like an anchor. Holding her wrist with an iron grip, he took his dagger in his other hand and ducked under to slash at her skirts, kicking the rags free as they tangled around his legs. He dared not let go of her to use both hands—he would never find her again. God knew it was incredible luck that he'd found her the first time. At last, the skirt and petticoat had been cut free. Cerissa had swallowed enough water already, he didn't dare let her stay under any longer. He let the knife float away out of his hand and slid that arm under the girl's chin and across one shoulder, drawing her up as high out of the rippling water as he could, then turning on his side to strike out diagonally across the swift current, carrying Cerissa's limp, unresisting body with him. He aimed first for a single tall pine, but the numbing cold of the water and Cerissa's weight forced him past that before he had swum even half-way cross-river. Next, he fixed his gaze on a stand of graceful willows and kicked toward them, forcing his muscles to keep straining, keep reaching, resisting a growing impulse to simply relax, let go, and sink into the peaceful sleep of the soothing water. At last, he felt the mud buttom under his feet and he halted a moment, still chest deep in the river, to glance at Cerissa's face. It seemed obvious, even in the pale light that she was breathing normally, that the color was returning to her ashen face. In a moment, the girl began to move restlessly under his arm and he hurried to carry her free of the water before she fully awoke. He was under no illusions just now about his own physical condition. The night's worry and the exertion of the swim had exhausted him utterly. Ordinarily he would have felt a reserve of strength buoying him, but tonight, for whatever reason, that reserve was not there—or perhaps he had used it already without realizing. Anyway, if Cerissa awoke in the water and began to struggle to free herself, he would never be able to hold her. Perhaps, if she were already on land . . .

Brett slipped in the deep mud and stumbled to one knee, struggling desperately to keep his balance. Cerissa's movements grew stronger and he lunged forward for the grassy bank in a last, gasping effort, falling full-length upon it, letting his cramped, numb arm relax at last around the girl's body. For long minutes he was aware only of the heaving gasps of his lungs, the violent shuddering of his body, and the roaring of his blood in his ears. At last he raised his dark head to rest it on his folded forearms, still stretched belly down on the long, rank marshy grasses, turning only far enough to see Cerissa's face in the dappled moonlight.

"Oh, Brett" she murmured softly, her words barely audible to his ringing ears. "Couldn't you at least have let me die in peace?"

He merely stared wordlessly at her for a moment, too drained to even feel resentment or surprise at her question. "No," he mumbled, at last, still struggling for even breath. "I want to marry you."

Cerissa's eyes opened wider, and incredibly she began to laugh, choking yet on the river water she'd inhaled as she shook her head slowly. Of all the times in the three and a half years she'd known him... perhaps she was only dreaming this... perhaps she was still in the Thames and drowning and her last conscious thoughts were only to cause further bitterness within her soul..."Oh Brett, not now, I'm not so stupid as that. What about your wife Elizabeth? Is she aware that you're proposing to another?"

"Elizabeth's dead. She died in France—of a fever."

Cerissa dropped her gaze, feeling a quick rush of guilt at her thoughtless words. Gradually, the cold air and the tickling, waving grass were convincing her that this was reality... somewhere, somehow Brett must have leapt in the river after her and dragged her out. "I'm sorry, Brett, I didn't mean to sound so..."

"No apologies, Cerissa, they aren't needed. She was overjoyed that God had seen fit to deliver her from our disastrous marriage she even gave us her blessings on her death bed." Brett's words continued to be spoken so low, and so oddly slurred, that Cerissa had to strain to hear them. She fell silent a moment, thinking, still staring at the wet, black curls framing his face only a foot away from hers. "Then it's because Ardsley told you that I'm quality. I'm no different than I was a week ago except now I've got the necessary pedigree to be acceptable as a match for the blue-blooded Lindseys."

Brett shook his head more at the bitterness of her tone than the meaning of her words. "I decided as soon as Elizabeth died. I buried her and sailed straight for home. I don't give a damn about your history. Ardsley can verify that. He went to your house this afternoon when I arrived to ask you to see me. You didn't give him the chance."

Cerissa shivered as a cold gust off the water struck her. What was wrong with her? She still felt more dead than alive? Her brain was responding to Brett's words but her heart was still numb and unmoved. "And what about Edward, my husband? You haven't forgotten..."

"I'll have your marriage annulled," he replied wearily, still resting his head on his arms as if it were too heavy to hold upright. "The marriage hasn't even been comsumated so it shouldn't prove too difficult..."

"No, Brett, I can't embarrass him like that—reveal his impotence. It wouldn't be fair, he's been so kind," amazed to realize a tiny tear was rolling down her cheek. Suddenly, as if the dam had burst, she dropped her head in her hands in a gasping sob, all the horror and the hurt and the tearing, agonizing love bursting free of her soul. She felt Brett's arm slide around her and she burrowed her face in his shoulder, hearing the strong even pounding of his heart in her ear, the river-wet linen of his shirt against her lips.

"Hush, sweetheart, it'll work out somehow," he murmured quietly, his head bent close above her.

Cerissa shook her head in sobbing denial, not knowing anymore whether she wanted his words to prove true or not. This was the height of irony. That now it was Brett, the once callous, unfeeling, cold-eyed lord who believed in love's power to conquer all obstacles. While she, who had taught him that philosophy, was too bitter, too hurt, too frightened to risk her heart any longer.

"Hush, sweetheart, don't cry so. We don't need to do anything tonight—or even tomorrow. All I'm asking is that you think about it. If you decide you will still have me, I'll get it done somehow, I promise."

At last, Cerissa managed to control her wracking sobs and she nodded mute agreement, reluctant to lift her head away from the embracing security of Brett's arms.

"Let's get back now to Ardsley's. No use both us catching our deaths out here soaking wet," Brett murmured, dropping a hesitant kiss on the top of her cold, wet hair. The girl nodded again and sighed, reluctantly, he guessed with growing hope. Then she drew away and pushed herself to her feet, walking back toward the bridge now several hundred yards upriver of them.

Cerissa paused after several steps to wait for Brett, turning her head to see him get slowly to his feet, his movements strangely awkward for a man of his grace. As he caught up to her though, he managed a faint smile, offering her his arm for the climb up the uneven grassy slope of the embankment. Cerissa was shivering violently in the raw autumn wind by the time they reached the tethered horse and she huddled thankfully against it's warmth as Brett walked ahead to retrieve his sword and boots, shaking his velvet coat free of dirt before offering it wordlessly to the trembling girl. Cerissa accepted it gratefully, forcing a small strained smile up at his weary face as she slipped it on. She stared at Brett a moment longer in sudden concern, her heart lurching fearfully within her. Even in this faint light, the dark shadows ringing his eyes were plain to see, yet the eyes themselves were over-bright, almost fever-bright. She shuddered and thrust the thought firmly from her mind. Of course he looked exhausted. Burying a wife, sailing home, chasing her tonight, then pulling her out of an icy river. She half turned in his arm where she sat in front of the saddle, leaning her forehead a moment against the hard line of his jaw, relieved to see his quick smile and downward glance as he turned the horse slowly toward Ardsley's. He was all right, she assured herself hastily. Some dry clothes and a good night's rest after a glass of brandy would take off his exhaustion and his chill. She smiled faintly to herself, leaning back against his chest, letting herself begin to believe again, to hope for some kind of future. In growing contentment, she pressed against his chest as they rode, finally glad of his insistence that she continue to live. Thoughtlessly, her hand strayed down to touch the ragged bottom of her bodice, and suddenly she froze again, realizing the truth . . . my God! she thought the baby, Brett's baby, that he doesn't even know of yet. How could she annul her marriage when she was with child? How would she convince anyone, Edward included, that an impotent husband had managed to get his wife with child?

Chapter Eighteen

Ardsley opened the door himself, his face drawn and pale with worry and shock, his eyes opening in silent disbelief at the half-dressed girl, the water still dripping around both of their feet as she and Brett stood in the doorway. "Jesus Christ!" the blond lord breathed, his mouth gaping open. "What in bloody hell happened to..."

"Just let us in, Ardsley," Brett mumbled, pushing Cerissa into the marble tiled hall. "I'll explain it all when I get to the fire."

"Go ahead into the drawing room then. I'll run upstairs and get a robe for each of you." Still shaking his head in confusion, Ardsley turned and hurried for the stairs.

Cerissa stood shivering by the crackling fire, rubbing her icy hands together near it's heat before turning to strip her soaking clothes off. She undressed hurriedly, feeling oddly uncomfortable being naked in front of Brett, in such a large, unconcealing room. As the last rag dropped to the floor she slipped Brett's velvet coat back on to cover herself, glancing furtively at the dark haired lord. He too seemed to share her unease undressing, for he had slipped his wet shirt, boots and hose off, but had left his breeches on, dragging a straight back wooden chair nearer the fire to collapse wearily upon it, exhaustion evident in every slumping line of his body as he rested his head on the chair's back, his eyes already closed. Cerissa stooped to pull her one wet shoe off—the other had been lost in the river earlier—then stepped nearer the warmth again, grateful for Brett's silence. Silly that they should feel so awkward now when they had sported for hours in the Jamaican sun in total nudity enjoying the cooling waves and the browning, tropical sun. Cerissa looked again at Brett, noting the shadowed circles ringing his wide set eyes, the drawn pallor of his face. Firmly, she resisted a sudden instinctive impulse to go to him, to take his tired head in her arms, let him rest against the cool softness of her breast. She knew if she did that, her love for him would come flooding back, overwhelming her head and her logic. Just now she needed to keep both in balance. Probably the most important decision of her entire life lay before her now—she intended to make that decision with a clear mind. Why? she asked herself again, stealing another sidelong look at Brett. Why should he propose marriage now? Because I'm quality, and therefore acceptable, where I wasn't before? So what if it is that, a small part of her heart argued, you were willing enough to marry Lord Ramond to acquire a title and gain that acceptability. So why balk now? What's the difference? I don't know, she thought wearily, I only know there is a difference. I don't want to marry him unless it's truly his love that has forced a proposal. I need to be sure he loves me enough to defy both convention and the crown to gain me. If it is anything less, it isn't enough. What of Edward's reaction? And what of the baby she carried? How would she explain a pregnancy by a supposedly impotent old man? How explain the child's birth scant months after her marriage to Brett? If she could be as callous as the other Court ladies she could flush it from her womb, destroy it and . . . no, she revolted instinctively against the thought. She would never solve her dilemma at the innocent's expense . . . though God alone knew what the baby might be like. Everyone realized a child reflected it's conception. Look at Jamey, conceived in a loving of infinite joy and tenderness. How much he reflected that fact. Yet this one . . . conceived in violence and anger and bitter hurt, how would it turn out then? Suddenly remembering she turned swiftly to face Brett, her eyes watching his face intently. "Brett, did you send me violets that day after Lord and Lady Millford's party?"

The smile that fleeted across his lips was answer enough though he said nothing, didn't even open his eyes. Cerissa turned back to stare into the fire, feeling a small smile play on her own lips in response to his. "I thought it was you. You always did pick flowers to match my eyes..." she murmured softly, her heart warming despite her efforts to remain untouched. She glanced back at him, expecting some explanation but Brett remained silent and motionless so long that at last she began to turn away, thinking him asleep.

"I've regretted that night more than you could know, sweetheart," he murmured at last, his eyes opening a fraction to catch hers, his sincerity written plainly in them. "I would have sent a note but... I didn't know what kind of relationship you had with your husband then. And I was afraid you'd slam the door in my face if I came in person. Anyway, I'd promised Elizabeth I wouldn't see you again until we returned from France."

Cerissa blinked in surprise, dropping her gaze to hide the confusion of her thoughts. Strange... people often said lovers grew alike. She and Brett had, each changing the other slightly. A promise was worthless to him when they'd first met. It was his broken promise of waking her by midnight that first caused all the trouble. Now, he considered a promise a solemn, binding responsibility. Once given it would never be broken. So that's why he had not seen her all that time... at last, the pieces of the puzzle were beginning to fall into place. "Then Elizabeth did know?" she asked softly, unwilling to meet his eyes.

"Yes," he replied slowly, his voice barely above a whisper. "When it came time to leave, she came into the gardens looking for me. I guess I'd fallen asleep—too much brandy... or too much love... maybe both. Anyway, when I felt her hand on my shoulder shaking me awake I simply assumed it was you."

Cerissa felt her heart lurch again, remembering. Then the sweetness, the tenderness which had ended the loving—she hadn't simply imagined it as she'd thought she had. For his wife to realize...

"She insisted we return immediately to France, Cerissa. I felt I owed her that at least because I had already decided to continue seeing you—if you'd allow it. Elizabeth was a very religious person. She took adultery very seriously. I believe she wanted to discuss the repercussions of my wickedness with the Mother Superior of her convent school."

Cerissa was silent, digesting Brett's words. They'd hurt each other so deeply—and all in innocence. If only they'd had a single hour alone together to explain... "There's something else about that night you ought to know," she murmured hesitantly, her hand dropping to rest on her belly, her eyes turning from the flames to seek his. "I believe I..."

Ardsley's knock at the door interrupted her and she stopped at once. Brett frowned slightly, his eyes coaxing her to continue but she shook her head, turning for the door. "I'll get it." she mumbled, not really unhappy to leave her disclosure for a later time. Perhaps Brett, too, had had enough shocks in one day. He certainly didn't look as though he was fully himself. She opened the door and Lord Ardsley came hurrying in, shaking his head as he carried two robes to the fire.

"You two keep me waiting longer in hallways than anyone I know," he grumbled, tossing the robes to the sofa. "Now I'll go out again—for only a moment, I warn you—so you can get these on."

Cerissa shed the damp velvet coat as soon as the door closed and looked expectantly around to Brett, frowning in surprise to see he hadn't even made a move yet for his. She waited a moment longer, then walked toward him, slipping between him and the hot fire to touch his raven hair gently with one hand. It was unusual for Brett to sit so close to the flames—he was invariably too hot there. Even now, his bare arm and forehead felt burning to her fingertips. "Get out of your wet breeches, Brett," she coaxed gently, leaning across his lap to fetch the robe over. "You'll catch your death sitting around in those cold things."

Brett forced his eyes open and he gazed wordlessly up at her, smiling a singularly sweet and tender smile. Cerissa felt her heart ache in swift response and she smiled back, letting his love wash over her like life-giving nectar. "Still playing little mother?" he mumbled at last, the light in his eyes taking any possible sting out of his words.

Cerissa shrugged and nodded, faintly embarrassed but still determined to get him into the dry robe.

"I'm not sure I can get up again," Brett sighed, lifting his hands to rub at his eyes.

Cerissa frowned briefly, then forced a smile. No matter how tired he was, this wasn't like Brett to be so sluggish. He had been weary before, even wounded, yet, with his force of will, he always managed to keep going as long as he needed to. "Try, love," she whispered. "I'll help you."

With another deep sigh, Brett leaned forward, resting his head for a long moment in his hands, his elbows balanced on his knees. Cerissa waited wordlessly, her throat closing in the grip of fear's icy fingers. Dear God! Don't let him be sick! Not now! Not when we might finally have a chance! She leaned forward, sliding her arms under his and began to heave backwards. Brett resisted a minute, then leaned with her, using his hands against the chairs' arms to force himself up, swaying against Cerissa before he gained his balance. The girl reached cautiously for the robe, keeping one arm around Brett's back for support, terribly aware of the dryness of her throat, the pounding terror of her heart. At last, Brett managed to slip the buttons of his breeches and he stepped awkwardly out of them, shrugging his wide shoulders into the robe Cerissa held for him. She urged him gently toward the long sofa, feeling her arms beginning to tremble from his weight even though he was supporting most of his own, sighing in relief as he sank down onto the cushions and leaned back into the plump pillows.

"All right, Ardsley," Cerissa called over her shoulder, her eyes never leaving Brett's ashen face, her hand reaching out to touch his brow tenderly. Brett caught at her hand and forced a faint smile as he took it in his. Even here, away from the fire, Cerissa could feel the heat of his skin, the warm moistness of his palm.

"Jesus Christ, Brett, you look awful." the blond lord frowned down at his friend in quick concern. "I'm sending you up to bed. No more excuses."

Brett opened his eyes and shook his head in quick denial. "No, James, I have to talk to Cerissa yet about . . ."

"No," Cerissa interrupted instantly, "No more tonight. Ardsley's right, you should be in bed. I'll come by tomorrow and . . ."

"Stay here." Brett urged, his eyes pleading with hers. "So I know you're safe. Or I swear I . . ."

"All right, Brett." Cerissa smiled overbrightly. "I'll stay right next to you all night if that's what you wish. Just promise you'll get a good night's sleep."

"No, not with me," the dark haired lord disagreed hastily, glancing over at Ardsley. "In another room."

Cerissa noted with growing unease the glance of understanding that passed between the two men before Ardsley nodded. "Why?" she demanded abruptly. "Why another room?" She stared down at Brett but he only returned her gaze wordlessly. Ardsley shrugged and shifted uneasily as she turned to him.

"If the fever's contagious, sweetheart..."

"Fever?" she breathed in horror, feeling the blood draining out of her face. Oh my God! Hadn't Brett said his wife had died of fever? "Oh Brett, no..."

"I'm only tired," he murmured, obviously trying to smile encouragement, glancing again at Ardsley for agreement.

"Of course," the blond lord agreed. "We'll let him get some rest. If he doesn't feel better in the morning, I'll call a physician then."

Cerissa swallowed hard and nodded, blinking to keep the welling tears from falling on her cheeks. She wasn't fooled for a moment by either of the men's insistence. Brett wasn't tired, he was sick. But she kept silent until she'd seen Brett into bed, kissing his forehead softly, feigning a confidence she did not feel. Alone in the hall with Ardsley, as she turned for her room, she grabbed his hand and stared solemnly up into the lord's troubled eyes. "That fever... the one his wife died of... how did she get it?"

Ardsley frowned, then shrugged, deciding to tell the girl the truth. "Some of the crew had it, Cerissa—on the yacht they took over to France."

"And of the crewmen who got it, how many of them lived?" Cerissa stared still at him, her eyes beseeching honesty, holding her breath for the answer.

The blond lord's eyes shifted away, his hand taking hers in a brief grip. "None of them, sweetheart, they all died."

Cerissa stared at him a moment longer in sick horror, then closed her eyes, forcing her breath slowly from her lungs. Sick with a deadly fever! Oh my God! And she had thought she'd known the bitter sting of irony before.

"But Brett's strong, sweetheart, he's lived through half a dozen situations a lesser man wouldn't have. We'll get him the best care..."

"Oh Ardsley... that icy water tonight... getting me out of the river..."

"Hush, girl, he was sick before that. You mustn't blame yourself," he smiled faintly, his eyes gentle with pity. "Anyway, don't give up on him so easily," he shrugged, trying to force some levity into his tone. "He's tough. We'll pull him through—wait and see."

Cerissa stood a moment longer, then nodded, realizing she had already made her decision. Yes, if Brett lived she would do whatever she had to to be with him. And she wouldn't let him die, that was all there was to it. By God! After all they'd been through together, she wouldn't let go of him now. Unconsciously in the dark hallway, she raised her chin in determination. "First thing in the morning then we'll get the king's own doctor for him James."

The blond lord nodded, envying the girl's hope for he had none. "Right, sweetheart. First thing in the morning."

Cerissa awoke as the first grey streaks of dawn were touching the horizon, feeling even more exhausted than she had when she'd gone to bed. She hadn't slept well. Half a dozen times during the night she had awoken, wondering how Brett was. Once she had even climbed out of bed and slipped her robe on before forcing herself to patience. If she went in, and he was sleeping and her entrance disturbed him she would regret it. If he weren't sleeping, her coming would only upset him—he would be fearful to exposing her to the disease. So, better to wait, she'd cautioned herself. Wait until morning.

Now, as she tiptoed cautiously into his room, moving slowly in the dim light of the shuttered windows, Cerissa searched Brett's face anxiously, holding her breath lest even that slight sound wake him. He was sleeping at least. Not too restfully perhaps, from the sign of the rumpled sheets and disarrayed pillows—and his breathing was rapid and more shallow than normal—yet at least he slept. She leaned closer, holding her unbound hair back lest it swing forward to brush his bare shoulder. A first faint flush of fever was spreading on his cheeks. Cerissa bit her lip to restrain tears—she hadn't realized until that sudden plummeting of her heart that she had still hoped he was not sick. Ironic how fever let a dying man masquerade for the first few hours as an exceptionally healthy one. The vibrant color in Brett's face reminded her of the Indies, when he would return from the sea with new sun. She stared at him a moment longer, achingly aware of how compelling an attraction he held for her despite all that had passed between them. Then, silently, she turned to go.

"Sweet?"

The girl turned quickly at the sound of Brett's low whisper, forcing a smile as she looked down into his drowsy, half-open eyes, reaching tenderly to smooth the black hair back from his burning forehead.

"Love me?" he murmured with the ingenuousness of a child, his mouth curving in a lop-sided smile.

Cerissa nodded hastily, bending down to kiss his dark curls. "I do love you, Brett. I'm sorry I woke you. Go back to sleep."

With another faint smile, he closed his eyes obediently. Cerissa remained motionless until she guessed he was sleeping, then stole cautiously out of the darkened room and down the hall. She would borrow some clothes from one of the servants and go fetch the doctor. Perhaps, with immediate care, he would live.

"Here, darling, drink this," she urged the dark haired lord firmly, repressing her own instinctive revulsion for the greasy looking concoction. Doctor Broughlin had said he must drink it—and Ardsley vowed he was the best physician in London—so drink it he would.

Brett stared at her silently, a half smile on his lips. "Will you feel better if I do?" he asked at last, raising an eyebrow in question.

"It's not for me," she frowned, glancing quickly at Ardsley in puzzlement at his words, "It's for you. It'll help the fever."

Brett glanced at the cup again, grimacing, then shrugged, smiling strangely as he met her gaze. "All right, sweetheart, I'll take it for your sake—though I don't believe it will help." With an obvious effort he drained the cup, gagging at the end on it's foul taste.

Cerissa watched anxiously as he turned suddenly away from her, vomiting into a silver basin on the other side of the bed, then choking for breath before vomiting again, and still again until his shoulders shuddered from the spasms. Cerissa watched helplessly for a few moments, then turned angrily to face Ardsley, her blue eyes hard and hurt in confusion. "Ardsley, what's going on? You said that doctor was the best in..."

"He is, sweetheart, you've got to trust him," Ardsley replied gently, his own face showing no surprise at the potion's effect. "He isn't poisoned. The doctor's got to rid his body of the bad blood—of the fever poison—it's the only way."

"Then why didn't you warn me?" she accused with a half-sob. "At least I could have told Brett what to expect."

"Brett knew," Ardsley assured her. "He's been doctored before. That a purge, and some bleeding... it's not pretty, perhaps, but..."

"Brett knew?" the girl echoed in disbelief, gaping at the blond lord. "But why did he drink it so..."

"For your sake, sweetheart."

Cerissa stared wordlessly at Ardsley another minute, then with a violent shudder she turned away. In the country, they'd had no real doctors. Sickness was treated with grandmother's recipes or witchwomen's potions. And Liza, in the islands, she hadn't made

Brett sicker making him well. Nothing she'd every prepared had torn his insides apart like that foul, inky liquid of Doctor Broughlin's. If she'd known the results of that draught she'd never have asked Brett to drink it. And the way he'd looked at her before he took it—as though he was sure it was all for nothing anyway.

"Move back a step, sweetheart," Ardsley touched her arm, beckoning her away from the bed. Cerissa flung a quick look at Brett who lay motionless now in the bed, his eyes closed, then obeyed, watching the doctor extract a sharp looking silver instrument from his black satchel. As he made several small cuts into Brett's limp arm, she gave another small cry, starting forward toward the bed.

"Hush, girl, he's only going to bleed him now. Brett's all right."

Cerissa watched incredulously, with a sense of growing horror as the doctor reached again into the bag for several glass bottles, extracting a roundish brown lump from each one, laying a glistening lump on each of the bleeding incisions. Suddenly, as she stared at it, one of the lumps moved and she cried aloud her revulsion, jumping forward to knock frantically at Brett's arm with the back of her hand.

Ardsley leapt behind her, catching her arms and pulling her bodily away. "Jesus, Cerissa, what the hell are you doing?"

"Get them off!" she cried, trembling on the brink of hysteria, fighting against the lord's restraining grip. "Get them off of him, whatever they are!"

"Cerissa, for God's sake," he snapped, thoroughly out of patience with her. "They're leeches! How the hell else is Doctor Broughlin supposed to bleed him? Those creatures will suck out the poisoned blood, sweetheart," he added, more kindly. "Just stay calm."

Cerissa leaned helplessly against him, tears burning her face as she stared in fascinated horror at the small, evil looking creatures on Brett's arm. At last, the doctor decided he had bled the sick man enough, and he sprinkled some white powder over the leeches and gathered them back up, returning each to his own separate bottle with great care. Cerissa sighed in relief, feeling nauseous and weak, glad the doctoring was finally over. Liza hadn't done anything like that—and she had said something once about pulling Brett through a fever. She had used roots and herb leaves, wholesome things. Now that Doctor Broughlin was through she would tend Brett her own way—as best she could. She might not help him very much, but then, she was positive, instinctively, neither had Doctor Broughlin, celebrated physician though he might be. She shuddered again, watching the man's fingers fumble to close his satchel. The fingernails were broken, and lined with dirt underneath. Lisa's hands had always been clean when she'd tended him—she'd even washed her hands each time with an odd, pungent lotion before she'd touched the open wound on his leg. Damn! she thought in desperate frustration. Why didn't I pay more attention to Liza's remedies while I was there? Why didn't I ask her more questions, find out what she used in...

"I'll return this afternoon," Doctor Broughlin announced to Lord Ardsley, his eyes flickering contemptuously over the still trembling girl.

"Fine, I'll be..."

"No!" Cerissa blurted, feeling her stomach heave in renewed rebellion. She'd thought he was done! She'd never let him touch Brett...

"Cerissa, he's got to," Ardsley argued, his voice gentle and patient but still firm. "He's got to keep treating Brett as long..."

"No, James! No more, I won't let him!" Cerissa's voice broke as a sob escaped her lips and she shook her head defiantly. "I don't care what you say, that can't do him any good."

"Of course it does."

Cerissa shook her head more forcefully, her chin setting mulishly. She could remember now so clearly, sitting with Liza one evening on the veranda, asking her about Brett's earlier fever. "Shucks, chile," the round, black woman had chuckled, her black eyes sparkling in mirth. "I didn't work no miracle. Just used some stuff my momma told me 'bout and kept de chill off him. You white folks now, you got de damnest way of fixing a sick man I ever seen, taking blood away from him just when he needs it de most!" She hadn't understood then what Liza had meant, but now she did. "I mean it, Ardsley, please. No more."

"I'm sorry, Cerissa. Doctor Broughlin is the finest physician in London. I respect your rights in making a decision but Brett's my friend too. I've got to do what I think best for him."

"How did they treat Elizabeth... and the others that died?" she challenged desperately, her hand clutching his beseechingly. "Didn't they have the same sort of care?"

Ardsley frowned a moment, glancing at the doctor and then at Brett's motionless body, before returning his gaze to the girl. "All right," he sighed, shrugging. "Do what you want. He's likely to die no matter what we..."

298

"No, he won't," she denied determindly, feeling her breath return to nearer normal in relief. "I won't let him."

"You're discharging me?" Doctor Broughlin asked stiffly, his eyes registering disapproval and surprise.

"Yes, doctor, but thank you. The girl's his...his fiancé," Ardsley lied easily. "She has the final say."

With a curt bow, the doctor left the room, his overstraight back and too quick stride expressing his irritation. With a weary sigh, Ardsley turned back to face Cerissa where she sat on the bed beside the unconscious lord, wiping his face gently with a wet cloth. "What now then, sweetheart?"

"I don't know," she answered slowly, her eyes dark with thought. "Liza, Brett's housekeeper in Jamaica, knew so much about curing fever. Oh, I wish she were here."

"Hell, the Indies are near six weeks away. I'm not sure Brett's got six days let alone six weeks."

"Well, maybe I can find another black woman here in London," she argued, "There must be some here brought over from the tropics."

"It wouldn't help you if you could," Ardsley grunted dispiritedly, dropping beside her on the bed. "The Negroes don't all know about healing. They have witchwomen and medicine chiefs who have that knowledge locked up tight. Most likely that Liza learned from one of them."

"Well there must be somebody else who might know! Someone who's lived in the islands, or... I know!" she cried softly, turning to catch Ardsley's hand, "Maybe the surgeon on Brett's ship. He'd had to have seen plenty of fever cases! He might know how the natives would treat the sickness."

Ardsley smiled faintly, wishing with all his soul that the girl was right and that there might yet be hope for Lindsey. "Good. What's his name? I'll send a carriage..."

Cerissa dropped her head quickly, feeling new tears sting her eyes. "Oh damn, Ardsley, I don't remember his name now... it was years ago. Oh damn." she bit her lip, feeling the tears start to fall anyway, and she leaned her head helplessly against the blond lord's shoulder. "Oh damn it, Ardsley, I can't remember anything. I can't remember what Liza said she used. I can't remember the surgeon's name. I feel so damned stupid and useless."

"Hush, sweet, don't start giving up. Think some more. Who would know the ship's surgeon's name and location? Isaac Benjamin? Or is there a ships log somewhere?"

"Jake Oates, the mate!" she remembered, feeling hope lift her heart again, almost laughing aloud in relief. "He would know, I'm sure of it."

"Good, where does he live?"

"I'm not sure but I know it's in the city, James, I remember Brett saying so. He said he could always find him at...at the...the Mermaid's Palace, that was it!"

"Mermaid's Palace?" the blond lord echoed in disapproval. "That's in Cheapside, Cerissa, near the docks. You can't go about alone down there looking for some sailor. Are you sure he even returned with Brett from the Florida wreck?"

"Yes, I asked about him," she replied without hesitation. "Ardsley I've got to go. I'll take a manservant with me. But sailors are funny. He might not help unless he's sure it's really Brett that's ill. He'll remember me though. I'll leave now."

Ardsley nodded agreement and she stood up, reluctant to leave Brett's side but eager to find help. Oh, please God help me find Oates! she prayed, fervently "I know he can help me! I know it in my soul! If he should awake, James, don't let him worry. Tell him I went home to gather some clothes and I'll be right back. And tell him...tell him I'm sorry...and I love him."

Ardsley smiled and nodded again, urging her to caution as she turned to leave. "I'll watch him carefully for you, I promise."

"Yes, Jake, the ship's surgeon. Brett's terribly sick of a fever and the London physician we called..."

"Surgeon's dead, missy," the weathered seaman shook his head regretfully, taking another sip of his ale as he glanced across the crowded tavern room to glare a warning to an over-interested young seapup. Making eyes at the Captain's wench! He'd gouge the man's impudent eyeballs out if he...

"Dead? Oh, no, Jake he can't be!"

The girl's disappointment sounded plainly in her voice, and he turned his full attention back to her, frowning at the quivering lower lip that presaged tears. "Now, no need to be crying, little darling," he cautioned hastily. "He died in the Florida swamp. Pretty little black snake with red and orange rings crawled in his bedroll one night, and ppfett! by next sunset, he was gone. He wouldn't have been no help to ye anyways. He was drunk often as not, 'specially on land. 'Course the Captain didn't allow him boozing aboard ship."

Cerissa could only stare at him, unable to think rationally of

300

what next step to take. Fate mocked her, thwarted her at every turn. Just as she had thought help was in hand, finding the old seaman so luckily as soon as she'd arrived . . .

"You say Captain Lindsey's bad off?"

She nodded, not trusting her voice, feeling defeat wash over her, unable to resist it any longer. "Dying," she admitted at last, gathering her gloves to leave again.

"Well, hold on there, missy," the mate frowned. "Give an old man time to think. You know I think the world of the Captain, I'll not be letting him go if I can help. As I said, the surgeon what died . . . he wouldn't have been no help to ye anyway. And the ones shipping on the Captin's other boats aren't much better. Them black bush women in the islands are about the best I know for fevers and such, but we ain't got time enough to go picking one of them up. Seems to me, though, that I remember the Captain saying something once about some foreign fellow what lived here in the city. Said King Charles ought to have had him instead of the butcher he did. But most folks don't take kindly to foreigners, 'specially them oddball Turks and such, always muttering about Allah, and Mecca, and carrying little rugs around to . . ."

"What's his name?" Cerissa interrupted breathlessly. If Mate Oates was talking about a Moorish physician . . . how many times had she heard Brett argue how valuable their skills and knowledge might be if only the English could disregard their prejudices against their religion and their strange customs. Centuries of fighting the Moslems in the Crusades had left a legacy of hostility that was so slow to die . . .

"His name? Hell, missy, they all got such peculiar names," Oates frowned a moment thoughtfully, then looked around the tavern, banging the flat of his hand on the scarred wooden table top for attention. "Hey, blokes! I got all the free ale ye can drink for the man what remembers where to find that Turkish doctor. Any takers?"

Cerissa stared in astonishment as the tavern exploded in noise—ten, maybe twelve men yelling at once. Finally, the leathery mate seemed to make sense of the chaos and he beamed happily, pointing a gnarled finger at a burly, young man in a striped cotton shirt. "Aye, Smitty, that be the one I was after! Drink yer drinks, man, and thanks."

Cerissa memorized Oates' information carefully, repeating it twice to be sure she had it correctly. Then, impulsively, she smiled, hope restored, leaning across to kiss the mate's wind-toughened

301

face. "Thank you so much, Jake. Oh, I hope he can help Brett."

"Maybe he can, maybe he can't, missy," the sailor philosophized with an answering smile. "But at least ye gave it yer best shot. Let me know how things go if ye will."

"Yes, of course, Jake. And here," Cerissa offered several gold coins to the sailor, meaning to pay for the young man's ale, but he shook his grey head."

"No, thank ye. T'is the least I can do fer the Captain, lass. Give him my wishes."

Cerissa smiled again and nodded, hurrying back to her coach to call the precious name and address to the driver. "The Knightbridge Arms," she called, "Doctor Hajamin. And hurry!"

Hurry he did, and the girl bounced unmercifully in the small compartment, not minding the bruises or the bumps in the slightest. Now, she thought hopefully, only one more obstacle. That he be home when we arrive. And that he agree to undertake the treatment. The carriage lurched to a stop, and she flung the door open, hurrying to the door of the narrow brick building herself, knocking on it loudly. "Doctor Hajamin?" she questioned breathlessly, as a swarthy looking, black-haired, black-eyed man opened the door.

"Yes." The man merely stared at her, his eyes distant, his manner unencouraging.

Cerissa felt her heart begin to hammer with fear that he would refuse to help. "Please, Doctor, my . . . my fiancé is terribly ill of a fever. I've heard he spoke highly of your skills as a physician so I . . ."

"How did you find me?"

Cerissa stammered a moment, taken back by the man's manner and his queerly accented English, uncertain how to respond. "One of the sailors on my fiancé's ships remembered your name," she began hesitantly. "And I . . ."

"Who is your fiancé?"

"Lord Lindsey," she answered promptly, praying the man would not recognize Brett's name enough to wonder at such an abrupt change in his marital status . . . if he caught her in a lie about being betrothed . . .

"I thought you said he was a captain."

"He does . . . he is," Cerissa stammered. "He's both, does it matter? Please, I'm afraid he's dying and I . . ."

"Haven't you called a physician? If he is a lord you must surely have your choice of the city's finest."

302

Cerissa paused a moment, puzzled by the man's whole attitude. He stared at her now most intently, a strange expression in his black eyes. "Yes," she breathed gambling on the truth. "I did. A Doctor Broughlin. I'd never seen a physician at work before and I didn't know what to expect. Perhaps I'm wrong, but I don't believe such treatment can help Brett...Lord, Lindsey, I mean. I was in the Indies with him several years ago, and saw a different sort of medicine used there with great success against fever. I hoped perhaps you might be able to propose an alternative to Dr. Broughlin's poisoning and bleeding. Brett's often remarked that you...that the Moslems have greater knowledge than we in some things."

The man studied the girl's flushed face silently for some time and finally nodded, sending waves of relief bursting through her soul. "Oh, thank you," she murmured, turning back to the coach.

"Wait, please, I must gather some things before I go. And one more thing. Can you gather some few items I may require? I will write a list for you."

Cerissa nodded, trying to wait patiently while the man disappeared inside the house for a seeming eternity. Her whole soul cried out to be back with Brett without delay, but she would do as Doctor Hajamin requested. It wouldn't take long.

"All right, I'm ready, I shall take a coach to what address?"

"Take mine, I'll hire another for..." she paused, glancing down at the list. It read like a grocery inventory. Lemons, limes or oranges...sugar...various herbs.

"My methods will seem strange to you," the man smiled faintly though his eyes now seemed kind. "But I do need what is on that list. Find as much as you can, but don't take over long. If your lord is so very ill, time is important."

Cerissa nodded again, feeling a growing confidence in this strange man. "I know," she agreed. "And thank you again."

Cerissa jumped from the coach in great haste, dragging her purchases with her under each arm, turning to toss the hired driver a generous wage. As she stepped in the door, both Ardsley and Doctor Hajamin confronted her.

"He wants to move Brett to the country." Ardsley protested immediately, frowning his unease. "He says he needs clean air and spring water. You can't really..."

"Please, James," she interrupted at once, her eyes pleading with his. "If he says move him..." She hesitated, glancing at the silent

Moslem, wishing she could be sure. Everyone knew fresh air was dangerous for a sick man, it only let more bad air in. Yet, come to think of it, hadn't Liza left Brett's window open down at Sweetwater? She'd tacked some netting over it to keep out the insects, but..."Liza let fresh air in too, James. And it didn't hurt him then. Please. What other choice do we have? I'm certain he'll die under Dr. Broughlin's treatment."

The blond haired lord frowned at her for long minutes, finally shrugging a reluctant agreement, though he was obviously unconvinced. "My wife's family has a small cottage in Windsor. Is that country enough?"

"Does it have a window in the bedroom? And a fireplace as well?" The swarthy doctor met the lord's eyes calmly, apparently unperturbed by Ardsley's unease.

"Yes, and a spring fed well."

"Fine, we'll leave at once."

"Is Brett going to live?" Cerissa could not help blurting the question that trembled on her lips.

"Kismet," the Moslem shrugged, his dark eyes compassionate as he met hers. "You would call it fate. Perhaps...if he is strong enough...if we are clever enough...perhaps, yes, he might live."

Cerissa smiled radiantly, blinking against the hopeful tears that filled her eyes. At least, there was hope. With Doctor Broughlin, she'd sensed he was performing only what he knew to be a useless ritual. "May I see him?"

"Yes, if he is awake yet. But hurry. We must leave at once."

Cerissa leaned over Brett, delighted to see him turn his head and open his eyes in recognition. "Hello, darling," she whispered, repressing the impulse to ask how he was feeling. The fever had flushed his full face scarlet and the shadows surrounding his eyes had darkened. Obviously, he was no better. "Oh, Brett I'm sorry about Doctor Broughlin," she blurted helplessly. I didn't know he would do...I didn't know what to expect."

"All right," he whispered huskily, trying to force a smile as he met her eyes. "Is he here again?"

"No, I...we...Ardsley and I discharged him. I couldn't help but compare how he was treating you with what I remembered Liza doing down at Sweetwater. I hope I'm not wrong, Brett, but I felt so sure Doctor Broughlin couldn't help you. So I went to the Mermaid's Palace and I..." her voice trailed off as she saw Brett close his eyes again, already beginning to drift away from her. "We're moving you into the country," she murmured. "Doctor Hajamin suggested it."

Brett nodded slightly on the pillows, his lips twitching in a ghost of a smile. Cerissa relaxed, sensing that he was pleased, smiling her answering pleasure. Brett moved his head restlessly again, forcing his eyes half open to catch her gaze.

"Jamey?" he breathed, every word an obvious effort. "Like to see him again."

Cerissa felt her earlier gladness turn sour in her mouth, and she dropped her gaze, nodding wordlessly. He hadn't said he'd like to see his son once more before he died, but he may as well have, the meaning was clear in his eyes. "I'll ask the Doctor," she promised. After a moment, as she brought her gaze back to Brett's face, she saw his eyes close again. Even as she watched, the muscles of his neck relaxed and his dark head drifted sideways deeper into the pillows. Oh Brett, she thought hopelessly, don't give up. My love, my darling, you never gave up so easily before. You always bent Fate to suite your wishes, do it again. Fate, she mused fearfully, kismet Doctor Hajamin had called it. Fate would decide whether he lived or died . . . and Fate was no friend to them, had never been. Yet she would forgive all of the past cruelties if Fate would only be kind this one time and spare his life. She wouldn't even ask for their love to continue, or the marriage to be possible. Only Brett's life. Heavily, she rose to her feet and went to seek the Moslem physician.

"Jamey? Who is that? Lord Ardsley?"

"No," Cerissa shook her head. "My . . . his son. He lives here."

The man studied her a long minute, his black eyes shrewd. "Your son also?" he questioned at last.

Cerissa felt a red blush creeping up her neck, but she forced her chin up, forced her eyes to continue meeting his without shame. "Yes," she admitted at last, taking a deep breath, "I was not altogether truthful with you concerning our—Lord Lindsey's and mine—relationship. I have been his mistress for several years now, Jamey is our son. I'm sorry I lied to you. It just seemed easier than explaining.

"But Brett loves me," the girl said quietly, feeling the sweet serenity of that certainty in her soul, "He would marry me despite the world's censure if he could."

The Turk nodded, his teeth flashing startlingly white agains this swarthy skin in a rare smile. "A man who loves a woman will do many things for her. Perhaps if you ask him, he will live for you when he would find it easier to die.."

Cerissa gaped at him, feeling a sudden shiver touch her her spine. Before she could speak, the man continued, taking her hand kindly to lead her toward the carriage.

"I do not think we should risk exposing the boy, Cerissa. Usually, by the time a disease is apparent, it is no longer contagious, yet... why take such a chance? Besides, we do not wish Lord Lindsey to make his farewells. He must use his strength for living, not for dying."

The girl nodded slowly, climbing into the waiting coach, then watching anxiously until she saw several manservants carrying Brett out. The ride to Windsor was a short one, they should be settled before sunset. What a strange man the Turkish doctor was... and yet she liked him, trusted him. If anyone could save Brett, he could. No, she amended silently with a faint smile, *they* could. She and the doctor together.

Chapter Nineteen

Cerissa stirred the thick beef broth again, watching the faint steam that floated up away from the surface of the bowl. This too was different. Doctor Broughlin had said no food whatsoever except an egg or a custard. Hajamin insisted Lord Lindsey have rich beef and chicken broths, with the fat skimmed clean from the top, but no eggs or milk, he'd said. A fevered stomach would only sour such foods and make him sicker. And, even while Brett drifted away in a strange half-sleep, half-coma, she must spoon cold spring water mixed with sugar and the juice of the fruits he'd ordered into Brett's mouth. She'd tasted the concoction herself and found it pleasant, sweet and tart at the same time, and refreshing. From what the Moslem said, the extreme heat of the fever would use up Brett's body water. It must be replaced constantly. And another oddity, though the fireplace burned low, the window was open slightly as well, letting the cool, fresh October air into the bedroom. With a sigh, Cerissa set the cup of soup to one side and reached for the soft cloth to dip it again in the ever present, freshly drawn ice cold water of the spring fed well. Several times, Hajamin had reminded her of the necessity of keeping cold cloths on Brett's forehead constantly, even soaking his black hair with the water as well. And he'd thrown only one light cover over him instead of the thick woolen quilts Doctor Broughlin had requested. Cerissa found it strange, for she knew a main danger during fever was to catch a chill. But she had to admit Brett seemed more comfortable this way. His sleep was less restless and he did not fight the covers constantly. Frequently the Moslem doctor had come in to check his patient, feeding him doses of tea made of pungent herbs. He often held his fingers tightly against Brett's wrist, or leaned over to place his ear to the lord's chest. It was nearly noon now and her head ached with weariness. She would feed Brett this soup and then sleep a while herself.

She awoke to the sound of murmured voices, and blinked sleep quickly from her eyes, searching the darkened room. Ardsley and Doctor Hajamin stood between her and Brett's bed and she suddenly bolted to her feet, her heart squeezed in instant fear, running desperately back to where her lover lay. Ardsley caught her as she moved, holding her back from the wide, rumpled bed, restraining her frantic struggles to reach Lord Lindsey. "It's all right, sweetheart, Brett's all right," he whispered loudly against her ear. "Hush now, don't wake him."

At last Cerissa quieted, allowing his words to calm her thudding heart. Ardsley beckoned her to follow him into the hall and she glanced at Doctor Hajamin in mute question. As he nodded, she turned to follow the blond lord out of the room.

Out in the hall, Ardsley turned swiftly to the Moslem doctor, his face creasing in a reluctant smile. "I owe you an apology, Doctor. I confess I doubted your ability to treat Lord Lindsey successfully, but now I cannot doubt you any longer."

The swarthy Turk frowned slightly, shaking his head thoughtfully. "You should not congratulate me too soon, Lord Ardsley."

Cerissa joined Ardsley in staring at Hajamin in shocked surprise. "Not congratulate... but, my God! man. All the others were dead before sunset of the third day. Brett—bull-headed as he is—spent the first day walking around with it, jumping into icy rivers for a midnight swim. It's dark now... beyond the third day already. Surely..."

"No. He is no worse, perhaps, but he is no better," the Turk's voice held an odd note of compassion and his black eyes darted quickly to the girl's face to note her reaction. "I do not understand this fever. I have seen no others like it. It resists medicines which ought to help and responds to others which should not affect it. No, we have not won. At best we have managed a ... what term is it you English use in the chess game? Ah! yes, 'stalemate.' We are at a stalemate, the fever and I."

"Well, what's wrong with that?" Ardsley protested instantly. "Eventually the fever will pass and ..."

"No, I don't believe so. The fever will continue to slowly sap your friend's strength. He may live a week, even two, yet in the end, when his strength is worn down, he will succumb."

The silence grew stifling in the narrow hall. Cerissa could feel the sick scudding of her heart, and she swallowed twice to force moisture into her dry throat. "Well, then ... there is no hope?" she managed to whisper at last, her voice amazingly calm. "Can you not suggest an alternative treatment ... or is it totally impossible that he might outlast the fever's length?"

Doctor Hajamin met her gaze with thoughtful eyes, spreading his hands in a hopeless gesture. "Who can say yes or no to that for sure, my dear? Such knowledge belongs to Allah alone. I am only mortal. I can only guess. My guess is that if we continue as we have, your lord will live another week or longer, growing slowly weaker with each passing day."

"And the alternative treatment if there is one?" Cerissa forced herself to ask with apparent composure.

"Unpleasant and dangerous," the Turk replied bluntly. "To force the fever higher and higher in hopes it will break before it kills him."

Cerissa forced her breath slowly from her lungs, trying not to allow the spreading numbness of her despair from clouding her mind. "Ardsley? What do you think?"

"I think we should wait it out," the blond lord replied slowly, a frown creasing his brow. "Raising the fever is precisely what we've been struggling to avoid. The risks of such treatment may be as great as the other. Plus the higher fever is liable to send him half crazy with delirium, we'll be roasting him alive. At least he's fairly comfortable this way."

Cerissa considered his comments silently, tempted to agree with him even though she had great faith in Hajamin's skill. "Can we not try both?" she asked the waiting Turk at last. "Keep this care up for a week or so ... then, if he hasn't started to improve, try more drastic measures then?"

309

The doctor shook his head, regret showing in his troubled eyes. "No, each day will take more strength from him, Cerissa. To wait a week...What I have in mind would surely kill him then."

"Couldn't we give it another day or two at least?" she pleaded, fearful of making such a choice. Suppose she agreed to Hajamin's suggestion and Brett died? Would she ever be sure he wouldn't have lived the other way? And if she refused the change, how would she feel in a week or two if he slipped slowly away from her as the Moslem guessed he would?

Hajamin sighed, shrugging, his eyes full of pity for the girl. "Every day lessens our chance of success, but perhaps...one more day might not make too great a difference."

Cerissa glanced sharply at his eyes, reading there what she guessed she might. One more day might very well mean a great deal of difference. The man only sought to spare her a while longer...and perhaps give her a last day with the man she loved. But even knowing that, she was helpless to make a decision. She was fearful and she was selfish. If Brett was to die in either case, she wanted every last precious moment remaining. "One more day then," she murmured, unable to meet either man's eyes. "Perhaps by tomorrow night our choice will be clearer."

Doctor Hajamin nodded acceptance of her decision, and Ardsley squeezed her hand briefly in wordless consolation as he turned to leave for bed. Cerissa walked back into Brett's room, with a sick cold knot in her belly, her mind torn by whirling, conflicting demands. Dispiritedly, she leaned to check Brett before drawing a chair up near the bed. The moonlight was bright tonight, and showed the growing gauntness of his face with dreadful clarity. His lips were parted slightly as if in sleep, but the restlessness of his movements belied that state. It was not true sleep he wandered in, she knew, but a sort of drugged trance induced by the Moslem's medicines. Oh God! she prayed silently, help me make this terrible choice. Help me know what to do.

She would not have believed it possible, but she slept again, waking in the greyish light of near dawn with the uneasy awareness of being watched. She opened her eyes immediately, surprised to find Brett's eyes open again and meeting her gaze clearly and with recognition for the first time since leaving Ardsley's London home.

"Brett?" she breathed questioningly, moving closer to rest her hand upon his, reaching automatically to freshen the cool cloths on his forehead.

His eyes left hers for a moment to travel around the room, a faint frown of puzzlement forming between his dark brows. "Where am I?"

"In a cottage in Windsor. Do you remember my telling you we were moving you to the country, darling?"

He sighed, nodding slowly, his gaze swinging back to her, an expression strangely apologetic lingering in them. "I'm sorry, sweetheart," he mumbled softly. "For all the time I've wasted..."

Cerissa stared at him in confusion, not understanding his words. "Time you've wasted?" she echoed quizzically. "You mean being sick? I don't count it wasted, Brett. Any time I have with you is..."

"No," he managed a fleeting smile and the barest shake of his dark head. "Not that. Before. I resisted loving you for so long—God only knows why—and then I should have married you in Jamaica when I finally admitted to myself I did love you. But I was too greedy, sweet. I thought we had so much time. I could coax Charles' consent to our marriage and gain everything...lose nothing. But off Florida...and then Gerard died...and Charles died...Again, I should have married you at Whitross last summer, but I wanted to wait...see if King James might not consent to the match given time...and I was in no hurry, Cerissa, I should have learned but I didn't. I always thought there would be so much time..."

Cerissa stared into his grey-green eyes in astonishment, unable to fully comprehend what he was saying, her heart filling with bittersweet joy. "You mean...you would really have married me...you were planning to marry me? Oh Brett," she whispered, her voice breaking with anguish and remorse, "Why didn't you ever tell me? I never guessed...I would never have married..."

"No...no regrets, princess," Brett murmured, moving his hand with an intense effort to clasp hers. "I never told...didn't want you to be disappointed if it didn't work out...I would have married you anyway this summer but I wanted Jamey to inherit..."

A choking sob burst from Cerissa's throat and she leaned her head helplessly against Brett's forearm, letting her tears wash over his burning skin to fall dark on the white sheets. Hadn't she done the same thing? Hadn't she also wasted their time together by being so greedy? It was not enough to have his love, to have his son, she must have his name as well. So she'd married Lord Ramond in her selfishness—she too believing there would be plenty of time for all her schemes to bear fruit. Hadn't she too been content to wait, preferring a future perfection to present sacrifice? Why hadn't she

311

seized on every day they could have had together? Why hadn't she followed his return? Always he had waited and always she had waited and now they had run out of time.

She lifted her head, tears still blinding her eyes, shaking her head in inexpressible agony. Brett's eyes were still seeking hers though he was obviously struggling hard to keep awake. "Plenty of money, sweet..." he murmured, his words soft and slurred. "In my will...to you and Jamey...raise him to..."

"No!" she sobbed, raising his hand to clutch it possessively to her chest with both hands. "No don't leave me, Brett, promise me you won't leave me..."

"Can't...promise," he mumbled, his eyes haunted by sorrow. "Everyday...harder for me to even talk to you...make sense of your words, sweetheart...sorry..."

"Brett, wait, there's a chance," she cried intensely, willing him to stay aware, to listen to her, "Doctor Hajamin wants to try something different—to force your fever so high it will break. But it's dangerous, love, and you may be horribly ill. He asked me and I didn't...

"Try it," he breathed, his eyes already closing slowly. "At least you'll know then...no more waiting..."

"Brett!" she cried again, knowing even as she opened her mouth that he was gone away from her back into his heavy sleep. "Oh Brett, you didn't give me time to tell you I loved you. Oh damn!" she swore, sobbing, still holding his fever hot hand against her wet cheek. "There's never enough time, never enough..." At last, her sobbing grew less bitter, less frenzied, and Cerissa laid Brett's limp hand gently back on the bed, stroking it tenderly as she let it go. At least one decision had been made for her. One she agreed wholeheartedly with. She could realize now, recollecting, that Fate had not always been unkind to them. When they had been willing to risk something to gain each other, Fate had been generous. It was when they had grown cautious, when they had grown greedy that Fate had turned her face from them. When they sought to gain life's most precious gifts without being willing to sacrifice anything in payment—that's when they'd been thwarted, time and time again. Cerissa lifted her head with growing determination and growing hope. Hadn't she begged God's guidance just before she'd slept? And hadn't He, by the clearest signs possible, directed her to the answer? If she wanted Brett's life she must be prepared to risk something equally precious to gain it. That was how the world was. There was no acquisition without payment. Even love was not the

312

heaven-sent, freely given gift she had imagined it three years ago. Love too must be sought and gambled for. So she would gamble now. She would risk Brett's agony and the security of the few precious days she knew she would have left with him if she followed the cautious path. She would risk that in a gamble for his life. And someway, somehow, whatever it cost, she would gain it.

She walked quietly down the dark hallway, not wanting to disturb Ardsley or the servants nor raise a false alarm on Brett's condition. At the doctor's door, she stopped, then hesitated, reluctant to wake him. For a moment she stood motionless, deciding to wait until later, then she heard a faint sound from within and knocked softly. hearing an immediate answer from inside the room.

Obediently, she pushed the door ajar and slipped in, seeing the Moslem sitting cross-legged on the floor, reading a book written in unfamiliar characters by the light of a burning lantern.

"I was afraid I'd wakened you," the girl murmured apologetically. "Perhaps I should come back later."

"No need," the physician sighed, getting to his feet with a wan smile. "I was just looking through some old records seeking some counsel on this fever we are battling. What can I help you with?"

"I . . . I decided to try that new idea you proposed. I thought you might wish to begin at once."

"There is no need for haste," Hajamin replied, glancing at her shrewdly in the growing light. "I gave him a dose of herb tea several hours ago to restrain the fever. We must let that medicine dissipate now before we turn the treatment around. But tell me why you changed your mind."

"Well . . . I spoke to him about it . . . and he seemed to favor . . ."

"He was awake? And clear headed?"

"Yes," she shrugged, noting the Turk's slight surprise. "Not very long, but . . ."

"What did he say?"

Cerissa frowned uneasily, shifting her gaze. What had been said should remain a private matter, only between she and Brett. She didn't want to share it.

"Please, my dear, I do not ask for idle curiosity," the man smiled encouragingly, his black eyes patient. "But it may tell me much about his attitude and his condition."

"He . . . he apologized to me for wasting the time we could have had together," the girl replied reluctantly, in a soft voice. "And said something about his will—and money for Jamey."

The Moslem frowned and turned sharply away, uttering what Cerissa guessed to be a curse in his native tongue. "I do not understand it," he thought angrily aloud. "Lord Ardsley has told me much about your Lord Lindsey these past few days. An independent man, he said, with an iron-will, often stubborn with a fierce temper. He told me about Lord Lindsey's rescuing you from the Thames, Cerissa. In weather like this, with the water so cold, I would have been astonished to hear of a healthy man accomplishing such a difficult feat. For a man already in the grip of fever it should have been impossible. He must have used his will to force his body beyond all reasonable limits. Yet now . . . nothing. He speaks of wills and makes farewells. Why does he not fight this disease, Cerissa? Why does he not help us save him?"

"I don't know," the girl answered helplessly her own eyes clouded with surprise. "I asked him not to leave me, but he wouldn't . . ."

"You must not ask him, Cerissa, you must demand it of him. This lies beyond the range of my skills or knowledge. This lies within his soul. You have the key to that—unlock it and seek within to find the spark he's let die. Coax him, scream at him, storm and weep, even strike him if you must—anything to raise him from his lethargy. Lie if you must. Use any weapon you have. Too many times as a doctor I have seen two men ill of the same disease, both equally sick. One lives, one dies. Who can say why? Was one unable to tolerate the pain? Was one perhaps less determined than other? With my knowledge and my medicines I can give him a chance, but only that. If he is not willing to fight as well, then . . ." he shrugged disgustedly, his frustration bitter on his face. "Then we may as well begin to dig his grave."

Cerissa stared at the swarthy Turk a long moment, her mouth gaping open in surprise at his unusual vehemence, her blue eyes haunted with fear. "But . . . but I don't know what I can do," she whispered, her words ending in an anguished half moan.

"I do not know either or I would tell you," Hajamin replied more gently. "I do not love him—I do not know him as you do. What has keyed his determination in the past? What can you offer him to make him tolerate the agony he will undergo? What can you promise as a reward if he endures the unendurable to live?"

"I . . . I . . ." Cerissa stammerd helplessly, her heart frantic, her thoughts desperate.

"Think on it, dear child," the doctor advised softly. "We must begin in a few hours. Soon after that he may be raging in hopeless

314

delirium, unable to hear your voice or see your tears. And you, Cerissa, don't weaken for a moment. Don't allow his suffering to touch such pity in your heart that you are willing to see him lost to you to cease his pain. Be cruel and selfish and demanding."

Cerissa dropped her head slowly into her hands, feeling huge silent tears trickle between her fingers as she nodded understanding. Doctor Hajamin was right of course. She could not force all the responsibility for Brett's care on his shoulders. If anyone would know the key to Brett's soul it must be her. She would have to think of something.

Cerissa watched anxiously as the Moslem physician and Lord Ardsley struggled to move Brett's bed closer to the now roaring fire, both men sweating profusely in the stifling air. Hajamin turned to check the huge steel cauldron hung directly within the flames, filled with water, already sending billowing clouds of damp warm mist out into the small room. The window now was locked and shuttered, eliminating any possibility of a cool breeze of relief from that quarter. Cerissa pushed the already curling, wet wisps of her hair back from her forehead and reached up to anchor the pins holding her heavy hair up off her neck. Drastic, she reflected grimly, had been an appropriate term for the change in doctoring. Only two things remained the same. The bucket of cold water for Brett's forehead, and the lemon-sugar water she must force constantly down his throat. If Doctor Hajamin's gamble paid off, the extreme heat would force Brett's fever to break at last, allowing him to sweat the poison out of his body. But the other part of the treatment, Cerissa's responsibility, thinking of something which would force Lord Lindsey's incredible will power to work for them . . . that part still eluded her.

"What's the cauldron for?" Lord Ardsley bent to ask Cerissa, glancing nervously at the steaming mist issuing from it. "This is the damnest piece of doctoring I've ever seen."

"The steam," Cerissa explained absently, staring across the short space to Brett's flushed face, watching the doctor heap quilt after quilt over his already restless body, "will help Brett breathe when the fever grows most intense—it will keep enough moisture in his lungs."

Ardsley nodded and shrugged his incredulity. "I guess the doctor knows best," he murmured, looking skeptical, still staring uneasily into Cerissa's weary face. "Sweetheart . . . one last thing," he said gently, placing a hand on her shoulder to capture her full attention. "If this doesn't work . . . I've thought about it. I think you're right to try it anyway. Brett's never been a man for the cautious approach. He wouldn't want to linger, half-alive half-dead for weeks. He's never done anything halfway in his life. So what I'm trying to say is—whether this works or it doesn't work, whether he lives or dies from it—I think you made the right choice for him."

Cerissa blinked away the tears that came instantly to her eyes, squeezing the blond lord's hand in silent thanks. Regardless of Ardsley's words, or Hajamin's assurances, if Brett died . . . then it would not have been the best choice. At least, not from her point of view anyway.

Lord it was hot! she thought grimly, wiping the back of her neck with a cool rag before moving to refreshen Brett's. He was growing restless already beneath the piled covers, his breath rapid and heavy, almost panting in the close, steam filled air. Suddenly, Brett mumbled something unintelligible and moved his arms, trying to push the blankets away. Cerissa caught at his hands, amazed at how easily she could control his incredible strength, waiting until he grew quiet again before reaching to pull the quilts back up around Brett's chin. Immediately, he began to resist again, moving his head restlessly on the pillow, pushing at the covers with greater strength. Cerissa struggled to keep him covered, murmuring soft comfort as she reached quickly to dip a fresh cloth in the cold spring water, thinking its touch would calm him. As she straightened up to set the linen on his forehead, Brett sighed raggedly and opened his eyes, blinking drowsily, frowning faintly in surprised annoyance.

"So hot, sweetheart" he mumbled petulantly, pushing feebly at her hands. "Too damn hot."

Cerissa forced away the compassion that flooded her heart, and met his gaze firmly, keeping a tight grip on the blankets. "I'm sorry, Brett, but it's necessary. Don't you remember we talked about changing the treatment last night and you agreed? Please Brett, it's the only chance."

Brett frowned again, shifting under the blankets, letting his gaze shift to wander the room, coming to rest on the fire blazing only scant yards away. "Remember . . . when you were too stingy . . . with wood," he murmured, swinging his gaze back to her face, trying to force a smile.

Cerissa smiled tenderly, touching his face gently, knowing no words were necessary while their eyes could meet and speak the sweetness of their hearts. But in a moment, Brett turned his head away restlessly again, swallowing and licking his dry lips as he moved, the frown returning to his face.

"Can't stand this heat...sorry," he breathed. "Never been so bloody hot...even in Florida...that damned swamp that summer..."

Cerissa bent to bring another sopping cloth up, raising his black head in the crook of her arm to bathe the nape of his neck, letting the icy water trickle down into the thick waves of his hair, running the cool rag over his face and throat. She reached wordlessly for the cup of cool lemon-water, tipping the edge of the mug against his lips.

"Drink this, love," she coaxed. "This will help."

Greedily, he swallowed it, almost choking in his haste. Cerissa began to mumur a warning and suddenly held her breath, echoes of his words touching a dormant memory. Florida! her brain raced furiously. When he had returned from there, hadn't he told her why he had forced himself to live through that? What had it been? For her...and Jamey...

"Brett, I never gave you an answer to your question the other night, about marrying you," she began breathlessly. "I will now. If you will live for me. I'll do anything you want me to do, I swear it. We'll live together the rest of our lives. And Jamey with us. You can teach him to shoot and use a sword, and take him riding with you..."

Brett smiled faintly, his eyes resting wistfully on hers. "Jamey...all right with Ardsley...he'll raise him as his own. And you...your husband will protect you...fond of you...good to you...and money..."

Cerissa stared helplessly at him, reading surrender in his grey-green eyes. She took a deep breath to still her hammering heart and decided to risk a desperate gamble, praying it would not backfire and work against her. "And the new baby, Brett? How about him or her, whatever it may be? How shall I explain him to my impotent husband?"

Brett stared back at her, his eyes clearing slowly under his frowning brows, the line of his jaw muscles clenching as he fought to concentrate. "New baby?" he muttered slowly, his face reflecting confusion.

Cerissa felt her heart lurch in sudden hope and she dropped her eyes hastily, fearing it would show in her face. Please God! "Yes, Brett...that night in the garden house...at Millford's," she whispered, moving her hand to rest gently on his shoulder. "Don't

317

you see?" she improvised hastily, her heart thudding in mixed hope and fear. "That's why I had to...to jump into the river. When I hadn't heard from you...and knew you had married..."

"Oh Christ," Brett murmured, his voice surprisingly stronger, his eyes searching hers with anguished remorse. "Oh Cerissa, forgive me..."

She forced a nervous smile, raising her gaze again to cling pleadingly to his. "That's why I couldn't answer you...and I was afraid to tell you, Brett because I knew it would ruin your plans..."

"Oh hell..." he swore, moving his head restlessly on the pillow, his mouth set grim and pale in his flushed face. "No, sweet...mustn't...mustn't worry. We'll figure something...sail for France or winter in at Whitross...sail for Jamaica when the weather breaks..."

Cerissa felt her heart explode in sudden joy, feeling the blood rush to her face in giddy relief. Finally, she'd made Brett talk about a future. She'd done it! She'd found the key after all! Now Brett would work as hard as she or Doctor Hajamin to beat this fever..."Whatever you want, my darling," she whispered, her voice breaking as tears of joy began to wet her cheeks and tremble in her long lashes. "But don't talk any more just now. You'll get hotter, be even more uncomfortable before the fever breaks. Sleep now, my love. Save your strength." She leaned over to kiss his burning forehead, staying motionless beside him until she flew to the door, calling for Ardsley and the doctor. She must tell them at once, let them know of this new, incredible hope. They would be as relieved as she was.

Ardsley swore as Brett's forearm hit his shoulder, knocking him back a step toward the raging fire, then tenaciously lunged back to struggle again with the dark haired lord's fever induced violence. Cerissa watched anxiously, trying to read information in the Moslem's inscrutable face. Brett's restlessness had increased gradually throughout the day, but this was by far the most violent struggle she'd seen. For Brett to be able to throw off Ardsley's not inconsiderable weight and strength. Plus, as his delirium deepened, Brett raged and cursed in language she'd never heard before, even aboard the ship where she'd thought she'd heard everything. Once or twice, even the worldly Ardsley had looked shocked, glancing quickly sideways to note the girl's reaction before returning his full concentration on the raving lord.

She bent to pick the cloth off the floor where Brett's struggles had thrown it, dipping it hastily into a fresh bucket before replacing it. Suddenly, as Brett writhed violently, Ardsley fell against her, knocking her back with him as he gasped for breath in the hot, steamy room. Immediately, the delirious lord threw the stifling blankets off, wrestling with the straining Moslem for total freedom. With a cry, Cerissa leapt toward him, throwing her full weight across his face, grabbing frantically for the covers to haul them into place. Without conscious thoughts, she screamed at Brett, ordering him to be still, demanding he cease his struggling. Whether he heard her or not, the dark haired lord relaxed again, falling back into a motionless unconsciousness once more, leaving both Ardsley and Hajamin panting in exhaustion, the sweat streaming down their faces.

"Jesus!" Ardsley muttered incredulously, his chest still heaving for breath. "Where's that strength coming from? I've wrestled Brett all my life and never..."

"Fever strength," Hajamin muttered wearily in reply, trying to force an encouraging smile Cerissa's direction. "We wanted him fighting remember?"

"Huh," Ardsley grunted. "Fighting the fever not us."

Hajamin smiled, shrugging as he took a long swallow of cold water. "He must do both perhaps. And his struggles will only increase as his fever rises. We must be prepared for that."

Cerissa slumped wearily on her chair, too tired to even move her hand for the water she craved, staring numbly at Brett's face. Whether the doctor admitted it or not, she knew Brett couldn't withstand too many more such violent struggles. The strain of them, combined with the fever, would weaken his heart too greatly. Oh damn, she thought silently, come on Brett! Throw the fever off before...

Lord Lindsey's sudden thrashing interrupted her thoughts, and she leapt instinctively to her feet, leaning her full weight behind the arm she laid at the back of this throat, trying to keep out of the blond lord's way as he strained to keep hold of Brett's arm and shoulder. She felt herself being thrown back and forth, one section of her mind numb in astonishment at Brett's seemingly inexhaustible strength.

Suddenly, with an almost animal snarl of frustration, the dark haired lord pulled free of the Moslem's grip and swung viciously at his friend's face. Ardsley managed to block the blow somewhat by flinging his forearm up as a shield, yet even the partially deflected blow sent him reeling backward. Cerissa locked her arms desperately around Brett's neck, dropping to her knees to force her full weight on the man's shoulders but he scarcely seemed aware of her as he struggled half free of the blankets and nearly out of the bed. With a muttered curse, Ardsley regained his balance and leapt forward again, grabbing Brett's right arm with a vicious grip, twisting it to force the dark lord down again. Cerissa watched in helpless horror as Brett snarled and swung again, Ardsley ducking the blow without releasing his arm. Then suddenly, without warning, Brett's body shuddered and he went totally limp, collapsing heavily back onto the bed, his black head jerking forward as it hit the pillow. Doctor Hajamin jumped forward, his face drawn in apprehension as he flung the blankets back and bent his head over his patient's chest, pressing his ear to the man's heart. Cerissa stood frozen with fear, aware only of the crushing grip of terror which stopped her heart, her eyes fixed desperately on the Turkish doctor's grave face for what seemed like a timeless eternity. At last, Hajamin sighed his relief, raising his head to nod slowly to the stricken girl, before drawing the blankets back up to Brett's chin.

The breath exploded from Cerissa's lungs, and she closed her eyes momentarily, aware of the hammering of her heart as it started again. "Thank God," she murmured, not even realizing she spoke aloud.

Doctor Hajamin smiled faintly at the ashen faced girl, catching Lord Ardsley's eye before speaking gently. "Yes, thank God and Allah, Cerissa and pray for the next time."

The startled girl met his black eyes for a moment, then dropped her gaze to Brett's face as the two men moved silently away from the bed. She did not need to see the slump of Ardsley's shoulders to realize what the doctor meant. Their gamble hadn't paid off. The combined strain of the high fever and Brett's fierce struggles were too much for his weakened heart. This time, perhaps by the merest edge, Brett had managed to live through the attack. Next time...

She gazed silently at his beloved features, noting the breadth of his forehead, the thick ebony lashes framing his dark shadowed eyes, the ashen pallor of his parted lips. Tenderly, in farewell, she bent to place a gentle kiss on his flushed cheek. Brett frowned faintly and moved his head away from her touch and she drew quickly away, fearing to begin another fit of delirium. Suddenly, she froze, her blue eyes widening as she stared down at Brett's throat where it joined his shoulder. His head had been laying toward her, creasing the skin there, refusing to blink her watering eyes for fear the tiny beads of moisture on his skin were only an illusion that would pass if she looked away. Finally, with a trembling finger, she reached out to touch him, shivering convulsively as she felt warm wetness beneath her hand. Not daring yet to believe, restraining herself from hoping too greatly, she forced her hand away, sliding it gently beneath his averted face to turn his head toward her. One small spot of moisture might be from the dripping cloth, or even the perspiration of her own palms as she'd touched him. Holding her breath, she forced her gaze down to the line of Brett's neck as she moved his dark head gently with her hand. Again, the golden blaze of firelight caught and gleamed in a faint line of wetness. Her heart lurched in incredulous joy! Just when she had believed him lost to her..."Ardsley! Doctor Hajamin!" she called softly, not taking her eyes from Brett's quiet face. "Look."

Ardsley leaned over her, his sharply caught breath reassuring her that what she saw was no illusion. The swarthy Turk stared, then muttered incredulously in his own tongue before reaching to catch Brett's wrist between his fingers, bending the lord's limp arm tightly over as he frowned for silence. After a long moment, he smiled wearily, laying Brett's arm again on the rumpled linen covers. There, in the crease of his elbow, was further proof of the fever's breaking. Even as Cerissa looked, the tiny droplets grew in size to merge together and roll slowly down his forearm to drop onto the sheet. Hajamin reached beneath the blankets and brought his hand out with a wan grin of satisfaction, reaching for his cup of cold water to hold it aloft and mutter in his strange language.

Cerissa didn't need to understand the language to realize he was proposing a toast, and at last she let her heart leap free to soar with joy. Ardsley grinned and handed her his mug of water laced with rum, letting her return the physician's toast before draining the rest of it himself. For long minutes, the three just stood beaming at one another, grateful and astonished that such a triumph had indeed occurred. Finally, Ardsley yawned and glanced at the shuttered windows, seeing the sun's light pale as sunset approached.

"I know it's not considered fashionable to retire so early, but I'm doing so anyway. I don't think I've gotten three good hours sleep in so many days. What's next, good doctor? May I seek sweet slumber or play nurse a while longer?"

The Moorish doctor smiled, shaking his head. "Go to sleep, Lord Ardsley. I intend to follow you shortly. But before you go, help me slide your friend's bed several feet farther from the flames.

It is vital now that we not reduce the heat too swiftly or we risk a chill. Still, I believe he will sleep easier a bit cooler."

Cerissa waited patiently, while the men followed through on this, still smiling in almost dizzy relief, watching Brett's face grow wetter with a sense of incredulous gratitude. At last, the men turned to leave, and Hajamin paused a moment to issue instructions. "Keep him covered, Cerissa, though you may remove one blanket in an hour or so. Keep the cold cloths on his forehead still, they will soothe him. I will send broth in to you—if he wakes even halfway, feed him what you can. I will prepare a sleeping draught for him tonight that will keep him quiet so you may rest as well."

Cerissa nodded, letting her eyes speak shining thanks as he left. She turned to Brett at once, bathing his gaunt, but still handsome face gently to give her an excuse for touching him, caressing him, sending the sureness of her love to him through her tender fingertips. The sweat rolled off his forehead now, trickling down his throat, soaking his black curls until they lay limp against his head. Yet he seemed oblivious to it, never stirring, his breathing changing gradually from the ragged pant of fever to a slow, even sign of deep sleep. At last, when her weary eyelids insisted on closing, she drew her narrow cot over against Brett's bed, watching him until she slept. Morning would dawn fair and fine and bright with joy, she thought drowsily, just as sleep took her. Morning would see her love out of danger and on the road to healing.

The slanting sun swore late morning before Cerissa opened her eyes again, and she stretched luxuriously, feeling fully rested for the first time in days. A quick sidelong glance showed Brett still sleeping quietly, one arm thrown carelessly across his waist above the blankets, the other above his black, tousled hair. The girl rose and tiptoed to the washbasin, smoothing her sleep rumpled skirts, picking up her sterling and mother-of-pearl inlaid toothbrush, wetting it in the pitcher before dipping the bristles into tooth powder. Then, she pulled Brett's brush through her long, tangled chestnut tresses and pinned it quickly in a bun at the top of her head. One thing she had planned for the day was a good bath. Between sleeping in her gown and the constant heat of the small room, she felt like a well-used dishrag.

Doctor Hajamin shouldered the door open, his hands filled with a tray of steaming food. Cerissa smiled and returned his cheerful nod of greeting, finishing her hair. As she turned, she noticed the Moslem pulling another of the heavy coverlets off Brett, leaving only one now. She moved to the table where he'd left the tray, waiting to thank him for his consideration until he finished with Brett, nibbling hungrily on the edge of an iced sweetroll. Hajamin chuckled as he turned and saw her, his black eyes gleaming with amusement.

"A fine nurse!" he snorted. "Stealing her patient's breakfast."

Cerissa dropped the roll hastily, flushing guiltily and feeling foolish. It had never occurred to her that the breakfast could be Brett's! Usually, beef broth and watered wine followed illness! "I'm sorry," she smiled apologetically, "I never guessed . . . Can he eat such foods already? I would have thought . . ."

"I wouldn't recommend a slice of rare beef and Yorkshire pudding just yet, but these foods he can eat," the Moslem grinned, flashing white, perfect teeth under his full mustache. "If you're hungry, I'll ask Dora to bring you a tray up. In fact, I believe your friend, Lord Ardsley, may be collecting your breakfast even now."

A sudden low chuckle from behind her brought Cerissa around quickly, and she beamed to see Brett smiling at her.

"Lucky you woke, Lord Lindsey," Hajamin laughed. "Your nurse here would have finished your breakfast shortly. As it is, there's a morsel or two left."

"Good lord! I'm ravenous." Brett nodded, heaving himself up to a sitting position on the bed. Then he glanced over to the Moslem's dark face, and his gaze grew serious. "I gather you're the man to thank for saving my life."

Hajamin smiled and shrugged. "Hardly. Your life was in Allah's hands. I but gave you a better chance to survive."

"Well, whatever you say. I have the feeling Allah's decision about my life might have been different without your treatment," Brett protested solemnly. "Thank you again."

"You ought to thank me too," Lord Ardsley's low voice boomed from the door as he stepped forward, balancing a pair of heavily laden food trays. "My jaw is sore as hell this morning from getting in the way of your fist, Lindsey. Damn me for an addle-brained idiot if I ever wrestle you in a delirium again."

Brett laughed, seemingly unabashed by his friend's grumbling, knowing the blond lord too well to take him seriously. "When I am recovered sufficiently to stand, you may take a free swing for revenge if you wish." Ardsley chuckled, already eating his breakfast and Brett arched an inquiring eyebrow at the smiling doctor. "Seriously, when can I get up?"

"That depends how you feel."

"Well, last night I felt as though a dozen carriages had rolled over me, or that I'd done back somersaults down the marble steps of St. Paul's. But today..." Brett shrugged, flexing his arm muscles experimentally, "All right, I think."

"Brett, don't rush things," Cerissa frowned uneasily. She knew only too well how completely he despised weakness and sought to push his strength beyond reasonable limits.

"The girl is correct, Lord Lindsey. Your sense of strength is deceiving. While your strength returns quickly, your endurance will not. For today, at least, I suggest you keep abed. Tomorrow, perhaps, if you wish, you may dress and even try a short walk in the garden if this warm sunshine continues."

"And when may I resume my...ah, normal activities?" Brett asked, tossing a wicked grin in Cerissa's direction, his eyes flashing a familiar message.

Cerissa blushed and dropped her eyes hastily to her tray, not needing the answering stab of heat from her own loins to realize his game.

Hajamin's black eyes sparkled with mirth and he flashed a sidelong glance at the embarrassed girl before returning his patient's broad grin. "I have no way of knowing what your normal activities may include, my lord. But I suggest you wait at least a week before engaging in...ah...strenuous exercise."

"Then you'd better trade nurses," Ardsley grinned with a low chuckle. "Believe me when I tell you that these two will never..."

"Excuse me, Lord Ardsley," Mary, the cook and cleaning servant stood nervously by the open door, wringing her hands nervously, flinging anxious glances over her shoulder toward the main room of the small house.

"Yes, Mary," the blond lord frowned, rising quickly to his feet. "What is it?"

"It's...it's a Lord Ramond, sir, asking the whereabouts of his wife, Lady Ramond," she stammered, frowning fearfully at Cerissa's astonished face. "I didn't know what to tell him, whether you wanted it known she be here or not, so I pretended..."

"What did you tell him, Cerissa?" Ardsley interrupted impatiently, already starting for the door.

Cerissa stood slowly, trying to make her wits function again in the face of such an unexpected turn of events. "Well...I...." she stammered softly, her eyes wide with surprise. "I didn't tell him anything...I only stopped home to get a few clothes and told Lina I was going to your home to treat a sick friend of yours..."

"Good Lord, woman!" Ardsley swore, "You mean he had no idea where you've been all this time? He must have searched the city high and low..."

"I know, I simply forgot all about him," Cerissa explained weakly, casting a pleading glance at Brett's scowling face. "Please, Brett..."

"We'll tell him I sent a note—pretend the boy didn't deliver it. That might soothe him. Or perhaps we should simply deny you're even here, send you back to..."

"No," Brett interrupted firmly, his voice low and firm. "Why put off a confrontation that's got to come soon anyway? Go speak to him Cerissa, I'll come in as soon as I can get decently dressed."

"You stay in bed, Lindsey, I'll go with her," Ardsley amended, with equal firmness. "I'm better at soothing ruffled feathers than you are anyway, Brett." Without waiting for his friend's sure argument, the blond lord seized Cerissa's arm and hurried from the room, pausing only to whisper in her ear. "Follow my lead, whatever I say, sweetheart. We'll soothe the old gent's injured feelings."

Cerissa nodded breathlessly, uncomfortably aware of the wild thumping of her heart and the nervous wetness of her palms. Helplessly, she stopped still at the sight of her aged husband, angrily pacing the small parlor.

"Cerissa!" Lord Ramond exclaimed in angry surprise. "Where the devil have you been?"

Cerissa opened her mouth, but no words would come from her suddenly parched tongue. Gratefully, she glanced at Lord Ardsley who stepped forward with a courteous bow to answer for her.

"Your pardon, my lord," Ardsley apologized smoothly, "I was in sore need of your wife's aid. A good friend of mine was stricken with fever, and..."

"I went to your house, Lord Ardsley," Edward snapped. "And no one there seemed to have the slightest idea where you'd all gone. Couldn't you at least have had the decency to inform us of your plans?"

"But I did," Ardsley feigned surprise, turning innocently to Cerissa for her supporting murmur of agreement. "I sent a note to you upon our departure—a hasty one, albeit, but..."

"I received no note."

Ardsley fell silent a moment, a white line of anger touching his lips at the man's rudeness, then forced a depreciating shrug. "I am sorry for that, my lord, yet it is no fault of ours. As I said, my friend was most gravely ill and every minute was of the essence..."

"And how did my wife come to be such a noted physician that her aid was indispensible?" Lord Ramond's sneer was unmistakable, his eyes cold with anger and disbelief and Cerissa flinched unconsciously, wondering at his astonishing behavior.

"Your wife spent several months in the tropics, Lord Ramond. Surely you are aware of the high incidence of fever there."

Cerissa laid a cautioning hand on the blond lord's arm, hearing the answering anger that threaded his deep voice. A scene now would only make matters worse. Her husband's transformation from the kind and gentle man she'd known was frightening enough. She didn't want to press his bad humor farther.

"May I speak to my wife alone, Lord Ardsley?" Edward's request held the cold ring of command and Cerissa stared at him in wonder, only barely able to nod her head in response to the blond lord's questioning glance.

"It's all right, James," she murmured softly, though her hands trembled with sick apprehension. "Leave us for a moment."

With obvious reluctance, Ardsley bowed and exited, contenting himself with a swift warning glance at the fuming older lord. The door had barely closed behind him when Edward stepped forward, his eyes snapping anger as he stared at his ashen faced wife.

"How dare you be so thoughtless, Cerissa?" he hissed, stepping threateningly toward her. "Did it never occur to you that..."

"Ardsley told you we sent a note," she defended herself lamely, shrinking fearfully away, still unable to meet his eyes in her lie.

"Damn the note! Had I received it, I would only have been here sooner!" he snapped, his lip curled in an unpleasant way. "Did you never consider the consequences of galloping off into the country, unchaperoned, with only men and servants for company? You bear my name, woman, and, by God, you will take care not to dishonor it in such a frivolous manner!"

Cerissa's head snapped up, her own blue eyes sparking with defiance. "Frivolous? You consider it frivolous to aid a man dying of fever? Aren't there a few instances where honor might reach deeper than bows and court manners? Are you honestly criticizing me for choosing to help a man..."

"First and foremost you are my wife!" he snarled, "You will comport yourself as I see fit, woman!"

"You weren't so full of arrogance when you met me in Lichester Spa, Edward," she reminded him rebelliously. "You said little then about how I was to conduct myself! How much honor would your name have carried had I not offered to marry you and assume your debts?"

"That matter lies in the past, Cerissa," he hissed. "I speak of the present. I have kin in distant Yorkshire, my dear. Perhaps a few years of living there with them will change your thinking!"

"You're mad," she sneered, "What makes you believe I'd go to York if I didn't want to?"

Lord Ramond took a deep breath, smiling slowly with little mirth, his eyes cold and pitiless as ice. "You forget, dear child. I do not require your agreement. Under law, as my wife, you will go where I direct you to go. Your gladness or the lack of same matters not a whit. You were kind enough to pay off my debts, and clever enough to set up a small dress shop which produces a comfortable income. If you displease me now, wife, I can most easily teach you a lesson or two at my convenience."

Cerissa caught her breath, staring at the aged lord in utter astonishment, totally aghast at his unbelievable change of attitude. "But, Edward, you know as well as I do our marriage is only one of convenience," she spluttered, struggling to understand this new and totally unpleasant aspect of her husband's character. "Why do you . . ."

"You bear my name, Cerissa, as I said before. I have no intention of allowing you to disgrace it." he replied coolly, with a faint, triumphant smirk. "You have been introduced in high circles as my wife, and for that reason, I shall determine your comportment."

Gradually, Cerissa felt slow realization break upon her. "I see now, Edward. You enjoy having everyone believe I am truly your wife, don't you? You enjoy the envy of the younger men when they admire me at parties. You feed on that for your damned ego. Of course, you don't want anyone to suspect the truth—that would make you a nobody again, wouldn't it?"

Lord Ramond only stared at her coolly, lifting one shoulder in a half shrug, a faint smile still lingering on his thin lips. "You sought to use me for your own ends, my dear, whatever they might be. I only play turnabout."

Cerissa felt the blood draining from her face. "And now, Edward?" she questioned coolly, still forcing her chin to remain high and proud though her lips trembled as she spoke.

"You will behave according to my direction Cerissa, or you will take a lengthy country vacation with my cousins in the north. So long as you are my wife, you will act the part of a loving spouse. Understood?"

Cerissa could only stare helplessly at her husband's unrelenting face, unable to think of any rebuttal. What he said was true enough. When she'd married him, she had given him absolute power over her, never thinking for a moment that the meek, gentle Edward Ramond would ever seek to use the power against her. If she refused to accede to his demands, he could indeed send her to virtual imprisonment in York—far from Jamey, far from Brett.

"You are my wife, Cerissa," Lord Ramond continued with a smile, sensing his advantage and pressing it home. "Now then, wife, your first lesson in acting the part."

"She could just as easily be made your widow, Lord Ramond."

Cerissa turned with a gasp to see Brett standing at the doorway, dressed in breeches and a loose, linen shirt, leaning one shoulder against the wooden door jam in a deceptively casual stance, though his eyes were emerald dark and flashed dangerous sparks. "Brett, you shouldn't be out of bed," she protested, hurrying to his side, almost forgetting Edward in her concern for the dark haired lord.

"Lord Lindsey, I believe," Edward drawled slowly, his eyes narrowing again in annoyance.

Brett smiled slowly, his eyes still locked to the older man's in silent warning. "You believe correctly," he nodded.

"May I ask by what right you intrude upon a private discussion between a man and his wife?" Edward sneered coldly, secure in the knowledge of his power.

"By the most ancient right of all," Brett answered easily, a faint smile still playing on his lips. "Cerissa is carrying my child."

Cerissa gasped, her eyes flying open in stunned disbelief at his announcement. Behind her, Lord Ramond's face registered the same initial shock, then slowly changed to scarlet rage. With a muttered curse, he turned swiftly to the girl, bringing his hand back full length before letting it fly forward to strike her face, knocking her to her knees against Brett's feet. "You slut!" he hissed, stepping forward to strike again.

In an instant, Brett had moved with the quick, cat-like grace, grasping the older man's outstretched arm in an iron grip. "Touch her again and you're a dead man," he treatened softly, his eyes promising he spoke the truth.

Cerissa cried aloud, struggling to her feet to press herself fearfully against Brett's chest. He was still far too weak from the fever to force a fight. Even his legendary skill with a sword would not avail if he fell in exhaustion.

Lord Ramond stared slowly from one to the other, nodding at

last. "I should have realized upon meeting you at Millford's, my lord. The boy, Jamey, is yours as well."

"Correct."

"And you planned the girl's marriage to me to give a name to your bastards?" Edward lifted one grey eyebrow in mocking admiration, but his narrowed gaze was ugly.

"No. I was forced to France for a short time," Brett shrugged, dropping a protective arm around Cerissa's quaking shoulders. "Had I been here, she would not have married. But..." Brett frowned, hesitating. "I never meant to wrong you, Lord Ramond. And Cerissa did not betray you either. She was not with child when you married. It was when I returned from France... and then, it was through no fault of hers."

"Fault or not, I do not intend to pass my name on to your bastard child," Lord Ramond's soft voice was laced with menace, and he bent his head to scowl down into Cerissa's face. "Filthy slut. You will simply seek medication to abort your bastard seed. Either that, or carry and bear the brat in Yorkshire and leave it there with a wetnurse for the rest of its days."

Cerissa cried an instinctive denial and felt Brett's arm tighten around her simultaneously. She glanced up to see his emerald eyes flare for an instant with unbridled rage, the line of his jaw growing white and clenched. "Lord Ramond, there is another solution. I know your marriage has not been comsummated. Let it be annulled. I have no wish to dishonor your name by forcing it to cover a child not of your getting. Set Cerissa free from her vows. I will marry her myself and claim the child that is rightfully mine."

Cerissa held her breath, hoping against hope that Edward would agree. "Please Edward," she begged, her eyes searching his. "You had been so kind to me, so good... please..."

For a long moment, the absolute silence grew. Then, with a sudden laugh, Lord Ramond shattered it. "There is but one flaw in your plan, Lord Lindsey," he sneered. "A most simple one. I have no wish to have the entire Court snickering behind my back. They will all be counting the months backward when the child arrives, we both know that. And they shall discover it's conception came when the girl was yet married to me. I shall be proved a cuckold for all the world to see, while you two... you shall have all the best of the bargain."

"Not entirely," Brett snapped, his patience at an end. "Part of that bargain saw my money pay your debtor's claims, my lord. Had it not been for my 3,000 pounds you'd be rotting now in

Newgate—though in that hellhole you'd have scarcely lasted this long. How would your honorable name have taken to that disgrace, Lord Ramond?"

Cerissa's husband only smiled and shrugged, turning away to step toward the door. "This has truly been a most enlightening conversation, Lord Lindsey, but I fear t'will have to close now. I intend to make London before nightfall, so we really must be off. Come along, Lady Ramond."

Cerissa hung back, shaking her head beseechingly, tears heavy in her yes. "No, Edward please . . . try to understand . . . I love Brett. I've loved him for years. Why must you be so selfish now when you've been so kind to me before?"

The aged lord turned slowly back, no pity in his clean silver eyes. "It is very simple, my dear. Before this man returned from France, you were a model wife, always cheerful, always decorous, always obedient to my wishes. As for the freedoms I offered you before our marriage, well . . . suffice to say I did not realize then how much I would enjoy having a pretty young wife to hang on my arm at social gatherings. Now that I've grown to appreciate your charms, I'm naturally loathe to part with you. Come! Come! You'll get over this lovesick nonsense in time. Lord Lindsey shall find another mistress who pleases him as well and forget all about you. In the meantime, you and I shall have many satisfying years ahead of us together."

Edward reached out to clasp Cerissa's limp hand, tugging at her to follow along. The girl cast a last, helpless glance up into Brett's dark face, seeing already the growing pallor in his face, the weariness in his eyes. She stretched her hand up to touch his cheek tenderly, willing him to let it go for now, to rest until he regained his strength before pursuing the argument farther.

Brett's eyes flashed in frustration and helpless anger as he caught her gaze, then snapped back to fasten on Lord Ramond's smiling face. One hand reached forth to seize the aged lord's shoulder for an instant, forcing his complete attention. "Make no mistake on one thing, Lord Ramond. You may have lawful rights over Cerissa just now—though you will not always—but you have no right on her unborn babe. The child is mine. If you lift a finger against it's mother, or seek it's harm in any way, then I swear to God, I'll see you dead and in your grave. Do I make myself perfectly clear?"

Lord Ramond's face paled just a fraction, and for an instant, his smile faltered as he nodded and turned again for the door, dragging Cerissa with him. Only for a moment, he doubted the wisdom of his choice. Had he accepted Lord Lindsey's plan, he would doubtless have been dealt with generously—he would have had a handsome income for the remainder of his days. And finding out about the child Cerissa carried—that had been a shock as well. Luckily, he could farm her out far to the north country for a year or so with little stir created. Yet it all was worth it. Worth the lost income. Even the loss of the girl for a year. To see the handsome young lord smoulder with helpless anger. To see him grovel, to lower himself to pleas with him, Edward Ramond. Well, he had something that all the man's fancy family, his looks, his money, even his sword could not acquire. While he lived, he would have the pleasure of knowing one of the most famous men of the realm was under his boot heel. He had only to set it upon the girl, or the babe she carried within, and he would see Bretegane, Lord Lindsey hasten to do his bidding. Suddenly, as he handed Cerissa up into the waiting coach, he threw his head back and laughed aloud. Inside the coach, the girl glanced at him fearfully, hearing a note of high hysteria in his mirth. She shivered and drew herself away into the farthest corner of the velvet seat. Rest and get strong, my love, she prayed silently, her blue eyes straining to catch a last glimpse of the dark haired lord through the narrow cottage window. Whatever Edward may think to do, you will anticipate him and forestall his every move. Only be quick, my love, my darling Brett, for time speeds by while we must yet live apart.

Chapter Twenty

The days passed slowly in London while Cerissa paced her lodgings restlessly. Lord Ramond had forbidden her to venture past the parlor, even hiring a huge, bullshouldered man to guard her door lest she plan escape. Lina, her maid, was sympathetic to her mistress' plight when Cerissa had tearfully related the dilemma—remembering no doubt, the strong, handsome face of the dark haired lord, the burning concern in his grey-green eyes the night he'd sought so desperately for Cerissa. One time, Lina had managed to slip out alone for errands but she had returned with no news. And after that, perhaps guessing the maid's loyalty, Edward had confined her to the house as well.

"Pack up, my dear," Lord Ramond's brittle voice called through Cerissa's open bedroom door. "We leave tomorrow for the north. I have decided to travel with you, isn't that a pleasant surprise? Take warm clothing. That close to Scotland, the winter is fierce."

Cerissa glanced swiftly at her husband's face before turning wordlessly to the wardrobe. Even now, he continued to astonish her. He always acted as cheerful and relaxed as though they were, in truth, a loving couple. Never did he refer to the scene at Windsor with Brett. Never would he even acknowledge hearing her tearful entreaties on the subject of annullment. It was as though he was determined to pretend the confrontation had never occurred. Cerissa sighed silently, Edward honestly believed what he had said at the cottage. That in time, she and Brett would forget their love for each other. And in the meantime, she could sense that her husband was greatly enjoying the idea of possessing something the dashing young adventurer desired so strongly. And now, she was being shipped off to some place in York where Brett would pay the devil trying to trace her. Edward would make sure of that. Cerissa dropped a hand lightly to her belly, and felt her lips curve in a swift, gentle smile. So long as she carried the babe though, so long as she would be with it in Yorkshire a part of Brett would be beside her. Even Edward's stubborn perversity could not change that.

"Have you a fur-lined, hooded cape of sufficient warmth, Cerissa?" Edward's voice interrupted her reverie, and the girl half turned to give him a mocking glance.

"Really Edward, why pretend such deep concern for my welfare? We both know that if you were truly anxious for my happiness or well-being you would simply unlock your hold on me and leave me go to be with the man I love."

Her husband frowned, lifting one hand to brush petulantly at his meager grey mustache. "I believe I have heard enough on that particular subject, my dear. Even my patience wears thin after ten solid days of such complaints."

"Ten days?" Cerissa laughed derisively. "Why, husband, ten days is but the start of it. T'is a tune you will hear whistled the rest of your days unless you relent."

"Why paint me such an ogre?" Edward protested, shaking his head in disapproval. "Pray remember child, it was you who sought me out at Lichester to offer marriage. If you find yourself now caught in a trap of your own making, who's to blame? Surely, not I."

"Since your memory of the incident seems so clear, Edward, how can it be that you've forgotten the conditions of that marriage offer?" Cerissa remarked over-sweetly. "Was I not to be allowed affairs with the man of my choice, Edward? Your freely admitted impotence, and your agreement to let me seek outside our marriage..."

333

"I might remind you that my agreement on that score required discretion on your part, Cerissa. You can hardly call getting with child discreet."

Cerissa felt the hot blood flush her face and her eyes sparkled with anger. "Brett told you—as I did—that my pregnancy was hardly planned, Edward. I've admitted to our mistake."

"Mistake or not, your belly will grow every bit as swollen, my child. Now, let's leave off this wearisome talk. If you would only allow me to continue to be the kind, loving spouse I had intended..."

"You were only kind and loving when the advantages of our marriage lay all on your side." Cerissa flared, her long-building frustration bursting free. "When you found your debts paid, your income assured through my efforts! When it came time to pay your part of the bargain, then suddenly you balked."

"You were willing to remain my wife until my death, Cerissa. Why such impatience now? Nothing has changed. You will remain my obedient, loving wife until I die. Then you can run off with whomever you care to."

"I was willing to be your wife, yes, so long as I could continue seeing the man I loved as well!" she retorted. "Since you are unwilling to hold to that premise, so then am I. If you think I intend to continue this masquerade with you any longer, you're grossly mistaken. You think I will hang meekly to your arm now when you would flaunt your pretty young wife to your friends? Hardly!"

"Be reasonable, Cerissa," Edward sighed, looking not at all perturbed by her anger. "You certainly will do just that and whatever else I bid you do. You and your Lord Lindsey are both young while I am old. You will have years together after my death. I have no lands to oversee as he does, I have no fleet of ships to be cargoed. My sole pleasure is the social gatherings of my peers. Why can you not show some compassion for me?"

"Compassion?" Cerissa breathed in utter disbelief. "Such as you show to me perhaps? No, Edward. Brett nearly died of that fever he contracted in France. And as he lay dying, he apologized for all the time he had wasted being apart from me. He has not been the only one who's wasted time, I am equally guilty. But no more, Edward, if you would seek to keep me from him, then by God! You shall see your triumph turn sour in your mouth. Go ahead! Take me to your friend's houses, I shall scream to the heavens of your impotence and your selfishness. I shall tell everyone I see that you are a cuckold and I carry the seed of another man's child in my belly! If I am trapped, as you say, in a snare of my own setting, then so will you be, Edward. That I swear on God's name."

The surprise on Lord Ramond's face, turned slowly to petulant stubborness, and his eyes held a crafty glint. "You should be grateful to me that I have not insisted you terminate your bastard pregnancy, dear wife. Continue with such threats and I may yet change my mind."

"Change it then," Cerissa laughed mockingly. "And then try to enforce such wickedness upon me! I have dealt fairly with you, Edward. In your heart you know that. My real sin was to so debase the sacred vows of marriage that I uttered them with you, knowing while my lips said them that I was bound already, heart and soul, to Brett Lindsey. Perhaps this is God's punishment for that, that even while I realize finally how precious every day of love can be, only now when I can finally admit my love for Brett is sufficient unto itself and would no longer even seek a wedding ring—now I find myself entrapped by a gentle old man I thought to bargain with." Cerissa paused, her chest heaving, her eyes hard with comtempt. "So I have tolerated your imprisonment of me, Edward, thinking it was God's will for me to learn my lesson from it, hoping still that I might reason with you and spare us both further humiliation. But when you dare even imply a threat against the innocent life I carry within me. Did you not hear Lord Lindsey's warning on that score, Edward? Or are you so unacquainted with his prowess in duelling that you set his caution at naught? Believe me, Edward, Bretegane Lindsey would hunt you down and see you dead though crown and kingdom told him nay! And if he failed somehow, then I surely would."

For a long moment, Lord Ramond stood motionless, staring at his wife's enraged face. He'd never seen the girl so spirited before, so chillingly determined. For the merest fraction of a moment, he hesitated, doubting for the first time the wisdom of his action. But suddenly, with a nervous toss of his grey head, he strode to the door, gesturing toward the waiting carriage. Cerissa had always been a gentle girl, easily handled. Once they were in Yorkshire, she would forget all her defiance and settle down properly again. Lord Lindsey might seethe all he like. While he had the girl and her unborn babe under his hand, the dark haired lord could do nothing but dance to his tune. "Into the coach, Cerissa," he ordered with a faint smile. "We must be going if we're to reach Oxford by nightfall."

Cerissa kept her face turned resolutely toward the coach wall, ignoring Lord Ramond's attempts to solicit conversation from her. Obviously, he did not yet realize the depth of her determination to see Brett, but he would eventually, she assured herself. Until then, she would not say a single word to the man though the journey take six months. A faint smile curved her lips at that thought, and she had to struggle to withold a soft laugh. So far, the trip looked as though it very well might take a full six months. Though they had left near dawn, thinking to reach Oxford sometime after supper, they were still many miles from the town and the moon was already high and silver in the star-studded sky above. It would be dawn most likely now before they reached the inn. Even longer, if one of the horses should throw a shoe again or the carriage wheel find another muddy sink hole to stick in.

"Hold! Draw up your horses!"

Cerissa's eyes flew open, all traces of her smile vanished at the sound of the harsh voices coming from outside the carriage. Highwaymen! Of course, traveling so late into the night on the desolate, forest lined path. Her husband seemed transfixed with terror, his mouth flapping wordlessly open and shut like a hooked fish's. Cerissa grabbed for her small purse, stuffing it into the pocket of her cloak, then swiftly she pulled the hood up to cover her face and high piled hair. However badly she wished for escape from her husband, leaving him only to be mauled by savage outlaws was hardly an improvement. Of course, she'd been lucky with highwaymen before, when Sean St. Michael had been masquerading as one, but fortune would hardly favor her so greatly twice in a row!

The coach lurched to a bouncing, bone-jarring halt, and almost immediately the narrow door was wrenched open from without.

"Lads and lasses both, outside please," one of the outlaws, richly dressed in jet black velvet, his face covered by a full mask, leaned inside, a long barrelled flintlock pistol in one hand to enforce his request. His voice was low, scarcely above a whisper, but the heavy Scottish brogue was easily heard.

Cerissa followed Edward and her maid, Lina, out of the coach, the hood of her cloak pulled so far forward that she could not see the narrow metal steps and nearly fell, catching her heel on the hem of her gown. The highwayman reached swiftly to catch her elbow, murmuring a caution as he helped her dismount from the carriage.

Cerissa frowned quizzically, she knew no one who spoke with such a strong Scotts accent, yet aside from the brogue, the masked man's voice held a familiar timbre. Puzzled, she glanced sharply sideways around the edge of her hood, searching the black velvet mask for some hint of identity. Suddenly, the man's gaze shifted back to meet hers and she found herself staring into a pair of clear blue, blonde lashed eyes. Incredibly, as he met her gaze, the highwayman winked, and with a sound barely above a breath Cerissa heard his softly chuckle.

Ardsley! Her astonished brain cried. Dressed in black velvet to masquerade as a Scottish robber! She bit her lip hard and dropped her gaze, fearing to laugh aloud and spoil whatever scheme was afoot. At once, the blond lord stepped away, demanding Lord Ramond's wallet, kicking open their baggage trunks, brandishing the pistol threateningly.

Cerissa dared to raise her eyes at last, in control finally of her mirth, glancing once at her ashen faced husband before letting her gaze swing widely over the moonlit roadside. There, with Ardsley, was another man, also clad in black helping the blond lord search for loot. And there, sitting silently aback a restive black stallion, silhouetted on the crest of a slight mound nearer the forest, was still another. Cerissa's breath caught in her throat, her heart soaring with joy. Brett! More than any visual sense could tell her, cloaked and masked as he was, her heart knew by instinct. The careless grace with which he sat the horse, his hard-muscled thighs clamped confidently to the barrel of the pawing steed, one gloved hand steadying the reins with arrogant strength—these spoke of Brett. She stared at him a moment longer, allowing her greedy eyes to drink their fill of him before turning back to the others.

"T'is hardly worth the trouble," Ardsley was grumbling in his feigned accent, the burred "r's" slurring the words together. "This canna be all ye've been taking."

"It is, I swear it," Edward protested fearfully, his wide eyes still locked to the pistol in the highwayman's hand. "I am not a wealthy man, sir, please believe me."

Ardsley strode quickly to Cerissa, flinging the hood of her cloak back to her shoulders with the flick of a wrist. "Is this yer lassie?" he asked gruffly, turning again to stare at the nervous lord.

"No," Edward mumbled. "My wife."

"Yer wife?" the mask muffled voice was heavy with disbelief and he chuckled his doubt. "The girl's less than half yer age, old fellow and pretty as the blossoms of springtime. Why now would such a rare creature be married to an old man—a poor old man? Would it na make more kin to think ye be rich as the good king Jamey himself and holding out on us?"

Lord Ramond seemed unable to reply. The only sound his fear

frozen lips could utter was a faint, shrill squeak. Cerissa bit her lip again, smothering a laugh.

"Methinks we'll be taking the lassie here—and perhaps her maid as well—for ransom," Ardsley drawled, his cold stare drilling into Edward's ashen face. "Mayhaps ye'll be willing to part with more money when ye've had a few days to be missing her."

"But sir, I have no more money, I swear it," Lord Ramond pleaded again. "I could not meet even a miserly ransom!"

"Then maybe her father'll be willing to help ye out. Or ye've friends. I do na care a whit where the money be coming from, only that's its there. Ye'll be hearing from us at our pleasure."

At Ardsley's last statement, Cerissa managed a small cry of dismay, realizing belatedly that she too ought to show some fear of being kidnapped by such ruffians. At her cry, the mounted man spurred his horse away from the forest and toward the huddled group, hauling the stallion back in a rearing stop several feet away.

"Pardon-moi, madame," Brett's deep, rich voice spoke in flawless French, and Cerissa could follow only scattered phrases as he continued to give orders to the two other men.

Ardsley nodded at length, glancing swiftly at the quaking Lord Ramond who did understand the language, before turning to Cerissa. "He says ye're na to be worried, lassie, he will na treat you ill. Ye may bring yer maid along wi' ye to see to yer needs, and ye can select a change of clothing as well if ye wish."

Cerissa nodded and bent swiftly to her trunk, thinking Brett meant her to bring it all along.

"Pardon-moi, madame. Un peu-seulement," the deep voice cautioned her.

Cerissa nodded again, understanding. Only a little. She pawed through the clothes, finding an aquamarine blue satin gown and an extra shift, then pulling an extra cloak out of the trunk as well. They might well be camping outside tonight and the mid-November air was chilling. "All right," she murmured at last, "I'm ready."

Ardsley lifted her to Brett's horse, and she felt the familiar strength of his arms slide around her waist. A moment later, Ardsley had led his horse out and hoisted Lina up in front of the saddle, then mounted himself, waiting while the third man followed suit. At last, the small party was ready to fly.

Brett, turned the horses' head around, seemingly on an impulse, to toss Lord Ramond's wallet back at him, gesturing that he might reenter the coach and be off. "You may need this, my lord, to see you back to London again. I believe I have stolen enough of your treasure," he smiled, still speaking French. With, a half bow from the saddle, Brett tightened his arm around Cerissa's waist and spurred the horses forward into the forest shadows.

For long minutes, they galloped along a fairly wide, even path and the horses were moving too quickly to allow conversation. At last, Brett slowed the snorting stallion and gestured toward a lesser track, bending his head well down to avoid a low hanging bough at the path's entrance. As he straightened, he reached up to pull the mask from his face, glancing down at Cerissa's sparkling eyes with a wide grin of pleasure.

"You make a dashing highwayman," Cerissa complimented with a throaty laugh, reaching up to brush a stray lock of ebony hair back into place.

"You think so?" Brett chuckled in return, stopping the horse momentarily to bend his dark head down for a kiss. "Ah...If treasures like you are there for the taking, I've been foolish not to pursue such a line before. Pirates have more gold, but they don't kiss nearly as well."

Cerissa laughed in response, glancing over his shoulder to be sure her maid was also aware of the game. "Edward nearly died of fright," she murmured at last, unable to feel anything other than merriment yet at his reaction. "But weren't you taking a dreadful chance, Brett? What if he'd recognized you or Ardsley?"

Brett shrugged, seemingly unworried. "We thought...with the full face masks and our voices disguised..." he chuckled, squeezing her waist. "I'm sure he didn't even suspect, sweetheart. By the time he gets back to London he will remember only Ardsley's Scottish brogue and my French. Even if the authorities bother to search, what would there be to connect them to us?"

"Me."

"Yes, but you'll be with me at Whitross, my sweet. And even if someone should discover you there, I shall simply say I ransomed you from the thieves."

"Won't Edward be expecting a ransom note though, Brett? Surely, you don't expect him to simply let me go forever without even an inquiry. And once he discovers that I'm living at Whitross with you..."

"I don't intend him to discover that, Cerissa," he replied seriously, meeting her quizzical gaze directly. "I've had time to think this situation out, sweet, and I've come to several conclusions. One, as long as he lives, he won't give you up. So, short of murdering him on the duelling fields, he's got to believe you beyond his grasp. Two, so long as he won't agree to an annulment—and with your being with child there's hardly any way for us to prove the marriage isn't consumated—Cerissa Hammond Whitestone must remain his wife. Three, if we remain in England, eventually he will discover you're with me. Then we'll be back to where we started. And I can hardly continue indefinitely to abduct you from him. This sort of a thing is fine once or twice, but it would grow wearisome after a while."

Cerissa sighed, her eyes troubled, as she leaned against Brett's chest. "Well, what can we do then Brett? Are we truly as trapped as Edward believes we are?"

"Yes and no," he smiled. "I think I've figured a way out, but the escape is difficult and twisted. Suppose these wicked highwaymen did send Edward an exorbitant ransom note that he was, of course, unable to meet. Such blackguards could threaten to toss you into the Thames if their demands were not met. Then, a few days later, your clothing washes up along the banks of London. Wouldn't everyone—Edward, Lord Ramond included—believe you dead? Then, very quietly, a marriage license for the young, newly rediscovered Lady Lakeland and Bretegane, Lord Lindsey might be issued. We would sail for Jamaica in the spring as man and wife."

Cerissa furrowed her brow, thinking of too many risks in the plan. "Oh, Brett, anyone who saw me would know at once that it was a sham. Besides, I can't marry you when I'm already married. Even if the name is different, I'm the same person."

"Well, sweet, to answer your first objection, you'll simply spend a long, reclusive honeymoon with me at Whitross. The few times I have to introduce you to anyone, you'll wear a heavy veil—as though you've had smallpox and the scars are still healing. I doubt if Edward Ramond will have the audacity to ask to be presented to you, and most of his friends are mere acquaintances of mine. Actually," he mused aloud, "I believe your husband will keep a respectable distance between himself and me. He might well suspect my displeasure when you're supposed death is announced. By the way, I assume your maid is fairly loyal to you?"

Cerissa glanced upwards in amusement. "Yes . . . very," she replied "Why did you bring her along with . . ."

Brett nodded, interrupting her words, "Good, we shall ask her aid in convincing Edward of your death. Perhaps she can say she saw you enter the river."

"But, Brett," Cerissa objected softly "Don't you realize? We'll be fleeing from my husband the rest of our lives? Whether England, or

Jamaica, we'll always be in fear of discovery. I can't ask you for my sake..."

"You didn't ask, sweetheart," Brett smiled gently. "This is my own decision. Nothing is worth spending another single day away from you—not my lands, not Whitross itself, nor the Court, not even Sweetwater. Trust me, sweet, I'll work it out."

Cerissa fell silent, feeling her joy swell in her throat. Unconsciously, she reached a hand up to her neckchain to clasp Brett's emerald ring in her hand. Ever since her return with Edward, when Lina had offered the ring, she had strung it on a fine gold chain and worn it around her neck, feeling closer to him for it. "All right, Brett," she murmured, tilting her head to lay a soft kiss against the beating pulse of his throat. "I'll stay with you then. But I won't marry you. I won't put you in that kind of jeopardy."

His soft chuckle sounded loud in the forest's silence. "I can't believe my ears," he grinned. "Isn't this exactly what you've schemed for since I first tumbled into bed with you at Mrs. Tyler's? Are you seriously denying my proposal?"

Despite herself, Cerissa smiled, acknowledging his jibe. "But Brett, please be serious. I just can't have two husbands, you..."

"Not two, sweet, one," he amended. "Only me. I don't intend to share you with another living soul. Now listen. Once you're thought dead, it would be comparatively simple for Ardsley to have your marriage to Lord Ramond annulled. Ardsley has plenty of influence at court, plenty of clerks anxious to do him such an easy favor. Then, with your marriage annulled, what obstacle would bar your wedding me? Under your different name, of course. It would be difficult for me to marry a ghost, and the honeymoon less than entirely satisfactory. Our souls might get along well enough, but I've a few more earthly pleasures planned for you as well."

At last, Cerissa allowed a tiny spark of hope to light her heart, following Brett's words and finding no fault in them. It hardly seemed possible that what she had dreamed of for so long—what she had finally dismissed as impossible—could actually now be within reach.

"Well, Cerissa Hammond Whitestone Lakeland, will you marry me?" he asked softly, his lips touching her ear in a gentle kiss.

Cerissa pressed closer to him, reaching one hand out to entwine her fingers in his, swallowing hard against the giddy joy that closed her throat.

"Do you want me to coax you? To court you and woo you as I might in a different circumstance?" he murmured softly. "Then I will. Shall I tell you my heart was cold and dead until you touched it with your love and gave it life? But then, I know you know it so. Shall I then remember that I scoffed at the very existence of that emotion, love, until I saw it shining in your eyes and found it while laying in your arms? But you know that too. Shall I tell you you are the sun of each day's dawning and the clearest, most constant star of each night? That your single smile is a treasure I would not trade the throne of England for? That I would have no other woman beside me through my life? To bear my children? To grow old in contentment with? Marry me. Cerissa, be my wife. Though I would lose the world, even my life, for such a promise I would still count it only joy."

Cerissa pressed her face tightly against Brett's beating heart, nodding helplessly through her tears, feeling Brett's kisses fall amidst her curls as he realized her answer.

Suddenly, above her head she heard Brett's husky chuckle and she lifted her face for his lingering kiss. "We celebrate tonight," he called back to Ardsley and the maid riding just behind. "We've a betrothal to toast."

Chapter Twenty-one

The seasons turned slowly from autumn to winter, bringing the scarlet and golden leaves fluttering from the boughs of the trees to litter the ground like a silent carpet. At Whitross, Brett and Cerissa welcomed Lord Ardsley's Christmas visit, especially as he brought Jamey, and his own two sons, along with him. Marian, Lady Ardsley, had elected to remain in London for the Court Yuletide merriment, even though the Court festivities, under the sober King James, would not be nearly so gay as in the preceeding year under the "Merrie Monarch" Charles. With him, Ardsley had brought scattered news from London. Edward had received the bogus ransom note and had evidently resigned himself to the loss of his young wife, for he had reportedly made small effort to secure the sum named. Faced with the choice of selling the dress shop—and losing his income—or losing Cerissa, Edward's romantic attachment to the girl had been easily overcome by practicality. Though Brett had greeted that report with a dark frown and eyes that sparked anger, Cerissa had felt only relief. A faint, lingering sense of having mistreated her elderly husband had persisted, bringing the only shadow that had darkened the halcyon days with Brett at Whitross. Assurance of Edward's utter selfishness and lack of devotion toward her had obliterated those feelings, and Christmas had passed in beautiful perfection.

Now, with the warming breezes of March blowing gently into the carriage through the half opened window in the door, Cerissa put a hand up to draw a fine gold neckchain from beneath the bodice of her gown. She had relinquished Brett's emerald ring to it's rightful owner, sliding the heavy gold mounting on his finger herself. In it's place, among the small mountain of gifts she had received Christmas morning, was an emerald studded wedding ring. Brett had suggested she wear it around her throat until she could wear it on her finger and she had agreed with a joyful heart. It should not be long now, she smiled patiently to herself, slipping the ring half onto her slim finger. Ardsley's last letter had assured her the annullment was nearly final already. Edward—and indeed, London itself—had accepted the news of Lady Ramond's supposed death without question. Jake Oates already had the "Cerissa" fully careened and cargoed and ready for departure. Doctor Hajamin was planning to leave with them, intrigued by Cerissa's accounts of the miracles of Liza's bush medicine. Lord Ardsley had promised to sail down for a long visit the following fall. So, the exile from England that she and Brett had anticipated would not be so total as it might have been. Jamey would be with them in Sweetwater, of course, and in June another baby to love and share. She would miss the gentle, greenly rolling hills of England, the huge, proud oaks, the whisper of the Thames and the patchy fog which covered most of the southlands each morning, yet the exile seemed a small price to pay for the promise of a life spent with the man she loved. Brett too seemed pleased with his choice, though she knew he, more than she, was giving up much in leaving. His seat in the king's council, his influence at Court and in the House of Lords, his enjoyment and the challenge of selecting cargo from among the countless variety that daily flowed in and out of London's markets. Perhaps, Cerissa mused, after five or six years had passed, if Lord Ramond were dead, she and Brett might dare a cautious visit back to England. They had known so much happiness, at Whitross especially, she would like to return occasionally, she wanted the children to grow to love the old house as she and Brett did.

The coach stopped suddenly, interrupting her thoughts, and the door opened wide. "Here Jamey, best ride inside with your mother for a while. She'll be getting lonesome for company."

Cerissa smiled and reached out to take the boy from his father's arms, laughing softly at the child's excited account of all the wonders he'd seen perched atop his father's saddle. She touched Brett's hand with wordless love, the emerald wedding ring swinging free to brush the velvet of his coat as she moved.

"Soon sweetheart," he promised with a grin, catching the ring in one hand to slip it back into her bodice, his green eyes lighting with a familiar expression as his fingers lingered a moment against her breast. "We'll be in Bainwater within the hour, and Bywater tonight. Within a week, we'll be aboard "Cerissa" with full sails set. Once we're out to sea, Jake Oates will be promoted to captain long enough to read our vows to us. And then, Lady Lindsey, you'll set your mind on becoming a loving, dutiful wife to a dull Jamaican planter."

"Planter?" she murmured in teasing disbelief. "Pirate again most likely. Either way, once I've delivered this most recent addition to our family, I shall not expect to find you dull."

Brett laughed, his white teeth flashing as a mischeivous grin creased his face. "For a lady not yet wedded, I believe you entertain exceptionally lewd thoughts. Now, be patient sweet. I'll ride ahead and warn your Aunt Mary that we're nearly upon her."

Cerissa nodded, still smiling faintly as the coach door closed and Jamey clambered over to sit on her lap, eager for her attention. "No Jamey," she replied patiently to the child's endless questioning. "Aunt Mary isn't truly my aunt, just as your Uncle James isn't truly your uncle. Aunt Mary raised me though, and she has some papers and things of my mothers I wanted to have. Besides, I wanted her to see you, and to say goodbye before we left on our long trip."

Goodbye forever perhaps, Cerissa reflected sadly, as she kissed the woman farewell at the steps of the tiny cottage. Her foster mother had aged quickly since the death of her husband, and Cerissa guessed the woman might not live the half dozen or so years it might take before she and Brett could return. She turned to watch Brett lift Jamey into the coach, then shook her head as he turned expectantly to her. "No, love, I'd like to walk down to the field where I first met you. I'll not be long, I promise."

"All right, sweetheart, but be careful you don't turn your ankle on a loose stone. Those velvet slippers are hardly working shoes," he cautioned gently.

Cerissa nodded, lifting the hem of her satin skirt up out of the dirt as she walked, her mind intent on reflections of the youth she'd spent. Leaving Whitross had been hard, leaving this cottage again was hard as well. She swallowed against a sudden surge of premature homesickness, breathing deeply of the fresh, misty English air, engraving it on her memory. For long minutes she was silent, walking slowly amidst the furrows, stooping once to pick a wildflower just poking it's graceful color through the earth. Finally, she heard the sound of horse's hooves along the road, and she turned, squinting against the sun to see Brett riding slowly toward her, his eyes gentle, and his lips curved in a tender half smile.

"Excuse me, sweetheart," he murmured, reining the stallion to a halt. "But is there an inn here in town?"

Cerissa stared, then smiled quickly, dropping her knee in an awkward curtsey, remembering. "With the best strawberry tarts in town, my lord," she answered. For a long moment, their eyes locked needing no words to communicate the feelings that flowed from soul to soul.

At last, Brett sighed and nodded. "Ready to go, sweet?" he questioned softly.

Cerissa paused, turning for a last, slow look around the country side, then nodded, starting toward him. Suddenly, she stopped, bending down to pick a round, brown pebble up from out of the dirt. "I think I'll keep this," she murmured aloud. "To remember that first day I saw you, looking up from this field with you on that black horse. I think I fell in love with you at that very instant. When I'm old and grey, I shall take this little stone out to remember by. And I'll show it to the children as they grow, Brett, to teach them that dreams still come true if the heart pursues them patiently enough."

She reached up, laying her hand against his muscled thigh, her blue eyes clear but filled with thought. "What would have happened, Brett, if I'd gotten back before midnight do you think?"

The dark haired lord smiled a moment, dropping one hand from the reins to caress her thick hair. "I don't know, sweetheart," he answered slowly at last, shrugging his shoulders. "You'd have missed much of the pain of your life, I think . . . but perhaps, much of the joy as well. I'm sure I would have missed the joy of mine."

Cerissa smiled, staring down at the pebble in her hand, turning it over with her fingers before dropping it into the pocket of her cloak. At last, she raised her head, her eyes meeting Brett's tender gaze with radiant, serene, assurance. Yes, she decided reflectively, whatever the price of their love in past pain, whatever lay before them in Jamaica or in the Carolinas where Brett seemed so eager to settle, she would pay that price ten times over for but a single day of the glorious joy. "All right then, love," she smiled, "I'm ready to go now."